No Shortage of Evil

by David S. Rosenberg

PublishAmerica
Baltimore

© 2004 by David S. Rosenberg.
All rights reserved. No part of this book may be reproduced, stored in a retrieval system or transmitted in any form or by any means without the prior written permission of the publishers, except by a reviewer who may quote brief passages in a review to be printed in a newspaper, magazine or journal.

First printing

This book is a work of fiction. All characters and descriptions are a product of the author's imagination or are used fictiously.

ISBN: 1-4137-6412-6
PUBLISHED BY PUBLISHAMERICA, LLLP
www.publishamerica.com
Baltimore

Printed in the United States of America

For the fine women and men of the Federal Bureau of Investigation who work tirelessly here and abroad to keep us safe.

Chapter 1

Tuesday, September 28, 2004, 5:17 PM

After running up a flight of stairs with Agent Joel Grivner, Donald Corbbitt adjusted the miniature speaker perched in his right ear. They took a moment to catch their breath, but Corbbitt felt the stress mounting as they drew close to their objective.

"I feel like I've been running since they declared the Code Red," Grivner said.

"This one's for real, Joel. The Department of Homeland Defense mobilized everyone," Corbbitt said. "Ready for this?"

Joel nodded. "I guess we'll know soon enough if all the training was worth it."

"All units, report your status," Corbbitt said into the tiny microphone extending from his right ear to the corner of his mouth.

"Delta Ready," an agent said over the radio.

"Alpha Ready."

Precious seconds ticked by as the rest of his team attained their positions around the apartment complex in the south side of Bayonne, New Jersey.

Verified intelligence information located a new terrorist cell and determined that an attack in the northern New Jersey-New York City area was imminent. Thousands perhaps millions of people were at risk, and his team's actions in the next few minutes might prevent the gruesome agony of another September 11.

"Bravo Ready."

"Charlie Ready."

Corbbitt acknowledged the units positioned at stairwells and across the street. "We're ready," Corbbitt said into his microphone to Communications Specialist, Jocelyn Hafner, who served as a focal point for relaying operational status back to Homeland Security staff, FBI supervisors, and the President of the United States.

Her delayed response indicated that something else was brewing. "Did you copy?" he said, when she failed to respond.

"Hold."

He acknowledged her instruction.

A minute later she spoke in his ear. "Be advised that additional information may require your team's immediate relocation. Proceed with your current operation."

He acknowledged her transmission and drew his weapon. "All units, we have a 'Go'." Corbbitt said.

One second later his size eleven shoe slammed into apartment door 227 sending splintered doorframe into the room and leaving the door partially open. He kicked it again to gain full view of the living room.

"No one yet," he said, speaking into the microphone. He entered just ahead of Grivner and surveyed the immediate area overlooking the mattresses, porn magazines, and dirty paper plates on the floor. Quickly they searched the kitchen, bathroom, and two bedrooms.

"This place smells like wall-to-wall armpit," Grivner said. "Looks like we missed them."

"Yes, but not by much. Notice the smoke?" Corbbitt asked, pointing to an ashtray. "Someone's cigarette is still burning "

"Status?" Jocelyn barked in his ear.

"Vacant. No one injured."

"Proceed to vehicles. Departure immediate, precise directions shortly," Hafner said.

"Copy," Corbbitt acknowledged. "All units proceed to vehicles. Move, move, move."

Chapter 2

Tuesday, September 28, 2004, 5:31 PM

Bayonne police barely had enough time to block traffic at intersections along the twelve-block route from the apartment complex to a self-storage facility. Hafner advised that the Radiological Emergency and Control Unit would respond to support their team's efforts but only after they captured the terrorists and then only if it was safe. Corbbitt saw their brown van and noted how well government agencies were responding to this emergency.

Information flowed continuously from Hafner to the three vehicles transporting Corbbitt's team. Jocelyn Hafner spoke as rapidly as she could without distorting her words. Torrents of relevant information flooded the communications center, and it was unlikely there would be enough time to use standard communications protocol. Her team's job required quick decisions to supply field agents with only relevant information. Too little or too much information often contributed to injury or death of field agents under fire.

As they made the last turn a block away from their destination, they saw the four small flatbed tow trucks that Hafner mentioned. "I think we've caught up with them, Don. What are the metal caskets on those trucks? Do you think the bombs are that large?"

"That's my guess, Joel," Corbbitt responded. "Hafner, any mention of eight foot long metal boxes?"

"Nothing about them yet. Why?"

Before Corbbitt could describe what he saw, four men came from the rear of the storage area carrying identical brown envelopes. The men were all tearing open the envelopes as they approached their respective trucks.

Corbbitt, famous for his lightening fast ability to process information and perform the correct action, barked commands at the agents in the other vehicles. Seconds later the team pulled up beside the trucks. Ten agents swarmed the trucks with guns drawn.

Instead of attempting to escape or fire the handgun that each of them carried, the surprised drivers merely raised their hands. When the drivers failed to move, the agents yanked them from their trucks and threw them to the ground.

Corbbitt struggled to hear Hafner over the yelling of the other nine agents who handcuffed the hapless drivers on the pavement. Corbbitt, sensing something vital from Hafner's tone, tried to quiet the other agents.

"Hafner, I only heard 'fifth, leader, dangerous'. Repeat your last please."

"You filthy, Jew-loving, American pigs. You think you have stopped us, but you are wrong. Allahu Akbar, Allahu Akbar–God is great."

Several agents looked up from their charges to see an olive-skinned man standing forty feet away. The man moved quickly to extend a short antenna from a black device the size of a small cell-phone. Without hesitating, Corbbitt fired three shots. Two found the man's heart and one entered his right eye. The expression on the man's face never changed but three high velocity bullets caused him to fall backward. For a few agonizing seconds the black electronic device flew in the air. Ten agents watched helplessly as it hit the ground first on its side and then roll on its back away from the buttons.

"Let's make sure that there aren't any others lurking about," Corbbitt commanded. He pointed to two of the agents. "Stay here and baby-sit these guys. Agent Grivner and I will search the driveway on the right, the rest of you spread out and check the area."

Corbbitt walked with Grivner toward their area. "Ya know, Don, there's something 'bout these guys I don't understand."

"What's that, Joel?"

"If God is so great in their eyes, and they believe that heart and soul, why do they think that God needs them to run this planet?"

Chapter 3

Tuesday, September 28, 2004, 8:56 PM

Virtually the entire population of the United States knew by six o'clock in the evening that terrorists tried and failed in their attempt to attack helpless citizens. The air seemed to resonate as an anxious nation exhaled together. Secure and safe in their homes, many waited for assurance that no other hostilities were in progress. The major television networks added crawlers to the bottom of their broadcast picture notifying news hungry viewers of a nine o'clock news briefing concerning the thwarted attack. In the absence of detailed information, the networks provided viewers with theories and speculations for three hours.

Pundits and politicos clamored for television time to praise or condemn government policies. Supporters praised the multi-disciplined coordinated effort to locate and prevent another terrorist induced crisis, while those critical of the current administration, blasted away at our inability to prevent terrorists from entering the country. None of the breast-beating or finger pointing made much sense, but it did fill airtime while facts fell into alignment.

At nine o'clock three men and one woman appeared on the screen. The tallest of the men walked towards a podium to begin the news briefing. The smile in his eyes advertised that nothing sinister had happened in the three hours following the dramatic events in Bayonne.

"Good evening, my name is Michael Bayard, Under Secretary for Emergency Preparedness & Response. My organization is part of the Department of Homeland Security. I am here to present the preliminary information concerning the thwarted terrorist attack in New Jersey late this afternoon. The Homeland Defense Secretary is meeting with the President to determine the current risk to the United States on a minute-by-minute basis.

"With me are Arthur Mills of the Nuclear Incident Response Team,

Donald Corbbitt, FBI field agent, and Jocelyn Hafner, FBI communications specialist. Each of us has some information concerning the terrorist's attack. Let me stress this point, information gathering and analysis continues. We will present only what we know and not extrapolate, assume, or surmise beyond those details that we currently have.

"We have not had much time to prepare and organize our presentation, and we're still sorting through the available information. Still the Secretary felt we should reveal what we have as soon as possible.

"A little less than a day ago the entire country was put on a Code Red status indicating that a terrorist attack was likely. This information originated from a terrorist prisoner at our Guantanamo detention facility in Cuba just five days ago."

"This information convinced us that a dirty bomb factory was in operation in the wilderness between the town of Salalah, Oman and the Yemen border. A subsequent ground strike against that facility occurred yesterday. They discovered vast quantities of high-level radioactive materials and a significant quantity of C4, a very high-grade explosive.

"They found three completely assembled bombs and another six in various phases of construction. Experts worked continuously with drawings and other information captured at the site to determine the strength and nature of these bombs. Additional information obtained from personnel at the site indicated that the facility delivered four bombs. Records indicate that the bombs left this facility twenty-seven days ago. This led to a massive investigation and the declaration of a Code Red and the arrests made today in Bayonne.

"The United States sent a small task force from ships stationed in the Arabian Sea. Initially there were protests from the governments of Oman and Yemen. I believe the President, through diplomatic channels, obtained a measure of cooperation in this matter."

"You mean the President made them an offer they couldn't refuse," a reporter commented loud enough for the dozens of microphones to detect.

"I won't speculate on the President's methods." Bayard grimaced, but he knew the entire nation chuckled at the reference to a famous line in *The Godfather* movie. "That's all I have for you at the moment. Let me introduce Arthur Mills who led the nuclear response team," Under Secretary Bayard concluded. He backed away from the microphones and a portly bald-headed man with a gray chin beard took his position.

"Thank you, Mr. Bayard, and good evening everyone. Let me begin by introducing a few basics that will help you understand the potential consequences of what almost happened in the greater New York-Newark metropolitan area this afternoon. The bombs, four of them, contained high level radioactive isotopes and C4 explosives. We believe these bombs are the ones from the facility that our attack force discovered. If I may have the slide please."

Again, the reporters laughed as a graph with two large hill-shaped curves appeared on the screen. "Yes," Mills interrupted their laughter. "This has been called the Jane Mansfield curve in the nuclear arena for decades. What it really represents is the relative percentage of various isotopes that appear after a quantity of fissile material such as Uranium-235 undergoes the fission process. The atomic weight of isotopes increases along the X-axis, while the percentage of each isotope is displayed on the Y-axis.

"This is the nature of the material that is likely to be found in each bomb. Most of the isotopes are radioactive and together they emit a range of various energy gamma, beta, neutron, and alpha particles. Each bomb contains five cylindrical canisters of radioactive material with individual explosives placed to propel the radioactive material into the air. This would contaminate everything in the immediate area.

"We are developing a computer simulation to provide estimates of the contamination field that would have occurred if these bombs had exploded. This will provide a benchmark to help us determine how to manage a crisis in the event one of these devices explodes in the future.

"I am sorry if this is a bit complicated but the concerns here are many. While the explosives themselves would no doubt kill anyone within the immediate area, the radioactive material would devastate the surrounding area. When I say devastate, I mean making it useless for habitation until extensive cleanup procedures are complete. Those caught in the plume of this explosion might suffer various forms of radiation sickness or even death depending upon the type and quantity of ingested radioactive materials. Aside from the radiological effects, many of the isotopes are toxic to living creatures and could well act as a poison."

Mills stopped for a moment, to see if he still had the reporters' interest. "These are not the only consequences of exploding these devices in a populated area," Mills said and waited until the general rumble of the reporters diminished. "Far more serious is the widespread panic that would ensue when thousands of people try to flee indiscriminately away from something they cannot see, but fear.

"Panic would breed panic, many would die from heart attacks or from being trampled to death during massive stampedes. Remember the hordes of people peacefully crossing bridges and milling about trying to get home during the last widespread power outage. Their peaceful departure from work sites to their homes provides a visual picture of the number of people potentially affected. Now picture them all panicking. No doubt, panic would kill more than the direct results of the explosion or the radioactive material.

"The only way to minimize panic in a situation like this is through information. Informed people are far less likely to panic and more likely to follow instructions when and if this situation occurs. The Department of Homeland Security has pledged to provide educational materials to the general population. In addition, emergency service personnel training to manage large crowds of people without inducing panic is in progress. That's all I have," Arthur Mills said and nodded toward Jocelyn Hafner and Donald Corbbitt who in turn looked at each other.

Corbbitt indicated with a wave of his hand for Hafner to go next.

She stepped in front of the microphones tentatively but soon gained composure. Many of the television cameramen zoomed in on her flawless skin. In the sea of blue suits that seemed to surround her, Jocelyn's beauty was hard to ignore by the cameras that sent her image to millions across the country.

"Hi everyone, I'm Jocelyn Hafner a communications specialist out of the FBI's center in Washington, D.C. Frankly, I'm a little surprised to be here, but I'll do what I can to shed some light on what happened this afternoon from my perspective.

"First, let me say that I only relayed information to Agent Corbbitt's team who successfully stopped what could have been a disaster worse than what we experienced on September 11. I work at the communications center that collects, interprets, and analyzes information gathered from all sources both domestically and internationally. Once we get the information, we sift and present it in a way to support, capture, or stop those who would do us harm.

"Without well-coordinated information gathering, this terrorist cell would have succeeded. Early this afternoon sufficient information allowed us to determine the nature of this terrorist cell and their location. We also had some idea of what they were going to do. Clearly al Qaida planned to explode four dirty bombs in the New York-Newark metropolitan area. The four men with four trucks, four bombs, and four destinations had a plan designed to create death and havoc in our country. About five o'clock, with the help of the

Brazilian and Canadian governments, a fifth man, Ibrahim Al-Din, known as Allah's Death Angel was traced to the New York area. Al-Din is currently number six on the FBI's most wanted list. This man personally organized al-Qaida terrorist activities in Indonesia, Philippines, and Sudan. He is responsible for murdering and maiming hundreds of innocent people. Today, thanks to Agent Donald Corbbitt, he lies in a morgue.

"None of this could have happened without the complete cooperation of many government agencies working together. Fortunately, we located them before the four trucks started to roll. Imagine how much more difficult it would have been to stop the detonation of these devices if they were in separate locations." The reporters stirred in their seats wondering if she knew what targets the terrorists had in mind.

Sensing their anxiety, she continued. "I am sure everyone wants to know where these bombs were going to be placed. Oddly enough, that is one piece of information we didn't have. This operation followed a similar pattern to other al-Qaida operations. Only Ibrahim al-Din knew the locations and he arrived in the New York area yesterday. The only other thing I know at this point is that he checked out of a hotel near LaGuardia airport this morning.

"Perhaps I should turn this over to Agent Donald Corbbitt. He certainly was a lot closer to the action than I was," she said and left the cluster of microphones. For a second she made eye contact with Donald Corbbitt as he approached the podium.

Reluctantly, Donald Corbbitt took her place and began while reporters were still murmuring about Hafner's presentation. "It's been a long day, so I'll try to make this brief. Our rapid response team had approximately four-hours to plan and get in position for the operation that we executed this afternoon. I've been in law enforcement for seventeen years. I've never seen such coordination between various levels of government agencies and their personnel. Perhaps that is the only reason we were successful in stopping the five terrorists from launching their attack. Ms. Hafner and the entire staff that provided information to my team allowed us just enough time to stop a major disaster.

"Initially, we intended to capture these ruthless men in their apartment. Fortunately, additional last minute information redirected our efforts and we located them in four trucks at a self-storage facility in Bayonne, New Jersey. These trucks are small flat bed type trucks that can carry and remove single automobiles. These trucks have flatbeds that tilt toward the ground. Each one has a motor-driven towing cable used to drag a disabled vehicle onto the bed.

"Instead of an automobile, each of these trucks had a large metal casket shaped container lashed to the flatbed. These containers were the dirty radioactive bombs that Mr. Mills described. Apparently, these men operated a legitimate towing business in northern New Jersey for over three years.

"We rushed the four men just after they climbed into their trucks. After throwing them to the ground and handcuffing them, a fifth man appeared. This man turned out to be Ibrahim al-Din, the same man that Ms. Hafner described.

"He began yelling 'God is great' in an Arabic dialect and also in English while he prepared to use a device to detonate at least one of the bombs. I fired my weapon with the full intent of killing him. The actuator flew from his hands and fortunately, it didn't detonate any of the bombs.

"We found three other actuators in a small case that al-Din was carrying. Inside the trucks, each man had a 45-caliber pistol, additional clips of ammunition, and a brown envelope. Each envelope contained a single sheet of paper with text written in Arabic and a map that apparently designated the individual truck's destination. A translation of the Arabic text provided exact driving directions, specific parking locations for each of the trucks, and precise time of 9:11 PM to detonate the respective bombs.

"It is very likely that al-Din intended to control the actuators as long as possible to avoid accidental detonation. We think he was ready to hand the actuators to each driver and send them on their way." Behind him, Arthur Mills cell-phone chimed with an incoming call and Corbbitt paused for a moment to ensure he had everyone's attention.

"The maps and instructions indicate that they intended four simultaneous detonations at JFK Airport, Yankee Stadium, Port Authority Bus Terminal, and Newark Airport. Had they succeeded, no doubt thousands of people would have been injured or killed, directly from the blast, the radiation, or the ensuing panic. And the economic implications from this attack are beyond my capability to estimate."

Corbbitt paused again. Many of those present thought he was through with his portion of the presentation. "One other thing. Several agents have called me within the last two hours. According to them, there has been some widely broadcast concerns about me acting in haste or using excessive force." Suddenly the room was quiet again.

"I just want everyone to understand. I am not some cowboy with a gun. Ms. Hafner warned me just before Ibrahim al-Din appeared. I recognized him from pictures of the FBI's most wanted terrorists. I attended FBI training and recognized the type of actuator he had in his hand. Furthermore, he had a cellphone in a holder on his belt and since he was proclaiming 'God is great' the typical proclamation of those about ready to martyr themselves, I decided he wasn't calling God on the telephone."

The television cameras zoomed in on his face and the anger in Corbbitt's eyes was clear for the nation to see. "The danger was present. We were one button away from death and a major crisis. I killed that man and have no regrets about doing it. This was not some Hollywood movie. Ibrahim al-Din was not going to recover and use his last moments of life to push a single button to kill my team members, other citizens, and wreak havoc in New Jersey.

"Those of you who want to Monday morning quarterback my decision to kill this man, go right ahead. Those of you who do, ask yourself what would happen if he pressed the button."

With that he left the microphones and Under Secretary Bayard stepped forth. "I believe Mr. Mills has some additional information for us. Go ahead, Arthur."

Mills joined Bayard at the microphones. "The telephone call I just received came from the secretary, who wishes me to relay two other items to everyone. First, a barge will take the four trucks and their bombs from the Bayonne area. A Coast Guard cutter will escort the barge to an undisclosed area for further transport to a facility capable of dismantling the bombs in a safe manner. This immediate action minimizes the possibility of an accident. Second, the current threat seems to be over. Because of this, it is likely that the current Code Red status will be downgraded to a Code Orange."

Under Secretary Bayard checked briefly with the others and announced that there was no further information and that the press briefing was over.

Immediately after the press briefing, Corbbitt felt the vibrator on his cellphone. Harold Pincher ordered him to fly back to Washington with Under Secretary Bayard and Jocelyn Hafner.

After an hour flight and three hours discussing the day's events with the FBI Washington Field Office Assistant Director, Harold W. Pincher, Donald Corbbitt finally made it to a hotel room on the Arlington side of the Potomac River. The twenty minute hot shower did very little to help him relax. Persistent thoughts of the previous afternoon's brush with personal annihilation, the news conference, and Pincher's five-minute ass chewing lingered.

Pincher was the type of man who delighted in finding flaws in others, and who would remark about a spot on your tie even if you single-handedly saved the whole world from cracking in half. He knew one agent who described a meeting with Pincher as a visit to a Civil War doctor; you just knew you were going to lose a body part.

Now as he tossed and turned in his bed, Corbbitt wished he had never mentioned the criticism he received. He had only drawn more attention to himself and additional criticism towards the FBI. In slow motion, he began retracing the operation, every detail and action that led to his decision to shoot to kill.

"Shit! This isn't helping me to get to sleep."

He turned again on a hotel mattress that was far too soft for his two-hundred-and-twenty-pound, six-foot frame and became tangled in the sheet and blanket. "Damn it." He punched at the pillow and tried to flush the day's ugliness from his mind. Needing something pleasurable to think about, he searched desperately for something else.

The only thing he could think about that was at all pleasurable in his life yesterday was meeting Jocelyn Hafner at the news briefing. While Ms. Hafner was a pleasure to look at, he listened to Bayard's and Mills' discussion while gazing into the sea of cameras and reporters ever watchful for some small detail that might yield another act of violence.

Then for only an instant their eyes met while trading places at the bank of microphones. What was in her eyes? Perhaps she had a similar distaste for the limelight and the hoard of clamoring reporters. Perhaps it was something else.

During the short flight back to Washington on the Under Secretary's airplane, her fine features soon became apparent. He noticed her delicate hands and fingers that she moved while discussing something with the Under Secretary. Other details seemed to come now in torrents. He remembered her silky light brown hair and her glowing face with a dentist's daughter's smile. And legs, beautiful long legs that she crossed when she accepted bottled water from an attendant.

He could feel the great wave of sleep coming closer as he turned toward the empty, cold side of the bed. The cold side of the bed only reminded him of the perpetual emptiness in his life. Rather than try to find an answer, he allowed sleep to flood over him.

His cell-phone chimed and without opening his eyes, he groped to find it on the bedside table. "Yes," he grumbled.

A man's voice spoke in his ear.

"Yes, sir," Corbbitt responded.

The man continued to speak.

"Thank you, sir," he mumbled.

He heard a few more words and somehow in his foggy state of mind understood that the caller was through.

"Thank you, Mr. President," was all he could manage to say before the telephone clicked in his ear.

Chapter 4

Monday, October 18, 2004, 9:45 AM

Company employees and the investing public were shocked at the latest corporate financial debacle. Financial newswire services and business networks presented the gruesome details:

> Common Cause Communications Corporation announced today that it is considering seeking protection from creditors under Chapter 11 of the United States Bankruptcy Code. Corporate spokesman, Howard Digman, said the company's financial problems stem from the inability to realize anticipated revenue from operations and unexpected increased operating costs of its recently acquired low-earth satellite company, Transistar. Common Cause will not be able to meet bondholder interest payments due on November 1. Eighty-five percent of the company's 9,385 employees will be terminated immediately. The remaining vital employees will maintain communication service to the existing customers.

Monday, October 18, 2004, 9:46 AM

Financial newswires report that Common Cause Communications Corporation stock and corporate bonds lost ninety percent of their residual value.

Monday, October 18, 2004, 11:15 PM

New York City Patrolman, Peter Chambers, pointed his flashlight through the chain link fence that enclosed Common Cause panel trucks. He pulled his service revolver, called for backup, and ordered the Caucasian male to lay face down on the pavement. Later he placed the boy under arrest for slashing the tires on thirteen company vehicles. The youth, who was angry over the company's bankruptcy, said that he could not attend college next semester because his two thousand shares of Common Cause stock were now worthless.

Tuesday, October 19, 2004, 10:15 AM

Junior stock analyst, Bill Stone stood in the unemployment line. His sudden termination resulted from his recommendation to purchase Common Cause stock last month. He knew now how foolish he had been to believe company senior executives that Common Cause would weather a temporary decrease in revenue. He had no idea who might hire him. He just knew that he would never work for another securities firm. None of them would dare take the chance. He dreaded the thought of moving back in with mom and dad in Mansfield, Ohio, and starting his adult life over again.

Wednesday, October 20, 2004, 7:13 PM

Except for the company of a single bottle of twelve-year old malt scotch, Frank Purcell was alone in his three-bedroom house in Johnson City, Tennessee. His loving wife failed to understand how he could have invested so much of their hard-earned money in a company that no longer existed. The notebook of press releases, magazine articles, and company annual statements did little to support his cause. Forty-one thousand dollars down the toilet was too much for her to bear.

Frank wondered if she would come back home or if their loving relationship would ever return to normal.

Thursday, October 21, 2004, 11:20 AM

Margaret Jensen sat on a Battery Park bench looking across the water to Ellis Island and the nearby Statue of Liberty. She had the urge to don concrete shoes and try to wade out to the statue that seemed to know she was there. After losing her Common Cause marketing job, pension money, and the doctor's diagnosis of liver cancer, she certainly felt tired, poor, and weak.

Until this point in her life, she dealt with life's adversities. Her psoriasis, her mother's early death, and father's abuse—somehow she managed to deal with it all. Now the bastards at Common Cause with their greed and their self-aggrandizing nature managed to destroy a company filled with growth and promise. Their decisions and policies duped thousands of employees and investors.

If she was senior vice president of marketing instead of that vixen Yvonne Taylor, she might have been in a position to make a difference, to raise hell and prevent the corporate death spiral. The pretty slut, who smiled, flirted, and eventually slept with the right man, magically received the promotion. After all, who would want a short, frumpy-looking gal with scaly blotches on her arms and legs in the front office, no matter what the qualifications?

Who was there to complain to? Where was the justice? Would it even matter? The longer she sat on the bench, the more inviting the water looked.

Thursday, October 21, 2004, 3:12 PM

Brenda Talmage cried as her husband, Jason, called the mortgage company to tell them that they no longer had the down-payment required to get the $125,000 loan for their dream home in St. Petersburg, Florida. Jason lost control and slammed the telephone down when he heard that the eight hundred twenty five-dollar application fee was not refundable.

He stormed out of the house vowing to get even with the bastards who stole their money.

Friday, October 22, 2004, 12:18 PM

Junior law partner, Jeffery Iverson, felt a little uncomfortable lunching with senior partners, Williams, Clayton, Rosencrantz, and Martin. He had the feeling these experts in tort litigation knew the answer and that his only purpose was to display his analytical abilities and manage personal butterflies. He fingered the water glass while he listened to the other partners talk about previous class-action lawsuits that they labored over and earned fees from thousands of clients by successfully winning one case and the subsequent appeals.

During his second bite of grilled chicken, his mentor Clayton finally turned the conversation in his direction. All the partners focused their laser beam eyes in his direction.

He forced the half-chewed bite down hard and began, knowing that they did not want to waste much time on this issue. "Gentlemen, I've looked at the assets and liabilities of Common Cause. It seems the common stockholders do have a case against the company management. To be sure, the senior executives made some incredible mistakes. Phony earnings forecasts accelerated stock prices to incredible levels only to sink even faster when the company failed to achieve those promised profits. Subsequent acquisitions placed an additional debt burden on the company."

Without saying a word, Clayton looked at his watch indicating that it was time to get to the chase of the matter.

"The aggrieved stockholders have a case, but there is virtually no money. Taxes, bondholders, and banks will force a sale of the company or break it up into its constituent parts. There's simply nothing left to grab for the stockholders."

"Thank you, Mr. Iverson, I think we agree with you. Now if you'll excuse us there are other matters we must discuss and we do make use of our lunchtime to run the firm," founding partner, Williams, said.

Friday, October 22, 2004, 5:45 PM

"Stupid bastards!" Joshua Koweleski said as he read the article to his live-in girlfriend, Bethany Parker who showed him about his former employer Common Cause. "I told you the company was filled with crooks."

"Sweetie, I've known you've been right all along, but don't get so upset over it."

"Upset, I was making six figures with that company plus tremendous stock options. I was the technical brains of the outfit."

She put her hand on his forearm with the hope of keeping him from losing his temper again. "Yes, but that is history now and now you've got a wonderful job—that voice synthesizer software is pretty cool. How's the latté?"

"Well, it looks like they all might get indicted," he raged, purposely ignoring her attempt to divert the subject and control his outburst. "But so what! Look at all the damage they did to both the employees and investors. Well, I have no faith in the justice system. Remember the mortgage scandal where loan officers granted extremely large loans for properties that were no way near the value of the loan? Credit union and bank officers were in the scandal up to their necks. The government had to step in and bail out the whole mess. Who got punished for that one?"

After hearing this again, Bethany just rolled her eyes. "Yes, Joshua, I remember."

"What about the Abscam business where elected officials were convicted of taking bribes for political favors. Four congressmen and one senator did time for that."

"I remember reading about that in my nursery books, Josh, geez, I was almost a baby when that happened."

"I'd like to show those senior execs the business end of my hunting knives."

Several patrons in the coffee shop turned in his direction.

Bethany knew there was only one way to extract him from his bitterness. "Josh, if you're through with your latté, please take me home. It's been a tough week," Bethany said as she looked in his eyes and moistened her lips seductively with her tongue. "I'd love to spend some time in your arms and relax."

Friday, October 22, 2004, 8:45 PM

After calling her stockbroker and cooling off for a few hours, Mary Jane Murray of Lansing, Michigan, sent emails to her congressman, two senators, and the governor. She complained vehemently that Common Cause Communications Corporation intentionally deceived investors, and that gross mismanagement of company assets led to the bankruptcy at the expense of common shareholders.

Approximately three minutes later she received email form letters from her elected officials. They all said about the same thing: that it was always good to hear from voters and that her suggestions and concerns were of great importance.

"No doubt I'll get on their mailing list for future campaign contributions," she said as she deleted the useless emails.

Friday, October 22, 2004, 10:45 PM

Common Cause President and Chairman of the Board, Gerald W. Pendergast, placed calls to business partners in Kuwait City, Dubai, Singapore, Frankfurt, Germany, Tokyo, Japan, and other concerned individuals in Washington, D.C. All of the partners spoke the common language of money and wanted reassurance that fortunately he was able to provide. If all went according to plan, their individual asset growth would be astronomic.

Monday, October 25, 2004, 5:45 AM

Common Cause Communication Corporation surprised the business community and thousands of common share stockholders with another news release.

> Common Cause Communications Corporation announced today that a group of international investors pooled their money to purchase long-term and short-term bonds. The company canceled research and development programs and additional expansion programs. Affected banks have tentatively agreed to restructure existing loans allowing the company to repay the loans on a relaxed payment schedule.
>
> A spokesman for Kuwaiti industrialist and investor, Jobran Al-Tarabolsi, states that one proviso of Common Cause's return from bankruptcy wipes out common shareholder equity. This eliminates any possibility of shareholder asset recovery even if the company returns to profitability. Common Cause share-price dropped from $2.25 a share to $.03 since the company's declaration of financial insolvency a week ago.
>
> Common Cause spokesman Howard Digman said Company President Gerald Pendergast is unavailable for comment.

Chapter 5

Monday, December 13, 2004, 2:44 PM

Three police cars parked outside the hotel. The officers in the lobby had a difficult time controlling hotel guests who seemed to know about the body found in the hotel pool area. Amherst, New York, Detective Albert Burnside pushed through the crowd but felt a hand on his right shoulder.

"Are you the detective?"

"Yes, I'm Detective Burnside. Who are you?"

"The hotel manager, Vincent Lann. What can I do to help? Some of these people want to checkout."

"It really looks like you need the help. I'll get the officers to calm these people down before some one gets impatient. For now though, tell your desk clerk that nobody leaves until we've taken a statement. I'll need a list of names of hotel guests and the staff that is currently on duty. Tell them that as soon as I get the crime scene secure, we'll start taking statements. I'll need to talk to you again very soon."

"Sure, Detective, I'll get the lists as quickly as possible. Oh, if you need a quiet phone, you can use my office."

"Thanks."

Detective Burnside finally reached the pool area and was glad to see that one of the officers had already cleared the vending area outside the pool entrance.

"What's the situation, Jerome?" Burnside asked his friend, Officer Jerome Bailey who was guarding the door.

"A dead Caucasian male, late fifties or early sixties. It looks like someone cut his carotid artery. I'm not sure how many times; there is simply too much blood. We roped off the immediate area and blocked access to the three outside doors. I don't think the crime scene has been disturbed."

"Okay, good so far. How long ago was the body discovered?"

Officer Bailey referred to a few hastily scribbled notes. "Approximately forty minutes ago, Detective. A hotel guest, Helen Gilbert, signed in to go swimming. One of the maintenance men got the key at the desk to let her and her three children into the pool area."

"Three children?"

"Yes, sir. The maintenance man rushed back to see what was wrong because all of them were screaming."

"Pretty hard on the kids," Burnside said.

"Yes, sir. The mother is really shaken by it."

"Any idea who he was?"

"They keep a sign-in sheet at the front desk. Since the pool opened at nine this morning, several dozen people have entered. If he's a registered guest, it should be fairly easy to find out the guy's name."

Burnside pointed to a set of large glass doors with a black frame and simple key-lock. "You're sure that everyone uses this door to get into the pool."

"No, sir. There are three outside doors with push bars. They keep those doors locked so that no one can enter from the outside but anyone in the pool area could let someone in."

"Looks like someone's taped the mechanism to keep this door from automatically locking."

"Yes, sir. The maintenance man says that happens several times a week. The guest wants a can of soda, so they find a way to defeat the lock."

"Not much security here, Jerome," Burnside said.

"No, sir. And there aren't any security cameras in the pool area either."

Burnside just shook his head. "I'll have a look at him now."

"Oh—the medical examiner is on the way."

"Good. See if you can get dispatch to direct her to one of the other entrances. The lobby is packed and a sea of chaos."

"Sure thing."

He pushed the door open with his foot to avoid touching the glass and possibly smudging any fingerprints. Two steps inside the doorway he saw the dead man lying on the green tiled floor. A trail of sticky blood trailed away from the dead man's body a few feet towards a floor drain. Blood spatter stains covered the tile on the right side of the hot tub. The handrail leading from the hot tub had similar stains. He figured that some one cut or stabbed the man in the neck and he managed to crawl a few feet from the tub before losing consciousness.

Monday, December 13, 2004, 9:13 PM

Detective Burnside took the last cold sip from his coffee cup before entering more information in the hotel homicide case file. The department's new software made case file documentation much easier and made it possible to instantly transfer records, pictures, and information to other law enforcement agencies. He leaned back in his swivel chair and wondered what additional details needed recording.

Statements from hotel guests and staff revealed little additional information. The killer simply picked a time when no one else was around. None of the people questioned so far seemed like the type to commit a crime of this nature. The dozens of statements obtained so far amounted to nothing; not a single clue that might lead to the person who sliced into Bertram Nagel's carotid artery?

It was easy enough to find out the dead man's identity, because unlike the killer, Nagel followed hotel rules and signed in to use the pool. By process of elimination, one of the officers isolated Nagel's name from the pool sign-in sheet. They reviewed individual hotel registrations to determine his room and license plate numbers.

A thorough search of Nagel's room added another dimension to the case. Everything in his room appeared normal until they opened his briefcase where they found five thousand dollars. That is a lot of pocket money for any traveler unless the trip is very long or banking is difficult to obtain.

A roadmap on the passenger seat of his 2003 Dodge Concorde indicated he planned a trip to Owens Sound in Ontario, Canada. Four suitcases found in the trunk seemed to be excessive for a single person on vacation. It looked like Nagel was running away from something and that someone had to stop him from leaving. Burnside decided to dig deeper in order to discover what Nagel planned to do in Canada, or see what he had done already in the United States.

With a few keystrokes, he queried the Internet seeking information about Bertram Nagel. Seconds later the information search engine revealed hundreds of items. Burnside grimaced at the number of identified articles. He knew that either there were several newsworthy Bertram Nagels, or for some reason, the deceased Bertram Nagel captured a lot of attention.

After reading several articles, Burnside confirmed that Nagel was on the run. Mr. Nagel's employment termination from independent accounting firm Stegleman, Schwartz, and Mahoney stemmed from Nagel's gross negligence in verifying the accuracy of Common Cause Communication Corporation's quarterly and annual financial statements.

The stockholders from many corporations routinely elected this accounting firm due to decades of pristine service to the investing public. Until Nagel's malfeasance, the firm's reputation for accuracy was beyond question. Since the scandal, most of the accounting firm's corporate clients canceled service immediately. Stegleman, Schwartz, and Mahoney started downsizing the company, while anxious partners tried to reassure the investing public that it would never happen again. The once mighty accounting firm was on the verge of closing its doors forever.

The ringing telephone interrupted his web surfing and Burnside instantly recognized the raspy voice of Mary Ellen Davis, the Erie County medical examiner.

"Hi sweetie, I was beginning to think you forgot about me," he said to the matronly woman who loved to flirt and keep things light before discussing the gruesome details of a homicide case.

"Don't sweetie me, big guy, you haven't been around to see me. Is it my rubber gloves you're afraid of?"

Burnside pictured the rotund woman chasing him with a rubber gloves and chuckled. "Learn anything important about Mr. Nagel?"

She laughed in his ear. "Don't think I didn't notice how quickly you changed the subject, but to answer your question—no. Any tenth grade pimply-faced biology student afraid of frogs could have determined the cause of death here."

Burnside waited for her to start the technical discussion.

"Some one cut his carotid artery twice. There was also a deep cut on his left thumb. It looks like the first cut came as a total surprise. He then raised his hand to either stop the bleeding or to defend himself from another attack. The second cut wasn't as deep but it wouldn't have mattered. Frankly, I can't believe he crawled as far as he did."

"Anything else?"

"No, this all happened in less than ten seconds, there wasn't much of a struggle. I don't think the person that did this got cut in the process. All the blood samples are the same as the deceased. Did you get any solid evidence so far in your investigation?"

"No—nothing that amounts to anything. We interviewed hotel guests and staff but it could have been anyone. Maybe some one from a nearby hotel drifted in. Oh—one thing I did learn, it looks like the deceased was ready to run and hide in Canada, I'm just beginning to learn the reasons why."

"Hey, maybe we could get together and do a little close investigating ourselves," Mary Ellen chuckled.

"Sure sweetie, I've got your home number. Just remember if the phone rings, it's not me."

"Pity," she said in a tone that indicated her loneliness.

Chapter 6

Saturday, January 15, 2005, 6:33 PM

Jocelyn Hafner finished setting the table for her dinner date with Donald Corbbitt. She took a final look to make sure everything was in its place and turned down the oven heat in case Donald had trouble driving down from New York City.

She looked in the mirror and plucked a solitary gray hair from her head, a subtle reminder that at age thirty-five, time was not on her side. Still, she vowed this new relationship would be different from the others. Other men came and went. They were nothing but passengers in a revolving door in her life. Sometimes she thought her beauty was her worst enemy. Most of the men in her life only wanted a quick thrill, to hold her for a moment, grope and paw, enjoy her body, and then be on their way to look for another conquest. Clearly, it was a mistake to let these men in her life, to love and respond to them on their terms rather than set terms and expectations of her own. Yet, she wondered if she would go bald extracting gray hairs one at a time until Mr. Real had sense enough to realize there was something more than sex between women and men.

She remembered getting a surprise telephone call from Donald Corbbitt just after he prevented the terrorists from detonating the dirty bombs in the New York area last September. After many hours on the telephone, she noticed a certain refinement about him. While they talked on a range of subjects from politics to ethnic foods, he never seemed overly aggressive, though his job occasionally demanded lethal force.

On a whirlwind one-day trip to New York City to attend a communications technology conference, she agreed to have lunch with him. Perhaps when their eyes met at the press conference, it was that sad emptiness in his eyes that caught her interest. It was the same emptiness, that ever-present sense of loneliness, that seemed so pervasive in her life.

At the time, she wondered if the brief encounter was a mistake. Manhattan restaurants, notorious for throwing lunch at you and breathing down your neck, hardly gave them any time for conversation and relationship building.

During that quick lunch, she inventoried his physical attributes as no doubt he had inventoried hers. However, many men had blue eyes, brown hair, a set of muscles, and tight buns. If he only wanted a quick fling, she would throw him back in the pile and look for another rather than waste precious time.

She sincerely wanted to believe in him even now at this early point in their friendship that he would be Mr. Real. Perhaps they held the key to each other's happiness. This time she would test the man rather than try to gain acceptance in his eyes. She knew she might scare him away, but she wanted a man who would make room in his heart and keep her there. She needed to know if Donald was the right man and hoped he was smart enough to stay on her honor roll.

Her cell-phone chirped. "Hello," she said.

"Hi Jocelyn."

"Hi Donald. Where are you?"

"I'm in a holding pattern circling the block. I'm trying to find a place for this rolling land barge that I rented. I'll be there in a few minutes. Okay?"

"Yes, of course, and thanks for letting me know."

She increased the oven heat and checked the apartment again to make sure everything was in its place. She dashed to the mirror to ensure that every strand of her honey brown hair fell into its allotted location. She checked her dark green turtleneck sweater and the well-coordinated emerald-green jacket and skirt for lint. Only then did she notice there was something missing. She dashed into the bedroom and selected a gold bracelet for her left hand and simple gold-loop earrings for her pierced ears.

She heard the security door buzzer sound, but checked to make sure it was him before she pressed the button that allowed him into the lobby. She suddenly realized that every action today, the apartment, the dinner, and her appearance revolved around this man. She was as perfect as she could be. She wondered if he would notice or if he would do the same for her.

The knock on the door broke her train of thought. She peered through the peephole in the door just to ensure it was safe, put on her best smile, and opened the door.

"Donald, it's so good to see you again. Thanks for making the trip," she said, noticing how his eyes lit up when he first saw her in the doorway. For a second this man of action just stood there as if mesmerized. "Come in. Let me take your coat."

He stepped through the doorway with a small box wrapped in gold foil. "Hi Jocelyn. This is for you."

She recognized the gift instantly.

"Wow, I know what this is. This is chocolate and not the type you get at the drugstore either," she said with genuine euphoria and an even bigger smile. "Thank you."

"You're welcome." He came close to her as if he wanted to kiss her cheek, but for the moment she dodged the attempt and hung up his coat.

"Hey, what's that smell. You've been cooking. I thought we were going out to eat."

"Guilty as charged, Agent Corbbitt. I just thought that our lunch in New York was so chaotic and since Saturday nights can be a restaurant's busiest night, we'd be better off eating here. Is that okay?"

"Sure, it's fine with me. With the job I have, I eat too many meals in restaurants anyway. So this is a real treat."

"We can have some chocolate later with the opera," she said while looking to see his reaction.

"Opera! We're going to the opera?"

"Well, yes, I haven't seen one in a while. Have you ever been to one?" she asked quickly, reinforcing her plan for the evening.

"Years ago, my dad took me to one, but it was in Italian and a mystery to me."

"If it's too painful, we don't have to do that," she offered.

"No, that's fine."

"Are you sure?"

"Yes, yes, it's just that I didn't think of you as an opera buff."

"I love theater and classical music, and with opera you get the best quality of both. Can I offer you a drink?"

"Well sure, thanks, I'm not fussy, anything with a little alcohol kick will do."

"I've got a few bottles in the kitchen, I'll be right back."

"You have a lovely apartment. Have you lived here long?" he yelled to her from the living room.

"Thanks, I've been here for nine years," she said as she removed the stuffed mushroom caps from the bake oven and gently warmed two snifters of cognac. She returned to the living room and noticed that he was looking around as if capturing details for a case he was investigating. She handed him a snifter and watched as he automatically swirled the light brown liquid.

She sat on the couch next to him and asked about the traffic on the trip from New York. She needed to get the conversation started. Donald kept referring back to work related items and she let him rattle on until she heard the oven's buzzer indicating that the popovers needed rescuing.

"If you'll excuse me again, I'll check on the dinner and we can eat in a few moments. The bathroom is down the hall if you need to wash up."

"You're really treating me like a king, Jocelyn."

"Well, my liege, perhaps it's because I'm selfish and want you to treat me like a queen," she said, observing that her declaration seemed to thump him in the chest.

She placed the salads and the bottle of raspberry vinaigrette on the table and poured ice water into two crystal goblets. "Hey Donald, why don't you put on some dinner music. I'm almost ready here."

"Sure, any recommendations?"

She moved to the doorway. "There's a few on top of the stereo, Chopin preludes, Mozart, Schubert, and there's more in the drawer below. Don't look for any Rap music in this house, you won't find any."

A minute later Chopin's piano preludes played softly and she called for Donald to join her in the dining room. She handed him a bottle of Merlot to open while she lit two white tapers and sat down. She watched Donald pour the red wine and noticed that he had sense enough to catch a drop on the outside of the bottle before it hit her white tablecloth.

She noticed Donald looking at her for a moment. His eyes somehow seemed mellow, the crows-feet of daily stress vanished, and his broadening smile was charming and somewhat disarming.

"The salad is wonderful, Jocelyn. Did you make the dressing yourself?"

"Yes, I did. I don't cook like this very often—really only for good company."

"Well thank you. Like I was saying in the living room, I eat too many meals in restaurants."

She nodded.

"We've been building a case file against eight people we suspect to be terrorists, perhaps part of the al Qaida network …"

"You know, Donald, we both work for the same company. I really don't want to talk about work this evening. I am much more interested in you and your family. We really don't know much about one another."

"I'm sorry. You're right, of course. There is more to life than work," he said, catching some salad dressing from the corner of his mouth with a napkin.

She listened to him tell her about his mother and father, his childhood, in Newark, Delaware. Then he spoke of his younger brother in the Air Force and a sister who married poorly, once to a high school football star, her subsequent divorce, and second marriage to a Pennsylvania dentist. While he talked, she noticed that he was immaculately dressed, knew which fork to use for the salad, and kept his elbows off the table.

She excused herself to serve the rest of the meal and she could feel his eyes studying her as she headed toward the kitchen.

"Anything I can do to help?"

"You can pour some more wine, if you don't mind. And please continue. I can hear you from the kitchen."

Moments later she returned with two dinner plates. "I hope you're not allergic to any of this, I probably should have asked."

He looked at the pork tenderloin slices swimming in pink apple sauce, with little heart shaped dollops of sour cream, asparagus tips, and a small baked potato. "This is too pretty to eat. It's like a valentine."

"Thank you, Donald," she said, smiling at his observation. "What is your favorite food?"

"A large medium-cooked steak, but this is wonderful, Jocelyn. Is this your favorite?"

"No, actually my favorite is something called Happiness Soup."

"Happiness Soup? It sounds Oriental to me."

She laughed. "No it's more international, something that everyone around the world enjoys."

"I've traveled a lot, most of it work related. Why haven't I heard of it before?"

"It's a simple recipe, one-half respect blended with one-half tender loving care, spiced to taste with passion, forgiveness, or kindness. It's served willingly, with no strings attached. It's sort of food for the soul."

For a while it looked like Donald had trouble digesting both the food and the food-for-thought. "Do you serve this often?" he said finally.

"I serve it only when I am reasonably sure, that I will have some of my own to enjoy. Happiness brings forth happiness."

For a while he concentrated on eating the dinner. "If you prepare happiness soup as well as you cooked this meal, then whoever is fortunate enough to partake of that delight will certainly be very lucky."

"Not lucky, he simply will have inspired the cook to make more. Unlike regular food, there is no limit to the happiness soup you can make or consume."

Again, he was quiet. She could almost hear his lighting fast mind processing the possibilities of her life's philosophy. She was quite content to let him think as he slowly consumed the food before him. Now she had doubts and wondered if she had pushed him too far into a corner. Her message to him was clear, poetic, and concise. How he responded next might determine whether they would continue to see each other, whether their friendship would strengthen and become love.

She knew that in a way this was nothing more than a negotiation and she was bargaining for equal status in shaping what future they might have together. Whether he understood that was the question of the moment. From her business psychology class, she remembered that the next person to speak yields the upper hand in the negotiation.

The silence lingered as they finished the last morsels on their plates.

"Jocelyn, the dinner was wonderful."

"Thank you, Donald, would you care for seconds? There's really plenty left. How about another popover?"

"No—thank you. I'm really quite full," he said, looking at her pendulum clock. "It's getting late. Aren't we going to be late for the opera?"

She laughed. "Actually, Donald, the opera-company will wait for us."

He looked skeptical at first, but realized that this woman was full of surprises and another one was on its way.

"Another confession, Donald, I have a collection of operas on videotapes. They all have subtitles. I thought we might enjoy one here, but I think I'd much rather spend the time talking with you," she said, looking for a sigh of relief on his face and was pleased when none appeared.

"You are a tricky one. I would gladly watch an opera, but we can do that anytime. I am curious, what opera were we going to watch?"

"Giuseppe Verdi's, *Rigoletto*. Are you familiar with the story?"

"No, I know a little about Carmen. That's all."

"*Rigoletto* is the tragic tale of a deformed court jester who boasts about the Duke's habit of debauching and deflowering maidens. Rigoletto forgets he has a daughter as he touts the Duke's behavior in front of offended noblemen fathers. Eventually Rigoletto is instrumental in his own daughter's death. Just think how you would feel if someone had no regard for your sister's virtue or feelings. May I interest you in some coffee and some lemon pie?" she said, not wishing to dwell on the message she just delivered.

"That is a tragic story," Donald observed. "As far as the pie goes, I'm pretty full. It does sound tempting, perhaps later. I'll finish my wine and help clear the dishes."

"Not in my castle, sire. I'll just put the dishes in the sink and come right back."

She returned and suggested that they would be more comfortable in the living room. She noticed now that he was asking questions about her background, family, and interests. Now she felt that the day's labor to make this evening special for him was not lost and they were a little closer for the time spent together and the mutual interests that were revealed.

Her eyes grew heavy with sleep and he soon took the hint by apologizing for staying so long. She smiled, retrieved his coat, and walked with him to the door.

"Donald, thank you for coming all the way from New York to spend the evening with me."

"Well, thank you for inviting me, and cooking such a wonderful meal."

"It was my pleasure, Donald," she said, noticing that he was staring at her lips.

"Jocelyn, my friends call me Don or even Corby."

She moved closer to him, looked up, and kissed his lips softly. "Don, my friends call me frequently," she whispered in his ear.

"Good night, Jocelyn. Thanks again."

"Good night, Don."

Sunday, January 16, 2005, 11:14 AM

Donald Corbbitt moved to the right side of the traffic lane as a large truck passed him on the New Jersey Turnpike. The trip back to New York City seemed long and the traffic extremely aggressive. The truck switched to his lane and he decided to stay behind it at a reasonable distance allowing the other driver's eyes and skill to lead him north while he reviewed the beautiful moments spent with Jocelyn.

Those memories appeared as a slow motion movie as his highly skilled mind recalled the details at Jocelyn's home. Now he realized that there was much more to Jocelyn than her well-proportioned figure. Her every movement seemed fluid and graceful as if part of a well-choreographed ballet. She was a total person who loved and enjoyed life. Her notable interests in art, music, and theater complemented her decorous apartment that she referred to as her castle. He realized that the blend of poise and charm did make her seem like royalty.

Whether she knew it or not, Jocelyn succeeded in presenting life to him again. The bleak highway suddenly felt like a de-orbit burn from heaven to mere existence. His world consisted of sterile hotel lobbies, phony desk clerks, and queen-less queen-sized beds. Now returning to his sparsely furnished third floor Hoboken apartment only promised to be a crash landing. After all, his only use for the apartment was a place to go when the demands of work eventually caught up with him. He never thought of himself as a prince or his apartment as a home much less a castle. He knew that unless he made a conscious effort to alter his life, his drab existence would only continue and he would never rise above peasant class. He certainly would never capture a woman such as Jocelyn.

He wondered why she changed the entire evening from having dinner out at a fine restaurant that would have been much easier than cooking and eating at home. That is what couples normally do on a first date. It seemed like she suddenly needed to control everything.

Suddenly he knew the reason. She not only wanted control but also the privacy. By eliminating interference from others, she made effective use of their time and filled that time with overt messages with covert intentions.

Big messages and little signals seemed to dominate the evening as if everything was preplanned for effect. The emerald green clothing, perfectly selected, to match her complexion, also served as a "go" signal, while turning to avoid a kiss when they met at the door clearly indicated a "stop" signal. Why have heart-shaped sour cream in his applesauce, while hers remained round? Was she sending a little signal that she liked him? Was she indicating uncertainty about his feelings? Why mention the opera, only to replace it with chummy conversation later in the evening? Finally, he decided it was a test and wondered if she was satisfied with the results.

What about the Happiness Soup that she described? Was it possible that the entire evening was his first taste, that her suggestion to call her was her way of saying that it was his turn to prepare and serve the soup? He smiled.

Unconsciously, his fingers touched his lips that only a few hours ago received Jocelyn's gentle goodnight kiss. Although the kiss ended their time together, no doubt she wanted him to think of her just as he was doing now. He remembered feeling entranced by her lips, her beautiful eyes, and the way her delicate hand caressed a crystal wineglass. He thought that the gentle arc of her little finger had more graceful elegance than all the other women he ever met. She was most enchanting.

His car automatically followed the truck as it arced slowly to the right and began to decelerate and then stop. Moments later it crept ahead and he saw a red light directing him to stop.

"Hey buddy, are you going to pay the toll?" he heard the muffled voice of the turnpike toll taker.

"Huh? Sure, how much?"

"Give me your ticket and I'll tell you."

He handed the ticket and a five-dollar bill to the toll taker and received his change.

"Are you all right, mister?"

"I think so," he said, somewhat dazed. "It's just that I've never been smitten before. Where am I anyway?"

Chapter 7

Wednesday, February 2, 2005, 10:15 AM

From: Guess Who
Date: 2/2/2005
Subject: Corporate theft
To: Gerald Pendergast, CEO, Common Cause Communications Corporation

No matter where you or your so-called senior executive thieves go, I will haunt you. No matter how long it takes. No matter what it costs me in time, money, or energy, I will make you pay and pay dearly. Start looking over your shoulder—all of you. You have much to fear.

I would sign this note, but it just adds to the mystery to leave it unsigned. Let's just say that I am one of the thousands of employees and investors you've screwed. Sleep well.

Joshua Koweleski, printed the memo to his former boss, folded it, and stuffed it in an envelope for mailing later in the day. He knew an email to the bastard, who destroyed a company that had infinite promise, would reach him instantly, but emails were traceable, while snail-mail made finding the source much more difficult. Maybe he could induce enough anxiety in Pendergast's life to induce a fatal heart attack.

He looked at his watch, grabbed the correct digital videodisc, and hustled down the long corridor to Ninth Generation's executive meeting room. The relatively new Boston beltway computer firm constantly surprised the computing industry with their new and powerful software. Since joining the company in November of 2004 his efforts led to the completion of project

NO SHORTAGE OF EVIL

Nightshade, the latest in advanced virtual reality software. His chief contribution was perfect computer duplication of the human voice.

Although Company President, Edward Hammond, had his usual scowl because of costly delays, Joshua doubted that there would be a big deal made over his late arrival. Innovation and the corporate profit stream that might follow seemed to buy a lot of grace these days.

"All right, folks, if we can begin now," Hammond said impatiently, to catch the attention of those engaged in idle gossip at the long rectangular boardroom table. "Joshua?"

Joshua looked at his assistant, Dale Perkins, who gave him the double-thumbs up signal indicating that his audio, video, and computer hardware was ready. "For those who don't know me, I'm Joshua Koweleski, Senior Development Engineer for the company's Nightshade Project," he said, pausing to take a sip of water. "Those of you who've heard about my former employment at Common Cause, let me assure you that I had no part in the decision-making process or the financial problems that caused that company to go bankrupt. I helped build their technical infrastructure and like many others I became an unfortunate victim."

President Hammond's stare became intense.

"Since my arrival in November, I've dedicated every available minute to Project Nightshade. In a very short time period, our company's innovative programmers made great progress. Technically, Project Nightshade is already a success because we've taken cyberspace to the point where it is indistinguishable from reality. Let me demonstrate what I mean. Dale, roll number one please."

Dale dimmed the lights. Soon the digital projector showed the company logo and a title: "Honing the Edge, Ninth Generation's Vision for the Future." An angry steel gray ocean with mountainous waves appeared on the screen with the persistent drone of a helicopter chopping its way through the air.

Soon an ice-bound shoreline appeared as the helicopter began its descent towards a single figure cloaked in a heavy parka. Wind-driven snow from the rotor of the helicopter temporarily obscured the lone figure on the screen. The camera kept rolling even as the cameraman left the helicopter. This made the picture bounce while he exited and walked toward a sign that read: "Hammond's Hide-Away, Future Home of the World's Best Software Innovators."

On the screen the image of President Hammond spoke. "Our company's products sales success prove that our software engineers are the best in the industry. A constant stream of our company's innovative products makes the computer more useful, more productive, and more entertaining, but we cannot afford to rest on past performance. In order to maintain our leadership position a new facility located on the shores of the Antarctic Ocean will enable our engineers to concentrate their efforts without outside interference from family, friends, or other sources."

The cameraman panned several Quonset huts with wafting black smoke from single rooftop stacks. A digital weather gauge showed the temperature at minus twenty-seven degrees Fahrenheit and a wind oscillating between twelve and eighteen miles per hour. The cameraman moved the camera again and focused on President Hammond's face.

Some of the viewers showed grave-concern.

"By isolating the best and the brightest people that we have for two years, we're sure that both the quality and the quantity of viable profit producing software products created at the facility will ensure continued company success." The cameraman zoomed in on Hammond's face. "Remember, Ninth Generation is counting on you."

During the last twenty seconds of the presentation, Hammond's beard grew from stubble to several inches long. The observers let out a collective sigh followed by laughter as they realized they had indeed watched a computer simulation designed to capture their attention and concern.

"This was made with our new three dimensional graphic rendering software, Ninth Space, and the improved version of Ninth Voice. With a little practice, some sample digital audio and video clips, our integrated software package can place anyone anywhere and cause them to say anything we want. Our software is user-friendly and reasonably inexpensive. So almost anyone can put together a video providing there is sufficient computer speed, memory, and storage capability."

He loved to see non-technical people in awe and smiled in triumph. "A little scary, isn't it?" He watched as some of them squirmed in their seats.

"Now let me show you something really neat," he chuckled softly while his audience whispered among themselves.

"We're all familiar with our company's voice command software, Ninth Command. It's been the industry leader for two years, but others are starting to catch up. So we've reviewed its capabilities and produced a superior product. The new release uses one microphone to detect background noise. The other receives the user's voice and processes the sound for conversion to text on the screen. The previous version had a limited vocabulary and often, high background noise interfered with voice commands. The computer either ignored a command or substituted an unwanted word. The new version uses the detected background noise, produces negative noise, and blends them together. This essentially makes the software error free."

"Then we looked at our company's text to voice software, Ninth Voice. Again, we found room for improvement. Now our software not only converts text into real human voice, but it alters the voice based on punctuation, emotion, mood, or even accent. Furthermore, we've included additional high quality male and female voices that permits the user to code blocks of text to alternate voices as required. Think of a radio-melodrama. That would probably be the best analogy."

He looked around the room and noticed most were unimpressed.

"I know what you're thinking, so what, we've just improved existing products, ho—hum. Consider the possibilities when you put these two products together?" He nodded for Dale to give a microphone to President Hammond and one to the Vice President of Marketing, Linda Prescott. Joshua gave each one of them a piece of paper. "If you'll just read your part of the script, I'll think you'll find this interesting. President Hammond you're first."

President Hammond adjusted his bifocal glasses and spoke into the microphone. "Mr. Hammond, I think it is time we give the employees a raise," President Hammond said. To everyone's amazement, the president's voice sounded just like Linda Prescott's voice."

Linda Prescott spoke. "Yes, I think you're right. Let's give them a twenty-five percent raise and an extra week's vacation too." Her voice sounded just like the president's voice.

Those in attendance gasped again.

"Technically, what we've done here isn't easy, but as you can see, we can make anyone sound like anyone else and in real time too. It's quite possible for one person reading from a prepared script to emulate an entire room of speakers."

"Who would buy this software, Joshua?"

He looked directly at President Hammond, "I think that's what we need to discuss. There is quite a range of possibilities. We should also be concerned that great harm might come from inappropriate use of this product."

Monday, February 7, 2005, 1:30 PM

Maggie Jensen closed her apartment door and looked at the remaining debris. Only the dregs of her fourteen years of comfortable living littered the floor of her eastside Manhattan apartment. An assortment of friends and neighbors came and went with armloads of her belongings. Some paid willingly for her treasures like Tiffany lamps, her computer, and a television. Others insulted her by bargaining for a lower price because they knew she was trying to reduce the tonnage and hassle of moving.

She washed her hands in the kitchen sink and returned to the living room picture window with a thermos bottle of hot tea. In the dimming daylight, she looked out toward the East River, Roosevelt Island, and the Queensboro bridge that were part of the often-enjoyed vista. They felt like dear friends to her and that she was saying goodbye forever. Without a job, there was not enough money to pay for the twenty-seven hundred dollars a month rent, medical insurance, and the drugs to combat liver cancer. Sustaining her previous lifestyle was a financial impossibility. She sipped the hot tea and watched the traffic creep across the bridge.

She felt the small hard mass on her right side just under her rib cage. It seemed harder and a bit larger today than yesterday, but perhaps it was her imagination running wild with the specter of forecasted pain and death from the living bomb ticking away within her body. She wondered if she would live another eleven months and drop out of life at age fifty-six.

The fighting spirit still rose within her. Somewhere deep inside some reservoir of strength remained. Perhaps it was the previous triumphs over a terrible childhood, her abusive father, and her cruel classmates that perpetually taunted her about her psoriasis.

She remembered that drunken red-necked father who demanded respect but deserved none. How he delighted in browbeating his mousy hillbilly wife and tormenting the children. The strict disciplinarian would quote the Bible, fondle a daughter's breast, and finally collapse on the floor in a drunken stupor.

When she had threatened to call the police to protect her mother, Janice, Clara, Brad, and Jimmy, her sisters and brothers, dear old dad put a loaded gun in her mouth and chipped her front tooth in the process. He threatened to pull the trigger. No doubt he would have spread her brains all over the dining room wallpaper, but mom's well-aimed blow with a frying pan across the back of his head changed his mind.

After her father's jail term and detoxification, guilt set in. He wanted desperately to have her chipped front tooth repaired. Every time she smiled at him, she knew he relived his despicable behavior. Her mother told her that the broken tooth was a blessing for them all because it helped keep him off the booze and corralled his anger.

He tried bringing her presents in an effort to regain her affection. The only thing she would ever accept from him was books and money to put her through college. With a Master's degree in Business Administration and an ever-present drive to excel, she thought recognition and reward would grace her life. Instead, the folks at Common Cause only added to her demoralization.

She looked toward the empty bedroom and remembered the many times she looked in the mirror and wished for those warm feminine features that most women possessed. Was it the sperm or the egg that caused the short frumpy creature with incurable skin problems? Did her mother jig instead of jag at the precise moment of insemination allowing the frump laden sperm to displace the sperm with genes of unsurpassed beauty? Was it that simple?

Her childhood, filled with taunts from other children, made her an outcast from all after school activities. Money for lotions or creams, drugs, and ultraviolet light treatment often was sporadic and frequently matched the ebb and flow of the scaly patches on her arms and legs. She lived in the social shadow of whispered names like Scaggie Maggie or Haggie Maggie.

People always made her feel like she was on the bottom side of the toilet seat in the great outhouse of life. Now in the last days of her life, she vowed it was time to do something different. To conserve money she leased a new van with deluxe features. With the available savings and the twelve hundred nineteen dollars from selling her treasures, she planned to travel, live in the van, and visit a few pretty people that needed to hear from the Haggie Maggies of the world.

She went to the kitchen, washed her hands again, and left the apartment with the scenic view she loved so much. Tears streamed from her eyes.

Thursday, February 10, 2005, 9:52 AM

Gerald Pendergast drove himself from the Baltimore International Airport to the northern Washington suburb of College Park. He turned left on Berwyn Road and drove to the end of the street. He looked at his watch. He had twenty minutes before the scheduled meeting with Adrian Horne, honorable senator from Illinois. He locked the car and walked east one block to the spiral ramp. The ramp led to a footbridge permitting safe passage over north-south railroad tracks and access to Indian Creek Park and Lake Artemesia.

He hoped the senator's demand for a private meeting was worth the risk. One published photograph of this meeting and the entire scheme would unravel. He walked quickly toward the lake to ward off the chill caused by a gusting wind in thirty-five degree weather. He stopped at the designated park bench and looked for the senator. Several hundred yards ahead a single figure huffed along the lakeside path with condensing vapor streaming from each nostril as the man approached.

"Adrian?"

"Yes. Gerald?"

"Yes. I thought this meeting was never supposed to happen."

"Neither of us can trust the phones or the email, but you know that. It's vitally important that you know about my colleague's change of heart."

"Don't keep me guessing, which one?"

"Our friend from New York says he's not going to run again and doesn't want to play," Adrian said as he motioned in several directions so anyone looking at them would think he was giving directions.

"Tell him it's too late. He's in up to his neck in this, and no one walks away from the table."

"He sent a one word message."

"What's that?"

"Double."

"In other words he's shaking us down as a price for his silence," Gerald said.

"It looks that way."

"Why didn't he talk to me himself?"

"Like I said, he doesn't want to play. He's trying to distance himself from you and the whole scheme."

"Tell me, Adrian, who gets to be chairman if the old man dies?"

"Probably me. I am reasonably certain, ninety-five percent if I had to guess," the senator said. "He's not planning to have an accident, is he?"

"Adrian, don't ask questions you shouldn't know the answer to."

For a few seconds the men looked across the small lake and the thin wisps of swirling wind-driven snow.

"It's cold out here," Adrian said. "That's the message. Are we done?"

"Not quite. How do I know you're not making this up just for political advantage or to become chairman."

"Look, I'm a team player, but ask him yourself if you don't believe me. Either way I don't care," Adrian said, looking directly into Gerald's eyes. "We've known all along he doesn't have the stomach for this. Do something or this is going to explode in our face," Adrian said, and then resumed jogging.

On the way back to his car on the other side of the railroad tracks, the president of Common Cause wondered what his friend Rudy Gambrelli in Jacksonville, Florida, would want for solving this personnel problem. Something told him that Gambrelli's service fee would be significantly less than the additional ten million-dollar payment that the honorable senator from New York demanded for his continued cooperation.

Friday, February 18, 2005, 8:21 PM

Senator Howard Champion met his driver at the Albany International Airport. The trip home every month seemed to take longer but after three terms in the Senate, he still had remarkable stamina for a man seventy-four years old. "Looks like the weather is going to make this difficult. I'd rather get home an hour late than spend the night in a hospital or in a ditch waiting for a tow truck, so take your time," he said to his driver and friend, Charlie Rayburn.

"Sure, Senator, but the roads were clear north of Saratoga Springs, so the last half of the trip should be all right."

He turned on the Towncar's backseat reading lamp to review the background information concerning Common Cause's bankruptcy. As chairman of the Senate Judiciary Committee charged with the responsibility of reviewing the corporate history and the behavior of the company's management, he realized that the many letters and emails flooding the Senate had justification.

The entire situation surrounding Common Cause's bankruptcy sickened him and he kept searching through the documents for some reasonable explanation to have his committee drop their inquiry. He thought for a moment about his big mistake of agreeing to help those responsible for the company's bankruptcy to get off the hook.

Clearly that decision was a mistake and it would be better just to bow out now by feigning ill health rather than hang with the other senators when the scandal hit the front page. He wanted nothing to do with these white-collar thugs or the money they offered. There was still time to get out, but every minute he delayed increased his exposure. He threw the reports back in his briefcase and clicked off the light.

He looked out the window. The highway only had a light snow accumulation and he felt safe enough with Charlie's driving to take a little snooze. Tomorrow his friends would arrive for another day of billiards and the traditional poker game. He closed his eyes and smiled. They had no idea of how many times he bluffed them out of their money.

Friday, February 18, 2005, 11:21 PM

Senator Champion loved the old Victorian era house near Bolton's Landing and the magnificent view of Lake George. Lake George was one of the most beautiful lakes in New York State. Generations of Champions graced its threshold for over a hundred years. To him, the most comfortable place on the planet was the master bedroom when the blazing fireplace warmed his legs and a winged back chair kept the draft from the back of his neck.

He fell into a chair with a sigh and closed the robe over his pajamas. He noticed the partially opened package Charlie put on the side table and wondered if he should bother with it now. He sipped a glass of red wine the doctors said was good for his heart, but then gave in to his curiosity and grabbed the package.

The plastic wrapped package was from some cigar manufacturer in Florida. He opened the box and looked at their six-page catalogue with colored pictures of the types and blends of cigars that he could buy. They described special discount prices if he enrolled in their cigar smoker's club.

The box contained several items. He found a tool that looked like a small pair of scissors, but upon examination proved to be a combination corkscrew and cigar snipper. There was a book of matches with the cigar company's name, address, web-site, and telephone number. A third item made him smile. They sent a free cigar in a hard plastic tube. He checked the product seal that ensured the cigar's freshness and safety.

He slit the plastic seal and opened the tube. The cigar had a nice heavy feel to it, solid, the mark of craftsmanship and fine tobacco. The doctors jumped all over him about smoking but since he routinely had red wine, he figured that it balanced out. He snipped the end off the cigar and placed it between his lips. He struck the match and pulled hard to get the smoke into his lungs. The first puff was wonderful. The second pull on the cigar had a strange bitter taste that he tried to flush away with the red wine. In disgust, he put the cigar in the ashtray and sipped the wine again.

Two minutes later he felt a tickle in the back of his throat. Then the coughing began. An hour later Charlie rushed in and found the senator on the floor gasping for breath and holding his chest.

Chapter 8

Saturday, February 19, 2005, 3:14 AM

The harsh ring of the telephone interrupted Donald Corbbitt's deep sleep and he fought his way back to consciousness. "Yeah?"

"Don't think you're the only one who was sound asleep, Corbbitt. It looks like there's been an assassination attempt," Harold Pincher, Washington Field Office assistant director in charge, barked in his ear.

Corbbitt suddenly alert wanted the details and fast. "The President?"

"No, thank God, Howard Champion, senator from New York. He's in a hospital in Glens Falls, New York, in critical condition. We need you to support the Albany Field Office. Over half the agents are down with the flu. The President jumped all over the Director and wants answers. We're notifying all congressmen, senators, hell, essentially the whole Federal government of possible attacks and we're mobilizing everyone."

"Terrorists?" Corbbitt asked, as he struggled with a pair of pants.

"There's not much information yet and nothing that ties back to the normal band of hotheads. The only thing we've got from the senator is something about a cigar. Local police have the guy who supposedly takes care of the senator. He might be involved in this. That's one thing we need to clear up, so get moving."

"I've got it. Any transportation lined up yet?"

"New Jersey State Police will get you to Newark Airport. We'll coordinate the rest. Just get there."

"Yes, sir, I'll be ready in fifteen minutes. Anything else?"

"Yes, a forensics team will probably be there by the time you arrive. Stay clear of the senator's home until we know what we're dealing with."

"On my way, but keep me informed if there is anything new."

"The information center is being activated as we speak. Just keep the lid on this, we don't want to get this on the airwaves until we know for sure what's happening."

He slammed down the telephone and dressed as quickly as he could. He filled a small overnight bag with two spare shirts, underwear, and toiletries to sustain him because this case was one of those high profile cases that you worked until you dropped. Everyone would demand answers and the pressure would only increase until the perpetrator was in custody.

Forty-two minutes later, a Beechcraft King Air 350 twin-engine prop plane was number-one for take-off for the fifty-minute flight to Saratoga Springs, New York. He needed a cup of coffee and none was available.

Saturday, February 19, 2005, 5:28 AM

Glens Falls' Chief of Police, James Carney, and two of his lieutenants greeted Corbbitt the minute he walked into the station.

"It's a real pleasure to meet you, Agent Corbbitt," James Carney said. "When we saw you on television and how you drilled that guy last fall, we just about burst our buttons here."

"Thanks, Chief, but I really had no choice. We were fortunate to get there in time," Corbbitt said.

"I've been told you're the eyes and ears of the President. Just know that you'll get anything we can give you."

"Thanks, Chief. What's this about the cigar?"

"It was the only word the senator said to Charlie Rayburn before the ambulance brought him to our hospital."

"Who's Rayburn?"

"Rayburn takes care of the property when the senator is in Washington and I guess the senator when he's here. The poor guy really likes the senator. We've finally got him calmed down a bit. He's over in interrogation room two."

"I'd like to talk to him myself," Corbbitt said. "Any problem with that?"

"Absolutely none, we don't consider him a suspect, but maybe you'll see it differently. I've never seen a man cry so much in all my years at the department."

"Okay, Chief, anything going on at the house yet?"

"Nothing much, we've got the area roped off. No one has entered the house. Your forensic team is about ready to go inside, but they're taking extreme precautions. Gas masks, protective suits—the works I guess."

"If you could keep tabs on that for me, I'd appreciate it, Chief. They're supposed to keep me informed if they find anything."

"Sure thing."

"What about the senator?"

"Not good, sir. They've got him stabilized, but he's real bad. You'd better get the details from the resident at the hospital. Dr. Emil Martinkowski is taking care of him. Here's the number. Just ask them to page him."

Corbbitt weighed the choices of going to the senator's house, to the hospital, or questioning the senator's friend. "Will you tell Charlie that I'm trying to get the latest on the senator's condition and that I'd like to talk to him in a few minutes?"

"Sure, anything else, Agent Corbbitt?"

"Not for the moment, but thanks for all you've done so far," Corbbitt said as he dialed his cell-phone.

The hospital telephone rang six times before a sleepy operator answered.

"This is FBI Agent Donald Corbbitt. I'm trying to reach Dr. Emil Martinkowski on a matter of national importance. Please hurry."

"Jeremy, is that you? If it is, this isn't funny."

"Ma'am, this is not some prank. Get the doctor on the telephone immediately. The Department of Homeland Defense and the President are listening to this call. No further delays please."

"Oh, wow! Okay, you're sure?"

"Yes, do it now!"

While he waited for the doctor to come to the telephone, he connected the cell-phone to his headset, and tested the connection ensuring communications with the information center in Washington, D.C.

"Specialist Hafner, this is Agent Corbbitt, can you hear me?"

"Yes, what is the status?"

"I'm at the Glens Falls Police Department. Senator Champion's doctor should be coming to the telephone. There was no point in me repeating his conversation, you might as well get it first hand."

"Copy, Corbbitt, good idea."

"Dr. Martinkowski, here. Who is this?"

"FBI Agent Donald Corbbitt, Doctor. I need to get information concerning Senator Champion's condition."

"I'm sure you would, Agent, but I am not authorized to give that information to just anyone, especially over the telephone. The senator is entitled to privacy concerning his medical status."

"There may be other people with this condition, Doctor. Please understand there may be a national emergency at hand, we need total cooperation."

"Sorry, Agent …," the doctor said.

"Excuse me please, Doctor Martinkowski. Do you recognize my voice?" the President of the United States said.

The telephone was silent for a few seconds. "Yes, Mr. President."

"Let's hear about the senator's condition. He's a public servant who would gladly yield his privacy rights to save his colleagues and constituents from harm. I'll take the responsibility, Doctor. Please tell us what you know."

Silence again. "Mr. President, this may be a little premature, but the senator's condition is getting worse by the hour. Apparently, he ingested some chemical or biological material. Severe lesions exist on the tongue, roof of his mouth, and throat. We've scoped his trachea and his esophagus; both are similarly affected. He's sedated, but clinging to life. Blood oximetry, blood oxygen level that is, is continually decreasing even though we have him on 100% oxygen."

"Anything we can get to you to help save him?" the President asked.

"Mr. President, I never try to predict the future. Decades of smoking weakened his respiratory system and now with this toxic exposure there is a high probability that the senator is going to die."

"Doctor, thank you …"

"Doctor, have there been any other similar cases like the senator? Anyone else this evening? Perhaps the ambulance personnel, hospital staff—anyone," Corbbitt asked.

"Good point, Corbbitt," the President said.

"Not to my knowledge, but I'd be glad to check and get back too you."

"Thank you, Doctor, much appreciated. Remember that we're all in this together," the President said.

"I will, Mr. President, and please stop who ever did this. I'd hate to think of thousands of patients like this," the doctor said.

"Specialist Hafner, any report on the forensic team yet?"

"Nothing yet, Agent Corbbitt. They've just entered the house with air sampling equipment."

"I'm going to talk with someone who lived with the senator and came to the hospital in the ambulance. I believe he remains unaffected. I'll confirm that shortly."

"Copy."

Corbbitt turned toward the nearby lieutenants. "Could someone please show me where interrogation room number two is? I'd like to see Mr. Rayburn now."

"Just down the hall and to the right, Agent Corbbitt."

"Thanks."

Seconds later he found Charles Rayburn, an exhausted man, with puffy blood-shot eyes, with gray and brown disheveled hair. "Mr. Rayburn, I'm FBI Agent Donald Corbbitt."

"The officer said you were checking on the senator's condition," Rayburn said with a trembling voice. "How is he doing?"

He looked at Rayburn and decided to delay telling him about the senator's condition. "I'm afraid that not much has changed," Corbbitt said, knowing it was far more important to hear what Rayburn had to say rather than quiet him down again after telling him the truth about the senator's condition.

"You know this is my fault. I should have inspected what was in the package before I gave it to the senator."

"Mr. Rayburn, I don't believe for a minute that you're at fault for what's happened to the senator. Let me ask just for the record, did anyone approach you with this package, or perhaps pay you to make sure that the senator received it?"

Rayburn looked back at Corbbitt in disbelief. "No, sir. The senator is like my older brother. I would have reported that to the senator and probably the police immediately."

"How did you get the package?"

"It just came in the mail. I take care of the house for the senator. Anything that's marked personal or private, I just give to him. This looked like some company promotion so I opened the package, just as I've done before. I didn't inspect the contents very well. Maybe I could have prevented this."

He looked at Rayburn and decided the man was close to losing control again.

"Mr. Rayburn, please try to remain calm. If someone sent him a package containing a toxic substance, I doubt very much whether you would have noticed it. Tell me about earlier in the evening. Did the senator seem all right to you?"

"I picked him up at the Albany Airport just like I've done many times. The trip from Washington is not as easy as it used to be for him. He read for a few minutes, and slept most of the way back here. Other than that he seemed fine."

"When was the last time you saw him?"

"When his work in Washington permits, he comes here about once a month—more often if there's a holiday. So about four weeks, I guess."

"Do you talk to him in between times?"

"Yes, about once a week, sometimes more if there is a problem with the house or something that alters his normal routine."

"Was there anything abnormal in those conversations? Did he talk about being threatened? Perhaps a change in the tone of his voice or mood."

"Some stress maybe, but that goes with his job. Some of those Washington jackals play pretty rough."

"Nothing that you can recall that might lead to an assassination attempt?"

Corbbitt saw something light up in Rayburn's eyes. "Well, the only thing, Agent Corbbitt... ."

When Hafner spoke in his ear, Corbbitt held up a finger indicating that Rayburn should wait a second.

"I've got Forensic Specialist Joseph Roscioli who is ready to report on what they've found at the senator's house."

"Copy, Specialist Hafner. Give me a few seconds please."

"Copy, Corbbitt," Roscioli said.

"Copy, Corbbitt," Hafner said.

"Excuse me for a minute, Mr. Rayburn. There's a report coming in from the forensic team that's pouring over the senator's house. Don't forget what you were going to tell me. Even the slightest detail might help us discover who did this to your friend."

Corbbitt stepped outside the interrogation room. "Ready now, Hafner, Roscioli."

"We've done an initial survey of the senator's home, there's no evidence of any widespread toxic gas, nothing in the way of radioactive materials. Biologics will take some time to incubate and analyze. The senator's bedroom was another story. We entered and immediately saw the partially consumed cigar in the ashtray. We've saved everything of course, including the ash that fell off the end. When we looked at the cigar's hot end, we noticed the end of a small metal container. This essentially confirms suspicions about the cigar. You getting all of this?"

"Copy," Corbbitt said.

"Copy," Hafner said.

"Copy," the President said.

"Preliminary indications from the table surface and the end of the cigar indicate traces of ricin. We're going to run the tests again to be sure. This is a very dangerous substance. Ricin is lethal when injected, swallowed, or inhaled. It's been used before in political assassinations."

"So it's likely given the mode of delivery with the cigar, that most of the ricin was inhaled or swallowed by the senator," Corbbitt added.

"Don't bet your life on it," Roscioli said. "It only takes a dose the size of a grain of salt to kill a human. Ricin stays airborne for several hours then falls or plates out like dust. But it is possible for it to become airborne again with agitation."

"So if I get this right, it's possible that we could have some secondary contamination," Corbbitt said looking back toward the door where Charlie Rayburn waited.

"Yes, the senator was coughing; no doubt he spread some of it around. It's best to take precautions."

"My God," the President said. "We could have others showing up at the hospital at any moment."

"Possible, Mr. President, but let's do our best to contain it," Roscioli said. "It still has to be swallowed or inhaled."

"We should notify hospital, ambulance, and police personnel then," Corbbitt added.

"Yes, start with washing hands first, changing clothes, and then showering. Minimize quick movements when undressing or washing clothes to prevent any ricin particles from going airborne again. Probably nothing would happen, but if I had to make the call I wouldn't take the chance."

"Good work, Roscioli. Keep us informed, will you?"

"Yes, Mr. President," Roscioli said. "That's all I've got for now."

"Wait! I have a question or two," Corbbitt said.

"What about the package the cigar came in?"

"We're going to send it in an evidence bag for analysis back at the lab," Roscioli said. "That's what we normally do."

"The more information we have, Joe, the better. This is not a case where we can wait. Suppose there are other such packages. We need to know what to look for," Corbbitt countered.

"What is it that you want to know, Agent Corbbitt?"

"Just describe the package, if you will."

"It's a light cardboard box approximately three inches by three inches, and eight inches long. It's white with multi-colored pictures of open cigar boxes with various kinds of cigars. It's from the New Havana Tobacco Company of Tallahassee, Florida."

"Copy that Roscioli. Did you get that Specialist Hafner?"

"Copy," she replied.

"Joe, one more thing. You've looked at the box as a whole unit. Now try scanning it inch by inch like you would at the lab."

"Sure, if you think that will help," Roscioli replied.

Corbbitt opened the door and motioned to Rayburn that he was almost done.

"Well, I do see three things. First, there seems to be a buildup in four areas on the front of the box where there are traces of some adhesive. Like something was stuck there before and was removed."

"Copy. What's next?"

"The box has a February, 15th post-mark from St. Petersburg, Florida, for one dollar and thirty-one cents."

"We'll have to check on why a Tallahassee company is mailing promotional boxes from St. Petersburg," Corbbitt said. "Who knows, maybe they have a contract with a marketing firm. What's the last one?"

"There are two labels. One gives the address of the Havana Tobacco Company and the other label has the senator's address. That label seems to be thicker than the return label."

"Is it possible we have a label underneath the other one, Joe?"

"I really don't want to pull them apart here in the field, Agent Corbbitt, but I'll do it if you insist."

"You've already taken pictures of it. Right? So whatever magic machines you have to do your testing and analysis with won't care if the label is torn or not. Right?"

"Well, yes, I see what you mean. Wait a second, I have to open the evidence bag and get some forceps."

"Copy," Corbbitt said over the headset while looking in on Rayburn again. Rayburn was rubbing his eyes. "Please get your hands away from your face. I'll explain in a minute."

"Am I in danger?" he asked with concern.

"No, I don't think so. It's just a precaution."

"Ok, I've got the upper label off, Agent Corbbitt and there is another address underneath. The name is Abdel Hassan, of Clearwater, Florida. The street and precise address came off on the backside of the other label. Give me a few seconds to reverse the letters I see."

"Sure, give it to Specialist Hafner, I'll get it from her in a bit."

"Copy," Roscioli said.

Corbbitt went back into the interrogation room. "I'm sorry, Mr. Rayburn. That took longer than I thought."

"Well, I'm not surprised, Agent Corbbitt. I'll sit here forever if it helps the senator."

"Would you tell me what you were going to say before I left?"

"Yes, of course. The senator asked me a strange question. He wanted to know if something really good could come from something really evil."

"Did he often ask you philosophical questions?"

"No, that's not in my league at all," Charlie said.

"Did you have an answer for him?"

"Yes, I said something like 'perhaps, but someone will always pay for the sin of evil'."

"You're more of a philosopher than you think."

"Me, a philosopher, not hardly. The senator took me off the streets when I was on my way down fourteen years ago. Gave me a job, a decent place to live, eventually I got my high school diploma."

"Now I understand why he means so much to you."

"You don't know the half of it. This man spends a great deal of his money trying to help children in Central and South America. He's got a lot of love in him for humanity and he never brags or takes any credit for it."

"Do you think that he wanted to extend the charitable work that he mentioned by some evil means?"

"Agent Corbbitt, I really don't know. Perhaps someone in Washington, someone that works for him has an idea."

"Thank you, Mr. Rayburn, you've been most helpful. There is one other thing and it is pretty simple."

"What's that, sir?"

"There is a very small chance that the ricin that injured the senator contaminated the room or his clothing. We're mobilizing personnel now to take every precaution so that no one else is affected. Your turn will come, but I think you may be here for hours yet, so I ask you to be patient."

"I don't have much choice in this, I guess."

"Mr. Rayburn—Charlie, since you don't have any of the symptoms I wouldn't worry. The forensic team will soon arrive with their equipment just to make sure you're not spreading ricin around. If they find it on you, I'm sure it won't be much more than showering and changing clothes."

"I hope you're right, sir."

"Just relax. If it's any help to you, no one else has reported any symptoms."

"Agent Corbbitt?" a police officer asked from the doorway. "There's a delivery for you at the front desk."

"Delivery? I didn't order anything."

"Looks like someone bought you breakfast. It's from the diner up the street."

"I'll be right there," he said and turned to Charlie. "You're a good man, Charlie, you've helped a lot. I'll do what I can to find who's responsible for hurting the senator."

He returned to the front desk where he saw a lanky young man with a white paper bag and a large cup of coffee next to him on the counter.

"Are you Donald Corbbitt?"

"Yes, what is this?"

"Just breakfast. Some gal called from Washington, D.C. placed an order for you. Normally we don't deliver. Would you sign here, please?" the young delivery man said, handing him a small blank piece of paper.

"Sure, let me borrow your pen," Corbbitt said while he tried to decide who his benefactor was. "Hey, this isn't a bill. It's just a piece of paper."

"I know, sir. I just wanted your autograph. I'd rather have that than a tip. I saw what you did for us on television. Thank you."

Corbbitt chuckled and signed the paper. "Well, I'll sign it, but I was just doing my job. Did the woman give her name?"

"Not to me, sir, but she paid using her credit card. She had everyone at the diner scratching their heads, 'cause she asked for something called Happiness Soup. We've got the largest menu in town, but no one had ever heard of that."

"I think it's sort of a gourmet item. Thanks, I'll go find a quiet corner somewhere and eat this while I have a chance."

He took a sip of coffee and opened the paper bag. Inside, a simple egg and cheese sandwich made him smile. He almost felt guilty eating while so much was going on, but he knew from experience that days that began so early in the morning never ended at noon. A little food and personal regrouping could only help him face the unknown rigors of the day.

Halfway through his egg sandwich, Hafner spoke in his headset. "Agent Corbbitt, be advised the President would like to speak with you shortly. Are you available to take the call?"

"Available—sure. I was just having a bite of breakfast someone was kind enough to order for me."

"Copy. Go ahead, Mr. President," Hafner said.

"Agent Corbbitt, thanks for responding to this situation so quickly and all the fine work you're doing. The Homeland Defense Secretary and I are considering placing the country on Code Red because of the attack on the senator. We wondered if you had any input from your perspective. We're really concerned about the hidden label and the Mid-East connection."

"Mr. President, I can't possibly have all the information that you have at your disposal. I am concerned about the second label too, but perhaps for a different reason."

"Please explain."

"It's too obvious. Either we're dealing with the dumbest terrorist on the planet or someone who is trying to divert our attention. In the absence of additional information such as other ricin attacks using the same delivery method or from others about perceived attacks, I'm inclined to believe this is not terrorism. Certainly, after we question Mr. Abdel Hassan we'll know more. Mobilizing the entire country in error will only desensitize the public for future emergencies."

"I was playing devil's advocate with you, Agent Corbbitt. We agree with your assessment."

"There is one thing, Mr. President," Corbbitt said while checking the wall clock.

"What's that?"

"We've known that it is ricin we're dealing with now for about forty minutes."

"And?" the President asked.

"Are we doing anything to try and save the senator?"

"I thought the doctor said he was going to die."

"At that time we didn't know what it was and more than likely the doctor wouldn't know how to combat ricin. It just doesn't happen everyday."

"Your point."

"Someone, perhaps in the Institute of National Health, should know how to deal with this. Perhaps a drug, or treatment plan could be used."

"Possible I suppose," the President agreed.

"Let me come at this a little differently. Won't the press want to know what is being done to help him? Even if there is nothing to be done, then you can at least say we've tried to help him."

"You're right again, Agent Corbbitt. Certainly the media and the opposing party would crucify me."

"It can't hurt to try. If there is something, you'd better get it up here fast. He's not going to make it much longer I'm afraid."

"I'll get one of the staff to start on this immediately," the President said. "Oh, I've asked the Director to keep you on this case. We need more agents like you, Corbbitt."

"Thank you, Mr. President."

"Agent Corbbitt," Specialist Hafner said. "What direction are you taking the investigation? Can we be of assistance?"

He thought for a second and realized that though the forensic team was very busy there was little else for him to do to do in Glens Falls and he could read their report later. "Try to get me down to Florida if you can."

"Copy," Hafner said. "Any specific location in mind?"

"Not at present. For now, get me to Atlanta by commercial jet. Try to get another private plane for the day so I can have some flexibility."

"Copy. Anything else?"

"Yes. I need the telephone number and address of the New Havana Cigar Company in Tallahassee, Florida, and the same for a Mr. Abdel Hassan in Clearwater, Florida. Also, let me know if forensics in Glens Falls learns anything more from their side of the investigation and the condition of Senator Champion."

"Copy."

Chapter 9

Saturday, February 19, 2005, 11:32 AM

From Atlanta's Hartsfield Airport, Corbbitt checked the available battery charge remaining on his cell-phone and placed a call to the New Havana Tobacco Company. Frustrated, he maneuvered his way through the layers of automated telephone answering selections before speaking to a human. Maybe calling would yield enough information to save time and avoid a trip to Tallahassee.

"Good morning, I'm FBI Agent Donald Corbbitt, please connect me with the company president, senior partner, or plant manager on a matter of national importance."

"I'll see if Mr. Marinelli is available. He is the plant manager," the operator said.

"Thank you."

"Marinelli here, who's this?" a gasping voice said.

"I'm FBI Agent Donald Corbbitt. This is more of a courtesy call but I have a few questions to ask."

"What's this about? I've got some labor problems brewing and a meeting in a few minutes."

"I'll be brief. Sometime today, local FBI personnel will pay you a visit. We will need samples of your promotional package that your company sent to people in Florida."

"Why?"

"It looks like someone tampered with one of your sample cigars and it caused severe injury to at least one person. That person might die."

"We're not responsible for that," Marinelli countered.

"We're trying to determine whether someone that's close to your company or someone else is responsible for this. If you cooperate with our investigation, we'll do all we can to minimize negative publicity that might hurt your company."

"Must have been some bigwig?"

"Does it really matter? But in this case, you're right. To save time and get me closer to the person that did this as quickly as possible I need to know exactly how your distribution center packages the cigar. I also need to know if you have a database containing the names and addresses of those who received your product samples."

"If you think someone here is responsible for this, you're wrong!" Marinelli said. "I've got problems with the workers from time to time, but no one here seems to be crazy or disgruntled to the point where they might do such a thing."

"What is the nature of your labor troubles?"

"Look, this is really company business, but I'll tell you anyway. We've increased sales because of better marketing and use of the Internet. Right now, I've got people upset because they're working too much overtime. I'd really like to hire more people, but growth is tricky.

"There's no violence associated with any of this. It's just that my employees want to spend more time with their families. Hopefully I can keep this from getting any worse."

"We will investigate all aspects of this case, sir. I'm just trying to see if there is someone working there who is motivated enough to tamper with a package you sent out that might do your company real harm."

"Okay, Agent Corbbitt, I understand. I do have to go. You'll get our full cooperation. Let me put you in touch with someone who can give you the answers you need. If you need more help, call me again."

"Thank you."

Marinelli gave him the telephone number that bypassed the automated system, routed his call to the company shipping department, and shipping clerk Angelo Santini.

"Santini here, Agent Corbbitt. The boss just told me on the portable radio who you are. What can I do for you?"

"I'm trying to compare a promotional sample that was found at a victim's crime scene that came from your company with the actual package you shipped. Would you describe for me what method you use to label and prepare a kit for delivery?"

"Pretty simple. One label does three things, recipient address, return address, and metered postage."

"One label, never two?"

"That's right."

"Anything unique about the label?"

"Nothing really, but they have quality adhesive and rounded corners so they won't peel back during shipping."

"Rounded corners?"

"Yes, the square edge tends to loosen and stick to other packages. At three bucks a pop, we try our best to get them to the prospective customers."

"Speaking of customers, if I give you a name, how hard would it be for you to find the name in your records?"

"Not very hard at all. If we've shipped to a customer, we got the name in the database. What name are you looking for?"

"Abdel Hassan," Corbbitt answered, but spelled it out slowly so that misspelling wouldn't yield an incorrect answer.

"Give me a minute to check, we have every person we ever sent a promotional sample to in the database. It's really the only way to prevent duplication and measure cost effectiveness."

Corbbitt waited but wondered about the database and the possibility of using it as a tool for tracking down the person responsible for injuring the senator.

"Agent Corbbitt, I'm sorry. I've checked twice. There's no record of a Mr. Abdel Hassan."

"Thanks for checking. I'm really not surprised," Corbbitt said.

"Why is that?"

"It's just that a little information came too easily," Corbbitt admitted. "Can you sort your database by shipment date?"

"Yes, and by location as well. That's one way we can tell where most of our orders come from."

"How many samples do you send out in a month's time?"

"It varies. Sometimes one hundred but usually never more than three hundred just prior to the Christmas holiday."

"Tell me about the cigar that normally comes in the kit? Do you use the same kind?"

"This year we used our most popular cigar. It's called the Barin, named for Fidel Castro's birthplace. It makes our rebirth of the Cuban cigar in the United States a little more realistic and the tobacco is as close to a Cuban cigar as we can make it."

"That's all the questions I have for the moment. There may be someone from the FBI visiting soon to collect additional information and to get the same sample you've been shipping for comparison purposes. Thank you for helping."

"No problem, sir. Good luck with your investigation."

He ended the conversation with the shipping clerk and checked the remaining cell-phone battery status. It was time to conserve a bit, but the cell-phone chirped again before he could get to a pay telephone.

"Corbbitt, here."

"Hafner here. Here is the update you requested."

"Thanks, go ahead."

"The senator is now in a coma, there is little hope he'll recover. The President did find several research groups that are working on ricin vaccines, but none is ready for trial. Dr. Martinkowski got a little testy with the force-fed help we pushed his way, but once he understood the possible consequences he calmed down. The forensics team at the senator's home has found a little ricin contamination in the senator's bedroom. Fortunately, that's the extent of the contamination. Since ricin is so devastating, everyone who's had contact with the senator is undergoing testing. No one has symptoms similar to the senator at this point."

"Is there any evidence of similar cases involving product tampering that resulted in ricin poisoning?"

"We're not aware of any at this time."

"Anything else going on?"

"No, the President returned to his scheduled activities, and the Homeland Defense Secretary is still worried about domestic terrorism, but is not going to Code Red yet. The FBI Director is another matter. He's got a team ready to capture this Abdel Hassan."

"On what basis? Don't tell me they're buying into this label business!"

"No. It turns out that Mr. Hassan is a chemistry teacher. They feel that justifies bringing him in for questioning."

"Perhaps, but teaching chemistry isn't against the law."

"Still the clamor is building to catch who ever did this to the senator."

"Don't we ever learn? The Bureau's done this before and taken quite a bit of heat from, harassing, arresting, or even killing the wrong person."

"The operation is about ready to go down."

"Who's in charge of this?"

"It's being coordinated by our Tampa Field Office, but Agent Milton Scrivner is just following the Director's orders."

"I'd still like to stop this operation if possible."

"Do you want to talk to the Director?"

"Yes."

"I'll try and patch you through to the Director. Wait."

Seconds later FBI Director Walter Lowery picked up the telephone; Corbbitt heard other telephones and a small army of people talking in the background. "Ok, Agent Corbbitt, go ahead, but we're kinda busy at the moment."

"Unless you have solid evidence that I am unaware of, Mr. Director, please delay an assault on Abdel Hassan's home. I've got information from the tobacco company that confirms product tampering and they've got a complete database that lists everyone that's received promotional samples. Mr. Hassan was not on the list."

"Look Corbbitt, thanks for the information, but this is not your call. I know you're the President's fair-haired boy right now and you're in charge of the case, but you're not on the scene yet. We need to act quickly before this guy evaporates."

"All right, Mr. Director, it will take me a few hours to get to St. Petersburg area. Can this be delayed until I get there?"

"No, they're ready to roll now. He'll be available for questioning by the time you get there."

"Mr. Director, I wish to go on record against this. I firmly believe that Mr. Hassan is not a part of this."

"You're not running the Bureau yet, Corbbitt ..."

"Mr. Director?" Corbbitt said into a dead cell-phone. "Shit," he grumbled and ran to a bank of telephones, punched in the number for the information center, and quickly fed the automated telephone answering system Specialist Hafner's extension.

"Corbbitt here," he spoke before she could identify herself.

"Very busy now, Corbbitt, I might be delayed in responding to you. Be quick."

"First, my cell-phone went dead, sometime soon please tell the Director I didn't hang up on him. Second, I'm on my way to St. Petersburg, I'll make the arrangements from here," he said as his mind raced. "Third, ..."

"Hold please."

"Copy," he said.

He looked around the immediate area searching for the departure monitors that would tell him the next commercial flight out of Atlanta.

"Agent Corbbitt, be advised that the subject, Abdel Hassan, is in custody."

"Copy, that was quick."

"Yes, no shots fired. Apparently the Hassans were having a birthday party."

Corbbitt grimaced, but refrained from making any comment. "Can we resume, our previous conversation?"

"Yes, continue. The other activity seems stable."

"Third, I'd like Forensic Specialist Roscioli's cell-phone or office telephone number. Fourth, I'm going on the assumption that whoever killed the senator needed some help to create a loaded replacement cigar. The quality of the cigar had to be good enough to fool someone like the senator who would know a damaged or bogus cigar in a second.

"Since everything points to Florida at this time, I need someone to research police activity, news articles, or other available sources for anything having to do with cigars."

"Copy, Agent Corbbitt. Be advised you're booked on the next flight from Hartsfield Airport to Tampa-St. Petersburg. Go to terminal D; gate D-38. The plane is on time and leaves in forty-five minutes. Here is Forensic Specialist Roscioli's telephone numbers," Hafner said, repeating each number twice.

"Copy."

"Anything else, Agent Corbbitt?"

He fought the urge to say 'I love you'. "How about a transfer to the Washington Field Office?" came out instead.

"Copy, request through normal channels please. If you wish, I can get the form number for you."

"Copy, but I'll take care of that myself, you're busy and I have to run across to the other terminal."

After flashing his badge to quiet several disgruntled individuals who had been in line to get their tickets, he managed to capture a ticket and boarding pass for his flight. Now he had the opportunity to jog to the gate rather than sprint to his connecting flight. Hartsfield was one of those places where little old ladies with canes became slalom cones for the more agile passengers trying to get to their planes at the appointed time only to wait another half-hour.

After making the mad dash across the airport, Corbbitt paused to catch his breath. Murphy's Law for airplane travel once again prevailed as passengers with the least time always seem to get planes assigned to the gate furthest away from the terminal entrance.

Corbbitt checked in with the gate attendant and identified himself as a FBI agent. The gate attendant said there would be a small delay due to airport traffic congestion. He begged her not to close the gate door until he was through with a short telephone call.

Roscioli's assistant answered the telephone but promptly handed the telephone over to his supervisor. "Yes, Agent Corbbitt," he said with a weary voice.

"Another favor please. I need to know more about the cigar."

"This doesn't surprise me. We were going to have lunch and then start examining the evidence in detail. What do you need to know?"

"I need to know if the senator's cigar was drilled and stuffed with the apparatus that dispensed the ricin or whether the tobacco was precisely wrapped around it."

"If it was drilled, it would probably have voids inside and feel soft to the user," Roscioli observed.

"Yes, and would be less likely to fool a frequent cigar smoker," Corbbitt added. "It takes skill to make a cigar and even more skill when you've got objectives other than producing a fine smoke."

"So either the assassin has skills in cigar manufacturing or there is an accomplice. Other than 'as soon as possible' how long do I really have?"

"I'm headed to the St. Petersburg area now. Let's say two hours."

"I'll try."

"Thanks," Corbbitt said and sat down to wait for his plane to begin boarding.

Saturday, February 19, 2005, 3:02 PM

The delays seemed endless to Donald Corbbitt as he waddled behind the other passengers deplaning at the St. Petersburg-Clearwater International airport. He moved to a second bank of telephones that offered a little more privacy and called Joseph Roscioli's laboratory number. Roscioli answered on the second ring.

"Well, Agent Corbbitt, I don't know why they pay us. You seem to have the answers before we dive into the evidence."

"Don't worry, Joe, your job's safe. To me the most logical things usually result in the most likely events. That's all. What did you find?"

"We took an x-ray of the cigar before we cut into it. There were two small containers connected by a small tube. The x-ray didn't show us anything about how the cigar was made, so we sliced it in half lengthwise. After a little research to compare normal cigar content, it appears that the installed apparatus displaced most of the filler tobacco. The inner tobacco leaves wrapped around the two containers without voids. I agree it took skill to make this cigar."

"Based on what you've seen so far, do you have an idea how it worked?"

"Just a best guess at this point, but here's what I think. The container near the hot end of the cigar had pressurized gas—probably carbon dioxide. When the cigar is lit, heat from the burning tobacco elevates the pressure within the container. The increased pressure ruptures a diaphragm at the other end of the container. The escaping gas pressurizes the second vessel containing ricin. The ricin is ejected with the cigar smoke into the victim's mouth."

"It doesn't look like the senator had much of a chance," Corbbitt said.

"Yes, even if he didn't have it in his mouth when the diaphragm blew it would still cause the ricin to go airborne. This took some real engineering. We're dealing with a professional assassin here."

"Yes, and assassins rarely work on their own accord. Someone really paid dearly for a professional."

"The 'who' and the 'why' is the tough part. Isn't it, Don?"

"I think the 'why' may lead us to the 'who' in this case, Joe. Anything else?"

"No, we're still examining all the evidence. I'll get back to you if anything unusual develops. We're waiting on the sample from the company so we can make comparisons."

"Thanks, Joe."

He began the next call to the Emergency Preparedness Information Center and requested Specialist Hafner's extension.

"Corbbitt here."

"Hafner, here. Glad you called in. I've squared it with the Director and assured him that you didn't hang up in his ear. So you're off the hook there. He'd like you to pay a casual visit to Mr. Hassan in Clearwater to express our regrets over our hasty action."

"So now it's in my lap for 'our' miscalculation. Ok, but I'll need to know what happened and why they're suddenly convinced he's one of the good guys."

"There's a lot to it, Agent Corbbitt, but Hassan proved his point. The man and his family have been practicing Coptics for decades. It's an ancient Christian sect, and in Egypt, that is a repressed minority. That's the reason he came to the United States twenty-five years ago and brought his entire family with him. Basically the man is a flag waving solid citizen and has no use for violence or anything to do with Islam."

"So now on top of everything else, I've got damage control to do. What else?"

"The Secretary of Homeland Defense decided the attack on the senator is an isolated case and no terrorism is involved. Be advised that we're deactivating the Emergency Communications Center at four o'clock. So return to normal Field Office and FBI headquarters communications systems."

"Thanks for all you've done."

"I'm not through yet, Agent Corbbitt."

"Oh?"

"You asked me if someone could check on Florida news and information sources for recent items involving cigars. I'm not sure if this is the kind of thing you want, but I'll give it to you anyway."

"Go ahead, right now I don't have anything substantial that might lead to the person or organization who tried to kill the senator."

"On February fifteenth, Mrs. Margarita B. Rosario, age 58, was found dead in an abandoned building formerly used in the manufacture of cigars in Ybor, Florida. I've looked at several of the articles; here are the basics. Mrs. Rosario is formerly a tobacco industry worker from the Dominican Republic and lived with her husband, José for the past twenty-two years in the Ybor area. Tampa homicide detectives are investigating her death. Another article said this woman was buried yesterday."

"Interesting, this woman is found murdered on the same day the senator's tampered package was post-marked in St. Petersburg."

"Any details on how this woman was killed?"

"No, just a short article and the obituary. It was very short on specifics."

"It won't hurt to touch base with Tampa police. Who knows?"

"That's all I've got for you except Agent Milton Scrivner of the Tampa Field Office should be waiting for you on the other side of terminal security. He can help with transportation and fill you in on the Hassan problem."

"Thanks, Specialist Hafner, I'll poke around here and see what I can dig up, then I want to talk to the senator's staff in Washington to see if they noticed anything strange in the last few weeks."

"Washington," she paused for a second. "Ok I'll make a note of that. For now I've got to go, we're going to review our effectiveness during this emergency."

Saturday, February 19, 2005, 5:22 PM (Atlantic Time)

Rudy Gambrelli sipped his third rum and punch and looked out on the azure blue water tickling the shore of St. Thomas, Virgin Islands. The bar's panoramic view of the surrounding water and several small islands captivated his attention until he heard the satellite fed television interrupt the program for the President's press secretary.

He waved to get the attention of the most popular resort bartender. "Please turn the volume up for a few minutes, Henry, I'd like to know what the emergency is back home."

"Sure ting, man. Every time day do this, it seem like der's big trouble," Henry said as his big smile disappeared.

He listened to the press secretary describe the attempted assassination of New York Senator, Howard Champion and that the senator was in critical condition at a Glens Falls, New York hospital.

"People does deeze terrible tings all de time," Henry observed.

Gambrelli removed a cigar from his shirt pocket. "Mind if I smoke this?"

"It's okay man, da wind blow da smoke outside."

Gambrelli pulled the plastic wrapper from the cigar and smelled the tobacco. He cut the end off the cigar and Henry came over with a match.

"I know what you mean, Henry, the world is turning into a violent place."

He watched Henry throw the New Havana Tobacco Company Seal in the trash can. He took several puffs and looked at the red and gold paper ring on the cigar that identified it as a Barin.

Chapter 10

Saturday, February 19, 2005, 4:05 PM

Corbbitt shook hands with Tampa Agent Milton Scrivner who returned a smile and led the way to a car parked illegally in the arrivals lane outside the airport terminal. Scrivner, like most of the Bureau's agents, had that tough square-jaw look that intimidated felons. Often, they knew by looking at him that it was far better to surrender rather than face the agent's coordinated application of strength, speed, and instinct.

He listened to Scrivner's report on the senseless raid on the Hassan home site earlier in the day. Scrivner described how all the agents knew in their hearts that Abdel Hassan was simply not a terrorist. Although agents rudely yanked Hassan away from his granddaughter's seventh birthday celebration, he answered all questions and managed to contain his anger. Their report noted he never spoke above a whisper.

The entire time he was in custody agents hurried to do a background check on him that included verifying each statement for accuracy. They soon discovered that Hassan was indeed a pillar of the community. Hassan was all he appeared to be—a gentle God-fearing man well loved and respected by friends, neighbors, and his family. Many took the time to show their support and vent their anger at the Bureau for harassing such a fine man.

"We really blew it, Don. Hassan had a way of getting his point across without anger. His eyes and soft spoken voice delivered his message even before you listened to what he was saying."

"I'll do what I can to patch this up, Milt, but I need to stick with the active side of my investigation. In my haste this morning, I left the spare cell-phone batteries on the kitchen table. So, if you don't mind, I'd like to stop and get some. After that I'd like to go to the Tampa Police department to check on a lead."

He gave his new colleague some of the accumulated details from the day's events and the trail that led to the Tampa police.

Once inside the Tampa Police Department, they presented their FBI badges to Desk Sergeant Tylo and asked about the Margarita Rosario homicide file.

"If you're going to take over the case, you'll have to present the proper documentation to Major of Criminal Investigations, Janice Utt."

"We're not here in that capacity. We want to talk with the detective investigating the homicide, and look at the file," Corbbitt said.

"What is your interest in the case then?"

"Have you heard about New York Senator Howard Champion's attempted assassination early this morning?"

"Yes, and we got a warning from the Department of Homeland Defense stating that a code change to Code Red might occur. Is that what this is about?"

"We're not sure if the two are connected. If they are, at least we'll know why she was killed. We'd be glad to share relevant information," Agent Scrivner said. "We'd like to bone up on the details and decide whether or not to talk to family members."

"The detective is not here at the moment. Let me talk to my supervisor," he said as he retreated to the back of the room to a desk telephone away from earshot.

Corbbitt and Scrivner waited patiently while administrative tumblers of cooperation fell into place. Finally, a junior officer came by with the file and handed it to the desk sergeant.

"I've been instructed to give you full cooperation, but that doesn't mean you can take off with this file. Use the desk over in the far corner and I'll get copies of anything but the photos if you need them. The entire file will be transferred on Monday morning to the FBI Records Department, and you can use your normal means to access the information electronically."

"Thanks, Sergeant, you'll get the same cooperation from us. Perhaps we'll solve two cases at the same time," Corbbitt said.

Tampa Detective Hernandez assembled the available facts in detail. Deceased name, Margarita Rosario; age fifty-eight; Hispanic female, approximately five foot six inches tall, weight approximately one hundred seventy pounds, wife of José Rosario. The file went on and on describing address and telephone number of next of kin. Cause of death: Exsanguination and asphyxiation due to aspirated blood from major eight-inch cut in the front of the neck. Approximate time of death 12:30 PM, February 15, 2005.

The agents read the file about two boys noticing the dark stains on a granite stoop in front of an old brick building where they often kicked their soccer ball. The file included a dozen statements from her husband, the two sons, friends, and neighbors all seeking the answer to the same question. "What do you know that might explain Margarita Rosario's death?"

Reading the documentation was one thing, but the photographs were quite another. How undignified Margarita Rosario looked lying in a pool of her blood with her legs spread on a dingy white tiled floor and the gaping neck wound that splattered blood over her simple housedress.

Corbbitt looked into the woman's dark eyes, eyes that even in death told a story of struggle and sadness. He wondered if after the initial pain and the realization that she was soon to die, whether she worried about who would prepare her husband's dinner or who would make sure her granddaughter's confirmation dress was properly ironed. No doubt, she thought about others, even in her last minute of life. Certainly, her killer never cared about any of this.

"Pitiful, what people do to one another," Scrivner said.

"No matter how many times you see a brutal homicide, you never get used to the idea that someone's life just got thrown away like it was nothing."

"Did you see the husband's statement?"

"Yes, very terse. He was either in shock when this statement was taken or he's not telling all he knows," Corbbitt said.

"Want to pay him a visit?"

"It won't hurt, but let's take it easy. The man just buried his wife. We don't want both the Hispanics and the Coptics mad at us."

Saturday, February 19, 2005, 5:34 PM

Milton Scrivner pulled into the short driveway in front of José Rosario's home. The yard, sprouting only weeds, matched the stucco house whose porch and window trim cried for paint, but was overrun with neglect. The house, like others in the neighborhood, gave visitors the impression that they were out of money or just tired of caring.

A rocking chair squeaked as a thin tan-skinned man rocked slowly while staring off into space. Corbbitt observed that the man's gaze never changed as they approached the porch.

"José Rosario?" Corbbitt asked.

The man suddenly jerked his head in their direction as if he mentally jumped a thousand miles. "Si," he managed to say.

"We're with the Federal Bureau of Investigation, sir. This is Agent Donald Corbbitt and I am Agent Milton Scrivner. Let me extend the Bureau's condolences on the loss of your wife, Margarita," Scrivner said very slowly so the Spanish speaking man had a better chance of understanding. "We would like to ask you some questions about her and what you might know about her death."

"Si, I have told the police what I know about this."

"We know you have talked with them, sir. We have read the police report," Corbbitt said. "Your wife's death may be connected with another case I am working on."

For a second José said nothing, but his frown seemed to deepen and moisture welled in his eyes. "Let us go inside. This is not the business of my neighbors."

They followed Rosario into a small living room filled with an old color television, well-used overstuffed chairs, and a three-cushion couch. Each had hand-made head and arm antimacassars. Beside one chair Margarita's knitting needles protruded from a yarn-filled plastic bag.

"I am bringing some iced tea. Margarita used to love iced tea."

Corbbitt looked at Scrivner who returned a subtle nod implying that this was necessary. Corbbitt nodded in agreement. From the kitchen they heard José sniffling and blowing his nose. When José returned with a tray and three glasses of iced tea, his back seemed straighter, his face seemed set as if fortified with some inner source of strength.

He put the tray on the table and pointed to many pictures hanging on the wall. "This was my Margarita," he said proudly. "She was my wife for twenty-seven years. She is also a mother, a grandmother, an auntie, and a great friend to everyone who knew her."

They looked at the pictures that showed Margarita as the central beaming figure of an assortment of children and adults. José handed each of the agents a glass, "Señors, please a moment of respect for a wonderful person."

They rose to their feet and sipped the tea.

"Gracias, señors, now I will tell you what you wish to know."

Scrivner looked at Corbbitt. "What is it you think we want to know, Mr. Rosario?"

"First, I am sorry I am not speaking English pretty good."

"That is all right, Mr. Rosario, I've been studying Spanish for years and your English is far better than my Spanish. Please continue," Scrivner said.

Rosario sat ramrod straight in his chair, "I will tell you now. I am responsible for Margarita's death."

"Mr. Rosario, did you cut your wife's throat?" Corbbitt asked.

José looked at them in horror. "No, señor, I would never do such a thing, but I am still responsible."

"How is that, Mr. Rosario?" Corbbitt asked.

"Since I was a little boy in the Dominican Republic I know right from wrong. My parents, like Margarita's parents, teach us about good and evil. My father, God rest his soul, told me on the day I left home to be a man, to be strong, and always spit in the eye of evil. Because I did not listen, because I was weak, my Margarita is dead."

"Continue, Mr. Rosario," Scrivner said.

"When you are living with the same woman for twenty-seven years, you are knowing everything. I knew last week so'thin' was wrong. I know so'thin' is wrong when I come home from pouring the concrete, just by looking in her eyes. I ask her. She said to me that nothing is wrong. I know she is hiding so'thin'. Señors, this woman lives in my heart, so I know.

"I wait and watch. Later, when we go to bed, I am worried. Señors, we had agreed many years ago, that there would be no lies between us. That in our bed there would only be love. I told her that until that time I felt it was as we agreed. I told her a husband should know what is wrong with his wife and that she could not lay in our bed of honesty and tell me nothing was wrong."

"What did she say?" Scrivner asked.

"First she cried. Then she begged my forgiveness. She was like that, Señors. Then she tells me about a man who talked with her in the market. The man showed her ten, one hundred-dollar bills. He wanted her to do something."

"What was that, Mr. Rosario?" Corbbitt asked.

"At first she thought he was some crazy tourist making a play for sex, but he only wanted her to make him a cigar."

"What day was this? Do you remember?"

"Last week, before the Valentine day. Maybe the twelfth."

"Did your wife know how to make cigars, sir?" Corbbitt asked.

"Yes, of course. She made them in the Dominican Republic as a young woman, and here in Florida. Like many of the other women around here."

"Did she take the money?" Scrivner asked.

"Yes, she showed me the thousand dollars. Then she said he was going to pay her another four thousand dollars, but she had to make the cigar in front of him."

"That is a lot of money for one cigar."

"This is what I told her also," Rosario said. "I felt the evil behind this. I told her that she was to return the money."

"Did she return the money?"

"I thin' so. She kept the money in her dresser next to her feminine things. I checked. It is not there. She was supposed to meet this man on Tuesday to return the money."

"That would be February fifteenth, the day she was killed," Corbbitt said.

"Si, the day after Valentine Day. On Valentine Day, we argued instead of kissing like lovers. Finally, she tired of arguing with me."

They waited while José dried his eyes.

"Señors, she only wanted the money to help Juan, our grandson, to stay in college. She was not a selfish or greedy woman."

"So you don't know what happened to the money or if she made the cigar?" Scrivner asked.

"No, the only money I know of was the fifty dollars police found soaked in her blood. It was an insult to leave such money after killing her."

"Did she ever describe what he looked like?" Corbbitt asked.

"No, only that he was a North Americano, with money. He dressed very well."

"Mr. Rosario, do not blame yourself. You have done the right thing by telling us the truth."

"No, señor. If I told you this last week, my Margarita would not be dead. By delaying the truth I am now a partner with evil."

"Mr. Rosario, I want to call social services and request some grief counseling to help you through this," Scrivner said.

"My family will help me, señor, the same as Margarita and I helped them. They just left. I was just trying to decide who to call with the truth when you drove to my door."

"I might have some more questions for you later, but here is my card. Call me if there is anything you want to tell me about your wife. You have our deepest sympathy, Mr. Rosario, on the loss of your wife. We will do all we can to discover who killed her and see that justice is done."

"Justice? Can justice give me back my Margarita? Can you give such justice?"

They left Rosario's home and drove back toward the Tampa Field Office. At a traffic light, Scrivner looked over in Corbbitt's direction. "I don't know about you, but I hurt over this."

"Yeah," was all that Corbbitt could say.

Chapter 11

Sunday, February 20, 2005, 6:23 PM

Jocelyn opened her apartment door to welcome her friend Don Corbbitt. "You're amazing. I don't know how you do it. You never seem to be in one place for more than a few hours. Come in, I'm almost ready."

Don laughed. "I haven't quite caught up with myself. I hope the rest of me gets here by dinner. I am sorry about the last minute invitation. I had no idea until late yesterday that I was coming to the Washington area."

"I understand, Don. The main thing is that you let me know as soon as possible. This time I was able to push things around a little, but I am very happy that you called me."

"Oh, here these are for you," he said as he handed her a large bouquet of cut flowers.

"Why thank you Don, they're lovely. I'll put them in some water and arrange them later."

"Good idea. We're just a little pressed for time. The reservation is for seven-thirty, but with the traffic around here you can never tell if you've got enough time."

"You haven't told me where we're going. Am I suitably dressed?"

"Jocelyn, believe me, you're perfectly dressed."

She stood in front of the closet full-length mirror to check for stray hair or lint on her black dress and decided that the cream white pearls did not look right with the dress's scoop neck. She stepped into her black pumps and grabbed her purse.

"One more thing and I'm all done," she begged.

"We're not that rushed, even so, they won't mind if we're a few minutes late."

She removed the single strand of pearls and dashed into the bedroom and returned a moment later with a thin gold necklace with a floating diamond and matching diamond stud earrings.

"Would you help me with the necklace, I just fumble with it when I try to rush," she said after putting the earrings on.

"Sure, but I've got fat fingers, those clasps are pretty small."

She handed him the necklace and turned to help him. The little hairs on the back of her neck sent tingles throughout her body as he touched her neck several times while closing the clasp. She hoped he paid more attention to the necklace than her obvious reaction to his touch.

"Thanks," she said and went to fetch her black dress coat.

"Here, let me help you."

She handed him her coat and slipped her arms inside. Then, just for a fraction of a second, she felt his hands on her shoulders.

"All set?"

"Yes, here's my keys. You probably drive better than I do, with all that training they give you guys. I've got a ninety-nine Honda Accord, well-christened with Washington area dents."

"Hey, not a problem. It beats having to rely on taxis, especially later in the evening."

After chipping a little ice off the windshield, Don pointed the car south on Wisconsin Avenue, while Jocelyn wondered what the evening had in store.

"You seem to know your way around the Washington area."

"I've been here many times, Jocelyn, especially since I've been with the Bureau."

"I know we agreed to not talk shop while we're together, Don, but I'm awfully curious about that fellow Hassan."

"She watched him frown for a second. You remember I was trying to get them to wait before raiding his house?"

"Yes, it was just yesterday."

"The Director sent the team in without any supporting detail other than the phony label on the tampered package, his Arabic name, and the fact that he had knowledge of chemistry. No one bothered to check who he was or whether there was any known connection to Hamas, al Qaida, or any of the other groups."

"Now the Arab community is upset over this."

"What about Hassan? Is he taking this to the press or to a lawyer?"

"You know, I don't think he will."

"Why is that?"

"He was more concerned about his granddaughter thinking of him as a bad man."

"What did you do about it?" Jocelyn asked.

"First I just listened to him. He spoke about the Coptic sect of Christianity. Up until that discussion, I just assumed all Egyptians believed in Islam. After that, I met his granddaughter, a real cutie pie, with dark hair and dark brown eyes. They called her Sarah."

"Sounds like she won your heart."

"Yes, believe me no one could resist. I just got down on the floor with her and asked her about her dolly friends."

"I would have loved to see Agent Corbbitt playing with dolls."

"Well, that was just a way to tell her that the police made a mistake and that her grandfather was really a very nice man. I told her that a bad man lied and how good people sometimes get into trouble when people lie. Then I said that the President of the United States sent me to say that we were sorry for ruining her birthday party."

"What did she say?"

"Well, that was interesting. She brought me a coloring book with biblical characters. She reminded me that Jesus said when people say that they are sorry, you are to be nice and help them smile."

"I asked her to help me smile by giving me a hug. Grandpa was very proud of her and he shook my hand before I left. I told Mr. Hassan that the world has a lot to learn from Sarah."

"I can see how this could melt anyone's heart," Jocelyn said.

"Ah, here's my turn," Don said, and took the right turn to cross the Arlington Memorial Bridge over the Potomac River.

"We're going into Virginia?"

"Yes, but just here in Arlington."

When he parked her car in the middle of Arlington's tall buildings, she had the feeling that he might be in the wrong area. Her apprehension grew when he took her arm and led her to a hotel entrance. Was dinner tonight supposed to be room service and a quick toss in the bed for dessert? She was about ready to protest but one step through the hotel's revolving door put them in front of a sign that read, Pegasus Room Dinner Guests, Please Use the Elevator on the Left.

The brass and glass elevator clung to the outside of the building and gradually revealed a spectacular view of the Washington skyline and the Potomac River. Don tugged on her arm after the elevator doors opened to tear her away from the panoramic city view.

From the elevator, they stepped on plush red carpet into a dark-paneled receiving room. A white marble statue of Pegasus with wings extended forced guests in circular paths to the outside of the room. The paths led to an illuminated wooden podium attended by a tuxedoed Maitre d'. "Good evening," he said softly with a warm smile.

"Good evening, I am Donald Corbbitt. We should be on your reservation list for seven-thirty."

"Yes, Mr. Corbbitt, I'll check to make sure your table is ready. You may leave your coats with the girl on the right."

"Thank you, sir," Jocelyn said as she began to remove her winter coat.

Don received a numbered ticket for their coats and returned to Jocelyn's side.

"Right this way, if you please," the Maitre d' said.

They followed him into the opulent dining room where others were enjoying drinks and food and engaging in subdued conversations. They passed a table with three elderly couples where the conversation stopped as they went by. Three gentlemen swiveled their heads.

The Maitre d' sat them at a table for two along the row of plate glass windows overlooking the Washington skyline. He presented the wine and dinner menus, and lit the single white taper on the table.

Jocelyn looked around the dining room and then out towards the nation's capitol.

"Don, this really is incredible. I had no idea that such a place existed."

He unfolded the linen napkin and put it in his lap. "Yes, it's like we're in someone's dream."

"Actually, Don, I feel a little out of place here. Look at those women with their furs and all that jewelry."

"Jocelyn, those women need the furs, a ton of jewelry, and a pound of makeup, but it was you who turned their husbands' heads. Your beauty needs no adornment."

"Thank you, Don. I am just me," she said, noticing the warmth in his eyes. She felt that his compliment was genuine and that there was no intent on racking up points for use later in the evening.

The waiter filled their water glasses. Another waiter brought a basket of fresh bread and rolls and a dish with three types of butter. Don passed the basket to Jocelyn.

"Don, they're still warm from the oven."

"Here, try some of the flavored butter. One is honey and the other is hazelnut, I think."

"Good evening," a man said as he approached their table with an open bottle and two small wineglasses. "I am the restaurant Sommelier. I purchase the wine for the restaurant. Just consider me as your ambassador to our extensive selection of fine wines. If this is a special evening for you, let me share a little of this fine four-year old Pinot Noir. Perhaps you'd like to make a toast."

"I think she is the wine expert among us, but yes, I think we are celebrating tonight."

The Sommelier poured the wine and retreated to allow them privacy.

"A celebration, Don?"

Don already had his wineglass raised. "Yes, tonight a personal celebration. To an awakening and the beautiful woman who rang the alarm to make it happen."

Jocelyn smiled, but deep within her heart soared. "What do you mean by an awakening, Don?"

"Jocelyn, we all have our strengths and weaknesses, things that we advertise to others and things we keep hidden. Sometimes we hide things from ourselves. I realize my biggest fear is that some day I will look in the mirror and see an old man who will have nothing but a retirement watch. A fear that there will be no one to love me because I never really loved anyone. It's like you've turned on a light deep within me, Jocelyn, and I thank you so much for waking me up."

The Sommelier returned to see if they enjoyed the mini-wine tasting. Jocelyn ordered cabernet and Don ordered a Manhattan straight up. With the slightest flare of the nostril, the Sommelier bowed slightly and told Don that he would tell the waiter about his cocktail selection.

The dinner was a blizzard of gourmet entrées served on fine china with the utmost care and accompanied by subtle semi-classical Spanish guitar. Sliced Caribbean lobster with shaved almonds bathed in delicate honey mustard sauce, a Caesar salad prepared at tableside, filet of sole stuffed with crabmeat, and apricot glazed pork loin on a bed of rice. They shared the main course to compare each other's dinner and decided that it was impossible to decide which plate had the better tasting food. The waiter took away their plates and returned with an impressive pastry cart.

"Don, I simply cannot hold another bite, but go ahead and have a dessert."

"Coffee?" the waiter asked.

Jocelyn nodded.

"Two coffees, please. And one of those," Don said, pointing to a seven layer tort with dark and light chocolate icing.

"Don, I've been in a few fine restaurants in my life, but this has to be the best dinner I've ever had. Thank you so much for bringing me here tonight."

"Like I said, I felt like celebrating and I am really pleased that you enjoyed it."

The fresh coffee appeared with the tort. Jocelyn used her spoon and nibbled around the edge of the dessert.

"Wonderful," Don said to the waiter as he removed the dessert dish and coffee cups from their dining table. Don caught the waiter's eye and pointed with one finger toward the ceiling. The waiter understood and nodded. The purpose for the gesture soon became evident when he stood and reached for her hand. At the end of the dining room, a spiral staircase led to a glass-enclosed dance floor on the rooftop. Small tables and chairs surrounded a large polished dance floor and musicians partially hidden by their music stands prepared to play. Don selected a table far enough away from the band so they could talk without having to yell over the music.

Again, the city of Washington and the Potomac River seemed to be at her feet, but now with the window glass in the ceiling the stars and the moon only added to the enchantment.

"Don, what a beautiful place this is."

"I think so too. Do you see the double doors over there?"

"Yes."

"There's a walk way with a high railing out there. When the weather is better, and it's not too windy, I'm told that gals often get kissed out there."

She laughed. "You know, Don, I bet they often kiss right back."

She ordered another glass of cabernet and he allowed himself one more Manhattan. Soon the band began playing, and a few couples ventured out on the dance floor.

"I guess I never asked you, Jocelyn. Do you like to dance?"

"Only with the right fellow," she said as she gave him her hand.

The music was moderately slow and permitted a range of dancing that included everything from vertical cuddling, the businessman's shuffle, and ballroom dancing. Their first steps together were a bit awkward as they are with most couples dancing for the first time. After a minute of acclimating to one another, Don's dancing skills soon became apparent. His lead was firm and decisive and soon their ability to move together without stepping on each other grew.

Whether Don realized it or not, he was passing other tests. She had danced with many other men. There were men who drew her close, squashing her breasts against their chests; men whose hands slid down groping her buttocks; men who checked bra hook location; and men who danced between her legs to rub her thighs. Those hapless creatures showed little respect for her as a person and a total inability to maintain self-control.

Don Corbbitt was not one of those men. He allowed her to maintain the space between them. He provided the direction and the platform for not only elegant dancing but joyous carefree floating under the stars. It was an evening of laughing, dancing, and talking. She noticed how easy it was for her to place her hand in his when the band played another lovely song and how good it felt to be in his strong arms.

At the table, she continued sipping the finest cabernet she ever had, while Don, who had switched to coffee ordered another cup. When the waiter left, Don looked into her eyes and she could sense the change in his mood from dreamy to suddenly serious.

"Jocelyn."

"Yes, Don."

"You know I meant what I said the other day on the headset."

"I'm not sure what you mean."

"When I said I wanted to transfer to Washington, I wasn't kidding."

"Are you going to tell me why, Don?"

He reached across the table. "You're the reason why, Jocelyn. As I was leaving your apartment after that wonderful meal you prepared, I saw something in your eyes that I hadn't seen in a long time."

She started to say something, but he raised his hand slightly begging to continue.

"I saw in your eyes a happy man. And that was me. I've spent the time since then searching my soul. I've examined my life and if nothing else I need to thank you for sharing a little time with me and showing me what life is really all about.

"Jocelyn, it's not right for me to swoop in and out of your life. Visiting the Washington area as work conditions may allow and expecting you to sit on the shelf waiting until I reappear is just not fair to you."

"Are you sure, Don? Have you thought about this thoroughly and what it might do to your career?"

"Yes, my career will just have to bend around this attraction I have for you. I do need to know that you're not unhappy with the possibility of us being together on a more frequent basis."

"Donald Corbbitt, nothing would make me happier," she said without the slightest hesitation.

The band started another song, he reached for her hand again. Soon her head found its way to his shoulder. They danced until the band played their last song. When the last note faded, they strolled back to their table and met the waiter who was impatient to go home. He stood close by until Don paid the handsome bill for the evening's food and drink. Reluctantly, they descended the spiral staircase and found their coats among the few remaining in the coatroom.

Don's hand felt natural and comfortable as he reached for her arm during the glass elevator's trip back to the ground floor and away from the enchantment of the restaurant's plush environment, delicious cuisine, and romantic dance music. She noticed the strange silence that seemed to grow between them. She wondered what he was thinking. Perhaps, as he tucked her neatly in her car, he felt the same sadness because their evening and time together would soon end. During the short drive back to her apartment in Bethesda, she felt the tension building between them and with each step toward her front door, it became more ominous.

Don said wonderful things during the course of the evening, but she had heard similar promises and affectionate words from other men. She realized now there was a big difference between love talk and the actions that validated love. She grabbed her keys from her purse and turned to him. "Thank you for a beautiful evening, Don."

He stepped toward her and put one arm around her waist and the other higher on her back. In a fraction of a second, she decided to return the embrace that included a lingering kiss. It was a kiss that begged for other kisses and the passion that followed. She allowed the embrace to continue and felt his warm breath on her neck as his head turned toward her ear.

"Jocelyn," he whispered. "I love you," but his voice trembled as if he was afraid to speak.

Those words made her soar inside and she wondered in this close proximity if he could sense her heart pounding or the sudden weakness in her knees. She backed away a little so she could see his face.

"Don, how wonderful it is to hear you say that, but those are just words."

He started to say something, but she put one finger on his lips.

"I suggest we judge each other's affection not by often-spoken words, but by actions that make scripted words between a man and a woman unnecessary," she said as she removed her finger from his lips and kissed him softly. "It was a glorious evening, Don. You made me feel like a princess." She unlocked her door and stepped inside.

He stood there for a second and finally shook his head. "Good night, Jocelyn."

"Good night, Don."

She closed the door gently and said out-loud, "Yes!" Then she wondered if Don heard her excessive exuberance.

Chapter 12

Monday, February 21, 2005, 5:52 AM

Leon Andress bound out of bed and turned off the alarm clock before it rang. He began a review of those psychological props that he would use throughout the day to ensure victory over bad habits and re-enforce relatively new habits. In a year's time thirty pounds magically disappeared, blood pressure medication became unnecessary, and stress—the debilitating kind, that caused those dreaded panic attacks virtually disappeared.

He thought of his brother, Peter, and his fat sister-in-law Lillian snoring away in the bedroom next to his. While he loved his brother, and was grateful to be able to visit them during this traumatic moment, he knew a lifestyle change was out of the question for Peter, even if it might ensure better health and prolonged life.

He continued his routine of stretching his back and limbs to make them as flexible as his sixty-one years permitted. He learned that the sweat suit he donned was his armor-plated defense against temptation. His jogging shoes no longer protected his feet from slush, mud, and the rigors of running, but their real purpose was to stamp out the evils of complacency and procrastination.

At home, deluxe coffee would automatically perk while he stretched, but since last Wednesday, the local coffee shop provided the best they had to stimulate his gray matter before the morning jog. He jumped into his rented Chrysler to face his first challenge of the day.

He stood in line at the coffee shop; girding himself against the temptation of consuming those gooey donuts that he used to eat two and three at a time. Now it was easy maintaining control over past purchasing habits. When it was his turn in line, he ordered only coffee, because he made a mental picture of a fat baker urinating in the batter all night. The thought of eating one of those donuts now seemed disgusting.

It was a short drive to the peace and tranquillity that the North Chagrin Metropolitan Park offered. Eight miles of soft trails minimized impact on body joints and provided safety from suburban Cleveland traffic. Out of habit he automatically turned into the driveway for Squire's Castle and selected a parking place as far away from the trail as he could to help him flex his leg muscles a little more before running.

Usually at this hour of the morning, the parking lot was empty. This morning one unoccupied vehicle, the same one that he normally saw upon leaving, was already there. He wondered what the odds were for two New York licensed vehicles to be the first ones to visit the park.

He took a final pull on the coffee cup and then stepped out of the car into the twenty-five degree, Ohio, air. Air that he recognized as a bracing ally demanding that his body burn calories to produce the heat removed by the cold temperature. He stretched against the car and headed for the bridal path that led into the woods.

After the initial hill and a quarter mile into the woods his strides lengthened as he achieved a comfort zone that optimized speed and personal capacity. He tried to concentrate on his pace, the beauty of the forest, animal tracks in the residual snow, and the crisp air that refreshed his body with every breath. The thaw-softened path made running easy. The only sound he heard was his breathing and he wondered if he was quiet enough to surprise the doe that often grazed near the path.

After thirty minutes and what he judged to be three miles of running he saw the familiar group of picnic tables at the bottom of the hill. In his younger days he would just run by them and continue until he ran back to the car, but his knee joints had other ideas. From previous experience, he learned to respect body pain signals. It was time to sit for a few moments and to meditate. The meditation was necessary to prevent a new stress monkey from attaching and growing on his spine.

Now he wondered about the ten million dollars he received from Common Cause to be one of Chief Executive Officer Pendergast's yes-men. He realized almost two years ago that there was something perverse about Pendergast. Risky ventures, unprecedented expansion, and little concern for accumulated debt, all of this demanded by the CEO, placed the company in an impossible financial condition. This was the precursor to its extinction. It was his responsibility as chief financial officer to produce accurate financial statements based on realistic forecasts for income and expenses.

He stared through the trees trying to force all this away from him, but he knew an investigation into the Common Cause bankruptcy was inevitable.

What was the worst that could happen? Scandal, trial, prison sentence, and who knows what the lawyers might leave after they tried every legal trick to get him out of this mess. He raised his head toward the sky to flex his neck and concentrate on the serenity of the passing clouds.

The cold steel against his neck caught him completely by surprise. "If you move you're dead," a soft voice whispered in his ear.

He felt a hand sliding through his hair, then pulling it forcefully yanking his head backward. He could feel the keen edge of a blade pressing against the side of his neck. He knew the slightest movement might be lethal.

"What do you want? Money? My wallet is locked in the car."

"No, Mr. Andress, a wallet full of money won't undo the damage you and your band of crooks did to the employees and investors of Common Cause."

"Listen, it wasn't just me. Why single me out?"

"Single you out! Who says that you're gonna be the only one?"

"You're crazy!"

"Perhaps, but you're dead. Here, this is for all those 'little people' who trusted in you and you screwed, Mr. Leon Andress, Mr. Chief Financial Officer, Mr. Vice Chairman of the Board of Directors."

He felt the sharp twinge as the blade sliced into his neck. Immediately, his field of vision closed. "Oh God, forgive ...."

"Him," the soft voice added, completing Leon's plea to his Maker.

Monday, February 21, 2005, 9:33 AM

When Agent Corbbitt arrived at the Russell Senate Office Building, FBI agents from the Washington Field Office were already in Senator Howard Champion's office looking for some reason for the attempt on the senator's life.

Corbbitt flashed his badge to gain entrance to the outer office where a television provided continuous news reports. Special Agents David Thomison and Edward Gooding knew that he was coming and greeted him in the outer office.

"We haven't done much yet," Agent Gooding said. "The staff is very cooperative and most of them appear to be in shock from hearing that the senator is in critical condition."

"Have you taken any statements yet?" Corbbitt asked.

"I've talked briefly with two of the interns he employs, but they've only been here since the first of the year. So far they haven't provided any relevant information," Agent Thomison said.

"Well, don't discount anything they may have to say. His right hand man at his home in Bolton's Landing thought there was an issue just last week. I'd rather have too much information than not enough. It is hard to tell what pieces might be useful later even if they seem insignificant now," Corbbitt said. "Who are these folks?"

"The woman is Pauline Dryfus, his secretary and office manager. She's been with him since his days as a congressman. The two men are clerks, Ray Jackson and Bernard Lambert. They do most of the research and write everything from speeches to answering inquiries to the senator's constituents," Thomison said. "We have more help coming. The pressure is really on to get to the bottom of this. The President is taking heat from his political opponents. They're claiming not enough is being done to protect elected officials."

"Let's stay out of the politics," Corbbitt said. "We've got enough to do and we don't need the distraction."

"It looks like they're almost done assembling the recent files that we've asked for," Agent Gooding said. "Time to start wading through this."

"Yes, I'd like to start with the office manager, if you don't mind. No doubt, she was closest to the senator. When you start questioning the rest of the staff, pay particular attention to the senator's behavior in the last several weeks."

"Go slow with Mrs. Dryfus. She's been crying and had to excuse herself once since we've been here. She keeps saying over and over that the senator is a good man," Thomison said.

"Thanks, I understand," Corbbitt said.

Corbbitt walked over to Mrs. Dryfus who was busy sorting through a pile of legal-sized file folders that represented the past, present and proposed amendments and bills offered by the senator in the last year. "Excuse me, Mrs. Dryfus, I'm FBI Agent Donald Corbbitt. May I ask you some questions about the senator and his activities during the last several weeks?"

She turned a puffy face toward him; deep scowl lines marred what would have been an attractive face for a woman in her fifties. "Yes, whatever you want, anything to help the senator. I don't know who would want to harm such a kind and generous man."

"Is there somewhere we can go. I'd prefer to hear your statement in private, that way you'll feel more comfortable and your information will not affect the views of others."

"We can use the senator's office," she said.

He followed her into the senator's lavishly appointed office where they sat in winged-back chairs diagonally placed in front of the senator's mahogany desk. "It looks like the senator keeps a tidy office."

"If we left him alone in here for a week this place would look worse than a bedroom for a set of four-year old triplets."

Corbbitt noticed the cigar humidor on the senator's desk. "I think we need to check the contents of the humidor. There might be another loaded cigar in there."

"I doubt it, Agent Corbbitt. Everything gets checked pretty thoroughly before it's brought into the building."

"I'm sure it does, Mrs. Dryfus, but just to be safe, we're going to have them all tested. It doesn't take much ricin to kill a person."

"It's really that dangerous?"

"Yes, trust me, it's nothing you want to ignore," Corbbitt said. "What are your responsibilities here, Mrs. Dryfus?"

"I've been his secretary since he was a congressman from New York's twentieth district about fifteen years ago. But the way this office is organized, the senator expects everybody to do any task that is required."

"That includes the clerks as well?"

"Yes, we fill in for one another all the time."

"Are you aware of anyone who might harbor a grudge against the senator? Some one who might be angry enough to kill him."

"With Washington politics anything is possible, but other than the occasional hot head or disgruntled voter there is no one that I know of."

"What about his friends and acquaintances outside politics?"

"I stay out of the senator's personal life as much as possible. Everyone seems to like him."

"What about some of the legislation? Did he step on any corporate toes?"

"It's possible. He did have an ongoing battle with the pharmaceutical industry over the price of prescription drugs, but all of that is what I would call within the normal bounds of politics. You know they lobby, the constituents complain, and the senator tries to push back on the companies."

"Does he have any other activities that might cause some one to try to kill him?"

"Not that I know of. He's been busy getting ready for the Senate investigation into the Common Cause bankruptcy. He's the chairman of the Senate Judiciary Committee, you know."

"When you say busy? What does that mean?"

"He's been talking a lot with the other committee members, but as to the specifics, his door is always closed."

"Any change in the senator's habits, mood, anger—anything you've noticed in the last few weeks."

"Nothing that you could really take note of, but come to think of it, he did seem a little preoccupied. I just thought it was the pressures of the job."

"Did he ever confide in you about interacting with the personalities involved in day to day business?"

"No, the intricacies of what goes on between the senators stays behind closed doors like that one," she said, pointing to the door.

"Did you have any unusual conversations with him, perhaps something you thought was a little mysterious at the time?"

She thought for a moment. "No, I can't recall anything strange."

"Nothing?"

"I don't remember anything."

Corbbitt remain silent, to give her time to think back over interactions with the senator.

"Well—Well, this is probably nothing. He did ask me a question once that I thought was a little …"

"Strange?"

"Not so much strange, just a little out of the blue if you ask me."

"Please try and recall the precise words if you can, Mrs. Dryfus."

"He asked, 'Is it possible for significant good to be born from significant evil'."

"Interesting. Did you have an answer for him?"

"I said it might seem that it can, but there is always the conscience that will remind you if nothing else."

"Did he respond to your answer?"

"No. He just grumbled a bit to himself, and came back in here. Then, he told me on the intercom that he was thinking about something and to hold all incoming calls."

"Mrs. Dryfus, do you know Charlie Rayburn?"

"Yes, he takes care of the senator's property back in New York."

"What do you know about Mr. Rayburn?"

"Why? He isn't a suspect I hope."

"Do you think he could be part of a conspiracy to kill the senator?"

"Absolutely not! If there was any person that loved the senator and held him in high regard, it would have to be Charlie. He's proven this for years."

"Have you ever met Mr. Rayburn?"

"Sure, he's been here in the office several times and the entire staff goes up to the senator's house for a holiday party in December. The man dotes on the senator."

"That's all the questions I have for now, Mrs. Dryfus. I'll give you my card, if you think of anything else that might help, please call me."

"Certainly, Agent Corbbitt. Just find out who did this and make sure they hang for it. The senator spent his life trying to make others happy and that includes his office staff."

Corbbitt opened the door and noticed instantly that something had changed, because the two clerks were drying their eyes. "Thomison, what's wrong?"

"The news channel just reported that Senator Howard Champion died at 9:32 this morning."

Monday, February 21, 2005, 10:06 AM

Maggie Jensen pulled her rental van into the rest area at mile eighty-eight in Pennsylvania. The rest areas on this road were just too far apart. She hated to get out of the van and expose her profile to people. Everyone thought she was pregnant because her winter coat could not wrap around her huge cancer-swollen belly.

She swore she could feel the tumor growing day by day, pushing on her stomach and bowels. Those organs pushed on others. It was difficult to roll in and out of the driver's seat, difficult to walk, difficult to breathe, and difficult to believe life was going to be much worse, and much more painful before this rampant growth snuffed her out. Those were just the obvious physical maladies.

Eating and digesting food became more difficult with frequent bouts of diarrhea and vomiting as her body's ability to metabolize the food waned. Food became less appealing. She was losing muscle tone and strength while the cancer continued growing.

She opened the windows a crack to permit some air circulation and crawled into the back of the van. She wondered if a protracted stay in a hospital bed would be better than the air mattress and sleeping bag.

She knew her life's calendar needed only months and it was doubtful she could be on her own very much longer. She had other places to go and others to see and maybe, if she was lucky, she could get someone to end it for her quickly. Anything would be better than the pain and agony of the last month of a liver cancer patient's life.

"God, I hate these night sweats," she said, knowing that no one heard or cared.

Chapter 13

Tuesday, February 22, 2005, 10:15 AM

"Good morning, Special Agent Clarke, this is Special Agent Donald Corbbitt calling from Washington."

"Good morning. This looks like a huge case from where I'm sitting. Our Jacksonville Field Office got the verbal cattle prod this morning to dig deep."

"The voltage is pretty high here too, Clarke. Are you getting all you need from the tobacco company manager Marinelli?"

"Yes, he's pretty hard-boiled, but he does cooperate."

"Good, I'm sure you can turn up the heat if he starts to waiver. Listen, I don't know where you're at this moment with the investigation, but it occurred to me that we can use the promotional database to contact the people who were supposed to get the samples."

"Yes, we've thought of that too."

"There are several possibilities, but I'm willing to bet the person who sent the cigar to the senator isn't on that list."

"I can believe that, but how would we know for sure?"

"Perhaps we can narrow down the perpetrator's location by checking to see who didn't receive a product sample from names on the list."

"That's a lot of running around to do. There's over a hundred names on the list."

"How about masking our inquiry as a customer satisfaction survey. Those that indicate they've received the sample and cooperate with a short survey most likely aren't part of this."

"And those that say they didn't receive the product or say they've given it to a friend or relative, are the ones we should interview."

"I guess it is possible for someone's Uncle Jimmy to be the perp," Corbbitt chuckled. "Anyway this might get us closer to the assassin. Check with Marinelli. See what he'd like to learn about his customer's opinions of their product."

"Sure, it won't hurt to get some real data for him while we're poking around."

"Let me know how it's going, will ya?" Corbbitt asked.

"You bet," Clarke said and hung up the telephone.

Corbbitt tried to wipe the sleep from his eyes and noticed that Agents Gooding and Thomison looked terrible. "Hey, let's stop and see what we've got so far. We've been going at this for quite a while."

They drifted into the senator's office; Thomison and Gooding collapsed in the wing-backed chairs. Corbbitt pulled the senator's large swivel chair around in front of the desk.

"Okay, have you discovered anything you'd consider a lead?" Corbbitt asked.

"Man, I've been through hundreds of letters from constituents and their corresponding answers. Outside of a few low-grade letters, there's nothing I consider really threatening. Most of the letters praised the senator," Gooding said.

"Same here, I've read through proposed amendments and associated supporting reports, inquiries, and correspondence until I'm seeing double," Thomison said. "Did you find anything, Don?"

"I'm not sure yet. I've been into the senator's computer. I'll tell you with these larger machines, you can spend forever reading all the stuff that accumulates there. I concentrated on the most recent programs and files that he accessed. I know how you feel, I'm a little dizzy from looking at all the Internet temporary files."

"Anything interesting?"

"I saw some banner ads for the Bank of Dubai. After checking a bit further, I found a reference to the Cayman Islands branch."

"Whew! That's an eye opener," Thomison said.

"Maybe, but it is easy to get ads on the Internet that you've had nothing to do with. After looking at thousands of these temporary files, I just had to look at something else. That's when I noticed the desk pad filled with doodles."

"Wow, he must have been pretty bored. Look at all the ink he's wasted," Gooding said.

"Either bored, or on the telephone a lot. Aside from all the geometric figures he was fond of there are a few things that he wrote and crossed out. Look at the pad. You'll see what I mean."

They left their seats to observe what Corbbitt described.

"See this patch of scribbles and how they're crossed out?" Corbbitt asked.

"I've looked at the underside of the paper where the pencil left indentations and found number BDCI 24770421."

"Maybe that means, Bank of Dubai, Cayman Islands, and the rest is an account number," Gooding suggested.

"Very possible," Corbbitt said.

"We certainly have to dive in the middle of this," Thomison said, stating the obvious.

"Let's assume it is an account number, there will have to be a password if it is a computer accessible account," Gooding offered.

"I've looked for that on the pad too, but I can't find anything that looks like a password."

"Yes, if it is a bank account we won't be able to hack our way through the security," Thomison said.

"When I was looking at the desk pad, I looked under the key board and found this list of the seventeen Senate Judiciary Committee members."

"Nothing strange about that, he was the chairman after all," Gooding said.

"True, but this list is marked up with an asterisk after eight names and there's a question mark beside his," Corbbitt said.

"Is it marked according to their respective parties?" Thomison asked.

"No, they're all labeled by one party or the other. The asterisked names are from both parties, so I'm not sure what it means. Besides, why the question mark next to his name?" Corbbitt asked. "That's all I've got to show for my night here."

"Pity we haven't found the keys to the kingdom," Gooding said. "The bank account business looks strange. We need to look at his finances thoroughly."

"His house manager in Bolton's Landing said he gives most of his money away to charity. Somewhere there has to be a record of this," Corbbitt said. "Let's ask Mrs. Dryfus."

Mrs. Dryfus dabbed at her eyes with a handkerchief and joined the agents in the senator's office.

"Mrs. Dryfus, do you know what this list is?" Corbbitt asked, handing her the piece of paper.

"Yes, it is just as it says. It's the list of senators on the Judiciary Committee."

"But what about the other marks made by the senator? Do they mean anything to you?" Corbbitt asked, continuing his line of questioning.

"No, I'm sorry they don't."

"What about the question mark next to his name? Was he considering stepping down as chairman?"

"Him, step down! I don't think so. In all my years with the senator, he's never quit anything. If he was planning to quit the committee, he never said a word about this to me," Mrs. Dryfus said.

"Do you know anything about the senator's finances?"

"No, since he spent a lot of time in the office, he decided to do all of his bill paying and banking from here. So it's all in the machine."

"Really. Is there a way we can access those accounts to see if there is anything unusual?"

"The senator is an honest man, sir," she said defiantly.

"I believe that, Mrs. Dryfus. This is just procedure. We're trying to reconstruct the senator's recent history looking for leads that might explain why some one wanted to kill him."

Her lower lip started to tremble. "He hated computers, but realized their usefulness. He always had trouble remembering the passwords for the accounts. So one of the clerks built him a file that lists all of them in one place. Give me a second," she said and abruptly left the office to talk to Bernard Lambert one of the two clerks.

"Bernie says to look for a file 'passwords-dot-doc' and to use the password 'helpkids' in lower case letters with no space between the words. That will open the file for you."

"Great, I'm sure that will save us a lot of time. Thanks, Mrs. Dryfus."

"Hope it helps. The senator would be rip roaring mad if anyone got into his private stuff like this. I suppose it doesn't matter now," she said, choking back tears. "Anything else?"

"No one has been to the senator's local residence. We're going to see if there is anything there as well."

"Well I can tell you, anything that might be involved with his business is right here. He made a point of using his home only for relaxation."

"Mrs. Dryfus, you seem to know a lot about how he lives. Have you been there before?"

She paused for a moment. "I might as well tell you. The senator and I have been keeping company since his wife, Millie, and my husband, Vincent, died eight years ago," she said as tears streamed down her face. "I am not ashamed to tell you. I've never known a finer man than Howard Champion."

Corbbitt whispered to Gooding to have one of the clerks to look after Mrs. Dryfus and see if she would like to go home for a while.

By the time Agent Gooding returned to the office, Thomison had Senator Champion's Bank of Dubai, Cayman Island account on the screen.

The account activity page showed a ten million-dollar deposit on November 22, 2004 and another ten million dollar withdrawal on February 18, 2005. "It looks like the money came from and returned to the same account number," Thomison said.

Suddenly, Don Corbbitt understood the senator's concern about good coming from evil. Apparently, rejecting evil cost Senator Champion his life.

Chapter 14

Wednesday, February 23, 2005, 8:42 PM

It was easy to find the village of Hastings-on-Hudson just north of New York City and the address of Common Cause's Chief Information Officer, Walter Mortensen. Hiding behind a large pine tree, while braving the cold February air, the full moon, and the barking neighbor's dog was uncomfortable and risky. Inside, an elegant chandelier illuminated the foyer and part of the large living and dining room. Here at the front of the house through a thin slit in the parted window drapes one might wait, watch, and listen for the perfect time to kill Mortensen.

From somewhere deep inside the house, a rumble of indistinguishable voices was barely audible through the double-pained windows. Long shadows moved across the foyer floor, stopping occasionally as arm shadows projected anger at some one else on the other side of the expansive home.

A woman's feet appeared in nylon stockings. A foyer closet door opened. Someone yelled far away from the front door. She flung calf-length winter boots toward the steps leading upstairs. A coat ripped from a hanger and a closet door slammed shut. A large shadow moved toward a smaller one, making the composite shape grotesque. Their voices grew louder as they approached the front door and each word was overheard on the other side of frosted window glass.

"Honey, don't go. Let's talk this over."

"Go to hell, you're never going to leave your wife."

"I will. I promise as soon as this business with the company is finished."

"What does one have to do with the other?"

"Plenty."

"You're nuts if you think I'm going to wait forever."

"Look Von, this will all be over in a few months. There will be a big investigation—maybe a trial. After that we'll be free to do what we want."

"You idiot! Go ahead and drink yourself into another stupor. I've had enough of that too," the woman said as she sat on the stairs to put on her boots. "We've got twenty-million between us. Let's take it and run like hell."

In the full light of the foyer, the hidden observer recognized Yvonne Taylor's beautiful face.

"Look, if we don't stick together on this we'll do jail time. The first ones who show weakness will be the scapegoats for everyone," Walter pleaded.

"Wait hell! I can't take this anymore Walter. I can't live my life sneaking around dodging your wife and family and running from the Feds because of Common Cause. All the Attorney General has to do is wave his magic wand and he'll indict every one of us."

"Von, honey, wait," he said, reaching for her hand.

"Get out of my way. I'm leaving," she said while struggling to her feet.

Walter grabbed her by the coat. "Von, we've had some great times together, don't leave like this. If we're patient, all of this will blow over."

"You're mad. You're forgetting the other little detail. All the good times and money isn't worth much if you get your neck cut."

"Look, it's just a coincidence, and that accountant, what's the guy's name?"

"Nagel," she added.

"Yes, Nagel. That happened six months ago."

"See what you know! It was two months ago, last December that someone tracked him down at a hotel and sliced his neck. Two days ago, Leon Andress got the same treatment."

Walter tried to use brute force to push her into the living room. Yvonne's knee was quick to respond and Walter dropped to his knees and then fell to his side in excruciating pain gasping for breath.

"Stay here and get your neck cut," she said and stormed out of the house leaving the front door wide open.

The observer waited until Yvonne Taylor walked in front of the house toward the driveway at the far end of the property and drove away in her gray Lexus. Mortensen, who was only beginning to draw a breath, started to crawl toward the living room sofa. With the door wide open, the streets and sidewalk deserted, and Mortensen barely able to move, the observer left the cover of the pine tree and entered the house.

"You've really hurt me, Von, after all I've done for you," Mortensen said, thinking the sound approaching him belonged to his guilt-ridden lover. "Help me up, will you, Von?" he said and then he felt the cold steel against his neck.

"Not what you expected, is it, Mr. Walter Mortensen, Mr. Chief Information Officer, Mr. Member of the Common Cause Board of Directors?" a soft voice said.

He felt a hand slide through his scalp and yank his head toward the floor. "What do you want?"

"I want you to tell me about the ten million dollars."

"You can have the money, just don't kill me," Walter begged.

"I don't want your filthy money. Tell me where it came from."

"Pendergast. It came from Pendergast," he gasped as the keen edge of the knife touched the nerves just under the skin on his neck.

"Who got the money?"

"All the senior executives, we just had to go along with Pendergast's plan for the company."

"Pendergast is a rich man, but he doesn't have that kind of money. Where did he get the money from?"

"I don't know! I swear I don't."

"Slide slowly on the floor, towards the foyer."

"Why?"

"Do it now or you're dead."

He pushed slowly toward the foyer.

"Why are you doing this?" Walter asked.

"I have several reasons, but I understand what a pretty woman can do to a man's sense of right and wrong, so let's keep it simple, Walter. If I don't give you what you deserve, nobody else will. This is for all the employees and investors you screwed, Walter. Did you ever think about any of them?"

A knee held him flat on the floor and the sharp knife pressed hard against his neck until a small rivulet of blood trickled down his neck and dropped to the tile floor.

"Oh Walter, I moved you to the foyer so the blood wouldn't ruin Mrs. Mortensen's beautiful Oriental rug."

With a slight increase in pressure, the knife sliced his carotid artery in half.

Chapter 15

Thursday, February 24, 2005, 7:12 AM

Joshua Koweleski hated telephones and hated them ringing in his ear at work even more. He answered after the seventh ring, "Yeah."

"I guess it's over," his girlfriend, Bethany Parker said.

"What are you talking about? Nothing's changed."

"Well, I tried calling you last night and all I got was the answering machine."

"I wasn't home, that's why."

"Did you find someone else? I tried this number, too, and you weren't at work either."

"Look, Bethany, just because you're in New York and I'm in Boston doesn't mean a thing. I'm still very much in love with you."

"Where were you? What am I supposed to think?"

"Bethany, please, I've had a very long night. Just because I'm not at my desk doesn't mean I am not at work."

"Oh," Bethany said. "I never thought about that."

"Bethany, I'm running out of time on this project. I promise the first weekend I can shake free I'll come to New York."

"Promise?"

"Yes, of course I promise."

"Oh, this morning's paper had an article about your old pals at Common Cause. It looks like two of them got murdered within the last week."

A smile crept over his face. "Well, this really doesn't surprise me, Bethany."

"Joshua, this doesn't sound like you. Show a little compassion."

"Compassion! Those guys never showed any compassion for the employees and investors they screwed. Look, Bethany, I'll call you soon. Take care."

Thursday, February 24, 2005, 8:29 AM

"This is your friend from New York, Senator," Gerald Pendergast said.

"I have a lot of friends from New York," Senator Adrian Horne said.

"I'm the one who met you by the lake. I'm calling from a pay phone and it's urgent."

"Interesting that you're calling me. Is there a problem?"

"I need you to expend some political clout, immediately," Pendergast said. "Two of the three pigeons I had lined up for the shoot have been killed this week."

"You haven't been out in the field shooting yourself, have you?" the senator said, continuing the evasive dialog.

"No, my license expired."

"What can I do for you?"

"I need the best game warden you can find to eliminate the danger. I need to find out who killed those pigeons. The illegal hunter is getting too close to my coop, and I'm very worried. My birds are getting nervous. Some may be ready to break out of the coop."

"I understand. I'll do what I can to get you some help."

"Please do, otherwise we'll lose the chance to win the prize."

Pendergast hung up the telephone and wondered if the whole scheme had already fallen apart. It was taking more people and more money to keep things on track and his slice of the five hundred million dollar budget was starting to shrink.

Thursday, February 24, 2005, 8:45 AM

Senator Adrian Horne turned slowly in his swivel chair to look out on the Mall and the Washington Monument in the distance. He mulled over Pendergast's request. Horne knew that in politics, snap decisions caused huge mistakes. Mistakes on something as large as the Common Cause financial debacle could cause scandals and end with prison terms for many people. Freedom was the real prize Pendergast alluded too. Now that the theft of investor assets was complete, the gang of white-collar thugs was a little nervous about suffering the consequences for what they had done.

He reviewed the Internet news articles that described in detail the recent and similar fates of Common Cause Executives' Leon Andress and Walter Mortensen and wondered what would happen if he did nothing. He tried to gauge the net affect of having fewer people involved against the mounting fear of the survivors. Would the possibility of extinction cause the survivors to crack and tell all they knew?

Maybe Pendergast himself would decide the risks were too great. That would be lethal to several of his fellow senators who suddenly and mysteriously backed away from campaign fund raising by deciding they no longer needed such activities and would end their careers. He knew that Pendergast was the only one who knew all the players in this high-stakes international game where the big money people stood little chance of doing anything but gaining and all the rest risked everything for relatively little.

In one respect, if the killer got all the executive players, the Senate Judiciary Committee's inquiry and the Attorney General's case would simply evaporate. That at least, would keep the government players away from prosecution and the shame of the public eye. This seemed satisfactory on the surface, but the outcome depended upon a killer's ability to strike quickly and thoroughly before one of the players got nervous and confessed.

He thought of several other options, but none seemed better than doing exactly what Pendergast wanted. He picked up the telephone and hit the speed dialer.

"Hello this is Senator Adrian Horne calling. Is the Director available? I need to speak to him on some matter of urgency."

"No, sir. The Director is teleconferencing with overseas FBI offices. May I take a message?"

"Yes, tell him to call me as soon as possible before all potential witnesses are murdered in the Common Cause inquiry we're supposed to conduct in a few weeks."

"I'll give him the message, Senator."

"Thank you. Oh, in case he didn't know, two of them were murdered this week and at this rate the supply is getting a little low."

He hung up on the Director's receptionist and for good measure made a similar call to the Attorney General of the United States.

Thursday, February 24, 2005, 2:15 PM

Corbbitt assumed that New York Field Office Assistant Director Peyton Bender, wanted to see him about the requested transfer to the Washington Field Office. Bender, hardened from decades of Field Office service, ran things by the book and with him, none of his agents' personnel files had room for mediocrity.

While the less experienced agents feared Bender, Corbbitt knew that Bender rewarded and recognized performance, efficiency, and results. Bender's chiseled-in-stone features softened and Corbbitt felt a little relieved.

"Are you responsible for this?" Bender asked, pointing to an aerosol can of hairspray.

"No, sir. If I was, I would have known to get you the 'super hold' strength," Corbbitt said to his boss who often took good-natured jibes from agents because of the flap of hair that he maintained to hide his baldness.

"I've read your summary of Senator Champion's homicide investigation. Anything new?"

"The Tampa agents are digging into the tobacco company's database. That might narrow down the perp's location. The lab analyzed the cigar, and they're chasing down tobacco types to see if it is possible to find the source. The same is true for the components in the cigar. They're also checking the market where Margarita Rosario met the man that killed her. The senator's brief interaction with ten million dollars in a Cayman Island account is the big unknown right now. Other than that—nothing."

"I've got something else for you while you're working on the senator's case and I'm afraid it's going to be a high profile case as well unless we get lucky very soon."

Corbbitt, who was hoping to discuss a possible transfer out of the department, tried not to show his disappointment.

"There is something in common with the senator's case, Don."

"What's that?"

"Common Cause Communications Corporation, the same company the senator's committee was going to investigate."

"Interesting, I know we've been ripping their financial files open to gather information for the inquiry, besides that, what's different about this assignment?"

"Murder," Bender said. "Have you been following any of the news lately?"

"Murder! No, really I've been too busy investigating the senator's case. What happened?"

"Two senior executives got their throats cut, one right after the other. A couple of months ago, the same thing happened to an independent accountant who worked for the company. Same MO on all three—quick cuts to the carotid artery. You'll need to touch base with the Amherst, New York, Willoughby Hills, Ohio, and Hastings-on-Hudson, New York, police departments for their homicide reports."

"That is pretty cozy when you come to think of it," Corbbitt said. "The previous chairman of the Senate Judiciary Committee and executives of the very company he's supposed to investigate are murdered. Very interesting."

"I thought that would peak your interest. Questions?"

"Maybe later," Corbbitt said, but failed to respond by getting out of the chair.

"Anything else?" Bender asked.

"Yes, I guess there is. What about my transfer request?"

"Is there something I've done wrong, Don?"

"No, it has nothing to do with you."

"What then? Do you really think I want to let the best special agent in the office escape to Pincher in Washington?"

"Thank you for the compliment."

"What is it? Are you trying to advance a career with FBI Administration? If so, let me tell you, you're not the type. Guys like you need the puzzle and the action."

"No, it's personal."

"Do you have family in the D.C. area?"

"No, it's someone special."

"Oh, a woman," Bender said.

"Not just a woman, she's 'the' woman."

"Is it possible that this dream woman might agree to come here instead?"

"I suppose, but …"

"Why don't you ask her? You never know, you might find out in her world you're 'the' man."

Chapter 16

Friday, February 25, 2005, 9:06 AM

Corbbitt took a seat outside Gerald Pendergast's office. Through large plate-glass windows, Corbbitt noticed Pendergast look at his watch when his secretary informed him that an FBI agent was waiting to see him. Even from a distance, Corbbitt noticed his eyes squint and a smirk spread across the man's face. Instead of being ushered inside the office, Corbbitt waited while Pendergast placed a telephone call and spun in his office chair to face one of the two windows in the corner office. Corbbitt hated gamesmanship, especially when it interfered with an investigation.

He decided it was time to begin this investigation with or without Pendergast. "I think I'll just stretch my legs a bit," he said to Heather Pollack, a svelte young woman with red hair, who advertised both a smile and an invitation with radiant sensuality.

He started to walk a few paces away from Pendergast's office. "Excuse me, there's not much to see, just a bunch of empty offices. Several of the execs aren't available and you already know about Mr. Andress and Mr. Mortensen," she said with no display of emotion about her dead acquaintances.

"Yes, that's what I'm here for, to investigate who might be responsible for killing them. Did you know them very well?"

"I am Mr. Pendergast's secretary. Since they have secretaries of their own, I didn't really get to know them very well, except for those times I filled in when one of their girls were ill or at meetings when I took notes."

"Do you know if either Mr. Andress or Mr. Mortensen received threatening telephone calls here or at home?"

Heather started to answer but stopped when her boss raised his finger to his lips.

"Mr. Corebutt is it? I would appreciate it if you would direct your questions to me," Pendergast said.

"It's Corbbitt, Special Agent Donald Corbbitt with the Federal Bureau of Investigation. I am investigating the Leon Andress and Walter Mortensen murders. I am empowered by Federal Statute to conduct this investigation independent of any interference. In other words, sir, I don't need your permission to ask your secretary questions."

"I'm the chief executive officer of this company and you'll treat me accordingly."

"You get the respect you deserve, sir. You're the one who turned his back on me. It makes me wonder why you stoop to petty games and you're not very concerned about your colleagues' deaths."

Corbbitt read the change in Pendergast's facial expression and realized he was backing down from playing hardball with a Federal agent. "Look, Agent Corbbitt, I've been under a lot of stress, your buddies have been swarming over our books and files, the reporters are pestering me to death, investors are screaming for my head, and my employees are very threatening."

Corbbitt noted that he put the investors and employees last. "Your stress level is not my problem or concern, Mr. Pendergast. We can stand out here or go into your office. Either way I'm going to ask my questions. You can decide whether to cooperate or not."

Corbbitt saw Pendergast's jaw tighten. "All right, Agent Corbbitt, let's go back to my office. Heather, get some coffee for us, please, decaf for me. Agent Corbbitt, would you care for anything."

"No thanks, I'm not here on a coffee break."

Corbbitt sat in one of the plush visitor chairs across from CEO Pendergast.

"Okay, Corbbitt, let's get this over with. With a reduced staff keeping the company's infrastructure running and maintaining service, it doesn't leave me much time."

Corbbitt wanted to tell him that he could care less about the demands on his time, but decided to begin the questioning. "Were you aware of any threats directed at either Leon Andress or Walter Mortensen?"

"There may have been some threats, but most of the anger came from disgruntled employees who got terminated or investors who lost money due to our bankruptcy."

"How many people are we talking about?"

"At the time of our bankruptcy there were approximately nine-thousand four-hundred employees and thirteen thousand investors."

"It's my understanding that the independent accounting firm elected by your stockholders also went bankrupt."

"Yes, that's true. Pity, it was a fine company."

"Do you know how many employees lost their jobs there?"

"No, I'm sorry. I don't know. You'll have to ask someone in their organization."

"But, you'll agree that any of them are possible suspects."

"Yes, I suppose so."

"How about yourself, have you received any threatening calls or mail?"

Heather knocked and entered with Pendergast's coffee.

"I've had a few phone calls, most of them were just people venting—understandable under the circumstances. If you want somewhere to start, you might consider what we've received. Heather, hand me the three hate files, please."

"Yes, sir."

"We've had letters and emails by the hundreds. Some of them are very threatening. We've broken them down according to perceived threat levels, that's why there are three files."

"Why didn't you report these threats?"

"We did report a few, but most of them are unsigned and frankly we didn't think that anything would come of it. Recent events proved us to be wrong."

"Can you correlate any employee behavior with the hate mail?"

Pendergast opened the top file. "Only one that I can be reasonably sure of."

"Why are you so sure?"

"Here look at this memo. There was one employee, actually one of our best employees—a truly brilliant man," Pendergast said, pausing a moment to recall the man's name. "A biblical name, Joshua, I think. Joshua Koweleski, yes, that was his name. He came storming into our meeting room, enraged—swearing."

"Was this typical behavior?"

"Not really, but he was very vocal within his work group. His manager had to jump all over him in order to get control of his department."

"The memo is from 'Guess Who'. How can you relate this to Mr. Koweleski?"

"That's what he kept saying. He made threats like, 'Guess Who is going to spill the beans on you guys," and, 'Guess Who is going to get even'."

"All right that sounds plausible. Do you know where he's at now?"

"I really don't know. We were just glad to get rid of him. It served another purpose, now that I think of it."

NO SHORTAGE OF EVIL

"What purpose?"

"Well, it kept other hot-heads in check. The gophers stayed in their holes after we canned Koweleski."

"I see," Corbbitt said.

"What about the remaining senior executives? Where are they?"

"Yvonne Taylor, executive vice president of marketing and sales, called in sick. I might as well tell you up front because you're going to find out anyway. Ms. Taylor and Walter Mortensen were very close friends if you know what I mean."

"I am not in the guessing business, Mr. Pendergast. So tell me exactly what you mean."

"They were lovers. I think Mrs. Mortensen caught wind of it and raised hell over it. You're better off getting the details from her."

"What about the others?"

"Edgar Pfost, executive vice president of research and development, is with a skeleton crew in Kansas City trying to get our satellite up-link system back on line. Oh, Koweleski used to work for him. He might be able to get Koweleski's new address for you."

"Thanks."

"Sidney Pelton, executive vice president of engineering and construction, is traveling to visit other offices in this country in an effort to keep others from jumping ship. We're in danger of not having enough people to maintain operations.

"Diane McKeevar, executive vice president of human resources and labor relations, is in Singapore, meeting with the new owners in an effort to rehire some of those who lost their jobs."

"Tell me about the foreign investors who took over the company."

"I don't really know that much about them," Pendergast said. "They came in at the last minute, negotiated with the banks who extended credit to Common Cause, and wound up owning the company, when the banks came to terms with them. Otherwise, we would have shutdown the entire network and there wouldn't be a chair for you to sit on."

"Mr. Pendergast, I need the list of your current and past employees including their addresses and telephone numbers. Soon please."

"I'll do what I can, but I don't have much staff as you can see."

"Yes, but expedite it. There is a killer to contend with here."

"Any more questions, Agent Corbbitt?"

Corbbitt decided that it was time to throw a shot across Gerald

Pendergast's pompous bow. "I need to know where you were at the times and dates listed here," he said.

Pendergast stood in amazement and did not reach for the paper. "Certainly you don't think I had anything to do with their murders."

"You're a suspect for two reasons, Mr. Pendergast. First, you don't seem to be upset that the line of murders points directly to your office. Maybe you're not afraid because you know more than you're telling me. Second, the other investigation regarding the Common Cause bankruptcy means that your executives know a lot about the downfall of this company. Perhaps with fewer people to testify at a trial or inquiry the safer you will be."

"I'm not going to be treated this way."

Corbbitt offered the paper again. "You don't have a choice in the matter, sir."

Pendergast took the paper and read the times and dates.

"Here's my card. Make sure your statements regarding your activities are accurate. We will check thoroughly to make sure you're telling the truth. You can have your secretary fax the information to my office. I'll probably be back with more questions after I've talked with Koweleski and the other leads I have involving this case."

"Anything else, Agent Corbbitt?"

"Yes, don't grow wings and try to fly away. If you must travel domestically, we need to know your itinerary."

"You can't restrict my activities."

"No, but common sense should tell you that more than one investigation is underway concerning you and this company. Any attempt to flee won't help you in court."

"Is that it?" Pendergast asked in disgust.

"I'll need Mr. Pfost's number in Kansas City and you should warn the remaining executives that they're potential targets for this killer," Corbbitt said. "Mr. Pendergast, be careful where you go so you won't get your neck cut too."

Friday, February 25, 2005, 10:16 AM

Only one light was on in Yvonne Taylor's College Point townhouse in the borough of Queens, New York. She looked at herself in the mirror and was appalled at the sight of heavy circles around her eyes from another night of fitful sleeping. Since the argument with Walter less than two days ago and the realization the next morning that someone had killed him, she pondered available options while fear attacked on multiple fronts.

The persistent worry about the Common Cause bankruptcy scandal seemed insignificant compared with the idea of being instantaneously murdered or if someone saw her leave his house just prior to his death, the prospect of being accused of Walter's murder.

The only safe option would be to call the police and confess all she knew about the Common Cause bankruptcy. She would have to include an explanation about the ten million-dollars that the executives received. It would mean plea bargaining with the district attorney to minimize her sentence involving the scandal. Walter's death was another matter. Would anyone believe that someone else killed him after she left?

Doing nothing might save the ten million-dollars as long as the killer decided to get someone else or stop altogether. She thought about the sequence of the murders. First the independent accountant, whose convenient oversight of financial wrongdoing failed to warn investors of internal company expenses and income inaccuracies. Next was Andress the financial officer, with the corner office, who prepared the phony financial statements. Next was Walter, the information officer, who prepared the phony system projections. His office was next to Andress' office.

Then she realized that she was in the next office. It mattered very little that she prepared the phony sales projections. It was very clear now that the whole scheme of phony reports required by Pendergast were nothing but a cover story and a way out when all of this came to trial. Concerning the scandal, whether he was responsible for the executives' deaths or not mattered very little and with each death there would be fewer people to sing the song that he ordered the phony reports to begin with.

She poured the last of the scotch.

"Out of drugs, out of booze, and soon out of time," she wailed.

Friday, February 25, 2005, 3:41 PM

To fly or to drive was always the question when travelling between New York and Boston. This time Corbbitt elected to drive because of a two hour delay leaving from LaGuardia and that his real destination, Ninth Generation Software Company, in Braintree, was at least a half an hour south of Boston.

Ninth Generation was one of many software companies that selected the Boston area and Corbbitt easily found the impressive eight-story building nestled with others along route 128. He pulled the rental car into a space reserved for visitors. A receptionist greeted him just inside the front door. Moments later, security escorted him to President Hammond's office.

"Security notified us that you were here. Mr. Hammond is expecting you," an overly officious secretary said. "You can go right in."

Mr. Hammond's handshake was a little stiff, but Corbbitt immediately noticed that he was cooperative and his cheerful demeanor advertised that business was doing well.

"Thanks for the courtesy call, Agent Corbbitt. I was able to clear my schedule and warn security that you were coming. Please make yourself comfortable," Hammond said, pointing to a nearby chair.

"Thanks," Corbbitt said.

"You mentioned on the telephone that you wanted to see Joshua Koweleski. Is he in some sort of trouble?" President Hammond asked.

"I'm investigating multiple murders of executives at Common Cause Communication Corporation, where he used to work."

"Murders! Do you really think he had something to do with murder?"

"President Hammond, I'm not sure yet, that is why I am here. What's been your experience with him since he joined your company?"

"He's only been here a short time, Agent Corbbitt, but let me tell you I've got no finer employee than Joshua."

"Did you realize that he was discharged from Common Cause because of his aggressive behavior toward management?"

"I'm aware there were certain circumstances concerning his former position, but you know, Agent Corbbitt, given the nature of what happened at Common Cause, I'm not sure I would have behaved differently myself."

Corbbitt handed President Hammond the same list he gave to CEO Pendergast. "Can you tell me where Joshua Koweleski was on those dates and times?"

Hammond took a minute to review what was on the paper. "Were all of these murders in the New York City area?"

"No, Amherst, New York; Willoughby Hills, Ohio; Hastings-on-Hudson, New York and actually a fourth one from another case in Ybor, Florida," Corbbitt said.

"Sir, I can tell you with one hundred percent confidence that Joshua Koweleski had nothing to do with these murders, unless of course he hired someone to do them for him. He's totally absorbed in the work and practically lives here."

"How can you be so sure?"

"See that couch. That's where Koweleski slept when he wasn't downstairs doing his job. He developed the fantastic software that increases our ability to duplicate reality in three-dimensional cyberspace. Our security system keeps a log of all personnel entering and leaving the building. I can have them cross-check these times and dates, but I'm willing to bet that you'd find it impossible for him to travel to these locations in the few hours he isn't here everyday."

"Thank you, Mr. Hammond. If security can place him here at work or near Boston during these times, it would certainly help."

"I'll have them look into this, just to be sure," Hammond said as he accepted Corbbitt's business card.

"Since he's been working here, we've got new products in the pipeline and new releases of our flagship software are selling well. Here, let me show you what I mean," Hammond said as he pecked on a computer keyboard. "It will come up on the television set."

Corbbitt guessed that Hammond had a background in sales and he watched the short video of Hammond's Hide-a-way that played for a few minutes. "Agent Corbbitt, just so you know for sure. I've never been to Antarctica and the voice that duplicated mine was totally computer generated."

"Very amusing and potentially dangerous I think," Corbbitt observed.

"Very perceptive, Agent Corbbitt. We've been kicking this around trying to determine the consequences of marketing this software. In the wrong hands it might contribute to extortion and fraud, or worse, instill panic similar to the Orson Wells radio scare. The video you just watched had our employees a bit nervous until they saw my beard suddenly grow."

"I see. Have you met with anyone in the government about this product?"

"Not yet, but that is scheduled next month. Anyway, in order to develop this software, Joshua essentially lived here. I've never had a project manager so dedicated to a product."

"I won't take much of his time, sir, but I would like to ask him some questions about his anger at Common Cause."

"Well, the time is not a factor as far as I'm concerned. With an innovator like Koweleski, you simply get out of the way. Basically he can work any hours he wants and with very little convincing on his part he develops projects and works on them as he sees fit," Hammond said. "We don't stifle creativity and dedication here, Agent Corbbitt. We feed it."

"It looks like that philosophy is paying off. May I speak with Mr. Koweleski now?"

"Sure, I'll get security to take you to his work area. Oh, Agent Corbbitt, we're trusting that you'll not reveal anything here to our competitors. We're developing some cutting-edge software. Most of the goodies are tucked away, but I mention that just in case someone leaves a door open."

"I'm here to do an investigation, not to spy on you," Corbbitt said. "You've got nothing to worry about."

"Thanks, I'll let Joshua know that you're coming."

He shook the president's hand and followed the security guard. They took the elevator down to the sixth floor and wandered through a sea of office cubicles to the far end of the building. The guard punched several numerical buttons on the security keypad and the door unlocked allowing access to the Innovation Lab and Koweleski's office.

An entire wall of Koweleski's office had a bank of forty-two computers. A sign with two languages apparently identified each computer's task. Koweleski, a man with dark brown hair, rimless glasses, and a well-trimmed mustache and chin beard, stared at a computer monitor.

"One second please, Agent Corbbitt, I just need to get this test started and it can run while we talk," Koweleski said.

Corbbitt watched Koweleski bang away on the keyboard at lightning speed and as promised he stopped. "Sorry for the delay," Mr. Corbbitt. "Schedules you know."

They shook hands and Corbbitt took a seat across from Koweleski's desk.

"Impressive lab you have here, Mr. Koweleski."

He chuckled. "This is my office. The lab is downstairs. These computers receive the results from the fifth floor language teams. We're trying to develop language translation software for the major languages. As you see we're working on English, Chinese, French, German, Spanish, Russian, and Japanese."

"Seems like a daunting task."

He laughed. "Daunting perhaps, but not impossible. Because of multiple meanings and differences in sentence structure between the languages, I don't think we'll be able to provide instantaneous real time translations. Who knows, there was a time when there were no color monitors in the computer industry."

NO SHORTAGE OF EVIL

"Mr. Koweleski, I'm investigating multiple murders of executives at Common Cause. How long did you work for them?"

"Almost twelve years. I was there to develop most of the initial fiber-optic network and control the modifications as new technology expanded the overall capability. Why?"

"I'm here because you are a suspect in the deaths of Bertram Nagel, Leon Andress, and Walter Mortensen."

"A suspect! You've got to be kidding."

"Mr. Koweleski, I would never joke about such a thing. Mr. Hammond says you were working on software projects when the men were killed. He's getting security to cross-check the times."

"Then you'll know that I was here at work most of the time. How can you possibly think I had anything to do with their deaths?"

"Gerald Pendergast ..."

Joshua slammed his hand down on the desk. "That asshole again!"

"Mr. Koweleski, I hope for your sake I can verify where you were when these men were killed. Gerald Pendergast and other managers at Common Cause documented your verbal abuse at meetings and the crusade against management through inciting discontent with your colleagues."

"Agent Corbbitt, I can explain why this occurred."

"In a minute," Corbbitt said. He handed Koweleski a copy of the hate-filled memo sent to Pendergast.

From:	Guess Who
To:	Gerald Pendergast, CEO, Common Cause Communications Corporation
Date:	10/15/2004
Subject:	Corporate theft

No matter where you or your so-called senior executive thieves go, I will haunt you. No matter how long it takes. No matter what it costs me in time, money, or energy, I will make you pay and pay dearly. Start looking over your shoulder—all of you. You have much to fear.

I would sign this note, but it just adds to the mystery to leave it unsigned. Let's just say that I am one of the thousands of employees and investors you've screwed. Sleep well.

Corbbitt watched Koweleski read the memo and noticed how he blanched.

"You can't prove that I wrote this," Koweleski said.

"I wouldn't bet on it. Your obvious hatred for the management, the similarity in the use of 'Guess Who' in both verbal and written dialog, and the Braintree, postmark on the envelope it came in, narrows down the possibilities. Don't you think?"

Koweleski's attitude shifted from the jovial to hostile. "That will never hold up in court," he shouted.

"You're forgetting one thing, sir. You're not the only one with a laboratory. Our forensics experts can do wonders with DNA testing, fingerprints, and numerous other methods to pin the tail on the guilty donkey."

Koweleski struggled to regain composure. "Agent Corbbitt, it is true that I hate the management of Common Cause, but I am not a killer."

"Tell me what you think about this, Mr. Koweleski," Corbbitt said. "I've highlighted the part that is relevant to you."

Koweleski read from a second piece of paper.

Title: 18USC0876, CRIMES AND CRIMINAL PROCEDURE, Mailing threatening communications:

> Whoever, with intent to extort from any person any money or other thing of value, so deposits, or causes to be delivered, as aforesaid, any communication containing any threat to kidnap any person or any threat to injure the person of the addressee or of another, shall be fined under this title or imprisoned not more than twenty years, or both.

> Whoever knowingly so deposits or causes to be delivered as aforesaid, any communication with or without a name or designating mark subscribed thereto, addressed to any other person and containing any threat to kidnap any person or any threat to injure the person of the addressee or of another, shall be fined under this title or imprisoned not more than five years, or both.

When the last trace of color left Koweleski's face, Corbbitt knew he found the author of the hate mail.

"I'm not going to admit to writing that letter."

"I didn't expect that you would," Corbbitt said. "Tell me, Mr. Koweleski, have you ever been arrested before?"

"No, sir."

"Be very careful when you answer my questions because every detail will be cross-checked. I have the resources at my disposal to find out the maiden name of the doctor's mother who gave you your shots when you were an infant. One lie and you're going to need a lawyer. Understand?"

"Yes."

"Have you ever struck anyone in anger causing physical injury that required hospitalization?"

"No, I was in a few fights in high school, but only in self-defense. The jocks didn't care much for nerds. I got pounded pretty hard."

"For now I'm going to assume that Mr. Hammond is going to be able to verify your location during the time of those deaths, but here's what I want from you," Corbbitt said. He noticed that Koweleski seemed anxious to find a way out of trouble.

"Agent Corbbitt, I'm not a criminal," Koweleski pleaded.

"I want you to enroll in anger management therapy. With all that occurred while you were at Common Cause, there is some basis for your anger. But anger is one thing, threatening is another. I want to believe that you're a decent guy, but there are decent guys doing life sentences because they couldn't control their anger."

Corbbitt handed Koweleski a business card. "You will provide evidence of your attendance in anger therapy sessions along with a statement from the therapist providing assurance that you are under control."

"You don't think I can control myself?" Koweleski challenged.

"Just do what I ask, Mr. Koweleski. I am trying to help you. I can see your deep-seated anger at the mention of Pendergast's name."

"You had to be there to understand why I am so upset with Common Cause's management," Koweleski scowled.

"Then tell me about the company, your experience, and what you think they did wrong? Besides, it will help you vent your anger."

"I can't really take the time to go into all of that."

"Mr. Koweleski, right now three company executives are dead, others may be in danger as well and I have some evidence there were others killed who weren't part of the management team. I need to know more about Common Cause than the fictitious press releases issued by the company. If you want to get even, here's a real chance to do it." Corbbitt saw Koweleski close his eyes as if he was deep in thought.

"There's nothing I'd like more than to help put these crooks in prison so they can get what they deserve."

"Then begin," Corbbitt urged, knowing that it was often better to get information voluntarily. Continuously prodding with questions often limited information flow.

"I started working for Common Cause about twelve years ago. At that time, it wasn't much more than a cell phone company struggling to get a network slapped together while other companies were doing the same. A good system and effective marketing kept us going. The company had plans that went far beyond the domestic cell-phone market. Implementing those plans required a vast amount of money. Gerald Pendergast was a master at raising funds, especially with his vision of connecting the entire world in a huge network using fiber optic cable.

"Management in those days was much like the management here at Ninth Generation. They hired quality employees and listened to them. My degrees in electronic engineering and computer science helped me land a job developing the network that would link the continents together with high capacity fiber optic cable.

"My break came when I learned about higher quality cable that required fewer amplifiers than previous cable. That helped drop the construction costs significantly. Suddenly I was in the limelight and asked to learn about and recommend other technological advances to improve the system and reduce costs. Basically this resulted in a better system because we waited just long enough to get the next technological improvements.

"Common Cause sought world-wide domination of the communications industry. To achieve this, Pendergast traveled constantly and twisted many arms around the world to enable our network to tie into existing networks. Given the nature of business, turf protection, and international differences, it's a miracle the network was built at all."

"So far so good," Corbbitt observed.

"Yes, think of it, because all communication such as television, voice, music, computer data, text, pictures could be digitized, anything and everything could be sent around the globe in a fraction of a second. Everyone in the company was thrilled to come to work. Salaries were up, so were bonuses, and stock options. From quarter to quarter, our business grew at double-digit rates with no end in sight. The stock price soared and many of us were wealthy beyond our dreams."

"Weren't you in danger of running out of capacity?"

"Not really, the fiber optic cable just acts as a pipe for light. Because we could use different light frequencies, we were able to expand capacity significantly. It's like owning a pipeline where you can pump milk, gasoline, and scotch all at the same time without spoiling the individual fluids."

"It seems like everything was going your way," Corbbitt added.

"For the most part it was. There were other companies laying fiber optic cable as well, but none had the world-wide connections that our network achieved."

"So what went wrong?"

"A little over two years ago a significant shift in the success formula took place at Common Cause. One day we were a loving family and it seemed like the next, we lost the magic that worked so well."

"What do you think caused this change?"

"Pendergast, who traveled often in the process of negotiating international connections agreements, frequently voiced that he was tired of traveling. Suddenly, he takes a month off and flies half way around the world, supposedly for an extended vacation. We knew he was over near Malaysia and out of touch. He turned company functions over to Leon Andress the chief financial officer."

"Did Andress make a mess of things during that month?"

"No, he just kept the pressure on the marketing and sales staff and kept the network running. Everything was fine. It was Pendergast who returned and suddenly demanded to take the company in a different direction."

"This came with no warning at all?"

"Mr. Corbbitt, please understand, I was not in the executive meetings. I am only expressing what the rest of us felt when he returned from vacation."

"All right, but what if you were wrong?" Corbbitt asked.

"Well, here's the rest of it, you can judge for yourself. See if you wouldn't have thought the same thing."

"What happened then?"

"Very shortly after his return, Common Cause started actively pursuing the purchase of other cell phone companies. Some of these companies overlapped our existing territories. Next, Common Cause gets involved with the purchase of one of the struggling spin-off companies from the old AT&T

Corporation. This one had marginal hope of sustaining growth even with minimal profit margin.

"All of this activity drained time, money, and energy away from our core business. Marketing and sales budgets were cut, subsequently our ability to maintain growth rate slumped dramatically."

Corbbitt started to say something, but Koweleski began again.

"The real kicker, and the one that got my blood boiling, is when Common Cause management decided to buy Transistar, the low earth orbit satellite communications company.

"Here was a company that had been hyped to death and we were purchasing it at a premium. All ready there were indications that their satellites were failing. I wrote a twelve-page position paper warning Pendergast and the others not to proceed with the purchase based on the difficulty of maintaining the two hundred and forty satellites. When they completed the purchase in the face of my objections, I began questioning the future of Common Cause."

"You felt it was a gross waste of company assets?"

"Yes, and the satellites were a technological nightmare to integrate into our network. Because of the satellite system's low bit rate and limited number of channels, it tended to bog corners of our main network down. We were supplying the few existing Transistar customers with service at tremendous expense to the company. Then the satellites failed either from solar radiation or poor design and ground based callers weren't transferred within the Transistar network quick enough and they'd lose the connection. The cost of bearing satellite replacement was totally out of the question."

"This led to the bankruptcy?"

"Yes, this focused stock analysts' attention on the company and soon all of these poor decisions came into focus and the stock price began to plummet. Stockholders and employees suddenly found their assets at risk. The stockholders began selling to retain their assets. Employees were not so lucky."

"What do you mean by that?"

"We worked our butts off to build the company and market its capability. Many of us got bonuses in the form of stock options. We also contributed significant amounts of our salaries to purchase stock directly from the company. This was fine while the stock continued to increase. The company pooled these shares in a common account and there were restrictions on selling the stock. Without exception employees wanted to bail out."

"And the stock price continued to fall and they continued to lose money," Corbbitt added.

"Yes. What was worse, when employees started to raise hell about it, they were harassed by management. I was one of several employees canned for actively challenging management. Others had to endure psychological testing and evaluation. Soon everyone learned to remain quiet or face dismissal."

"If this is true, you folks would win a law suit against management," Corbbitt said.

"We just didn't realize how bad things were at the time, when the company still had assets that could be awarded. After bankruptcy, there was nothing but debt, and the bank gets the remaining assets after the government taxes are paid."

"What about the new owners? Are they rehiring the old employees?"

"Some perhaps that are needed in key positions. Most have other jobs now or would rather starve than go back to work for Common Cause."

"It seems odd that the new owners appeared so quickly after the company filed for bankruptcy."

"That's exactly what thousands of employees and investors thought too. Before all of this happened, we were within two quarters of breaking even. Our capacity use at that point was under ten percent. Picture the same company when business expands while debt, corporate payroll, and construction costs decrease. The potential profits were enormous and just a few years away."

"So that's the real attraction for the new owners," Corbbitt said.

"Yes, especially when you consider they were able to renegotiate with the banks who were glad to capture some of their loaned money rather than losing all of it. Agent Corbbitt, owning this system is like putting a tollbooth on every road in the world. As long as information flows, Common Cause is in position to hold out their hand for money."

"Mr. Koweleski, it is important for you to tell the agents working on the bankruptcy investigation just what you told me. I think eventually my case and the bankruptcy case are going to merge."

"Is it possible that Pendergast is behind the murders as well?" Koweleski asked.

"I'm not sure yet, but I wouldn't be able to tell you anyway."

"Agent Corbbitt, I will do anything to help your investigation. Many people have really suffered because of this. It may have destroyed a beautiful relationship for me as well. My girlfriend is in New York and I am here."

"What you've just told me is most helpful. I'll remember your offer to help. Thanks," Corbbitt said. "Oh, you've reminded me, I think I'll send my gal some flowers. I'm based in New York and my gal is in Washington, D.C."

Friday, February 25, 2005, 8:20 PM

At the Connecticut-Rhode Island border, Corbbitt stopped for gasoline and checked messages at his office. With the help of another agent, he obtained Isaac Saltzman's telephone number and address from the Bureau's Database. Saltzman, a world renowned advisor, was available to presidents, prime ministers, corporate executives, or anyone willing to pay a thousand dollars and hour for his unique understanding of finance, business, and geopolitics. Fortunately, a law enforcement officer could ask questions without paying the consulting fee.

After four rings, Saltzman's telephone answering machine announced, "Due to the Jewish Sabbath, no calls are being accepted. Please leave your message, or call after sundown on Saturday. If you do leave a message, we will return your call at that time."

Corbbitt left a message on Saltzman's answering machine.

"Mr. Saltzman, I am FBI Special Agent Donald Corbbitt. I would like to talk to you about the Common Cause Communication bankruptcy and recent deaths of its executives. I will call again after your Sabbath."

Chapter 17

Saturday, February 26, 2005, 9:47 AM

With great effort, Maggie Jensen turned to redistribute her weight in the van's driver seat. All through the night searing pain tortured her body, forbidding all but a few hours of desperately needed sleep. In three days, she managed to eat only applesauce and drink fruit juices. She could feel the strength draining from her body. She had no way of knowing whether she had a day, a week, or another hour of freedom from hospital confinement and the final turn of the death spiral that was sure to follow.

From across the street the parking place near College Point Park allowed an excellent location to monitor Yvonne Taylor's townhouse and count departing airplanes from LaGuardia Airport to help pass the time. She wondered if Yvonne would win this waiting game by simply staying inside. After hours of staring at Yvonne's front door, Maggie thought she saw a shadowy figure move the lace curtain that covered the glass portion of the front door. Her arms felt heavy as she reached into the cooler to capture some cold water to freshen her face.

She watched the front door open and a portion of Yvonne's face peer through the opening as if studying the street and nearby cars. Yvonne, who dashed for her car checking right and left to ensure no one was nearby, paused to look in the back seat of the Lexus before thrusting herself into the car.

Maggie started the van but waited until Yvonne was half a block away before trying to follow her. Driving the van through the narrow streets with parked cars on both sides seemed extremely difficult. She was grateful for traffic lights and the few seconds they provided to allow her to draw on reserve strength needed to keep up with Yvonne.

Yvonne turned onto West 130th street and parked next to a fire hydrant. Without thinking, she carelessly opened the car door, causing the driver of a passing car to swerve abruptly and sound the horn. Yvonne, oblivious to the near accident, dashed into a medical-supply company. Maggie pulled the van into a nearby driveway to wait for the right moment.

From her rear view mirror, Maggie watched Yvonne dash to her car again. This time she wore a thick cervical collar. Yvonne gunned the car and peeled out of her parking space. With difficulty, Maggie backed the huge van into the narrow street and followed Yvonne who sped through a red light narrowly missing a crossing pedestrian.

Maggie felt the pain intensify again and wondered if she was up to chasing Yvonne through the city. Fluids secreted by her body in its desperate attempt to reject the cancer growth increased internal pressure in her belly. She felt like she would explode at any moment. The distended belly needed additional room behind the steering wheel and because of her short arms she had to lean forward in order to maneuver the van making vehicle control much more difficult.

Ahead she could barely see Yvonne's Lexus as it turned toward the ramp for the Whitestone Bridge. Fortunately, the ever-present traffic forced Yvonne to decrease speed and soon her fear of losing Yvonne waned.

Maneuvering from lane to lane Yvonne sped through traffic, taxing Maggie's strength as she managed to keep Yvonne in view across the Whitestone Bridge, to the Bruckner Expressway, Cross-Bronx Expressway, and then north on Interstate 87. It was clear now that Yvonne was leaving the city.

Yvonne continued north to Tarrytown and stayed on the highway as it crossed the Tappan Zee Bridge over the Hudson River and began to speed up as traffic thinned. Maggie wondered if her body would run out of gas before Yvonne decided that she was safe enough to stop running.

At mile marker thirty, truckers heading southbound began blinking their lights warning of a speed trap ahead. She felt the wrenching pain intensify. She knew that the nearly unbearable pain meant it was time to put an end to this misery. Instead of slowing down, she increased speed to decrease the distance to Yvonne's Lexus.

She waited several minutes and as promised a New York State Trooper pointed a radar gun in their direction. Once she passed the trooper she accelerated and brought her van next to the Lexus. Yvonne was too interested in putting miles behind her to worry about a van passing her.

Maggie studied the highway and noticed the guardrail on the right side of the road. She waited keeping Yvonne's car right beside her van. When they passed the end of the guardrail, Maggie pulled quickly to the right. The collision sent the Lexus off the highway and down across the grass toward the deer barrier and a small grove of trees. Maggie followed and managed to control the van until it came to a stop behind Yvonne's car.

She struggled with the seat belt and grabbed the razor-sharp knife. The van door seemed very heavy as she tried to get from behind the steering wheel. With very little strength left, she almost fell from the high van. Her legs were so weak they were barely able to support her weight.

She looked over at Yvonne's car. The front-end, crumpled from a collision with a small tree; billowed steam from the coolant system. Inside the car the driver's airbag deployed and Yvonne, still dazed from the collision, failed to notice Maggie's van.

Maggie waddled over to Yvonne's car and yelled.

"Open the door, miss, and I'll help you."

Maggie saw that Yvonne was still in shock from the accident. "Come on, lady. The car's on fire," she lied.

Yvonne fumbled with the door mechanism and unlocked the door.

The instant the door opened Maggie thrust her knife-wielding arm inside. Maggie smiled as she saw Yvonne's eyes widen in fear. When Yvonne opened her mouth to scream, Maggie inserted the knife in Yvonne's mouth until she felt it hit the back of her throat.

"Now that I have your attention, I'll pull back the knife so you won't gag. Blink once if you understand. Blink twice if you don't."

Yvonne blinked once.

"Your lips are already cut. If you move too much or try to fight, your tongue or throat will probably be next. So get control of yourself or bleed to death. I really don't care. Blink once if you understand."

Yvonne blinked once and whimpered as tears streamed down her face.

"I see you've taken some precautions to protect your neck. Unfortunately, that might not help you. Do you recognize me? Blink once for yes. Blink twice for no."

Yvonne blinked twice.

"I'm not surprised. Liver cancer does take its toll on a woman's figure. I'm Maggie Jensen the woman you screwed out of a senior executive job. Remember now?"

Yvonne blinked once.

Maggie touched Yvonne's smooth cheek. "Unlike you I've never been blessed with physical beauty. My only hope for a little happiness was to succeed in my career. You whored your way into the job, without thinking of anyone but yourself. Are you happy now with what you've done?"

Yvonne blinked twice.

Maggie listened for the trooper's siren and wondered how long she had before the trooper would come and end the searing pain in her body.

"What's worse is that you failed to blow the whistle on Pendergast. You didn't think of the consequences to the company, the employees, or the investors when you sold them out. Did you?"

Yvonne blinked twice.

"You can't imagine, Yvonne, how it feels to be on the losing end your entire life. God, I wanted to win just once. You have such a pretty smile, Yvonne. Should I make it a little wider for you?"

Yvonne blinked twice.

"Nagel, Andress, and Mortensen all died very quickly with minimum suffering. Pity, they were once good men, but they forgot that their real job was to keep the company strong. Tell me, Ms. Yvonne Taylor, Ms. Executive Vice President of Marketing and Sales are you pleased with the consequences of your actions?"

Yvonne blinked twice.

Maggie heard the trooper's siren in the distance. She pushed the knife to the right side of Yvonne's cheek slicing into the flesh just enough to make it bleed. Blood streamed down Yvonne's chin and dripped into her mouth.

"Too bad you won't look as pretty at your funeral as you did when you seduced Walter. Your relatives will probably want a closed casket by the time I'm through with you."

Yvonne suddenly grabbed Maggie's arm in a desperate attempt to remove the knife. The knife sliced into Yvonne's tongue sending a gusher of blood from her mouth, Yvonne pushed hard enough to back the knife partway out of her mouth. Maggie had the advantage of position. When Maggie slipped and fell forward the knife sliced through the back of Yvonne's throat slicing into her brain stem. Yvonne twitched for a few seconds as her body followed her brain in death.

Maggie pulled the knife out from Yvonne's mouth and slid on her knees to the ground. With the last of her energy, she pulled on the car door and managed to stand.

"Put down the knife now, or I'll shoot," the trooper said.

Maggie raised the knife and staggered toward the trooper. "For God's sake shoot," Maggie said.

The trooper, who had never fired his weapon at a human, took careful aim.

Saturday, February 26, 2005, 12:12 PM

His afternoon reserved for rest and relaxation ended with the New York Field Office duty agent's call. A half a day off at least gave Donald Corbbitt enough time to get clean laundry, throw away spoiled food from his refrigerator, and buy more food that he would probably throw away in a week. The call, describing the roadside murder of Common Cause Executive Yvonne Taylor and the capture of a Ms. Margaret Jensen, a former Common Cause employee, required immediate action.

After an hour's driving through very fast traffic, Corbbitt took the exit for the Sloatsburg Travel Plaza on the northbound side of the New York Thruway. There, as promised, was Trooper Wesley Power's State Police car parked at curbside in front of the travel plaza building. Corbbitt found Trooper Powers, a lanky, baldheaded man inside enjoying a well-deserved cup of coffee.

"Officer Powers," Corbbitt said as he approached Powers from behind.

Powers turned without getting up from his seat. "Are you Corbbitt from the FBI?"

"Yes, sir, I am," Corbbitt said, showing his badge. "I guess you've had a hell of a morning."

"Pleased to meet you, Agent Corbbitt. Want one of these?" he said, pointing to his coffee.

"No, thanks."

"You're right. I've seen a lot of things while patrolling the state's highways for the last twenty-five years. Most of it is related to accidents, this was my first homicide and the most pathetic thing I've ever witnessed."

"What transpired here, Officer?"

"I got an urgent call from our dispatcher about an accident involving a green dodge van and a gray Lexus. I swear I'd seen them pass me on the highway. I had the radar trained on the northbound traffic."

"I saw both the van and the Lexus about forty feet off the road. The Lexus had a crumpled front end. As I approached the vehicles I saw one woman leaning into the car and there was a short struggle. By the time I got within range, the driver of the Lexus was dead and the other woman struggled to stand. Ms. Jensen staggered a few steps toward me with the bloody knife raised high in the air. She had a very haggard look on her face. At first, I thought she was a dazed drug user. She said, 'For God's sake shoot,' and then collapsed."

"You didn't fire your weapon?" Corbbitt asked.

"No sir. The woman just fell in a heap. I doubt if I would have fired anyway because I didn't feel threatened, and I was concerned about her baby."

"Baby?"

"Yes, the assailant, a Ms. Margaret Ann Jensen, of Manhattan, New York looked to be seven to nine months pregnant. So, even if she charged me, I knew I could avoid the knife. There's something strange about this though, now that I think about it."

"What's that, Wesley?" Corbbitt asked.

"Well, her driver's license says she's fifty-six. That's a bit old for a woman to have a baby. Don't ya think?"

"Yes, but who knows these days. What about the deceased woman?"

"Yvonne Taylor, Caucasian female, age fifty-two, died instantly from a puncture wound in the back of her throat. There's very little room for doubt here, Agent Corbbitt. Ms. Jensen was the one who killed her. Can you tell me why the FBI is interested in this case?"

"The Bureau has several investigations running concurrently at Common Cause Communications Corporation. One of them concerns the death of three executives that had their carotid arteries cut. An accountant who worked for their independent accounting firm also died in a similar fashion. I thought you might have caught their murderer, but I'm not so sure now. Ms. Jensen used a different method for killing Yvonne Taylor."

"It could be because the deceased had on one of those protective neck collars, but you can find out for yourself. The ambulance took Ms. Jensen to a hospital in Newburgh. There's a police officer there just to make sure she won't escape."

"Anything else?"

"No, sir. I guess our end of it is about over if you guys are going to follow up on the case."

"That will sort itself out, but you can count on our cooperation," Corbbitt said. "I'll go pay a visit to Ms. Jensen and see what she has to say about all of this."

Corbbitt left his business card and thanked Officer Powers for providing the information that might put an end to the series of murders at Common Cause.

Saturday, February 26, 2005, 2:30 PM

Corbbitt found the Newburgh Hospital with little difficulty. Since the patient requested no visitors except immediate family, it took some haggling with the volunteer receptionist and permission from a hospital administrator before Corbbitt received Margaret Jensen's room number and directions to the Cancer Care Unit.

The hospital, in a desperate attempt to lighten the mood of the Cancer Care Unit, decorated corridors with bright colors. The cheerful decor did nothing to elevate the hopes of the ill nor did it dry the tears of those friends and relatives with heavy hearts. The Cancer Care Unit became a casino where patients played a crap game with life by relying on surgeons, radiologists, and chemotherapists to roll the dice for them. Some patients won while others merely accepted the roll of death's loaded dice.

Corbbitt found Newburgh Police Officer Janice Cartwright outside room 306, Margaret Jensen's hospital room. After showing his badge and a brief introduction, Corbbitt wanted to find out what caused Margaret Jensen to kill four people.

"Agent Corbbitt, there's a doctor and two nurses in with her now. You're going to have to wait awhile before you question her," Officer Cartwright said. "I did talk with her for a moment, and I think she's ready to make a statement about the incident on the highway. She was in a lot of pain and I rang for the medical staff. They asked me to leave."

"Any idea how serious her condition is?"

"I asked one nurse, who refused to comment about Ms. Jensen's illness. All she said was that the patient wanted to die."

"I may need your help to record her statement," Corbbitt said.

"Sure. What do I have to do?"

"I'll set it up for you. All you'll have to do is point the camera and press a button. This may save a lot of time and effort wrapping up this case."

The door to room 306 opened and a man emerged in a white lab coat with a stethoscope hung around his neck. Corbbitt missed seeing the nametag on the coat.

"Excuse me, Doctor? I'm Special Agent Donald Corbbitt with the Federal Bureau of Investigation. I need to talk with Ms. Jensen. She's a suspect in the deaths of four people."

"I'm the Resident Physician Arnold Flynn. Agent Corbbitt, Ms. Jensen won't be able to talk with you for several hours. She's exhausted and in severe pain. Her statement, I'm afraid, wouldn't amount to much."

"What's her condition?"

"All I can tell you is that she is very tired, and at the moment stable. I am sorry, but I cannot discuss her medical condition further without her consent."

"I understand, Doctor, with patient's rights and all, but is she going to be around in a couple of hours?"

"Agent Corbbitt, I cannot predict whether I'm going to be around in a couple of hours. If it's any help to you, she's in better condition now than when she first got here. All I can tell you is that she needs the rest. Give it to her, please," Dr. Flynn said. "Now if you'll excuse me please, I have other duties."

"Officer Cartwright, is there somewhere I can make calls with my cell phone without upsetting the electronic gadgets in the hospital?"

"Sure, you can use the cafeteria on the first floor, even the doctor's call from there. Don't drink the coffee though, I think they serve mud here to drum up business for the hospital."

"Thanks, I'll be back in a little while."

Corbbitt went back to his car, pulled the video camera from the car trunk, and grabbed his briefcase containing the case files for the Common Cause, Margarita Rosario, and Senator Champion murders. After another warning about the quality of the cafeteria's three o'clock coffee, he settled for a glass of water and selected a remote table away from the few mid-afternoon visitors and employees.

Even without talking to Margaret Jensen, it appeared to Corbbitt that the Common Cause murder case was over and it was time to make some progress on Senator Champion's assassination. He searched through the manila file folder labeled 'Champion' and reviewed the list of senators found in Senator Champion's office.

For a moment, he considered calling the individual senators and just asking in a direct manner why some are classified different from the others. If the list had some connection to the ten million dollars that Senator Champion rejected, calling the other senators would only warn them that they were under scrutiny.

He studied the list closely to glean some pattern associated with the asterisked names.

It was a simple list; a snapshot of the Senate Judiciary Committee as it existed when Senator Champion was the chairman. Of the asterisked names, there were three Republicans and five Democrats. All of the asterisked names were men. No bias based on geographical location was evident. Corbbitt wondered about the significance of Senator Champion, who had a question mark next to his name, and his replacement, Senator Adrian Horne, one of the asterisked names on the list.

The list meant nothing to Senator Champion's office manager and close friend, Pauline Dryfus, who had already reviewed the list and was unable to identify the reason for any special grouping of the senators. It was possible that there was nothing sinister and the list only identified those senators who liked to fish or support charity in the same way Senator Champion funded the betterment of children.

Corbbitt grabbed his cell-phone and the list of telephone numbers for those interviewed while investigating Senator Champion's death. He placed a call to another of Senator Champion's close friends.

"Mr. Rayburn, this is FBI Special Agent Donald Corbbitt. I am sorry about the senator's death and I want to assure you that we're still trying to find out who killed him."

"Thank you, Mr. Corbbitt. I went to the senator's funeral, there were hundreds of people there. Everyone liked the senator," Charlie Rayburn said.

"That's what I'd like to talk to you about, Mr. Rayburn. What about his friends?"

"His friends! No, I don't see how any of the regulars could have done such a thing."

"Regulars?" Corbbitt asked.

"Yes. About once a month, the senator's buddies came over for drinks, poker, and billiards. These guys are locals—men that the senator grew up with."

"What about other parties or meetings? Did he have any other special groups at the house last year?"

Corbbitt waited while Charlie Rayburn thought.

"There was one occasion. Let's see, last November. It was the weekend just before Thanksgiving. The senator invited some of his Washington colleagues here. He hired a caterer for that one. All I had to do was set the table for ten and make sure there was enough booze and cigars for the weekend. Then he insisted that I take a few days off."

"Was that unusual?"

"I thought it was at the time. The senator always liked to have me close by during social functions to keep things running while he entertained."

"Did he tell you who was coming for the meeting?" Corbbitt asked.

"No sir. I got the impression Senator Champion didn't want me to know either."

"Any speculation on who might have been to the meeting?"

"Not really. When I returned, the house was a mess. Apparently, most of them smoked and the ashtrays were full. There were dirty dishes stacked high in the sink. They consumed most of the available food and liquor."

"Any papers or documents left behind?"

"No sir. The only thing left behind was a man's dress shirt. It was hanging in the bathroom with a big coffee stain on the front. Too bad, it was one of the fancy tailor-made shirts with initials on the French cuffs."

"Do you remember the initials?"

"Yes, I'm pretty sure it was M R D on the cuff."

"What happened to the shirt?"

"Senator Champion said he'd take it back to Washington and return it to his distinguished but sloppy colleague."

Corbbitt scanned the senator's names on his list. "Were those his exact words?" Corbbitt asked.

"Yes, as far as I can remember."

"Thank you, Mr. Rayburn. If you think of anything else that might identify any of those guests, please call me."

"I will, Agent Corbbitt. I don't know how much longer I will be living here. There is some talk of selling the house. The lawyer is letting me stay here until it is decided. But when I move, I'll make sure you know how to find me."

"Thanks, Mr. Rayburn."

Corbbitt hung up the telephone and started playing with the numbers. With the three initials M R D he calculated there were seventeen thousand six-hundred and seventy-six possible combinations of initials. Assuming the population of the United States at three-hundred million, and that only half were male, dropped the number to one-hundred and fifty million. Calculating further that only eighty percent were adult males and an estimated five percent of those could afford a one-hundred dollar tailor-made shirt dropped the total number of potential deluxe shirt wearers to six million. Considering the three initials on the cuff narrowed the number to three hundred and thirty-nine potential owners. Allowing for the fact that the initials M R D were more likely than the initials AAA, QQQ, ZZZ, and similar low frequency combinations, he multiplied by three. This provided an estimate that in the United States one adult male out of one thousand and seventeen would have a tailor-made shirt with M R D cuff initials on it.

Corbbitt thought that any Las Vegas bookmaker would give ten to one odds that a senator would have those initials. Yet, there was North Carolina Senator Marvin R. Douglas's name with an asterisk, on the list. The fact that Senator Champion used the word colleague definitely lined the bookmaker up to lose a fortune.

Questions surfaced that needed answering. Why would senators trek all the way up for a secret meeting with their chairman? Why only some of the senators? If it was true, that Senator Champion only invited those with asterisks on the list, who was the tenth person to be served at dinner?

Corbbitt placed a call to Jocelyn Hafner's home only to get the answering machine.

"Hi Jocelyn, this is Don. It's Saturday afternoon 3:10. I'm going to be in Washington on Monday to continue the Senator Champion investigation. I hope we can spend some time together. I'll call again to confirm. Sorry to swoop in and out of your life like this. Talk to you soon. Love ya," he said and then wondered how long a beautiful woman like Jocelyn would tolerate the career demands of a FBI special agent.

Saturday, February 26, 2005, 4:45 PM

"Are you still on duty?" Corbbitt said to Officer Cartwright.

"Yes, I'm on until six. It really kills the weekend when it's your turn to cover."

"Anything new?"

"A nurse went in a coupla times since you've been gone. Other than that, nothing."

"She's had a chance to rest a bit, I'll see if I can get her to talk. Join me in a few minutes if I don't come right back out. Okay?" Corbbitt said.

"All right."

Although the hospital room was semi-private, because of Margaret Jensen's violent nature, the hospital would not use the remaining bed. The room shades, drawn to block the afternoon sunlight, made the room feel dark and ominous. Only a single lamp above Margaret's head provided a light that seemed too harsh for an ill person to maintain sleep.

Corbbitt sat in the chair next to the bed and looked at the sick woman whose brown and gray matted hair advertised that she had long ago given up trying to radiate feminine charm. In many ways Margaret Jensen became a battlefield where the attacking cancer waged war and advance while the body's defenses constantly retreated leaving in its path a bloated belly, puffy flesh, and a sickly yellow complexion. In bed on her back tied to a heart rate monitor, IV poles, and a urine collection bag she winced as pain bored through morphine's protective shield.

She stirred in her sleep and groaned from a spike in pain intensity as she tried to turn. "Who the hell are you?" Margaret Jensen asked. "And don't stare at me, I'm not a museum piece."

"I am Special Agent Donald Corbbitt with the Federal Bureau of Investigation. I need you to wake up if you can. Do you understand?"

She opened her swollen eyelids a little further, "I understand," she said, fumbling for the bed control to raise the head of the bed.

"Here," Corbbitt said, as he gave her the ice water that was just out of her reach on the bed stand. He could see the illness reflected in the yellowing of her eyes as she placed a straw between two cracked lips and took a sip.

"Not very pretty, huh?"

"No, and neither was the death of Yvonne Taylor," Corbbitt countered.

"Guilty as charged."

"Stop," Corbbitt commanded. He went to the door and asked Officer Cartwright to bring the video camera with her and join him at Margaret's bedside.

He returned to the chair and introduced Officer Cartwright to Margaret Jensen.

"Ms. Jensen, Officer Cartwright is going to record our conversation as part of this investigation. Do you understand?"

"Yes, let's get on with it," Margaret said.

Corbbitt checked the camera and showed the officer how to start and stop it.

"Ready?"

Officer Cartwright nodded.

"This is Saturday, February 26, 2005. It is 4:58 PM. I am Special Agent Donald Corbbitt conducting an investigation into the death of Ms. Yvonne Taylor that occurred earlier this morning around 10 o'clock. Officer Janice Cartwright from the Newburgh, New York, police department is in attendance and operating the camera. Officer Cartwright will you verify the time, date, and purpose for this recording?"

"Yes, it is Saturday, February 26, 2005, the time is now 4:59 PM, I am Officer Janice Cartwright from the Newburgh Police Department," she answered. "This recording is part of the official investigation into the death of Ms. Yvonne Taylor."

Corbbitt directed his attention toward Margaret Jensen. "You are Margaret Jensen a resident of Manhattan, New York."

"I'm Margaret Jensen, but I live in a van. I gave up my apartment because I could no longer afford it," she said.

"Ms. Jensen, do you understand that this conversation is being recorded and that anything you say may be used against you in court. That you have a right to an attorney…"

"I understand the Miranda rights, I waive my right to an attorney. I waive my right to a trial. I am guilty of the deaths of Yvonne Taylor, Walter Mortensen, Leon Andress, and Bertram Nagel. I am a menace to society and need to be executed immediately."

"Ms. Jensen, in this country we do have justice and due process of law that adheres to legal principles without favor or prejudice to all citizens."

"So you say."

"Ms. Jensen, we're not here to debate the nature of our justice system."

"Look, Agent Corbbitt, I'm willing to make your life easier with regard to these murders. I have little strength left. I may be dead in a few weeks or even days. I may slip into a coma. I am going to make my statement to you any way I see fit. If you have any brains, you'll record the whole thing."

Corbbitt knew he had no other choice but to agree. "All right, Ms. Jensen, within limits I'll record all of your statement, but I'll need answers to my questions along the way. Fair enough?"

"Yes, I suppose."

"We sometimes get people who confess to crimes just to gain notoriety, Ms. Jensen. Would you state for the record your involvement in the murders you say you've committed?"

"I killed Bertram Nagel in a whirlpool at a hotel in Amherst, New York. I used an ultra-sharp razor blade to cut his carotid artery. I ditched the blade in the crack between the elevator floor and the hotel floor. Go look and you'll find it.

"I killed Leon Andress in a park in Willoughby Hills, Ohio. He was out jogging but made a habit out of resting at a picnic table. I used a very sharp knife to cut his carotid artery. This knife I kept to use on the others. I switched to the knife because of my failing health. I was losing strength and I felt I might need it to defend myself in order to get the others on my list.

"I killed Walter Mortensen at his home in Hastings-on-Hudson, New York. Again I killed by cutting the carotid artery.

"This morning, I trailed Yvonne Taylor by following her from her home in College Point, New York. I forced her off the road using my van. Because

I'm terminally ill, I tried to arrange this murder so I would get caught in the act and get shot in the process. I saw the state trooper and hoped he would get there in time. That bitch Yvonne Taylor started to resist. She might have overpowered me, but I slipped and the knife pushed through the back of her throat."

"Ms. Taylor's death was more of an accident then?" Corbbitt said.

"No, I really wanted to kill her. I was waiting for the trooper to come. I just wanted to get shot myself so that I would escape the agony here in the hospital. Apparently, the trooper didn't have the balls to shoot me."

"I've talked with him myself, Ms. Jensen. He thought you were pregnant, but if he decided to shoot you, it wouldn't have been lethal. One in the leg would stop you in your tracks. State troopers can fend off a knife attack easier than you think. But let's get back to this list of yours and why you decided to take revenge on these people."

"List? Oh, yes—it's simple. I just wanted to kill them all, the senior executives and members of the board of directors," Margaret said as she sipped more water.

"You mean the executives and directors of Common Cause?"

"Yes."

"Why?"

"Because they were all paid to do a job and they purposely dismantled a thriving company. Common Cause was a company that people put heart and soul into, a company with incredible profit potential. Because of Gerald Pendergast and his gang of white-collar criminals, thousands lost their jobs and billions of investor dollars evaporated. I killed them because I was in a position to do it. I would do it again without hesitation. My only regret is that I didn't act before they destroyed the company. You see Agent Corbbitt I have very little to lose," she said, patting her enormous belly.

"Isn't it just your opinion that their professional misconduct caused the downfall of Common Cause. What about the company's enormous debt load?"

"Look, there's a lot that went on inside the company that never got printed in the papers."

"So enlighten me then."

"I know the Feds—you guys, are doing a big investigation into Common Cause's operation. Here's what they're going to find. Bertram Nagel, the independent accountant, the guy the investor's elected to check the accuracy of the company's financial statements, purposely overlooked major inaccuracies.

"Leon Andress purposely prepared inaccurate corporate financial statements by overstating earnings and understating expenses. With Walter Mortensen's help they exaggerated company growth rate and earning potential.

"That bitch Yvonne Taylor firsts sleeps with Mortensen to get into the senior executive row next to Pendergast. Then at Pendergast's demand she downsizes the entire sales and marketing staff. Agent Corbbitt, I developed a worldwide marketing program. I had dozens of people across the world delivering our message and the sales were rolling in because of it. Do you have any idea what that takes to appeal to vast differences in culture? Try doing that and solving the language and dialect problems too? By downsizing marketing, the downfall of the company was assured."

"So you're alleging there was a massive conspiracy to defraud investors?"

"Not only the investors, don't forget the millions of dollars worth of stock options that the employees had tied up in an account they had no control over," she said and paused to cough. The cough brought forth a surge of pain that made her grimace until it waned.

Corbbitt waited until he saw her recover from the pain. "Why would they do that?"

"For the money. For the ten million dollars each one of them got for going along with Pendergast's plan to destroy the company."

"Who told you about this?"

"There were rumors among the employees months ago that something strange was happening. The other night, Tues—no Wednesday night when I was outside Mortensen's home I heard Yvonne and Walter fighting. Yvonne wanted to take the twenty million they had between them and run. Later when I put the knife to Walter's throat he admitted that he received ten million dollars from Gerald Pendergast."

"How many executives received this money?"

"There are seven if you count, Nagel, the accountant."

"Seventy million dollars, where did Pendergast get that much money to spread around?"

"I had the knife to Walter's throat and he swore he didn't know."

"Where do you think Pendergast got the money from?"

"In business there are winners and losers, Agent Corbbitt. I have no way of knowing for sure, but my guess is that it came from the very people that own the company now."

Corbbitt sat back in his chair and thought about the implications of what

Margaret Jensen just said. "If that's true, they've already won, everyone else is just scrambling to stay out of prison."

"Welcome to the real world, Agent Corbbitt. Big money never loses," Margaret said.

"You realize, Ms. Jensen, that your actions are inexcusable in the eyes of the law. Our laws do not permit vigilante behavior in any form. Did killing these people result in reestablishing the company or the funds to the investors and employees?"

"No, Agent Corbbitt, and neither would putting these folks behind bars in a hospital clean prison resort for white collar criminals. What happened to all the watchdog government agencies in this case? Where was the Securities and Exchange Commission that is supposed to oversee the marketplace so that everyone has a fair and level playing field to invest? Clearly when the government fails to enforce its own laws it becomes a partner to the crime itself."

"Still society cannot contend with individuals ignoring the law and taking action on their own."

"Don't be so sure, sir. The Common Cause executives came close to collapsing the entire stock market. If it wasn't for the quick action by the Securities and Exchange Commission requiring every corporation to resubmit financial information to capture the remnants of investor confidence, every investor would have tried to dump their stock. The market would have collapsed."

"That doesn't excuse your actions," Corbbitt countered.

"Really, Agent Corbbitt, I think it's you who is skating on thin ice. Just think what a small group of intelligent terminally ill cancer patients could have done in the early thirties to Hitler and his henchmen. Twenty million people would have lived. Billions of dollars would have been saved by not fighting the war and repairing the damage afterward."

"Is there anything else that you'd like to tell me for the record, Ms. Jensen?"

"Oh yes. For the record, I admit that I am of sound mind now as I was when I killed each person. I stalked them with the intention of killing them. I've recorded my thoughts about all of this in my journal that's in the van and easy to find. I don't want an attorney; I waive the right to a trial. If you would just give me your gun and one bullet Agent Corbbitt, we can save a lot of time, trouble, expense, and agony. Just let me shoot myself and get it over with."

"I'm sorry, Ms. Jensen, but serial killers frequently don't get what they want. Law enforcement officers are not empowered to help anyone commit suicide."

"Oh sure, but if I was a rabid dog, a horse with a broken leg, or a fox with distemper, you'd have no trouble shooting me. You'd simply be doing the 'humane' thing. Frankly, I don't see much difference here. If I live long enough to go to trial, the end would be the same anyway."

"Except that due process and justice would be served," Corbbitt said.

"Due process! Justice! Agent Corbbitt, live with injustice your whole life and you'll understand what's wrong with 'our' system of justice."

"Ms. Jensen, remember that you're under arrest. There is an officer outside your door."

"Don't worry, I'm not going anywhere," Margaret said.

"This ends the interview with Margaret Jensen, February 26, 2005. It's 5:32 PM.

Chapter 18

Sunday, February 27, 2005, 5:22 AM

Jocelyn Hafner felt Donald Corbbitt's hard body pressed against her back and his fingers gently touched her neck. Then his lips slowly caressed the highway between her shoulder and neck sending shivers of delight through her body. She felt his hand in her hair, then her cheek, and then his fingers traced her eyebrows and eyelids. Every place he touched kindled the fire of passion until she hungered to be touched all over.

She felt his right foot move slowly between her feet bringing his knee just between her thighs, her heart beat faster in anticipation of the incredible pleasure that would soon engulf her body. Yet, he waited, content to kiss the back of her neck, and bury his nose in her hair, as if drinking in her fragrance. Perhaps he needed to remember this moment for some future time when a bliss-filled embrace might be prohibited by time or circumstance.

She felt his arm move carefully around her tummy. She knew that soon he would touch her breasts or slide down between her legs. Yet, he waited, kissing and nibbling on her neck and ears. Finally, the frustration overwhelmed her. She moved Don's hand to cup her left breast.

"It is natural for a man to want to touch a woman's breast," he whispered. "I cannot express my joy that you want me to do it."

"Don, it is not that I want you to touch my breast, it is my way of bringing you closer to my heart."

She turned slowly to face him, reaching out under the sheet and blanket to the empty side of the bed. She opened her eyes to see the murky light of another day sifting through the bedroom curtains and the shadow of Don's red roses that she put on her bureau the day before. The delicious dream vanished leaving only the stark reality of her loneliness.

"Donald Corbbitt, where the hell are you?" she cried.

NO SHORTAGE OF EVIL

Sunday, February 27, 2005, 11:45 AM

For a multimillionaire, Isaac Saltzman and his wife, Rose, lived in a modest one story Sayville, New York, home with a beautiful view of Great South Bay. The home had an elevated main floor and a ramp to the front porch indicating that someone required a wheelchair. He rang the doorbell and heard instantly from somewhere inside the house, "Rose, *tei-yerinkeh*[1], our guest is here. Would you get the door please."

"Don't yell, I'll get it already. I'm coming, I'm coming."

The door opened and Corbbitt saw a short, elderly woman in a simple flower-print housedress. He saw her looking him over with eyes that had a touch of sadness mixed with a hint of joy. Behind her, a large black Rottweiler snarled.

"*Sha Bubbe*," she said to the dog. "Some identification please, mister."

Corbbitt produced his badge and she studied it for a moment through thick glasses until she was sure of his identity. She spoke to the dog in a language Corbbitt thought was Yiddish. The dog seemed to understand and retreated allowing him to enter.

"I'm sorry, Mr. Corbbitt, but here we always check."

"That's fine, Mrs. Saltzman, everyone should take those precautions."

"*Yitzhak*—eh, Isaac is in the kitchen. He doesn't hear so well, so he yells. Me, I don't see so well, so I stumble and fall. Ah, but what can we do? It's no joy growing old and even less joy not growing old."

Corbbitt followed Mrs. Saltzman through their beautifully decorated home to a large sparkling clean kitchen. Isaac Saltzman, a thin elderly man in his eighties sat at one end of the kitchen table in a wheelchair. Newspapers littered one half of the table and he used his finger to track the text as he read. A six-digit tattoo stuck out from his unbuttoned sleeve indicating hellish concentration camp days earlier in his life.

"*Yitzhak*," Rose said. "Mr. Corbbitt is here."

"Ah, Mr. Corbbitt. Excuse me please if I don't get up, I don't walk very well anymore."

Corbbitt moved closer to shake Saltzman's hand. Immediately *Bubbe* growled.

---

[1] Yiddish: sweetheart

"*Sha, Bubbe.* It's okay," Saltzman said. "Sorry, she's very protective. A pleasure to meet you, Agent Corbbitt."

"Thank you for agreeing to see me on short notice, Mr. Saltzman."

"Sha, I should be thanking you. I had a big real estate deal in Manhattan, an office building, near the Port Authority Bus Terminal. One of those radioactive bombs would have killed the deal, but thanks to you it was sold without any problem."

"We were very lucky that day, Mr. Saltzman, with the push of one button the outcome would have been totally different."

Mrs. Saltzman busied herself removing the newspapers from the table, while Isaac frowned. "*Gib mir nit kain einorah!*[2] " So what do you expect Yitzak? Lunch won't be served on the papers in my house. *Yitzhak me redt zich oys dos hartz*[3], take Mr. Corbbitt into the family room, talk your hearts out. Then lunch when you are ready."

"*Dos gefelt mir, tei-yerinkeh,*"[4] Saltzman replied to his wife. "She's right, if you'll follow me, Agent Corbbitt. We're in her way," Saltzman said. Corbbitt followed him as he spun away from the table and wheeled himself into the family room. "Here, sit on the couch so I can park with my good ear next to you."

Corbbitt sat on the right side of a three-cushion couch. Saltzman maneuvered his wheel chair to his left. He had the feeling that many others sat in this same location to listen to the thoughts and opinions of this world-famous financial guru.

"Well, you're concerned about the monkey business surrounding the Common Cause bankruptcy and frankly I am not surprised. Please tell me why you are interested in it so I can get closer to the point without rambling too much."

"The Bureau has several investigations associated with the Common Cause Company. One involved the murder of three of its executives and one accountant from the independent accounting firm. We have a suspect in custody now, and that case is essentially over. That suspect's motivation for killing concerned the calculated destruction of a viable company and misconduct of its officers. The suspect alleges that these executives were paid millions of dollars to drive the company into bankruptcy. I need to learn more about how this came about and exactly who is involved."

[2] Yiddish literal: 'Don't give me a canary.' Used as: 'Don't give me the evil eye.'
[3] Yiddish: 'Go talk your hearts out'
[4] Yiddish: 'This pleases me, sweetheart'

"Given what's happened at Common Cause you've come to believe there's been an international conspiracy?"

"Yes."

Isaac Saltzman closed his eyes for a moment. When he opened them, the lower lids were heavy with moisture. "You must excuse an old man, Agent Corbbitt. Perhaps I've lived too long and seen too much, but I will tell you in this world there is no shortage of evil."

Corbbitt waited for Saltzman to regain control of his emotions. "Take your time, Mr. Saltzman."

"Since your call the other day I've done some research. I'll have a few things to say about Common Cause later, but let's start from the beginning."

"Fine with me," Corbbitt said already impressed with Saltzman's intellect.

"Someone gets a bright idea and that idea either creates a new industry or revolutionizes an existing one. In the case of Common Cause, their approach to communications did the latter. Their network, use of state of the art technology, and the arm twisting required to get international agreements is a sparkling business achievement. Of course, to create a worldwide network, brains are not enough. To fuel that idea requires billions of dollars. Often funding comes from venture capitalists who risk their money and expect a significant rate of return for that risk."

"In other words, an interest rate more than a bank account or certificate of deposit," Corbbitt said.

"Yes. Other money sources such as banks, who loan money with rates based on perceived risk, and investors, who buy corporate bonds and stock, provide the financial engine to move the idea into reality. This is normal business and it's done all the time."

"Okay," Corbbitt said.

"The venture capitalists often receive stock at the lowest prices since they are putting up vast amounts of capital to launch the idea. It is in their best interest for the idea to flourish and impress subsequent investors who sense the opportunity to make money on a speculative risk."

"Speculative risk?" Corbbitt asked.

"Yes, in the initial phases all companies are speculative risks until their operations consistently create goods and services that result in revenue that exceeds corporate expenses. Generally, as the stock price rises, the venture capitalists sell their stock at price levels that satisfy their reward requirements. They recover their funds and a handsome profit for taking the risk and move on to the next good idea. This is still normal business. Questions?"

"No, I'm with you," Corbbitt said.

"Good," Saltzman said. Bubbe sat beside the wheelchair and Saltzman obliged her by scratching behind her ears. "What happens when the idea is too good? What happens when the idea captures the attention of those with enormous funds, or in the case of Common Cause, you may add sinister motives?" Saltzman asked. "I'll tell you.

"The venture capitalists in this case have enormous capital at their disposal. To them, Common Cause was like a premium racehorse, but only an immature colt in the technological communications race to provide massive worldwide communications. When the common investors caught wind of the potential earnings, the stock price naturally increased. Instead of the venture capitalists bailing out and taking profits, they hyped the company's potential and actually timed additional stock purchases to drive the stock higher and higher."

"Hyped the stock? How did they do that?"

"They push in all directions at the same time. Independent analysts are inspired to tout company potential and the growth rate of the communications industry. Newsletters develop stories boasting of near term profit windfalls. Disreputable brokerage firms emerge hawking the stock siting recent gains supported only by the recent hype. Soon one investor tells another, then another, and eventually it reaches what I call the barbershop level where everyone knows about it and acts on it."

"All of this is based on management's inaccurate financial statements concerning revenues, expenses, and growth rate," Corbbitt said.

"Yes, exactly right, and now the big money venture capitalists slide out of the stock selling as the price goes exponentially higher. Then they sell short."

"Sell short?"

"They actually pay a fee to borrow other people's shares and sell them on the open market. Then guess what? The darling company suddenly falls out of favor, investors panic, the stock price drops dramatically, and then the venture capitalists purchase shares at a much lower price to replace the one's they borrowed. It's not unusual for the price to drop seventy-five percent or more during these contrived manipulations."

"Legal?"

"Selling short is perfectly legal. Manipulation through deception isn't. Some brokerage houses are guilty of pushing Common Cause shares to their customers while simultaneously selling shares from the firm's accounts. That, my friend, is highly illegal."

"So many investor's get caught by selling into the rising price and buying when the price is too high."

"You catch on quick, but we're not done yet."

"Not done?"

"No, remember the venture capitalists know the smallest detail about the company. What happens when they use those profits to bribe their way into management? With the millions they've already made they systematically destroy the company's forward momentum until it can no longer survive."

"Bankruptcy!"

Saltzman smiled. "Right again. Now the same venture capitalists buy the company's debt from despondent banks. The banks are happy to take pennies on the dollar for loans previously made or are at least willing to restructure loans to make repayment a breeze. Welcome to bargain basement financing."

"Incredible."

"And illegal," Saltzman said.

"Can't something be done?" Corbbitt asked.

"The big money players are all over the world."

"So we go to the respective governments, make a case, and indict the players."

"Don't bang your head on the concrete, Agent Corbbitt. The players already own the government and that includes the military. They have the money and the power to do what they wish. In the case of Common Cause, they exercised both."

Yesterday's review of the Senate Judiciary Committee roster and the ten million dollars that was in Senator Champion's Cayman Island account suddenly seemed very ominous. "Mr. Saltzman, what about corruption in our government?"

"Agent Corbbitt, as long as there are politicians making decisions for people there will always be corruption and abuse. It's because of government corruption that I learned about finance in the first place."

Mrs. Saltzman's sudden appearance in the doorway caught Corbbitt's attention. "Excuse me, the lunch is ready," she said.

"What do you think, Mr. Saltzman, is our government being purchased one congressman and senator at a time?"

"Where money flows like a river, integrity floats away," Saltzman said. "Let's have some lunch. Rose made some kreplach, and we've got some tongue, corned beef, and the freshest rye bread for sandwiches," Saltzman said and turned abruptly in his wheelchair and headed for the kitchen.

"Kreplach?"

"It's soup. Homemade noodles stuffed with meat in a beef broth," Saltzman said over his shoulder. "Usually we have it for our holidays, but Rose knows I love it so she makes it special for me," Saltzman said, as he locked the wheelchair in front of the kitchen sink and stood slowly to wash his hands. "*Barukh atah Adoshem, Elokaynu, melekh ha-olam, asher kid'shanu b'mitzvotav, v'tzivanu al n'tilat yadayim. Amen.*[5]

"It's the blessing for washing the hands. You may use the restroom in the hall if you wish," Mrs. Saltzman said. "He's required to wash his hands before eating and can't get the wheelchair into the bathroom."

Corbbitt took the hint and went to the bathroom to wash his hands. When he returned, Isaac and Rose Saltzman waited at the kitchen table.

"Here, while the soup is cooling, make a fine sandwich for yourself," Saltzman urged as he passed the rye bread and the meat platter. He took a small piece of bread and mumbled some words.

"The blessing for the bread," Mrs. Saltzman said.

Corbbitt felt a little on edge but nodded as if he understood. "Is it permissible to continue our discussion while eating, Mr. Saltzman?" Corbbitt said, trying to glean more information from Saltzman's warehouse of knowledge.

"Ah, Agent Corbbitt, I think the Jewish people invented the business lunch. Just be careful with the mustard, Rose is very fond of this tablecloth. Sure, let's continue."

"You said your father lost his money because of corruption," Corbbitt said as he deftly avoided the sliced tongue to make a corned beef sandwich.

"Yes, I was seven. I used to pull Rose's hair. She was a little younger and lived next door. Remember, *tei-yerinkeh?*

"My father owned a house that he made into a small restaurant. We lived in the back. We also raised some animals, to butcher and serve to our customers. We had the only radio in the village. People would come to eat, have a drink, and listen to music and the news. Simple village life is how it was in Hungary for us in 1923. Then a politician came by and offered my father a large sum of money for the property. My father sold the property and we had to move. Weeks later, that decision proved to be a mistake. Do you know about inflation, Agent Corbbitt?"

[5] Hebrew: "Blessed are You, L-rd, our G-d, King of the Universe, who sanctifies us with his commandments, and commands us concerning washing of hands. Amen'

"Yes, that's when the cost of everything keeps going up and up," Corbbitt said. "Mrs. Saltzman, the soup is very good, thank you."

"I'm glad you like it. There is more if you want it."

"That's one way of thinking about it," Saltzman said. "Those who print money would have you believe it was the goods and services that caused prices to go up. In reality, when there is too much currency available, prices rise because the currency is worth less. In 1923, Hungary had 100% inflation. My father lost an incredible amout of money. I still remember him crying out, *'In drerd mein gelt'*. It means, 'My money went down the drain'. I vowed I would never make the same mistake."

"Yet you're selling your real estate, Mr. Saltzman," Corbbitt said.

Saltzman paused for a second. "I was actually part owner of the office building. I am just trying to get my business in order before the last page of my life's book is read."

"I understand, Mr. Saltzman," Corbbitt said. "Great corned beef, Mr. Saltzman. I don't often order it and when I do it is never as good as this."

"We don't use the butcher in Chinatown and Rose steams it to bring out the flavor. May I ask you a question, Mr. Corbbitt?" Saltzman asked. "Do you know of government corruption associated with the Common Cause bankruptcy?"

"I'm not sure yet. There is some evidence that foreign interests have tried to influence certain individuals within our government. Why?" Corbbitt asked, noticing that Isaac Saltzman suddenly seemed deeply troubled.

"We think of terrorism as the use of violence or the threat of violence to achieve political objectives. It is possible that with Common Cause we are seeing the beginning of something new—Financial Terrorism."

"What do you mean?"

"Common Cause may be the first of many companies to be manipulated into bankruptcy. Subsequent profits from this company could be used to accelerate the illegal take-over of other companies."

"And this could destroy our country and our way of life?"

"I'm afraid so. If our leaders think they can accept money once from these devils, they're mistaken. They will find out there is no end to the demands placed upon them to further subvert our country."

"Blackmail?"

"Not for money but for the right vote, bending of existing law, or creation of favorable policies. Next, you have selective enforcement of law and harassment of minorities. This is exactly what happened in Europe before

World War II. Good people, people who knew right from wrong, permitted extremists to gain control and displace civility."

"What would you do to stop this?" Corbbitt asked.

"Act immediately. Think of corruption as a virus that multiplies unchecked until it kills the host. You see that I read many newspapers. They're maneuvering in the shadows because I don't see policy changes or any of the symptoms of widespread corruption that indicate they've gained much of a foothold. So if what you say is true, there is some time. Use what tools you have to expose them and prosecute them."

"It could be very difficult to flush them out. Proving complicity between foreign investors, company executives, and government officials certainly won't be easy. Law enforcement officers have to conduct their investigations without breaking the law themselves and it doesn't take much to get a case thrown out of court," Corbbitt said.

"No doubt, with the money and intelligence that's involved exposing such a network of corruption is going to be very difficult. Right now I don't know what I'm facing, but that will change soon?"

"Some more soup, another sandwich?" Mrs. Saltzman asked.

"No thank you. It was very good."

"Just remember that you have an ally here, Agent Corbbitt. It could be that system corruption extends to those in power. They might block your investigation or discount its results. The law becomes a toothless tiger unless enforcement is possible. I am on a select list of people who can contact the President of the United States and expect to talk with him within four hours."

"I'll keep your offer in mind, Mr. Saltzman. Thank you for educating me," Corbbitt said as he backed away from the table. "I've taken enough of your time and I have to be in Washington tomorrow to continue this investigation."

"It was not only my pleasure, Agent Corbbitt, but my duty as a citizen to help in this matter. As I said before there is no shortage of evil in the world. To me the way to combat such evil is by minimizing the ultimate source of it. But that is yet another problem, and for now you have your hands full."

Corbbitt followed Saltzman as he wheeled his chair toward the front door.

"I guess I have to know before I leave, Mr. Saltzman. What do you consider to be the source of evil?"

Corbbitt saw the old man's mellow smile. "To me it is simple. Compare the results of human behavior with the noble concept of loving our fellow man. Apply that concept in both directions globally. The difference is the breeding ground for evil."

Chapter 19

Monday, February, 28, 2005, 8:12 AM

Donald Corbbitt accessed his office computer from his apartment and read the email from Special Agent Franklin Clarke.

> From: Special Agent, Franklin J. Clarke
> Date: 2/26/2005
> To: Special Agent, Donald Corbbitt
> Subject: Follow up on Margarita Rosario and Howard Champion Homicides

We finished the New Havana Tobacco Company survey of potential customers receiving promotional kits. All but eighteen of one hundred-thirty seven customers indicated they received the product and used the sample cigar. Eight of the eighteen said they gave the product to friends or relatives. We're tracking down each one of these sample kits individually. Seven threw the cigar away. Of this group, all indicated they disposed of it in a manner that would make subsequent use unlikely. The remaining three customers cannot recall receiving the product. These individuals live in Jacksonville, New Symrna Beach, and Winter Haven, Florida.

We will follow through and do a background check on these individuals.

We checked the market where Margarita Rosario supposedly met the man who killed her. No viable leads resulted from talking with others who work or frequent the market. Do you have any thoughts or suggestions?

Corbbitt thought for a few minutes. He decided that the coincidence of the ten million-dollar payments to Common Cause executives and to the entry in Senator Champion's Cayman Island account needed examination.

> From: Special Agent, Donald Corbbitt
> Date: 2/28/2005
> To: Special Agent, Franklin J. Clarke
> Subject: Suggestion for Further Investigation of Margarita Rosario and Howard Champion Homicides
>
> Let's do a thorough check on Gerald Pendergast, current CEO, of Common Cause Communications Corporation. There is a possibility that he may have been involved in the senator's death. Check Pendergast, to see if he has a direct or indirect connection with criminal elements.
>
> If it isn't too late, you may want to delay direct contact with the three individuals who say they didn't receive the product. The killer somehow got one of New Havana's promotional kits. My bet is that the killer stole it from a neighbor's mailbox.
>
> Going in too soon might cause the killer to flee.

Monday, February 28, 2005, 1:34 PM

Corbbitt took a taxi from Reagan International Airport to the Hart Senate Office building on 2nd and C St, in the northeast section of Washington, D.C. After checking through the security checkpoint, he found Wisconsin Senator, Brian L. Seward's office. After another round of banter, Senator Seward shook hands with the ever-present Dairyman's Association representatives and ushered them out of the office. Senator Seward, a well-dressed man in his early forties, looked briefly at his office manager who pointed to Corbbitt and mouthed the letters 'F B I' to the senator.

The senator's gregarious nature switched on again with a warm smile and he offered Corbbitt a handshake.

"I'm Senator Seward, from Wisconsin. What can I do for you, Agent…"

"Donald Corbbitt. I'm investigating the assassination of your former colleague, Senator Howard Champion."

"Absolutely tragic. Why would someone want to hurt that wonderful man?" the senator said as he led Corbbitt into his office.

"That's what I am trying to find out," Corbbitt said. "I take it that you and Senator Champion got along all right."

"Yes, we certainly did. He was quite a man—the sort that teaches by example. Hey, even the other party likes the guy, though he'd argue his point into oblivion. New York never had a finer senator than Howard Champion."

"That's what I've come to understand from interviewing others, but someone didn't like him and they went to a great deal of trouble to assassinate him. There has to be a reason—some motive for his death. Can you tell me just before the attack on the senator, what was the mood on the Judiciary Committee?"

"Mood? What do you mean?"

"Was there any hatred, grudges, or animosity that was apparent between committee members and Senator Champion?"

"None that I'm aware of," the senator said.

"What about between other committee members?"

"Just the normal give and take between the Republicans and Democrats. All of it within limits considered normal in our wing of the Capitol."

"How about yourself? Were you comfortable as a committee member?"

"For the most part, I was."

"Care to elaborate?"

"It's really small potatoes," the senator said.

"Perhaps."

"It's funny you should ask about the mood, Agent Corbbitt. Several of us noticed a subtle pressure from some of the committee members to do damage control for the Common Cause investigation."

"Was the pressure along party lines?"

"No, and that is strange too. I can't say we really felt like outsiders on the committee, but there was definitely something divisive about the committee's approach to the investigation."

"Did that change in anyway when the new chairman took over?"

"Senator Champion was willing to look at the facts involving the bankruptcy in an objective manner. Senator Horne, his replacement, seems like he already has an opinion."

"Which way does he lean?"

"He's one who tries to tone down the Common Cause issue."

"Interesting," Corbbitt said.

"Now that I think of it, it's like each one of us who is neutral has an assigned senator applying this gentle pressure. Like having your hand held with just enough pressure to try to steer you in their direction."

"Would you tell me who the 'hand holders' are, Senator?"

"I could if it is relevant to your investigation. Is it?"

"Senator, the truth is that I don't know at this point. I'm not asking for inside committee information relative to an ongoing investigation. This concerns the death of your colleague."

"Well, you're implying that Senator Horne and the others might have caused Senator Champion's death. I simply can't subscribe to that notion."

"I'm not implying anything Senator, just gathering facts. It's what I do, collect facts from many sources and you know most of what I get is useless, but I still concentrate on the details."

The senator thought for a moment and frowned. "I don't want any ethics violation here, Agent Corbbitt, but Senators' Douglas, Yost, Malady, Petrie, McCabe, Wren, Brenner, and of course Senator Horne are the ones I'm talking about."

Corbbitt took down the names. "Thank you, Senator."

"Is that all, Agent Corbbitt? It's after one and I'm already way behind on the day's schedule."

"Almost, sir. Did you ever socialize with Senator Champion, at his local residence or perhaps his New York home?"

"No, I've never been to either place."

"Thank you, Senator. Here's my business card. If there is anything that you can think of that might help find who killed Senator Champion, I'd appreciate a call."

"Sure, but would you do me a favor?" Senator Seward asked.

"Yes, if I can. What is it?"

"Drink more milk."

Corbbitt laughed. "Okay, Senator, I know where you're coming from."

February, 28, 2005, 7:40 PM

Jocelyn greeted Donald Corbbitt with a beaming smile at her front door. Although Don looked ready to go out for the evening, she could tell instantly that something was bothering him. Even his overcoat seemed to sag at the shoulders as if he toted some heavy unseen burden.

"Come in, Don. Can I get you a drink?"

"You sure can. I'm afraid these investigations have worn me down."

She took his coat and hung it in the front closet. "Physically or mentally?" she asked.

"Oh, physically it's been nothing. What I've learned in the course of the investigation is the problem. But I don't want to get into all of that and spoil our evening together."

She poured an extra finger width of cognac in a snifter and warmed it for a few seconds in the microwave. "Here, see if this helps," she said, and handed the drink to him.

"Thanks," he said, taking a quick sip.

"So what brings you back to the capitol this time?" she asked, while looking at Don who seemed to be lost in thought. "Don, you seem like you're a thousand miles away."

"I'm sorry. I guess I'm not very good company tonight."

"Something's really wrong and I think you need to talk about it," Jocelyn said as she sat next to him on the couch.

"Jocelyn, what if I told you that I might have uncovered something that might be bigger and potentially much more damaging than the Watergate scandal. It's something that might affect everyone in this country, if not the world."

"I'd say you're scaring me, Don. No wonder you're having trouble being your normal self."

"Jocelyn, in the last three days I've interrogated a terminally ill woman who proudly confessed that she killed four executives involved in the Common Cause bankruptcy. And even through a morphine-induced fog she made sense and almost succeeded in justifying her actions. Then I talk with Isaac Saltzman, the world famous financial consultant, who describes in detail the systematic, ruthless, and illegal dismemberment of Common Cause by foreign investors."

"Incredible," Jocelyn said.

"Incredibly worse," Corbbitt added. "During the course of investigating Senator Champion's assassination, I found a marked up list of the Senate Judiciary Committee members. I talked with six senators today who all told the same story. Within that committee, there are members who don't believe there was much wrongdoing involved by Common Cause. They're pressuring their colleagues to limit the inquiry."

"Collusion?"

"That's what scares me. If there was a coordinated effort to destroy this company, and individuals within our government are positioned to allow it to happen there is real danger."

"I don't understand. Why do you think the judiciary committee is involved?"

"Not all of them, Jocelyn, but enough to soft-soap an inquiry. What bothers me is that these inquiries usually don't result in prosecutions. Sometimes they serve as the basis for a new law or revision of an existing law, but often they serve as a platform allowing the senators to do a bit of grandstanding for their constituents."

"What you're saying is that if it exists here, it's possible that it exists within the executive and judicial branches too."

Corbbitt looked at Jocelyn. "Now you know why I am troubled."

"If a conspiracy is this widespread, exposing it might be dangerous. A senator wields a lot of power and that might end your career."

"There are much larger issues here than my career, Jocelyn, and you know that I'm always one wrong decision away from being fired anyway. So I'm used to that possibility."

"What are you going to do?"

"I'm not going to walk away from this, that's for sure."

"What if you just put all of this in front of your supervisor and let him make the decision?"

"Peyton Bender is a fair man. I've got confidence he'd do the right thing, but he's going to need concrete evidence and right now, I only have loose pebbles. To me the key to this whole business is Gerald Pendergast. He's an arrogant bastard and it's not going to be easy to break down his defenses. All I really have against him is an allegation by a disgruntled and terminally ill former employee who's killed four people. She claims all the senior executives received ten million dollars to cooperate with Pendergast's scheme."

"What happens if you start interrogating the senators that you think are involved in the conspiracy?" Jocelyn asked.

"Red flags will go up all over Washington, and the Director himself will jump on me," Don said as he took a large sip from the brandy snifter. "I'm really sorry to dump all of this on you, Jocelyn."

"I'd be less than a friend if I wasn't concerned about you, Don. So don't worry about it."

"How is your end of the company anyway? Do they still have you breaking in the new Information Analysts?"

"Yes, the last batch they hired are as ready as they're going to be. But it takes years before they can learn to effectively put information pieces together. It takes skill and insight to form a reliable picture that might serve as the basis for policy changes or action."

"What's your assignment until the next batch gets hired?"

"For a while I needed six of me to get the various levels of law enforcement and supporting agencies to work together and share information. For the most part that's about done. There is some talk of taking our staff and farming us out to the Field Offices for investigative support. We'd scramble back in the event of another Code Red to combat the next terrorist threat."

"How do you feel about being relocated on a moment's notice?"

"Not good. It's not what I signed on for," Jocelyn grumbled.

"I have the reverse problem."

"How's that?"

"I requested a transfer from the New York Field Office to the one in Washington."

Jocelyn's smile advertised the euphoria she felt. Here was a man demonstrating his love, a man willing to make a huge change in his life to be with her. "Are they having a problem with that request?"

"I'm afraid so, Jocelyn. Bender must think it is strange request. I've been in that office longer than ten years and the Bureau's policy is that after you're in one location for ten years, they cannot force you to relocate. By requesting a relocation, I'm effectively restarting the clock."

"And you could be transferred at any time to any other Field Office?"

"Yes. There are also the high-profile cases I'm working on. He says I'm one of his better agents. With the heavy workload that's dumped on that office, he's going to make it difficult for me to get the transfer I want."

"What about after these cases are over? Can't you force the issue?"

"Jocelyn, there's always a high profile case or the burden is so heavy that even vacations get canceled."

She thought for a moment. "Don, somehow this will work out. The fact that you're seriously trying to relocate here to be with me, really makes me melt."

"I did that, Jocelyn, because I believe in us as a couple, that we are good for each other."

"Can I get you another drink, Don?" she said as she tried to hide her joy.

"No, but if we're going to put aside these difficulties and have a little fun, we'd better get going."

"You did say casual dress tonight, right?"

"Yes, there's a club over in Arlington. They have a group that plays rhythm and blues until the wee hours."

"We can go for a little while, Don, but I'm a working girl. I've got to get up in the morning. Okay?"

"Pity, there never seems to be enough time for us."

Jocelyn smiled. "I agree, but I know you're doing the best you can, Don. That goes a long way with me." She kissed him on the cheek and went to get their coats.

Monday, February 28, 2005, 8:22 PM

Rudy Gambrelli hated the thought of viewing his brother, Michael's, new home in swanky, West Side Jacksonville suburbia. Except for a little pretentiousness, Michael, was a great brother who swallowed his pride and paid monthly visits during Rudy's seven-year prison term. The problem with tonight would be contending with his wife, Sophia, with her fingernails-on-blackboard voice, meddlesome nature, and her in-your-face aggressive frugality. How Michael ever talked his wife into purchasing a quarter of a million dollar home and how they would pay for it was a mystery.

Dinner consisted of a the obligatory huge bowl of low quality pasta, high acid content out-of-the-jar spaghetti sauce, limp lettuce salad, and thrift store two day old Italian bread with a crust that needed a chainsaw for slicing.

It seemed to Rudy that Sophia Gambrelli, formerly Sophia Papini, gained tonnage and grew a mustache the minute his brother put a wedding band on her finger. Rudy looked at his brother hoping that Michael would get the hint and get Sophia to stop her endless prattling about Internet coupons and online shopping.

"Do you know what kind of furniture you're going to get for the house, Sophia?" Rudy asked to break her discount shopper's soliloquy.

"There's a furniture seconds store across town. I think we'll look there first and see if we can save a buck or two."

Michael grimaced.

The telephone rang and Rudy breathed a sigh of relief when Sophia volunteered to go into the kitchen and take the call.

"She's driving me nuts, Rudy," Michael said. "All day long rattling on about how much money she saves by careful spending. I told her she'd save more if she didn't insist shopping everyday and driving all over town to do it."

"I think she's out of control, Mike. It's not exactly fun eating dinner here, bro. It's up to you to reel her in."

"I've tried, Rudy. Usually it winds up in a fight or she drops a bucket of tears. I guess it serves me right for giving her everything and spoiling her."

Rudy pointed at the doorway when he saw Sophia enter to warn his brother that she was behind him.

Sophia returned to the table and gave the men the thumbs up signal. "Another triumph over big business."

"What was that call all about?" her husband asked.

"Remember that free cigar that I got from some tobacco company on the Internet, Rudy?"

"Yes. What of it?" Rudy asked.

"Well, you've got two more coming. They were doing a customer satisfaction survey. I lied to him and told him that I didn't receive the cigar. Right away he said that he'd send another."

"Okay, so you beat them out of another free cigar," Michael said.

"Oh it's better than that. The stupid guy wanted to know if I was really going to smoke the damn thing myself. I said no. I'll give it to my brother-in-law. Then he says he'd like to send another one directly to you and give you a twenty-percent discount on your first purchase. So I figure, what the hell, I gave him your name, address, and telephone number. Now you're going to get two free cigars. Cool, huh?"

The color left Rudy's face until the rage exploded. "You gave him my personal information, Sophia? Who the hell told you that you could do that?"

"Calm down, Rudy. She just tried to do something nice for you," Michael said.

"What other survey questions did he ask you?" Rudy demanded.

"Actually he didn't ask me anymore, once I said I was going to give it away to you. Why?"

Rudy looked at his watch. He could smell the police on the other end of this conversation and he knew he had a little time to get to his apartment, grab a few things, and run. "Mike, thanks for the dinner and good luck with the new house. Tell your wife not to do me anymore favors and stay out of my life!"

Monday, February, 28, 2005, 11:49 PM

Don Corbbitt checked for messages while he waited for the taxicab to take him back to a Crystal City hotel room near Reagan International Airport. "Urgent! Call Clarke. Case suspect," Corbbitt read from his cell phone message window. He dialed Agent Clark's number immediately. Clarke picked up the phone on the second ring.

"Sorry for calling so late, Agent Clarke, I was out enjoying life for a few hours."

"Don't make a habit out of it," Clarke chided. "We've got a possible suspect in the Margarita Rosario and Howard Champion homicides."

"Great, have you got the suspect in custody?"

"Not yet. We're watching an apartment complex for Rudy Gambrelli to return home."

"How did you come up with this guy's name?"

"We followed your suggestion and checked Gerald Pendergast's background. Pendergast's first wife Julia Carlson was once Julia Gambrelli. She reverted to her maiden name after she divorced Anthony Gambrelli citing spousal abuse. She died twelve years ago from a combination of alcohol and drugs. Anthony Gambrelli was a restaurant owner in Miami, but he had close mob ties."

"Was?" Corbbitt asked.

"Yes, apparently the people he did business with in the mob had a problem with him. Their heavy-hitters clubbed him to death with baseball bats."

"Usually the mob hits are quick. He must have really pissed some mob boss off to deserve the painful bludgeoning."

"Well, Anthony and Julia did have two sons, Michael and Rudy. Michael has no prior arrests, but Rudy did seven years for manslaughter at the Florida State Prison, near Jacksonville. He carved up a guy while trying to collect a gambling debt. Rudy Gambrelli was arrested one other time as a suspect in a booby trap murder, that case was thrown out of court due to insufficient evidence."

"So Gerald Pendergast is indirectly related to a thug with prior arrests. That's suspicious, but not enough to put Gambrelli away."

"True, that's why we ran the survey idea again. One of the three individuals who said they didn't receive a New Havana promotional kit is a woman. We made it seem like no one knew about the first survey. When we asked whether she would actually smoke the cigar, she laughed and said she intended to give it to her brother-in-law, Rudy Gambrelli. Eventually, Sophia Gambrelli, Michael's wife, gave us Rudy's address and telephone number."

"So either we have an incredible coincidence or Rudy Gambrelli is responsible for the homicides."

"That's what we think too. It will be interesting to question him. Are you flying in for the interrogation?"

"No, I'm going to pay another visit to Gerald Pendergast, just in case Mr. Gambrelli decides to go it alone in court."

"Well, that's it for now. If anything changes, I'll keep you posted."

"Clarke, play this one close to the chest. There are some side issues to this case that could really mushroom way beyond these homicides."

"Gotcha, any hints?"

"Let me work on it a bit, but I'll get back to you when the time is right. Thanks for your help. It looks like you've landed the right guy."

Monday, February 28, 2005, 11:47 PM

Margaret Jensen stared at the heart rate monitor indication. By relaxing and concentrating, she could only get her pulse rate down to sixty-one beats per minute. She wondered why human evolution insisted on preservation at all costs and why she must endure tormenting pain by continuing to embrace life. There had to be a way to end what was never pleasant.

Chapter 20

Tuesday, March 1, 2005, 11:12 AM

Donald Corbbitt approached the security guard in the lobby of the Manhattan skyscraper and presented his identification.

"Officer, I'm here to see a Ms. Heather Pollack. She works for Common Cause."

"One of the lucky few," he responded. "I'll call her and tell her you're down here."

"Wait, that's just it. I'm investigating a case and I don't want others nearby to know that I'm talking to her," Corbbitt said.

The officer thought for a moment. "We get flower deliveries here all the time. Now with tighter security measures in place, the deliveries are left here in the lobby and the recipient has to come and get them."

"Flowers, great idea. But I don't want to set her up in front of her boss…"

The officer raised his hand to interrupt. "If it's really that important, there's a small gift shop next door. You can get candy or flowers to help make it look good."

"Would candy be better?"

"Flowers might sit here for a while, but most of the time they zoom down the elevator for candy. If I tell her there's chocolate candy down here, she'll forget about the elevator and take steps two at a time to get here quicker."

"Thanks, I learned something," Corbbitt said.

The officer chuckled. "When it comes to chocolate, they're all sisters. I'll wait until you come back to tell her there's a package for her."

Twenty minutes later Heather Pollack asked at the security desk for her box of chocolate from an unknown admirer. The security officer told her there was an important visitor and directed her to the radio room where the backup portable radios were charging.

"Ms. Pollack, do you remember me? I'm Donald Corbbitt with the FBI."

"Yes, you were just here last week."

"Last Friday. I'm still investigating Senator Howard Champion's assassination."

"Yes, you started to ask me questions, then Mr. Pendergast interrupted."

"That's what I'd like to talk to you about. As his secretary you have a duty to show loyalty to your boss and of course perform duties assigned by him."

"That's right, and I really try to do that. There's a lot of things that require secrecy that might hurt him or the company if I wasn't careful performing my duties."

"Ms. Pollack, I'm going to share with you something that is very important. I'm trusting you with very sensitive information."

"Wow! This sounds serious."

"If you reveal what I'm telling you to Mr. Pendergast or anyone else, to the detriment of this investigation, and later Pendergast is found guilty, you might be charged as a co-conspirator. You have no obligation to maintain loyalty to Mr. Pendergast if his actions result in breaking the law. Do you understand?"

"Yes, I think so."

"Good. If I didn't need your assistance, I wouldn't tell you that Gerald Pendergast is a suspect in a worldwide conspiracy to force this company into bankruptcy and allow foreign interests to buy it."

"A conspiracy!"

"If I charge in there and ask questions relating to this, it's going to give those who are responsible for the Common Cause disaster a chance to escape prosecution."

"What do you want me to do?"

"I'd like you to decide which team you're on. Pendergast's team stole the assets and jobs from thousands of investors and employees. My team wants to put them behind bars for doing it."

"You want me to spy on him and give information to you, don't you?"

"That's one way of describing it. It is quite possible that other companies will have the same thing happen. I'm asking you to help protect others from a similar fate in the future. Instead of spying, I prefer to think of it as doing the right thing," Corbbitt said, handing her the box of chocolate truffles.

"Is this a bribe, Agent Corbbitt?"

"No, it is part of your cover story. This way you won't raise suspicion by being away from your desk too long."

"You don't give a girl much of a choice, Agent Corbbitt."

"I suppose not. It's the difference between what is right and what is wrong. You decide, Ms. Pollack."

"I'm on your team, Agent Corbbitt. I didn't like what happened to a lot of my fellow workers and personally I can't stand Gerald Pendergast."

"Thank you, Ms. Pollack. Specifically, I need to know what travel plans Pendergast had last November. I need you to find out without drawing attention to yourself. Here's my card."

"Agent Corbbitt?"

"Yes, Heather."

"Being on your team, already makes be feel better."

Tuesday, March 1, 2005, 2:19 PM

Gerald Pendergast's secretary, Heather Pollack, put the building security officer on hold and immediately called her boss. "Mr. Pendergast, security just called. There's a man down stairs who wants to see you. He claims he's a relative from Florida and that it is very important that he meet with you immediately."

Heather waited a moment for Pendergast's reply. "Sir, did you hear what I said?"

"Yes," Pendergast said. "All right tell security it's okay to send him up."

He paced in his office searching for some reason for Gambrelli's sudden appearance. Heather's soft knock on the door left him without a plan for confronting Gambrelli.

"Mr. Pendergast, your visitor is here."

"Thank you, Heather."

Heather backed away and suddenly Rudy Gambrelli, who's physique rivaled that of a professional football tackle filled the doorway.

Gambrelli closed the door and threw himself in a chair.

"What the hell are you doing here, Rudy? This place is crawling with Feds."

"Is that anyway to treat a relative after a long night's drive? Besides, it's not exactly a playground now where I live, thanks to my brother's stupid wife."

"What does that mean?"

"It means I just got out of town before they arrested me. It means that I've got three hundred and twelve dollars cash, and that I can't use credit cards for fear that I'll be tracked down."

"Well, this is your problem, not mine."

"No, I think you're wrong about that. You see if they grab me for last week's incident, I'm not going down alone. So it's in your best interest to make sure they don't."

"You're blackmailing me?"

Gambrelli smiled. "Let's just call it a one time payment to my retirement account. Then I can disappear."

"I've paid you already for the 'incident'."

"Yes, you did. Now you're going to pay again. Otherwise, you're going to prison with me. Who knows, we might get adjoining cells."

"Just out of curiosity how much does your 'retirement' cost?"

"I figure a million ought to do it, a million in cash that is."

"Where am I supposed to get a million dollars? Common Cause money is in the hands of the new owners. The Feds are reviewing our books and I'm in enough trouble trying to justify what happened here."

"Like you said before. That's your problem not mine. I want a million dollars cash, and I want it now."

"Even if I had a million to give you, getting cash at this point would cause instant suspicion. Eventually, they'd find you anyway and we'd both suffer. Like it or not, we're both married to the senator's assassination. Instead of making outrageous threats and demands, consider this for an alternative that might just get us through this without a murder charge."

"I'm listening."

"I'll hire you as a special consultant, give you a high-end salary with perks such as fine living accommodations. I'll even provide the business reports that you were supposed to develop for the money your salary. Just get out of sight and stay there."

"What kind of salary are you talking about?"

"Let's say twenty-thousand a month and I'll toss in nominal living expenses. The payment will continue until you've got your million dollars."

"Rental car and lodging?"

"Yes, but to make it legal, you'll have to submit bills for service and expense statements."

"Cash?"

"Look, I'll give you enough cash out of pocket to keep you going and entertained. We'll set up an offshore account in your name so you can hide the rest. Just don't get too eager to draw from it. Wait until the Feds back down. What do you say? Is it a deal?"

"This sounds pretty good. All I have to do is evaporate?"
"Yes, for the most part."
"What do you mean?" Gambrelli asked.
"It may be necessary to draw on your unique talents in the future."
"That will be extra of course."
"Let's discuss that when the time comes. Okay?"
"Yeah, sure. Don't forget your end of the agreement. If you have sudden loss of memory, I'll know what to do," Gambrelli said, drawing a line across his throat with an extended finger.
"Rudy, don't ever threaten me again."
Rudy stood up, grabbed Pendergast by the tie, and pulled him close. "What are you going to do about it, asshole?" Gambrelli asked in a hushed voice that rattled Pendergast. "Oh, by the way, I need some cash right now. Empty your wallet."

Tuesday, March 1, 2005, 5:44 PM

Gerald Pendergast, CEO of a world-wide communications network, had to walk across the street to a hotel lobby to make telephone calls without being monitored by possible FBI wire taps. He looked around before entering the telephone booth making sure that no one tailed him.
"Come on, Horne, you son-of-a-bitch, pick up the phone."
"Hello," Senator Horne said after the fourth ring.
"It's your friend from New York, you lying power-hungry bastard."
"This is not a good time to discuss this, I'm with other people, and dinner is about ready to be served," Senator Adrian Horne said.
"I've got an appetizer for you, that's going to kill the rest of your dinner. Let's talk now!"
"All right, give me a second to get some privacy."
A minute later Senator Horne spoke, "Go ahead."
"I finally noticed a little discrepancy in a special account, Adrian. It seems like your former colleague wanted to back out gracefully. He returned the ten million dollars, Adrian. You lied about his demand for more money."
"Like Nietzsche said, 'That which is falling should be pushed.' So?"
"So! I'll tell you what your quest for power accomplished. The guy who 'handled' the problem that you created by lying was in my office today. He tried to shake me down for two million dollars to insure that he'd have enough

cash to escape prosecution and evaporate. He's got us by the balls and he's squeezing."

"This was your man, not mine."

"Yes, but you invented the problem to begin with by lying. Fortunately, for you I've negotiated a better deal."

"Why me?"

"You don't think I'm going to pay the forty-thousand dollars a month?"

"Forty thousand a month!"

"Yes, in cash too, until he's paid his two million dollars."

"Where am I going to get that kind of money?"

"From the ten million dollars in your account, you dolt. He's no one to treat lightly and he'll need the money soon."

"What if I refuse to pay?"

"Simple, I've hired him as a special consultant. He doesn't know where the money comes from, unless I tell him. Unless you want to join your colleague, I suggest you cough up the cash."

"Can't we do something to get rid of this guy?"

"Oh, sure. What would we do then, start this all over again when the next thug gets the same idea?"

"Still this is really going to bite into my funds."

"You should have thought about the consequences before you lied to me."

"How do I know you're not shaking me down?"

"Well, Senator, I guess you'll have to trust me. Get the money and get it now," Pendergast said and slammed down the phone.

Tuesday, March 1, 2005, 6:53 PM

From his home in Hoboken, Corbbitt selected the computer screen icon that tied his home computer to his office computer to capture the latest information from other agents working on the Rosario/Champion homicides and Common Cause bankruptcy. He scanned his emails.

From: Special Agent, Franklin J. Clarke
Date: 3/1/2005
To: Special Agent, Donald Corbbitt
Subject: Follow up on Suspect Rudy Gambrelli

Gambrelli's neighbor was out walking her dog last night around 9:15. She saw Gambrelli loading suitcases in his car. Our surveillance team wasn't established until 9:40, so it looks like we've missed him. The fact that he suddenly decided to leave increases our suspicions that he is involved in the homicides.

Since our survey seemed to spark his departure, we interviewed his brother Michael and sister-in-law, Sophia. They confirmed that Rudy Gambrelli was at the house, learned of our survey inquiry, and abruptly left. They insisted they knew nothing of his prior activities or of his travel destination.

See the attached Gambrelli photograph and felony history obtained from the Florida State Prison records.

We're checking automobile license, registration, and credit card information now. We'll keep you informed.

"Shit," Corbbitt said and clicked for the next email.

> From: Joshua Koweleski
> Date: 3/1/2005
> To: Special Agent, Donald Corbbitt
> Subject: Confirmation of Requirement to Seek Anger Management Counseling

Agent Corbbitt, I've done exactly what you've required of me with regard to attending anger management. (See the attached information concerning the counseling program including its goals and objectives.)

My girlfriend, Bethany, called and said that it was in the news that you've caught the killer of the Common Cause executives. It looks like anger management counseling was a little late for Ms. Jensen.

On another matter, Mr. Hammond, Ninth Generation's President, and I want to present something to you that might be very helpful in solving future cases.

Since I feel I owe you for giving me a second chance, I'd like you to get the credit for introducing the FBI to a high tech way of ferreting out those who do us harm. Perhaps it is my way of redirecting my anger as recommended by the counselor.

Can we meet soon to discuss this issue?
Thanks, J. Koweleski

Initially, Corbbitt wondered what Koweleski really wanted, but then he remembered the short video presentation that President Hammond showed him when he visited Ninth Generation. From experience, Corbbitt knew that when an expert in any field of study knocked on your forehead, it was time to listen. Joshua Koweleski certainly qualified. He typed a short reply to Koweleski indicating that any meeting to alter current techniques affected policy. His supervisor Peyton Bender would have to approve the use of new techniques.

Tuesday, March 1, 2005, 11:07 PM

After four days, Margaret Jensen understood hospital routine. It seemed to her that the hospital staff, who vigilantly attended to her malady, were her enemies with their labors all designed to extend her agony while she only wanted to pull the plug on the treadmill of pain.

The first day she spent assessing the hospital room and its contents. Immediately, she discounted the idea of flinging herself from the window. Even without her huge belly, no adult could slide through the six-inch space offered by the window in its fully opened position. She looked in vain for pills or cleaning fluids left by errant hospital staff that might contain enough punch to stop her breathing.

Yet, she watched ever hopeful that some mistake in routine might give her the opportunity to die quickly. Why suffer the endless pain? Why lay in feces for hours until some poor soul came to clean up the mess? Why prolong the inevitable?

She studied the equipment tied to her body. The heart-rate monitor stood like a tireless sentinel, ready to broadcast any change in her condition. The green trace depicting her heart action had preset limits. With one signal from the sentinel, a team of well-trained professionals armed with equipment and ethics would swarm over her and save what she desperately wanted to lose. She knew if she unplugged the monitor, the green trace would stop. She wondered if somehow that action would reflect back into her body and stop her heart.

With the hospital's morphine and rest, the pain dropped to a tolerable level and she felt she had enough strength to get out of the bed, stand, and maybe walk a few paces. She knew that soon even this strength would leave, and this would further limit opportunities to kill herself.

She concentrated on the intravenous lines providing pain relief and nourishment to her body. While she could push a button to get pain relief, the device regulating the morphine limited the amount and the frequency, making it impossible for her to get a lethal dose. Whoever designed the system that locked away the blessed relief the morphine could bring had to be a sadist.

She followed the IV lines from the pumps to the puncture site on her right arm. There she saw the place where the nurse came to give her an injection by inserting a needle into a special port just before the IV needle penetrated her arm.

She looked at the site for a long time and suddenly knew how she would end her life.

Chapter 21

Wednesday, March 2, 2005, 9:42 AM

Corbbitt returned to the FBI New York City Field Office. On his desk was a request from his supervisor, Peyton Bender for a ten o'clock meeting to review Senator Howard Champion's case file. Corbbitt could read between the lines. The heat was still on to find the assassin, but the demands of the sprawling metropolitan area they serviced often overwhelmed their expanded staff.

Knowing the prime suspect for the Champion/Rosario homicides was completely different from having the suspect available for questioning. Without further information, Rudy Gambrelli might hide for weeks, but from Bender's perspective, it was a delicate balance between continuing the investigation with the current intensity or taking the political heat by diverting the investigative assets to other cases.

Corbbitt reviewed the existing interlaced Champion and Rosario files, and made some modifications from the previous day's findings. He stopped typing to answer his telephone, "Hello, Special Agent Corbbitt here."

"Hello, it's Heather," Pendergast's secretary spoke in a subdued voice.

"Thank you for calling, Heather. Before you say anything, do you have total privacy?"

"Yes, for the moment."

"Don't take any chances. There's a lot of money involved and with it there's an element of danger."

"I'll remember that," Heather said, in a seductive voice. "I checked on Mr. Pendergast's travel schedule for the month of November. Because of the bankruptcy and the holidays, he didn't do much traveling. There was one plane flight booked for him though from Long Island's MacArthur Airport to Albany, New York. I also have a bill for a rental car."

"Do you have the specific dates?"

"Yes, sir. Let me check," Heather said. "He left on Friday, November, 19th and returned on the 21st."

"Do you know if it was company business or personal?"

"Mr. Corbbitt, when you're the president, you don't have to justify your expenses."

"Yes, I guess so. Thank you, Heather."

"Oh, I did check into his cell phone charges for the month. Odd, the bill was not in the file like the others."

"Interesting, Heather, and that was good thinking. Anything else?"

"No, but all this spying makes me feel like one of those gals in the action movies."

"Just remember, Heather, in the real world people bleed and die. Just be careful."

"I will, Mr. Corbbitt."

Corbbitt hung up the phone. Immediately, he added to the Champion file two significant details: Gerald Pendergast was within two hours by car of Champion's home and the timing precisely matched Senator Champion's meeting with some of his committee colleagues.

Corbbitt checked his watch, realized he was four minutes late, and quickly gathered his files. Fortunately, Bender had four agents already atoning for unproductive hours on their assigned cases. After dismissing the other agents, Bender waved Corbbitt into his office. Corbbitt closed the door behind him, and took the inquisition seat.

"Before we get started on the case files you have, Don, what about this software company making a presentation here. They said you would know about it."

"Peyton, I'm sorry. I had no idea they were going to act so quickly. I did tell them what they have in mind required your approval. Probably they thought they were going through proper channels by contacting you directly."

"Okay, I'll accept that. What do they want with us?"

"I think they just want to show you their new software products. I saw a demonstration myself when I visited last week."

"We have all the office software we need and can afford."

"Believe me, this is not typical office software. Essentially, they can duplicate reality in cyberspace. When I was there, they were mulling over ways to market their product and possible consequences of how the product might be used."

"Do you think we need to meet with them?"

"Based on what I saw. Definitely."

"Well, they want to do a video conference tomorrow at eleven o'clock. Can you make it?"

"Sure, gee these guys don't fool around, but I guess now-a-days you can't wait or someone else will take your place."

"I just don't like sales people. I had their president, a guy named Hammond, and his fellow arm-twister, Koweleski, on the phone making the pitch. It's not our function to evaluate new products when we've already got a full plate."

"I know Koweleski, he's probably the brightest guy in the country with computer software. Peyton, believe me, this is cutting-edge technology. It won't hurt to see what they have in mind."

"All right, let's get down to our business."

Since Corbbitt filed frequent updates to his report, Peyton Bender knew most of the information concerning the Champion and related Rosario homicides. What he didn't know was the pervasive nature of money and corruption involved with the case.

"You realize what you're alleging here, Don. If what you say is true, it could permanently damage the administration, the legislative branch, and the people's confidence in our government."

"Exactly. That's why I've been very careful not to dig for dirt in the wrong corners. If we're going to strike out against this, we need to be very careful. No one knows how far this goes, or who is involved."

"You're assuming that we're going to dig further than the Champion/Rosario murders. Really, you don't have solid evidence to back up your claim of widespread corruption."

Corbbitt sat silently for a few seconds. "Peyton, you're really not an administrative type, you've come up through the ranks and know this business better than anyone in the Bureau. If you back me away from this, how are you going to feel later, knowing you had a chance to stop it now?"

"Frankly, this scares me to death, Don. If we proceed and are wrong, we're history."

"Right, Peyton—that's why I've not jostled those that are close to the action yet. No one knows except Isaac Saltzman, the financial wizard, who gave me an education into big money power games."

"You actually talked to him!"

"Don't worry, there's no consulting fee. He was actually glad to talk to me because of the successful capture of the terrorists last September kept a large real estate transaction of his together. I told him about the Common Cause executives and the possible corruption of the Judiciary Committee senators."

"He really thinks that foreign money is perverting our whole government?"

"He's not saying the whole government. But he is very concerned that once this reaches a certain level, it's almost impossible to stop," Corbbitt said. "Peyton, he's seen this happen before."

"Yes, and a good part of the world is run on baksheesh, favoritism, and corruption."

"Is that how you want to live here, Peyton?"

"No, certainly not. But this situation is bigger than both of us, Don, I'm going to have to talk to the Director about this."

"If you must, I understand. What happens though if he's in their back pocket?"

"You can't be serious."

"It was just a question," Corbbitt said.

"Now that I think about it, it was strange the way the heat got applied when the Common Cause executives started dying right and left. When was the last time you ever saw simultaneous demands from the Attorney General and the Bureau Director for investigating homicide? I found that a little odd."

"I really want to go after this, Peyton. I don't see where we have any choice."

"For the moment, continue doing what you're doing. Keep things low profile. I'll get back to you. I promise."

"I'll do what I can. Just remember, there's many people involved here. If someone else, like Senator Champion changes their mind, we might have more homicides to deal with. And don't forget about the media. One leak and all hell will break loose."

"I hear you."

"Peyton."

"Yes."

"Thanks for listening. Anyone else would have killed the messenger."

Wednesday, March 2, 2005, 8:08 PM

Getting the hypodermic syringe proved to be an easy task. Margaret Jensen waited until the evening shift nurse came around to administer the prescribed shot that she inserted in the intravenous line y-port. It was a simple matter of distracting the nurse by feigning a dropped contact lens. Begging the nurse to hunt for it brought forth a torrent of grumbles, but the nurse did exactly what Margaret thought she would do, place the empty hypodermic syringe on the bed stand. Margaret quickly tucked it safely under the covers.

The nurse finally gave up after a few minutes of searching; saying that it was not her responsibility to hunt all night when she had other patients who weren't murderers and needed care. To keep the nurse from thinking about the hypodermic, Margaret added further insult by whining for some juice.

Now it was a matter of waiting until the nurses were most busy and least likely to catch her in the act of committing suicide. This time she wanted no one, nothing interfering with the relief and eternal rest from a life filled with ugliness.

She began the procedure she decided to use to end her life. Phase one required recalling the beautiful things in her life. Those things once taken for granted now seemed distant, impossible to reach except for the wisps of memory she desperately sought in her final minutes of life.

She remembered walks through sculptured gardens, or on sandy beaches, or following narrow paths through pine-scented forests. Strange all these memories of beauty were shared with no one. She had no idea how much more these beautiful memories might have been if there was someone special in her life. Someone who would receive the torrent of love that she so willingly wanted to give. A lifelong gift to someone who would overlook her lack of physical beauty, who would see the aching-loving heart beneath the scaly patches of her psoriasis. How much sweeter would the blossom, the chocolate, or the music of her life been, if she had been born pretty instead of the way she was?

The sharp tug of pain ravaged her body again. She debated starting phase two that only required her to push the demand button so the IV pump would release another dose of morphine.

Outside her room there were voices laughing and giggling. Laughing? *When was the last time I really laughed? Why did it seem like joy was for everyone else?* She pushed the demand button to release the morphine. When the IV pump moved the morphine a few inches down the tubing and into her arm, phase three would begin.

She moved the hypodermic syringe carefully to protect the precious needle and turned slowly onto her right side. She pulled the plunger back on the syringe, filling it with air. Soon she felt the pain roll back like a huge tsunami wave, recoiling for the moment only to strike again.

Margaret paused for a second, knowing that the next phase would be the end. Air injected into her IV line, would either find its way into her heart or into her brain. The heart, that could only pump fluid, would stall and a classic heart attack would ensue. Air to her brain, would starve it from vital nutrients and within minutes she would be dead. A stroke or a heart attack was not much of a choice but she hoped the last dose of morphine might ease her through the last few seconds to make the intolerable tolerable.

She curled up into a ball and tugged at the sheet to cover her right arm and head. She inserted the needle into the y-port and pushed the plunger. "This one is for my mother, who should have stood up to my father to protect her children," she whispered. She removed the needle and reloaded the syringe with air. "This one is for my father who delighted in fondling his teenage daughter," she whispered, and injected another five cubic centimeters of air in her vein. She removed the syringe and reloaded it with air. "This one is for everyone who tormented me because I wasn't pretty."

The sentinel sent a signal to the nursing station indicating that Margaret Jensen's condition had changed.

She withdrew the plunger again, and reloaded it quickly. "This is for Yvonne Taylor, see you soon, sweetie," she said as she removed the plunger and reloaded it with difficulty. She struggled to maintain focus to insert the needle in the y-port. She pushed on the plunger again.

"This…one…is…for…me…I…deserved…bet-…"

Chapter 22

Thursday, March 3, 2005, 10:51 AM

Peyton Bender followed the procedure taped to the side of the fifty-two inch HDTV while Corbbitt helped a technician with the microphones. The technician would stay to operate their camera and maintain two-way audio and video communications with the Ninth Generation's software Company in Braintree, Massachusetts.

Bender, realizing that this was going to take a huge chunk out of his day, kept looking at his watch. "Are you sure about this, Don?"

Corbbitt, who received a call earlier in the morning from Joshua Koweleski, smiled. "Trust me, Peyton. It'll be the best part of your week."

The technician announced acquisition of Ninth Generations signal and the screen lit up with a picture of two men sitting behind a long table. Small signs in front of the men identified Ninth Generation President Hammond and Senior Project Engineer Joshua Koweleski.

"Good morning, Mr. Bender and Mr. Corbbitt, I'm Edward Hammond, president of Ninth Generation Software Company. With me is Joshua Koweleski, project manager, and I might add the brightest most innovative computer specialist in the country."

A smile spread across Koweleski's face.

"Please introduce yourself. It will also check that we have audio from your facility," Hammond said.

"It's a pleasure to meet you, President Hammond and Mr. Koweleski, I'm Peyton Bender, Assistant Director of the FBI New York City, Field Office. With me is Special Agent Donald Corbbitt and I have to add one of the most intelligent and aggressive agents in the Bureau today."

Corbbitt flushed on camera.

"Gentlemen we're here because we think Ninth Generations new software products, Ninth Space, Ninth Voice, and Ninth Command, have the potential to revolutionize the way law enforcement agencies capture felons. Enough talking for now; please let me show you a short demonstration, Mr. Bender. My apologies to you, Mr. Corbbitt, I believe you've seen it already."

The picture changed and immediately the icy waters of the Antarctic Ocean appeared on the screen. Bender viewed the video showing the bogus Hammond's Hide-Away and chuckled when he saw Hammond's beard grow in just a few seconds.

"Very impressive, Mr. Hammond. How are computer generated graphics going to help us capture criminals?" Bender asked.

"Mr. Bender, what you've just seen is something produced a month ago, and we saved it on videodisc for demonstration purposes. What is unique about our software is that we can duplicate reality in cyberspace in three dimensions with perfect audio in real time."

"I guess I don't understand," Bender said. "How is this helpful?"

"It means we can make anyone look like and speak like anyone else, Mr. Bender. You may use it for creating illusions, false assumptions, and numerous other possibilities to present to the criminal mind."

Bender rubbed his chin as he considered the possibilities. "I'm not a computer wizard, Mr. Hammond. What do you mean by, real-time?"

The telephone rang, and Corbbitt answered it quickly.

"Mr. Bender, we've sent two representatives to explain further the attributes and capabilities of our software," Hammond said.

"Peyton, apparently Ninth Generation's employees are right outside," Corbbitt said.

"I don't get where this is going, but okay, send them in."

"Thank you, Mr. Bender, for indulging our methods. It will be clear to you in just a minute."

The conference room door opened and two men entered. Peyton Bender did a double take, as he saw Edward Hammond and Joshua Koweleski stand before him.

The image on the screen spoke. "Did our assistants arrive, Mr. Bender?"

"Yes, they're here. They look exactly like you."

"Don't be fooled, Mr. Bender, our assistants are really Ninth Generation cutting edge robots."

Mr. Hammond offered a handshake to Mr. Bender. Bender reluctantly accepted the handshake in full view of the local television camera.

"Isn't the warmth and suppleness of his skin life-like, Mr. Bender? We have the best polymers to duplicate human flesh."

NO SHORTAGE OF EVIL

"Ah, well yes. It really is amazing," Bender said, with a great deal of uncertainty.

"Please forgive the theatrics, Mr. Bender," the real President Hammond spoke. "May we sit down?"

"Sure," Bender, who was still a little uncertain, said.

"I'm sorry that we had a little fun at your expense," Hammond said. "This is the real Joshua Koweleski, and what our technicians in Braintree said about him is absolutely true."

"How did you do this, Mr. Hammond? It was most impressive."

"Since it's his innovation, I'll let Joshua tell you about it."

"Good morning, gentlemen," Joshua Koweleski said. "The best way to tell you how this is done is to give you a behind the scenes look at some of the equipment used to create this little bit of magic."

Joshua leaned over to talk into the microphone. "Deborah and Dale it's time to end our charade here."

"Pity," Deborah Clements, who was playing the role of Joshua Koweleski on the screen, said. "We were hoping you'd open your shirt and show Mr. Bender the hatch where your robot power supply is located, but okay." Everyone had a good laugh at her response.

A Ninth Generation technician turned the camera input selector switch from 'Computer' to 'Real' to show two figures in full body stockings. "Mr. Bender and Mr. Corbbitt, on the screen now are actually Deborah Clements and Dale Perkins, two valued members of our innovation team. Deborah, controlled Joshua's mannequin and Dale controlled President Hammond's mannequin for this demonstration."

"Amazing," Bender said.

Joshua smiled. "We think so too. The way this works is that sensors attached to their body stockings relate to body control points in the software. Basically, sensor movements are monitored, translated for the computer, and fed as variables into the software."

"So their movements control the respective mannequin's movements," President Hammond added.

"But the likeness is incredible," Bender said.

"No, the likeness is exact," Joshua said. "Zoom in on Hammond's face and do a close up."

The Ninth Generation computer technician adjusted a virtual camera to zoom in on the Hammond mannequin's face. The television technician switched the camera input selector switch from 'Real' to 'Computer'. The

HDTV monitor now showed a close-up of the face on President Hammond's mannequin.

"Incredible," Bender said. "You cannot tell the difference."

"Yes," Hammond said, "we both have business-related crow's feet at the corners of our eyes."

"What about the voice?" Corbbitt asked.

"A module within this software uses Ninth Generation Voice software to convert spoken words from one person's voice to another person. Essentially, we can duplicate anyone's voice in real time. The two software programs work together seamlessly."

"And you're able to do two at the same time?"

Joshua smiled. "Two, twelve, twenty-seven, it really doesn't matter. Of course, the more you try to emulate the more time it takes for accurate scripting and the more people involved to direct individual mannequins."

"Certainly, you must have some accurate input to construct the three dimensional mannequins and emulate the voice. It must take a lot of programming to do this."

Joshua shook his head. "Not really, our competitors might try to write code for every aspect of a mannequin's feature. We're not computer Neanderthals so we naturally prefer our own methods."

"And our methods are proprietary," Hammond added.

"Still you have to have some idea to educate the computer, no matter how it's done," Corbbitt said.

"Yes, actually we can get reconstructed three dimensional information from two-dimensional video images such as tapes or discs. The same applies to the audio emulation. Simply put, the more input we have the better results we have constructing the mannequin and the associated voice," Joshua said.

"What's all of this cost?" Peyton Bender asked.

About fifty-three million to develop, but for you to use on its maiden voyage into crime solving, absolutely nothing for the software and equipment. Just provide the staff as required to create cyberspace productions."

"If we like it, we can buy it later?" Bender asked.

"No, but close," Hammond said. "If you like it, you may lease it. We must maintain very tight controls on the use of this software. Otherwise, unscrupulous people will use it."

"Mr. Hammond is right of course," Joshua said. "Picture this software used by attorneys to get the worst criminals set free by constructing video presentations of bogus conditions or statements supposedly made by persons who are now dead."

"Or a politician, creating scandalous real time smear campaigns to gain advantage over an opponent just prior to an election," Hammond added.

Bender thought for a moment. "It's just like anything else connected with technology, there's always a minus sign for every plus sign."

"Unfortunately, I have to agree with you, Mr. Bender," Joshua said.

They looked at the HDTV again and the cameraman transmitted the picture of the Joshua and Edward mannequins doing a sensuous slow dance together.

"I see what you mean, Mr. Hammond, it doesn't take much imagination to cause real mischief with this equipment," Peyton Bender said.

Corbbitt and Bender spent the next two hours picking Joshua's brain on how to best use the software to investigate crime.

Later in the evening over drinks, Corbbitt and Bender mulled over ways the software might be used to break through the wall of secrecy surrounding the takeover of Common Cause.

"All right, Don, I've bought into the idea of pursuing the corruption angle and frankly I think we're trying to do the impossible here. Since we have no idea how far the corruption has spread and who is involved, if you were me, what would you do?"

Corbbitt thought for a moment before replying, "I'd work on the weakest element of those we suspect, Peyton, and perhaps run a sting operation similar to Abscam."

"All right—so who's the weakest link?" Bender asked. "We've got quite a crowd to choose from."

On the back of a napkin, Don listed eight senators, three corporate executives, one company president, and one thug. With the wide range of suspects, numerous schemes were possible and each required analysis.

"On the surface it seems that Gerald Pendergast is the strongest member on the list, because he controls the money and certainly knows all the players," Corbbitt said. "I doubt if any of the senators know that Pendergast had a hand in the murder of their former Chairman, Howard Champion.

"It would make them all co-conspirators to murder," Peyton replied. "Look, develop several different approaches and see what yields the best possible response. Then I'll present this to the Director."

"Why, Peyton? He might be part of this," Corbbitt said.

"I can't authorize something that might affect the administration or other branches of government. The Director would grind me up into Bender paté and serve me as an example to quell other overzealous special agents or assistant directors in charge."

"Get authorization from the President then, Peyton."

"The President isn't that easy to approach and trying to get to him might destroy the element of secrecy we need to catch those involved."

"Isaac Saltzman says he can talk to the President anytime he wants. If I explain the circumstances, I think he can set up a meeting for us in secrecy."

"That might work. Saltzman is out of the Washington fracas and the President certainly knows you," Peyton said.

"It's worth a try, Peyton. The worst that could happen here is the President could be too busy or simply refuse."

"Or question our sanity," Peyton observed. "All right, Don, go for it. With this we either have to go all the way or do nothing."

"Look at it this way, Peyton, we're two guys caught in the middle trying to do what we think is right. I'll get on this right away."

Peyton laughed. "One other thing, Don."

"What's that?"

"Find out how much unemployment we're going to get if this blows up in our face."

Thursday, March 3, 2005, 8:42 PM

The gala party to honor the memory of Senator Howard Champion and support the senator's favorite charity soon degraded to another event where the powerful and pretty congregated to gossip, manipulate, and advance power play intrigue. Here in a grand ballroom under crystalline chandeliers, brilliant jewelry flashed and long-stemmed glasses filled with sparkling wine were raised to everything and everyone but the senator. Here, knowing wives gave air kisses to other women to avoid smearing their makeup and the reputation of the man they both slept with. At two hundred and fifty dollars a plate for standard banquet food, the Washington elite, in true Darwinian fashion did what was necessary to maintain or advance social status and climb the power ladder.

Senator Adrian Horne tried desperately from a podium to project his voice through the cacophony of hundreds of simultaneous conversations and the bustling activity of dozens of waiters serving the four hundred homage paying attendees. Finally, after yelling to get their attention, he managed to quiet the room.

He pulled three file cards from his jacket pocket and began a short review of Senator Howard Champion's accomplishments as a New York State congressman and senator. He reminded an uncaring audience of the senator's efforts to 'Champion' bills supporting the nation's elderly such as long-term health care and prescription drug assistance. Then he discussed at length the senator's love and support of children. After a few perfunctory stories about the senator's leadership as Chairman of the Senate Judiciary Committee, Horne asked the entire group to stand in tribute to a fine man and an outstanding senator. Two seconds later the room cacophony resumed.

He returned to his table where three committee members, the Vice President of the United States, and their respective wives and girlfriends sat. Before he could sit down, someone tapped him on the shoulder. Horne turned and saw the Attorney General, Eric Ethelridge, who gave him the slightest movement of his head, a non-verbal signal that they needed to talk in private.

Horne accepted affected congratulatory handshakes from his colleagues and the Vice President for his well-delivered comments, and excused himself from the table. He followed the Attorney General out of the banquet hall to a receiving area where several other private discussions were already in progress.

"I'm sure this will get the tongues wagging," Horne said.

"No doubt, I just needed some reassurance from you that the powder keg we're sitting on is still far away from the flames."

"Well, the FBI got the killer of the Common Cause executives, so at least no one is currently trying to whack our friend from New York. There's another problem though."

"What kind of problem?"

"It turns out that FBI Agent Donald Corbbitt is investigating both the Common Cause murders and Howard Champion's assassination. Is there anyway to pull him off the case before he learns too much?"

"Not a prayer. If I interfere with the investigation in anyway, I'll draw attention to myself. Is there something going on that I should know about?"

Senator Horne looked around to make sure no one could overhear their discussion. "That's just it, things are too quiet. Corbbitt interviewed some of the Judiciary Committee members about Champion's death. The interesting thing is that his investigation doesn't include anyone who supported the Common Cause takeover."

"The odds of him only talking with the others are astronomic, Adrian."

"That's what I mean. I think we should assume that he knows or at least suspects our involvement."

"But how would he know?" Horne asked.

"I really don't know. Perhaps from digging around in Champion's office he found something," Ethelridge said. "It may be time to get creative, Adrian. I've got a lot riding on this and I can't afford a scandal if I'm going to make a serious run for the Presidency in three years."

"One thing at a time, Eric. We've got to bury the Common Cause issue and keep it from resurfacing."

"Let's think about the problem for a bit and talk later. There's got to be a way to discredit Corbbitt's investigation or get him off the case," Ethelridge said.

Horne nodded in agreement and returned with the Attorney General to the banquet hall. Their departure and return did not go unnoticed by the scheming and curious.

Chapter 23

Sunday, March 6, 2005, 10:45 AM

Donald Corbbitt and Peyton Bender arrived at Camp David, Maryland; the presidential retreat nestled in the Catoctin Mountain Park. They were surprised to find Isaac and Rose Saltzman with their dog in the President's study. Bubbe enjoyed the President's gentle stroking of her neck but growled as the two men entered the room.

"*Sha Bubbe*, it's not polite to growl when you're with the President," Rose said.

"It's all right, Rose," the President said. "Gentlemen, Isaac and Rose Saltzman and their dog, Bubbe. Mr. and Mrs. Saltzman, may I introduce Assistant Director, Peyton Bender and Special Agent Donald Corbbitt from the New York City, FBI Field Office."

The men exchanged greetings and Rose insisted on taking Bubbe for a walk so they could discuss business important to the United States.

Corbbitt and Bender sat in the comfortable chairs next to Isaac Saltzman's wheelchair and declined the President's offer of coffee or water. They waited patiently while the most powerful man in the world sat and looked at them for a few seconds.

"Gentlemen, when Mr. Saltzman told me last Thursday what your concerns were, my initial thoughts were that the two of you were candidates for early retirement. Alleging that Common Cause was systematically dismembered by foreign influences and that certain members of government were involved was hard to believe."

Donald Corbbitt grimaced at the President's opening remarks.

"Mr. President," Peyton Bender said. "If I may explain."

"This situation resulted in a few hours of late night meditation," the President said before Bender could continue. "I knew Mr. Saltzman wouldn't trouble me with an issue like this unless there were real concerns. We've talked already this morning and after reading the reports you sent me on Friday, Peyton, I have to admit there are valid issues here.

"Mr. Saltzman, it takes great courage for men like Mr. Bender and Mr. Corbbitt to go outside the normal administrative structure of the FBI to bring this issue to my attention."

"Yes, Mr. President, and history is filled with the examples of what happens when good people choose to do nothing in the face of evil," Saltzman said.

"Quite right, Isaac. The consequences of not taking action are seldom thought of, especially by my critics," the President said with a chuckle. "Isaac, if you don't mind, there are some issues that we must discuss that are sensitive to national security that go beyond what you and I have already discussed."

"Certainly, Mr. President. I understand."

"Isaac, you're a great friend and advisor. Thank you very much for all you've done to make my job easier."

Isaac Saltzman moved his wheelchair backwards. "It is my pleasure to help, Mr. President. I vowed long ago to do all in my power to prevent another evil such as Nazi Germany from ever happening again."

Corbbitt opened the study door so Saltzman could get the wheelchair into the adjoining room. "Don't worry, Agent Corbbitt, the President is as concerned about this as you are," Saltzman whispered.

"Thanks, Mr. Saltzman," Corbbitt said with a sigh of relief and closed the door behind Saltzman.

Before Corbbitt could return to his seat, the President began. "The truth is, gentlemen, I would have ignored this totally but since you have a plan to take care of this problem, I gave it some more thought. Most people just try to drop stuff in my lap and run like hell."

"It's just a preliminary plan, Mr. President," Peyton Bender said. "We would welcome any suggestions you might have."

"Very diplomatic, Peyton, but I wouldn't presume to get in the middle of your investigation. I'll tell you the business about the magic software that duplicates reality scared me as much as the pending scandal with Common Cause."

"Because it could fall into the wrong hands and wreak havoc?" Corbbitt asked.

"Exactly. That's why I sent one of my staff up to that company in Massachusetts on Friday morning," the President said with a scowl. "They set up a video-conference and demonstrated the software for me later in the evening. It was beyond incredible."

"That was fast," Corbbitt said.

"With the possible danger here, Agent Corbbitt, I couldn't take the chance that someone else would latch on to their product. Even if you bomb out on the investigation, I'm very grateful to you for bringing this to our attention."

"Technology advances seem to come with hidden costs," Peyton Bender said. "The Internet, as useful as it is, has also opened the door to many flavors of computer-based crime such as fraud, identity theft, and child pornography."

"What these folks did at—what's the company name?"

"Ninth Generation," Corbbitt offered

"Yes, Ninth Generation. This software in the wrong hands could start wars, institute revolutions, or manipulate elections. Just so you know, the government is soon going to be Ninth Generation's biggest customer and probably the only customer for this fancy software."

"What happens if someone else develops a similar product, Mr. President?" Peyton asked.

"We might have to get the Congress to institute regulations similar to the one's governing the production and handling of special nuclear materials that might be used for nuclear weapons. It simply will become illegal to develop or own software that can precisely duplicate reality in real time."

"What about our proposal to use the software to corral those associated with the Common Cause fiasco?" Corbbitt asked.

"Timely question, Agent Corbbitt," the President said. "Peyton, this will be a great test of the software's capability. For this trial I'm placing you in charge of this operation and you're directly responsible for how this software gets used."

"I understand, Mr. President."

"It's very important that in the process of using this software you don't violate existing law or trample on the rights of suspects charged with a crime. Everything you do must be documented. I don't want any abuse of the power that I'm giving you today," the President said in a tone that defied anyone to contradict him. "Is that understood?"

"Yes, Mr. President," Bender and Corbbitt said simultaneously.

"Bender, when your team starts this portion of the investigation, I want detailed daily reports from you."

"Yes, Mr. President," Bender said. "Sir, may I ask something of you?"

"What more could you want other than the full support of this office that I'm giving to you?"

"Only one thing," Bender said nervously. "When the time comes, will you square this with the Director?"

"Here's what I think. If the Director is part of this, it won't matter. If he's not and you're successful, the Director will understand. If you're not successful and this blows up in our face, the Director will be the least of your concerns," the President warned. "If there's nothing else, gentlemen, I think lunch is ready. Because of the Saltzman's we're eating kosher food today."

"No pork then," Corbbitt offered.

"No, and they don't mix meat and milk in the same meal or eat shell-fish either," the President added. "They even brought a bowl for Bubbe. I guess the dog keeps kosher too."

Sunday, March 6, 2005, 3:45 PM

When Jocelyn Hafner opened her door to greet her friend Donald Corbbitt, she saw a totally different man than the last time he visited. "What's got into you, Don? You sounded so excited on the telephone."

"I just came from a meeting with the President at Camp David," Corbbitt said, and then tried to look past her to see if anyone else was in the apartment. "Are your girlfriends still here?"

"No, I shooed them out the door about twenty minutes ago. Candice wanted to stay and meet you, but she's definitely the vixen among us and there's no way I was going to let her near you," Jocelyn said with a smile. "Come in and tell me what this is all about."

Jocelyn took Don's topcoat and suggested that they talk in the living room. "Something to drink—coffee, juice? What can I get for you, Don?"

"Nothing, Jocelyn, I just want to tell you about this meeting and how it might affect you."

"Me!"

"Don't worry, I've not said anything to anyone yet—so you're not obligated."

"Fair enough, what's this all about?"

"We're forming a special team that will use incredible software to fool criminals and perhaps get them to incriminate others. The President was very concerned about the possibility of widespread corruption of corporate executives and government personnel in the Common Cause bankruptcy. With some restrictions, we're going to use technology to break up their organization."

"Where do I fit in?"

"Jocelyn, with your communications skills and knowledge of how we perform investigations you're perfect for the team."

"So, I would be working with you?"

"I would be on the team," Don said. "Look, I admit I have another motive."

"I'm listening."

"Jocelyn, I told you before that I believe in us as a couple. I meant what I said then, and if it's possible, I mean it even more today."

"A couple? We're hardly a couple, Don. You zoom in and out of Washington as your case investigations require," Jocelyn countered, but then decided to give Don the break he deserved. "I do give you credit for doing the best you can and you do call me."

"Jocelyn, that's because I like to be with you and feel empty when I am not with you," Don admitted. "Jocelyn, I love you. I'm not going to let my job or circumstances within my control get in the way of being the man in your life."

"Is the team going to be in New York City?"

"Yes, but it's only for the duration of the investigation," Don said.

"How long do you expect this to be, Don?"

"My boss, Peyton Bender, is all ready contacting the Software Company. We're going to begin immediately. I expect that this will only take one month."

"Don, are you asking me to move in with you during that time?"

Don paused for a moment somewhat confused by her direct question. "Jocelyn, as much as I would love that to happen, I'm not asking for that. You would have temporary living quarters, and of course decide how we might spend some time together."

A thousand thoughts swirled through her head. Don was certainly speaking from his heart and he deserved an answer.

"Jocelyn, there have been other women in my life, but until I met you, I never knew how it felt to be in love. I'm asking you to take one step in my direction. Believe me if it were possible I would walk miles in yours."

"I believe you would, Don. I know you've already tried to get transferred."

"Are you at least considering it, Jocelyn?"

"Yes, of course, Don, but you've thrown a lot at me in a few minutes. I need some time to think about this."

"That's just it, Jocelyn, there isn't time. The team will begin work as soon as possible. If I push Peyton Bender, he'll pull the strings necessary to get you from Washington to New York, but it will have to happen soon."

"What happens to us if I decide not to come to New York to be on this team?"

"Jocelyn, I know this is asking a lot, but if you decide not to participate, that won't change my love for you."

"Don, I want so much more than the temporary relationships that have crowded my life to this point. I'm so tired of the deceit and trickery—the love 'em and leave 'em routine."

"And I'm tired of the emptiness in my life, Jocelyn. That's why, I've talked plainly and honestly with you about this. I've put my heart in my hand and offered it to you."

Jocelyn knew the decision she was about to make might alter the rest of her life. She weighed the risk of giving her love to another man against the loneliness she felt each night in her apartment. Truly it was a defining moment for her and Don, filled with uncertainty and only a hint of love that he talked about but she desperately sought.

She stood and looked at her watch and reached for his hand. With a small grunt, Don got up from the couch and immediately accepted Jocelyn's warm embrace.

"Don, it's two minutes past four. I want you to remember this time."

"Sure, Jocelyn. Why?"

"Because it's the precise moment, I fell in love with you."

Chapter 24

Wednesday, March 9, 2005, 8:45 AM

"Please take your seats, so we can begin the meeting," Peyton Bender said, urging them toward the conference room table. "You've all had a chance to introduce yourselves, so we can skip the individual introductions. I'm Peyton Bender, FBI assistant director here in the New York Field Office. The President of the United States requires daily reports and strict controls over our activities. So let's understand from the beginning. All interactions this group has with investigation suspects must be approved. On this subject, I need your full cooperation. Is that clear?"

Bender looked at the team members individually to make sure everyone understood. "Here are your respective roles as I see them.

"Special Agent Donald Corbbitt is in charge of the investigation and will implement what this team develops to identify and capture those responsible in his assigned cases. You've read the team's mission statement so I won't elaborate on the scope of his investigations any further.

"Joshua Koweleski, will directly supervise Deborah Clements and Dale Perkins from Ninth Generation. Your task is to setup and operate your computers, equipment, and software, to develop audio and video materials in support of Special Agent Corbbitt's investigations.

"Jocelyn Hafner is here from our Washington Field Office. Ms. Hafner, since you have extensive communications skills, I'm relying on you to support and learn from Mr. Koweleski's team and assist in the development of his materials where possible. There is a great deal of interest in the use of this new method; therefore, I'd like you to keep a running journal of the activities. This will also help me monitor the team's progress and prepare reports for the President.

"Does everyone understand their primary assignments?" Bender said, and looked at each one of them again to see if there were any problems. "Within limitations, you may choose later to expand or share responsibilities as necessary. I am not into micro-managing every activity."

Joshua Koweleski sighed loud enough for everyone to hear.

"Is there a problem, Mr. Koweleski?"

"No, not really. I'm just used to a free hand in the development process."

"I understand, Joshua," Peyton said. "This is a little different than software development. Frankly, our necks are on the line here, but even if that wasn't the case, our investigation must follow well-established rules to keep us from breaking the law ourselves or violating a suspect's rights. In addition, there are time and budget considerations.

"I'm passing around a non-disclosure statement. Signing this document requires you to maintain all activities associated with this project secret. Inadvertent or purposeful disclosure of methods and techniques used by this team, or unauthorized use of Ninth Generation's software may subject you to criminal prosecution.

"Those are the rules for this project. I'm going to back away and let you start. Let me know if there is anything I can do to support the project and above all cooperate with one another. Any comments or suggestions at this time?"

Koweleski raised a finger to be recognized. "I'd just like to say thanks for the opportunity to work with you and Mr. Corbbitt on this. Right now there is a small constraint on progress, we brought several computers and most of our equipment with us, but the communications link back to our Braintree office won't be installed and functional until Friday. With the communications link I can direct additional Ninth Generation staff to perform elements of our task.

"I think we can use the available time to show Ms. Hafner and Mr. Corbbitt how we prepare our 'material' as you put it. Also, if I am not stating the obvious, we would do well to identify the end results and work backward in our development process. By this I mean we need to know who the targeted suspect is and what is necessary to get the desired information from the suspect."

"You're right on target with that suggestion," Donald Corbbitt said. "Given that there are several interlaced cases here, and multiple suspects, I've prepared several scenarios that might be useful," Corbbitt said, and passed copies around to the team members. "There's nothing set in stone here, just use this as a starting point. Your comments and suggestions are certainly welcomed."

Jocelyn, who thought at first that her duties as glorified note-taker somewhat demeaning, soon marveled at Ninth Generation's technical capabilities and the brilliance of Joshua Koweleski.

Wednesday, March 9, 2005, 2:15 PM

Corbbitt placed a call to Senator Champion's housekeeper and friend in Bolton's Landing, New York, from the back of a taxi en route to the Common Cause office building in Manhattan.

Corbbitt identified himself, and told Mr. Rayburn that the FBI was still actively pursuing Senator Champion's assassin. "Mr. Rayburn, you said before that you would do anything to help our investigation. If that's still true, we need some assistance now."

"Sure, I'm glad to help. What can I do?"

"I need to know if there is any videotape of the senator available."

"He wasn't much for home movies, if that's what you're looking for."

"No, I was thinking more of speeches he made, something more professional than home movies, especially footage that includes his voice."

"Wait, that's going to be very easy," Charlie said. "The senator was always making speeches at fundraising functions and the Senate floor."

"Wonderful, do you have the tapes there?"

"There are a few, but I think you can get more from that TV network that covers the Senate's activities every day."

"Great idea, Charlie. Why didn't I think of that?"

"Thanks, do you want me to rummage around and see what I can find and then send them to you?"

"If you can find them that would be great, but I am sending several people to get some video of the senator's home. We'll probably concentrate on his study. They can bring the tapes back with them."

"Sure, when are they coming?"

"Immediately. Charlie, you should know, that we're getting close to solving this crime."

"That's great. Anything else I can do?"

"Possibly, but it might be risky to get you involved," Corbbitt said.

"Within reason, I'll do anything to help you, Agent Corbbitt. They've killed a very dear friend of mine and made him suffer terribly in the process."

"I'll think about your offer. There may be a way you can help us."

He placed another call to Senator Howard Champion's office and talked with Pauline Dryfus, the senator's office manager. "Ms. Dryfus, this is FBI Special Agent Donald Corbbitt."

"I remember. What's happening with the investigation?"

"That's what I want to talk to you about. We're getting very close to solving the case and we should have someone in custody very soon and I'm sorry that I cannot tell you the specifics."

"I understand, Mr. Corbbitt. What can I do?"

"I wondered if you're friendly with the other Senate Judiciary Committee staff members, either during the course of daily business or informal communications."

"Sometimes I talk to them on the telephone to align meeting schedules between the senators. Occasionally, we get together for a gab session at lunch. Why?"

"I'd like to know if you overhear anything unusual among the staff members or you see any strange behavior from any of the Committee members."

"You don't suspect a United States senator in Howard's, er Senator Champion's death, I hope."

"There are several issues associated with Senator Champion's death, Ms. Dryfus. I cannot tell you more."

"Do you want me to probe around to see what I can dig up?" Pauline Dryfus asked cautiously.

"Just listen and observe, I don't want anyone to know what you're doing."

"Okay, I just wanted to know how you wanted me to go about this. I'll call you if I catch on to anything. I really miss the senator."

"I'm sure you do, Ms. Dryfus," Corbbitt said. "He was a good man. Thank you for your help."

Corbbitt paid the taxi driver and walked toward the building containing the remnants of the Common Cause Communications Company. He noticed someone spray painted the word 'BASTARDS' over the company plaque.

After checking through security, Corbbitt took the elevator to the eleventh floor to the Common Cause executive offices. Heather Pollack, Gerald Pendergast's secretary smiled at him as he approached.

"Mr. Pendergast is in the conference room meeting with the replacements for those who were murdered. Is there something I can do for you," she said and winked.

"Yes, there is something. I need videotapes of Gerald Pendergast. I'm really interested in something where he's talking for a long time."

Heather thought for a moment. "There's the tape of the company's last stockholder meeting and another one for welcoming new employees. The subject is kinda the same, corporate mission, vision for the future, that sorta stuff. Doesn't make much sense anymore now that we've been in bankruptcy. Say, what do you need them for anyway?"

"Believe me, you're better off not knowing, Heather. Can you get the tapes without him knowing that I've got them?"

"Sure, I'm sure he doesn't even know where they are. How long will you need them?"

"I'll get copies made and get them right back, so they won't be missed."

"No problem, I don't mind helping."

"That's great, Heather. This will all be over soon."

Heather looked over his shoulder and put her finger to her lips. "He's coming now, they're all bailing out of the conference room."

"Well, Corebutt. I see you're back. What are you doing lurking around here?"

"Mr. Pendergast, my name is Corbbitt and FBI special agents don't lurk, we investigate, and that's what I'm doing here."

Pendergast frowned at the rebuke given in front of his secretary. "So, why are you here? The person who killed my senior staff members has been found. What's left to investigate?"

"When I was here last, I gave you a list of times and dates so I could verify your location. Since you're an executive, I gave you a little leeway to get back to me with the answers and didn't press the point."

"What's the difference now? You've got the killer."

"The difference is that I don't like to be ignored. Your failure to provide the information makes me think that you've got something to hide."

Pendergast reeled at the accusation. "I've got nothing to hide. Heather, get my schedules for the last few months."

"Certainly, Mr. Pendergast."

"Let's not do battle anymore, Mr. Corbbitt," Pendergast said, more for the benefit of his secretary than anything else.

"I just ask the questions. You fail to realize that I'm not your employee. You've made this into a battle that you can't win because I have the full force of the government empowering me to do the investigation. So fight if you wish, just expect to lose."

"Here they are, Mr. Pendergast," Heather said, breaking the tension between the two men.

"What dates were you interested in now, Agent Corbbitt? I'm really very busy."

Corbbitt fought the urge not to ask Pendergast about where he was on the third weekend in November, the same weekend when the senators gathered at Champion's home, but he realized it was far better to trap Pendergast later. "Right now, there's just one date that I'm curious about Mr. Pendergast, then I'll leave you alone. Where were you, on February fifteenth, between the hours of ten AM to three PM?"

"What's so important about that date?"

"I'm asking the questions here. Just answer."

Pendergast fumbled with the schedule while he desperately tried to figure out why this date and time was so important to the FBI agent. While his corporate activities were on the schedule, he was worried about his involvement with the senators, executives, and Rudy Gambrelli. "Here, Agent Corbbitt, it says I was right here in the office the entire day, doing what I do every day. That particular week I was in the office every single day from sunrise to sunset."

Corbbitt took the relevant page that listed a week's worth of Pendergast's scheduled activities. There was nothing on the schedule that looked inappropriate or referred back to Margarita Rosario's death in Tampa, Florida. Corbbitt realized that Pendergast probably had no idea that anyone else but Senator Champion died at Rudy Gambrelli's hand.

"What about the schedule, would you say that the schedule represents the precise location of Mr. Pendergast on the fifteenth of February, Heather?"

Pendergast glared at his secretary, warning her not to contradict his statement to the FBI agent.

"Yes, sir. I remember, he was here the entire time."

"Thank you, Ms. Pollack," Corbbitt said.

"Is that all, Corbbitt? We do have other things to do around here," Pendergast said impatiently.

"Actually, my reason for visiting here this morning is to talk with the senior executives who were travelling the last time I was here."

"Edgar Pfost and Sidney Pelton are still on the road. Diane McKeevar just came back Monday. I thought you completed your investigation, Corbbitt. What do you want with these folks?"

"I'm just wondering what the motivation was for Ms. Margaret Jenkins to single handedly wipe out half of your executive staff, Mr. Pendergast."

"Isn't it simple, Corbbitt? She had an axe to grind because of losing her job. She was only one of many disgruntled people around here, only she decided to get revenge. It's nothing more than that."

"Right. I'd like to hear what Ms. McKeevar has to say about this. Perhaps then, I'll be able to conclude this portion of the investigation."

"All right, have it your way. She's down the hall and around the corner," Pendergast said as he threw up his hands in disgust. "Heather, tell Vice President McKeevar that FBI Agent Corebutt wants to talk with her."

Corbbitt ignored the slur on his name again and marched toward the executive's office.

He reached McKeevar's office just as she hung up the phone and noticed her deep frown magically convert to a beaming smile as if she had a separate face to hide and another to present to him. Corbbitt knew from experience that such people often had reasons for concealing what was really running through their mind. She looked up and waved him into her office.

"Agent Corbbitt," she said with her newly acquired smile. "I'm Diane McKeevar, vice president here in charge of human resources and labor relations."

Corbbitt entered and closed her office door and gently returned her handshake. Diane McKeevar, a highly polished woman in her mid-fifties, returned to the safety of her seat behind a large mahogany desk. She unbuttoned the jacket on her maroon colored business suit to reveal a cream colored silk blouse and ample bosom. "All right, Agent Corbbitt, what can I do for you?" she asked in a highly affected manner.

"We may be in a position to help one another out, Ms. McKeevar," Corbbitt responded. "But I'll get to that in a minute."

She tilted her head to one side and played with a single-stranded pearl necklace. Corbbitt noted the absence of a wedding ring on her hand. "All right, Mr. Corbbitt," she said in a soft and breathy voice designed to disarm and distract him.

"Ms. McKeevar, I'm interested in what might motivate someone like Margaret Jensen to commit multiple murders."

"Isn't it obvious, Agent Corbbitt, that she was a disgruntled employee?"

"Yes, and that is what I'd like to know about. What was the source of her anger here in the company?" Corbbitt asked, fishing for information.

"Look, she was just sore over losing her job. In that regard, she's not alone. Many others lost their jobs here, Agent Corbbitt."

"Do you think the relationship between Walter Mortensen and Yvonne Taylor had much to do with it?"

"Oh you know about that, do you?" she said as the smile suddenly thinned on her face.

"Yes, and it's a pity. Even under the influence of drugs and morphine, she seemed like an intelligent woman—too intelligent to be involved with murders. I'm wondering why she was so driven to murder these people."

"Look, Agent Corbbitt, regardless of what happened here concerning promotions and the bankruptcy, there was no justification for doing what she did."

"I learned a lot from Ms. Jensen before she took her life, Ms. McKeevar," Corbbitt said. "All right, Ms. McKeevar, just consider yourself lucky that you are the one I'm talking with today."

"Lucky! Why is that, Agent Corbbitt?"

"Because I know about the corruption within this organization. I know who's responsible for the bankruptcy and the money that's associated with it. Eventually I'll talk to Mr. Pfost and Mr. Pelton and make them the same offer. You're just the first one with the opportunity to make a statement concerning the vast payoff that affected the decision-making process of members of the board of directors and the senior executive staff."

Deep frown lines appeared on her face. "Are you threatening me, Mr. Corbbitt? I don't take this line of harassment from you or anyone else. If you're serious, my lawyer will have a lot to say to you."

"Ms. McKeevar, I'm not afraid of you or your lawyer. Here's my business card. If you change your mind, and decide you'd like to serve less time in jail for the crimes committed here, please give me a call."

"Agent Corbbitt, I have nothing to tell you. What happened here, happened. That's all."

"Ms. McKeevar, no doubt you'll report back to Gerald Pendergast with my offer and that's fine. You'll simply suffer the same fate," Corbbitt said as he stood and leaned across McKeevar's desk. "Right now, I'm offering you a helping hand. Be smart enough to take it before Pfost or Pelton decide they'd rather not spend the rest of their life behind prison walls."

"Are you through trying to intimidate me, Agent Corbbitt?"

"I guess right now you may look at this as intimidation, Ms. McKeevar," Corbbitt said. "I wonder what you'll think in your prison cell after the trial. Maybe you'll look back at this and see it was really an opportunity that you simply missed."

Corbbitt left her office without waiting for her response. He knew McKeevar would probably not accept his offer. The remaining executives were only a small part of Pendergast's scheme of corruption. The direct offer to McKeevar was a small shot across Pendergast's bow. Larger artillery would soon follow from another direction.

Corbbitt looked at Heather before he left the executive floor. She winked again and motioned with her thumb. Corbbitt understood that Pendergast was nearby that it was dangerous for them to talk.

He took the elevator back to the building lobby. The same security officer that helped him last week stopped him before he reached the lobby revolving door.

"Sir, there's a package for you," the officer said, giving him a familiar box.

"Thanks, Officer," Corbbitt said. "Keep this exchange a secret would you please."

"Certainly, sir."

Corbbitt opened the box and found two videotapes inside and a note that said, "Thank you for the chocolates, Agent Corbbitt. You've got good taste."

Chapter 25

Saturday, March 12, 2005, 5:45 PM

Jocelyn raised her arms over her head and stretched to relieve aching muscles. She was tired from endless hours of scriptwriting for their first production and monitoring the project for journal entries. Working with Joshua Koweleski was interesting and demanding. No one that she met in the Bureau was as task-driven as Koweleski. After three days of watching, learning, and writing, genuine fatigue and the spinal stress monkey were getting the best of her.

She waited for Don to get dressed after Koweleski's equipment performed a total body scan for assembling Don's virtual mannequin for possible use with case subjects. She looked at the computer screen and though his mannequin was only a wire-frame representation and lacked the skin texture. Don's trim and muscular physique was apparent. Ninth Generation's software did an amazing job and she studied his attributes and wondered how he found the time to keep himself physically fit.

Strong hands on her shoulders startled her and she flushed at being caught studying his computerized representation.

"Do you think I should get a calendar made?" Don asked, adding to her embarrassment.

"I'd like that," she replied, "but put your skin suit on if you want to drive sales up. And, yes, you can rub my neck and shoulders."

"I see," he said as he began slowly massaging her shoulders. "You're tight as a snare drum from too many hours at the computer."

His strong hands kneaded her shoulders, neck, and upper back with steely fingers that applied enough pressure to be therapeutic without causing pain.

"Aside from seeing you in the scanner in your underwear, Don, this has been the best part of my day."

"Yeah, I know. After I'm through here with these cases, 'Boxer Shorts 'R'

Us', wants to do a complete fashion line with me as the model," Don said, laughing as his fingertips caressed the gentle curve of her neck.

Jocelyn instantly noticed the change in pressure and the fire that he kindled within her. "I'm starving. How about some dinner and a dose of that quality time you promised? So far all we've done is work our butts off."

"I'd invite you to enjoy the cuisine at Chez Corbbitt Brasserie and Hash House, but if you're not in the mood for lumpy mushroom soup, me thinks m'lady would fare better elsewhere."

She smiled at his self-effacing humor. "Perhaps a reservation at the Elsewhere Bistro and Haute Beanery would be perfect," she suggested.

Don's brow wrinkled and then he smiled realizing that her quick wit continued his line of humor. "We'd better go now, Manhattan restaurants fill up quickly on Saturday night and we'll be lucky to get a seat in a decent place."

"Okay, but this girl needs a minute to freshen up a little."

A few minutes later they emerged from the Jacob Javitts building in Federal Plaza. The March wind whipping between the buildings sent street debris flying and Donald instinctively positioned himself upwind to protect Jocelyn while he tried to hail a taxi.

"So much for my hair," Jocelyn said.

"Welcome to the New York wind tunnel," Don said as he stepped off the curb toward an approaching taxi. "You just have to get their attention."

Jocelyn smiled as the taxi-driver passed by without stopping. "Yes, I guess, Don, maybe that one was blind."

Don came to the sidewalk and returned to her side. "The restaurant is only five or six blocks away, if you don't mind walking."

"No, actually the walking is perfect. Which way?"

"We're going over to Little Italy, there's a wonderful place I think you'll enjoy."

"Based on my last dining experience with you, I feel I'm in good hands," Jocelyn said, remembering the glorious restaurant Don took her to in Washington.

Don offered his arm as they headed north on Lafayette Street. "Did Joshua say when he'd have our bogus tape ready?"

"I talked with him earlier in the afternoon, Don. He thought all elements of the tape would be ready for your review Monday morning."

"Amazing, I thought this first product might take weeks to develop."

"He's had one of the computers he brought scanning Senator Champion's videotapes constantly since they arrived from Bolton's Landing on Thursday," Jocelyn said. "I guess we didn't factor in all the help we were going to get from the rest of his staff in Braintree. They're busy feeding the portion of the software that will duplicate Senator Champion's voice."

"Peyton Bender is really nervous about this project and frankly I can't blame him."

"Have you decided whether you're going to target one or all the affected senators?"

"We're still discussing it, but either way it's going to be traumatic," Don said with a frown. "If I've misinterpreted what's really going on here this is going to explode in my face."

"Don, what about trying to sequence the deliveries, so each revelation causes more and more angst in their group? Like an earthquake with a series of severe aftershocks."

"Delivering them in sequence would be reasonably easy, but getting them to actually watch them might be the most difficult problem."

"Perhaps you're right. There might be a tendency to push them aside as inconsequential."

"We have a plan in case they all decide not to watch the tapes we've sent them. So that shouldn't be a problem," Don said.

They turned the corner on Mulberry Street in the heart of Little Italy where the aroma from dozens of restaurants contributed to the atmosphere of the neighborhood.

"Unless Peyton Bender stops us cold, sometime next week we're going to raise hell with all those involved with Common Cause. Hey, enough of shop talk, here's our restaurant," Don said, pointing to Pasquale's Trattorria.

Inside the ancient wooden door, a small queue of people waited anxiously for admittance to the dining room. After ten minutes, the line diminished and Don whispered privately with the headwaiter. Jocelyn thought she saw him slip the headwaiter some money and wondered why that was necessary.

"We'll be seated in a few minutes, Jocelyn," Don said confidently.

Jocelyn looked into the dining room and saw the typical red and white checkerboard table clothes complete with demijohn candleholders for each table. The restaurant bustled with activities as tray-ladened waiters dodged patrons at breakneck speed in narrow aisles, while busboys hustled to clear tables for the anticipated throng of customers that would visit before the restaurant's midnight closing hour.

The headwaiter returned a minute later and seated them near a small stage and baby grand piano. The headwaiter presented the menus and wine list.

"Bon appetito," he said while pointing to the waiter assigned to the table. Seconds later, the waiter poured ice water in their glasses and placed a basket of fresh Italian bread and butter on their table.

Jocelyn looked at the wall tapestries that portrayed the Grand Canal in Venice, the Leaning Tower of Pisa, the Coliseum in Rome, and a view of Mt. Vesuvius from the ruins of Pompeii.

"This is a terrific place, Don. I wonder if Italy itself feels as Italian."

Don looked up from the wine list and laughed. "I think the owner would be pleased with that comment."

"It looks like a terrific menu."

"No one enjoys food more than the Italians. Have you made a selection?"

"No, I was just looking at the flyer inside the menu. It says there's going to be live entertainment by Annette Zampetti, soprano, and her brother, Marco, a tenor. Oh Don, they're featuring arias from Puccini operas."

Don smiled. "I know, Jocelyn. They're music students who earn their way through college by singing here."

"What a surprise, Don."

The waiter presented himself at their tableside and asked if they had any questions about the specials for the evening. After some interrogation on their part and a suggestion on his part, Jocelyn decided to have the fettuccine Alfredo and seafood combination while Don decided on veal saltimbocca with asparagus tips. Don chose a white wine to go with their dinners.

Just after the waiter poured the wine, the musical entertainment began. Tenor, Marco Zampetti, played the piano while his sister sang the first aria, "O Mio Babbino Caro" from Puccini's opera, *Gianni Schicchi*. Then she sang "Quando M'en Vo' Soletta", from *La Boheme*, and followed by singing the hauntingly poignant "Un Bel Di Verdremo", from *Madama Butterfly*. The room vibrated from the young soprano's strong and beautiful voice. Don noticed Jocelyn was so engrossed in the music, she hardly touched the crisp salad placed before her.

During the brief intermission waiters dashed between tables to refill water glasses, deliver entrées, and remove empty plates. When the majority of the dining activity quieted down, Soprano, Annette Zampetti took a seat at the piano to accompany her brother.

Marco Zampetti, a tall man with a barrel chest, took his place beside the piano and sang, "Che Gelida Manina" from *La Boheme*. Then he sang "Recondita Armonia" and "E Lucevan Le Stelle" both from Puccini's opera *Tosca*. Jocelyn's eyes watered as the tenor sang the last aria's soulful lament.

The entire room erupted with applause at the conclusion of the twenty-minute performance. Jocelyn turned back to face Don. "Wasn't that spectacular, Don?"

"By the look on your face, I'd say it was. Although I have to admit, I've got a lot to learn about opera before I can appreciate it as much as you do."

"Well, sir, I volunteer to assist your efforts to learn more," she said with a smile.

The waiter brought a cart next to their table and deftly prepared her fettuccini by blending and melting several cheeses over a low flame. Don's veal saltimbocca arrived just as the waiter completed making Jocelyn's dinner. Again Don saw the dreamy glow on Jocelyn's face and he knew his efforts to show her a good evening were successful.

Jocelyn wiped the corners of her mouth with the linen napkin and leaned back in her chair. "Don, you've treated this little girl to a wonderful evening. Thank you very much."

"Jocelyn, I could tell you were having a good time. Watching your face light up is a beautiful thing to see."

"I guess I'm not good at hiding my feelings," Jocelyn said.

"Nor should you be. It's very important that I know how you're feeling."

"Why is that, Don?"

"It goes back to the Happiness Soup you taught me about. How else will I know if my recipe is correct?"

Jocelyn could not express the joy she felt at hearing Don's simple explanation. "Don, if it's all right with you, I'd like to skip dessert. I'm really quite full from dinner."

"Are you sure? Their desserts here are as good as the main courses."

"Perhaps later, Don. I know a great place that specializes in such treats," she said in a way to make him anticipate what treats she might have in mind.

In typical Manhattan style, the waiter sensed that they were ready to leave and understood when Don waved off coffee and dessert. After paying the bill and leaving a generous tip for the service and the young singers they left the restaurant.

Jocelyn grabbed his hand and looked in his eyes. "Terrific selection, Mr. Corbbitt. Just for the record, I wouldn't mind going out with you again."

Don beamed at the compliment. "I'm really glad you enjoyed it, Jocelyn," Don said as they reached the sidewalk. "I'll try again for a taxi."

"Wait a second. You've taken care of the first part of the evening, now it's my turn," Jocelyn said as she stood next to him and waved at the next taxicab.

Immediately, the driver pulled over to the curb to accept their fare. Jocelyn looked at Don, "You're right. All you have to do is get their attention."

Don chuckled. "That's not fair, you've enchanted that poor driver. Where are we going?"

Jocelyn gave the driver instructions to take them back to her hotel near Madison Square Garden.

"I think our quality time is far from over," Jocelyn said before Don could ask any questions.

Don said nothing but reached for her hand as the taxi pulled away from the curb.

Jocelyn gave Don her electronic room key as the elevator rose to the eighth floor. Since she was going to be on the task force for a month, the FBI sprang for a larger suite with a sitting room and separate bedroom. Jocelyn turned on the light and was glad to see that the maid had been there and the room was clean and orderly.

"I've been in these clothes all day, Don. If you'll give me a minute in the bathroom and then a little time to change," she smiled, as Don's hand was a little slow in letting go of hers. "Meanwhile you might want to shed that sport coat and silly tie. I'll be right back."

After a quick stop in the bathroom, she pondered over the limited choice of clothing to change into. There were other factors affecting this simple choice of clothing. Was it too soon for something sensuous and provocative or should she wait? She searched her soul for a moment but her brain was already preparing her body for what she hoped would expand their relationship and enhance the new-found love in her life.

She heard the running water in the bathroom indicating that Don was tending to his personal needs and perhaps freshening up a bit himself. She hoped with all her heart that she was doing the right thing by peeling off her underwear and slipping into the lavender nightgown and robe. She looked in the mirror to apply lipstick and ran a comb through her hair. She slid into her matching slippers and looked at the door that separated her from her lover.

Sunday, March 13, 2005, 5:12 AM

The bed-stand clock radio read twelve minutes past five and Jocelyn turned slowly away from Don. She reflected on the past twelve hours with this incredible man who now shared her bed. If lovemaking was an art form, Don, certainly was a masterful combination of painter, sculpture, composer, and virtuoso violinist whose only concern throughout their experience was the beauty they shared together. She basked now in the exquisite afterglow this unselfish man provided. Clearly, his orchestrated and tender approach to touching, holding, and loving her left her with the feeling that he would sacrifice his own pleasure just for the sake of hers. She doubted if intimacy could ever be any better for a woman.

She moved again and immediately felt Don kissing the back of her neck.

"Jocelyn, if you don't mind, I'd like to have this square inch as well," he whispered.

"All this claiming of me one square inch at a time is wonderful. It certainly enhanced the delicious way you touched and made love to me," she said while trying to suppress a yawn. "Just so you know, I'd really prefer not to be carved up into little pieces and give myself to you one square inch at a time."

"I never looked at it that way, Jocelyn, but I do understand. Would you please turn toward me so I can see your face?"

She turned and lay on her back as he propped himself on one elbow. His eyes were moist and his lips formed a little smile. "Jocelyn, I respect what you just said, and I'd like to trade in all those square inches you gave me last night for just one square inch."

She frowned. "Is it really that important to you, Don?"

"Yes, it is. If I can have the one I want, I promise to never ask for another one."

She wondered what this was all about, but reluctantly agreed. "Okay mister, I'll humor you. Where are you staking your claim?"

"Close your eyes, Jocelyn. Where my lips touch your body, will mark my claim," he said as he yanked the sheet and blanket away exposing her body to the chill of the room.

She looked at him warily knowing this was a dangerous yet exciting situation. Then she closed her eyes as he requested. "I'm very nervous about this, Don."

She felt his breath on her legs moving higher from her knees to her hips. He was teasing her again by touching her mind and not her body. The sensation moved up along her belly to her breasts and she began to feel like a slab of meat inspected by a careful shopper. His breath now touched her neck and shoulders. His lips still failed to find their place on her body.

"Don, you're driving me crazy."

"Shhhh," he whispered. "You don't want me to lose my place or I'll have to start over again."

She was about ready to sit up and forget this little game, when she felt him move again. This time his breath slid along her left shoulder and down her arm, gently touching and tickling her along its path. He raised her left hand from the bed and gently kissed her ring finger.

"Jocelyn, I want you to know how much I love you. If it turns out that I'm not the man for you, I'll give this square inch back. Let's spend some more time together. Give me a chance to get an engagement ring, and sometime when we're both dressed and can talk and think rationally, I'll ask you a very important question. For now, allow me this one square inch as a pledge against that time."

She trembled, and tears streamed down her face from the corner of her eyes.

"I love you, Jocelyn," he said as his strong arm reached under her and he pulled her close. Her tears came in torrents because she knew his kiss was one she never had. It was from a man who was not afraid to declare his love. She felt it was the most beautiful and sincere moment of her life.

Chapter 26

Tuesday, March 15, 2005, 7:48 PM

Senator Marvin Douglas hated the drive from the Hart Senate Office Building to the five-acre palatial residence his wife, June, called home. The property, like their small yacht, matching Cadillacs and other possessions consumed most of his salary and occasionally nibbled at their precious savings. June, forever playing the role of the senator's wife, used their possessions as affluence icons among senators' wives. It was a never-ending and frivolous status-seeking game of ups-woman-ship.

From the middle of their winding driveway, he looked at the five-bedroom house, three-car garage, and in-ground swimming pool. He wondered why the two of them needed so much around them, especially when their three children were attending college. All of this forced him into the lap of Adrian Horne and Gerald Pendergast who brought with them ten million dollars and only wanted a little cooperation with the Common Cause inquiry during the Judiciary Committee hearings. At that time it seemed like an innocent flexing of moral principle, but now remorsefully he knew that taking the money was wrong. Eventually, scandal would end his career as a United States senator and they would turn-tail and hide in disgrace back in their home state of North Carolina.

He pulled the car in the garage and closed the door behind him. For a second he just wanted to end it all and leave the motor running, but there was no sense in adding shame to the scandal that his instincts told him was a growing threat.

He read the two messages his wife pinned to the kitchen corkboard.

"Marvie, big sales for summer wear. Went shopping with the gals, I'll be home late. Love ya, June."

"Shit!" he said, knowing the credit cards would be maxed out again this month.

The next message read: "Marvie, there's a package marked 'urgent' on your desk. Also Adrian called, said for you to call ASAP. Dear, keep the cell phone on. Okay? Love ya, June."

"I wonder what that bastard wants," he said to the expansive void in his empty house.

He went to the bar and poured a half a glass of bourbon. There he saw another note. "Marvie, you've been drinking a lot more lately. Is this drink necessary? Love ya, June." He grabbed the glass and the bottle and headed for his study.

He sat behind the desk in a large swivel chair and studied the light brown envelope that had his name and the word 'URGENT' stamped with two inch red block letters. With the possibility of a booby-trapped package, he squeezed the contents of the envelope and felt a one inch-thick rectangular object that had two holes. The object felt like a videocassette. He wondered who would be sending him a tape.

He opened the package and read from a piece of paper that was stuck to the side of the videocassette. "Watch the tape, then call Senator Adrian Horne. He'll be able to tell you what this is all about. Charlie."

"What kind of foolishness is this?" he asked.

He took the tape and glass of bourbon into the family room. After fumbling with the television and tape machine remotes, he sat in the recliner waiting for the mysterious show to begin.

The first seconds of the tape showed an empty desk and swivel chair with a personal computer positioned on the left side of the desk. The unoccupied office looked similar to his study and he had the strange feeling that he had been there before. An unidentified man walked in front of the camera, and a voice spoke. "Are we ready to do this, Charlie?"

"Yes, sir. The camera is on now," the voice said in the background as Senator Howard Champion took his seat behind the desk.

"Just check the focus and keep the button pressed while I'm talking. I don't want to have to do this again," Champion said.

Senator Howard Champion looked directly at the camera. His eyes betrayed his sadness, something that his friends and constituents rarely saw.

"Good evening, my family, friends, and constituents. Today is February 19, 2005. It's a sad day for me because it marks the end of a career as a public servant that I've found most rewarding. I'm resigning my office, immediately because of a gross mistake I made last November. After consulting with a few close friends about the moral predicament that my lapse of judgement placed me in, I understand now that no good can come from illegal behavior or tainted money."

The senator yawned and took a sip from a glass of water. "It's my hope by admitting my wrongdoing, those who have always relied upon me to 'Champion' a bill or to improve our lives through effective leadership, will understand a single failing of an old man. Perhaps you'll find it in your hearts to extend forgiveness.

"You all know that I'm the Chairman of the Senate Judiciary Committee. That committee will soon examine the circumstances surrounding the Common Cause bankruptcy. Last November, their president, a man by the name of Gerald Pendergast, approached a group of senators on my committee for the express purpose of purchasing influence within my Committee. To my shame, I accepted a sum of ten million dollars. A Cayman Island bank account in my name held the money. I'm sorry to say other senators were offered identical sums for the same purpose.

"Before you judge me too harshly, you should know that for years I've donated a good portion of my financial resources to aid impoverished children throughout the world. Very few people know about my charitable contributions to this cause because I chose not to make it public. I only mention it now, because that is what I intended to do with the funds. This of course is no excuse for my totally improper behavior. I've since returned all of the money.

"As to the other senators and their involvement in this messy business, I've given much thought to whether I should reveal their names. Although these men have similar career achievements as mine, they are no less guilty of the same wrongdoing. To attempt to hide their names would only add to my shame. In order for the people in this great country of ours to have any confidence in their elected servants, a cleansing of those tarnished with greed and avarice is necessary at this time. I sincerely apologize to their families for the pain that will ensue when I read this list of names.

"Phillip Petrie, Democrat from Massachusetts

"David Yost, Democrat from California

"Sandor Mahady, Republican from Pennsylvania

"Marvin R. Douglas, Democrat from North Carolina"

Senator Douglas's face turned ashen from the sound of his name on Senator Champion's list of felons.

"Adrian Horne, Democrat from Illinois

"Kenneth Wren, Republican from Alabama

"James McCabe, Republican from Ohio
"Raymond Brenner, Democrat from Delaware
"By providing these names I've violated a time-honored code of conduct that has no real basis in law. I'm confessing my great sin here and the sins of others for the overall good of the nation. Grant me forgiveness for trying to restore order to the great institution of the United States Senate.
"Good night."
Senator Champion wiped a tear from his eye and stood. "You can turn the camera off, Charlie."
"Are you okay, Senator."
"Actually a tremendous load on my conscience has just been removed," Senator Howard Champion said.
The tape ended and Douglas threw back the remaining bourbon in one gulp.
"Oh God, this is awful," he said as he reached for the telephone that rang in his hand.
"Douglas, are you there?" Adrian Horne asked angrily.
"Yeah, it's me. I just watched the tape. What's this all about, Adrian?"
"It's a shakedown. The others are on their way over here. We've got to decide what to do about this."
"How bad is it?"
"Bad! Get your ass over here. We're in trouble unless we can agree on what needs to be done."
"I'll be there in about an hour," Marvin said as he heard Adrian slam the phone down in his ear.

Tuesday, March 15, 2005, 8:32 PM

Vivian Rayburn had no idea why her brother-in-law, Charlie suddenly decided to pay a visit to their home in Nanticoke, Pennsylvania. Easygoing Charlie was much like her husband, Peter, who had the night shift this week at the power plant. Without Peter home in the evenings, managing a full time job as a convenience store supervisor and mother taxed her strength. She took a few minutes and fell into a comfortable chair, basking in the freedom provided by Uncle Charlie as he read stories to the kids and tucked them into bed.

Tuesday, March 15, 2005, 11:13 PM

When Senator Marvin Douglas joined the impromptu meeting, Senator Adrian Horne stood in the middle of the room and asked his colleagues to take a seat. "Gentlemen, I'm afraid we've got a crisis to deal with. I know you've all received and watched the videotape sent by a man named Charlie. The Charlie that called me earlier today was the same Charlie who ran the camera for the late senator. It turns out that we're being blackmailed by a household servant."

The senators moaned or gasped at hearing the news they feared. "How much does this fool want?" Senator Raymond Brenner asked.

"One million dollars," Adrian said. "From each of us." Seven senators gasped again. "See what I mean? We've got a real problem here, and what's worse he wants the money ten days from now, by the twenty-fifth."

"Is it possible this guy would take less money and leave us alone?" Senator Marvin Douglas asked.

"Would you? Look at it from his point of view. He sees a lot of money floating around. He knows what we've done is illegal and will cause a huge scandal. All he wants is to be an equal partner for his silence," Adrian Horne said.

"I've met this guy Charlie once at a Christmas gathering. Champion brought him down from upstate New York," Senator James McCabe said. "I'll tell you, I'm not going to be blackmailed by some over-age house boy."

All the others started to talk at the same time. Adrian Horne held up his hand. "Gentlemen, please, we can't afford the confusion." When a semblance of order returned, he continued, "All right, let's start with this line of reasoning. If we don't pay and he reveals the tape to the FBI or to the media, we're through as senators, the money will evaporate, and we'll all be playing bridge in a Federal penitentiary."

Again, they all tried to speak at once.

Kenneth Wren, the senior and most affected senator among them raised his hand to be recognized.

"Go ahead, Ken. What are your thoughts on the problem?" Adrian asked.

"It's clear to me that whatever we do, we must all do together. There's no middle ground," he said, pausing to clear his throat. "Based on our personalities and political views, most of us have trouble agreeing on anything. Gentleman, this cannot be one of those times," Senator Wren said and looked around the room for consensus.

"I agree," Adrian Horne said. "It just won't work for some of us to bail out and admit what we've done, hoping the others will not be discovered. Similarly, if we decide on a course of action that eliminates the problem, we'll have to be in it together."

"What do you mean by eliminate?" Senator Sandor Mahady asked. "If you're talking about murder, I cannot condone killing someone. Even if we got away with it, I wouldn't be able to live with myself."

"But if we pay this guy, what's to say that he won't come back demanding more money?" Senator Phillip Petrie asked not wanting to be drowned out by the rhetoric of his colleagues.

Adrian Horne sat back and let his colleagues debate the course of action. He only interrupted them when the discussion grew too loud or when tempers flared. He knew that collectively they were incapable of coming to an agreement they could all live with, but he let them rattle on until four in the morning before he ended the debate.

"It's clear to me that you've reached an impasse. Four of you want to quit and give yourselves up, and the remaining want to squash this little guy like the bug he is."

"I take it you're on the side that wants to eliminate him, Adrian," Senator David Yost said.

Adrian Horne did not answer Yost's question. "Let me propose this. There is one other possible path to take." Suddenly, the room was quiet as exhausted men hungered for a solution that would extract them from the crisis at hand. "There's another person who stands to lose as much over this as we do. Someone who got us into this mess in the first place."

"Pendergast?" Marvin Douglas asked.

"For now, let me talk to him. I'm willing to bet he's got some connections that might put pressure on Charlie to make him consider withdrawing his threat."

"If it doesn't involve murder, it might be worth a try," David Yost said. "We do have some time to experiment with this course of action."

"All right then. For now, I'll try that and for God's sake, everyone remain calm. Let's not say the word 'murder' again. When pressure gets applied, sometimes accidents happen. I think we can all agree that we don't want to be an accessory to that," Adrian said, breathing a sigh of relief. "Keep your mouths shut about this. If one whisper gets out, we're all sunk."

Wednesday, March 16, 2005, 5:27 AM

Senator Adrian Horne waited an hour before his friend from New York, Gerald Pendergast, could get out of his bed and find a tap-free telephone. Horne knew that the fragile agreement between the senators could fall apart if one of them got cold feet and decided to act independently. Action was required immediately, and Horne realized that Pendergast, who treated him with such distaste the last time they spoke, would require significant strong-arming to get him to do what was necessary to eradicate the blackmail threat.

The telephone rang and Horne picked up the receiver before the first ring had time to complete.

"Gerald?"

"Yes. Adrian?"

"What's so important that you call me so early in the morning?"

"The senators all received blackmail threats," Adrian said, and then told Pendergast about the tapes and the demand for millions of dollars within ten days.

"What do you want me to do about it?"

"We at least know who the blackmailer is and I want you to use your connection again to get rid of the guy."

"Dangerous and expensive, Horne. The FBI is already tracking this guy down. He came close to being arrested."

"That's his problem and yours," Adrian said.

"Mine! How can this possibly be mine?"

"Right now there are at least four senators who want to do a show and tell for the FBI on this matter. I've finally got them to agree to hold off until corrective measures can be taken."

"They want the guy killed?"

"No, that's just it. They don't want to line themselves up with a conspiracy to commit murder charge on top of everything else. Gerald, they're serious. You've got to do something and do it quick."

"Okay, let's say that I can get this done. Are you willing to pay for it?"

"Not a cent."

"Wait a minute. You guys are in trouble and you want me to pay for it? This is incredible."

"Gerald, first of all, I know you have access to some funds and can probably justify the expense. Second, you have as much to lose in this as we do. I don't believe for a minute that you've done all of this without a sizable fortune coming your way."

Gerald Pendergast's silence indicated to Horne that he was making progress.

"What if I refuse?"

"Then suffer the consequences, you'll simply be part of the huge scandal. So get busy and deal with this. The guy's name is Charlie Rayburn, Howard Champion's housekeeper in Bolton's Landing. He's threatened to release the tape to the media or the FBI."

"I'm not going to do this," Pendergast insisted.

"Yes, you are Gerald. You simply have no choice. I'm doing all I can to keep these soft-bellies here from spilling their guts. Think about it for a while, Gerald. Then you'll see that this is the best way. Just get it done soon."

Senator Horne only heard the word 'shit' as the telephone went dead in his ear.

Wednesday, March 16, 2005, 1:07 PM

Gerald Pendergast stood with a heavy briefcase outside the library in Stroudsburg, Pennsylvania, while he waited for Rudy Gambrelli. Since the stress-filled conversation with Senator Horne earlier in the morning, he felt queasy—as if he could throw up at any moment. The thought of dashing across New Jersey with a briefcase stuffed with sixty-three hundred dollars was enough, but dealing with Rudy Gambrelli again to propose another contract killing filled him with dread.

He looked up and down the street for Gambrelli but jumped when he felt a heavy hand rest upon his shoulder.

"You weren't followed, I hope?" Gambrelli grumbled.

"No, I kept checking. Frankly, it concerns me that I'm not being watched closer."

"How about a wire, you're not on their side now I hope," Gambrelli said as he put his hand on Pendergast's chest and stomach to feel for a recording device.

"No, I swear, I'm not wearing a wire or working with them."

"So what's up?" Gambrelli said while eyeing the heavy briefcase. "Ya got something other than a cheese sandwich and a pound of useless paper in there?"

"Rudy, there's sixty-three hundred dollars in the case for you."

Rudy frowned. "That's chicken feed compared to what you promised."

"That's what I'm here to discuss."

"This better be good or your neck is going to be too skinny to support your thick skull."

Gerald Pendergast looked around at the immediate neighborhood. "You must be getting tired of hanging out here."

"Funny you should mention that. This lifestyle is not what I expected, based on what you told me."

"Where would you like to be, Rudy?"

"Not in Nowhere, Pennsylvania, that's for sure. I'd prefer the Caribbean."

"I've got another task for you. If you do what we require, you'll be out of here and on your way within a week."

"Your credit is running a little thin. Not counting the morsel that's in the brief case, I haven't received anything but living expenses for the hotel and some food."

"I know, the cash is to help with part of that and I'll settle the balance for this month's payment in a few moments. You'll see the remaining amount for the month in your new Cayman Island account. You do realize that the Cayman Islands are in the Caribbean don't you, Rudy?"

"Yeah, I know that, I'm not illiterate," Gambrelli said. "All right, that will get you off the hook for a month, but what about this other task?"

Pendergast pointed to a secluded area with a bench outside the library. Gambrelli followed, knowing that the rest of the conversation required secrecy.

"Okay, before someone thinks we're a couple of faggots holding hands, tell me what this is all about."

"I need to get a very important videotape from an amateur blackmailer in Bolton's Landing, New York."

"Just the videotape?"

"No, the amateur needs to learn a lesson that he can't screw with Rudy Gambrelli's income."

"My income! How is it affecting that?"

"If this little man releases the tape to the police or the media, there's a lot of people going to be financially ruined. One of them is paying you your monthly payments. If he goes down, you'll get nothing."

"No, but I'll squeeze it out of you instead."

"No, you won't. I'm in danger too. The Feds will lock me up and you'll get nothing."

"How much of a lesson do you want this guy to learn?"

"Teach him to hold his breath for about ten minutes or since he's threatening you, you might want to do something creative. Just make sure he won't have the chance to effect the money transfers to your bank account," Pendergast said, as he handed Gambrelli a piece of paper from his suit jacket pocket.

"What's this?"

"It's your Cayman Island bank account number and password. Don't let anyone get this information or they'll drain your account."

"I don't do computers very well," Gambrelli said.

"If you do the job, you won't have to use a computer to get to your money," Pendergast said. "Just walk across the street from your ocean view apartment and get it."

"I take it the others are willing to pay dearly for this task."

"Everything has limits, Rudy, don't expect the moon. What's your price for the job?"

"Another million."

"For killing an amateur and recovering a tape! Come on, Rudy, that's quite a lot of money."

Gambrelli leaned forward and looked directly in Pendergast's eyes. "You'll pay it, and just so you know, I'm not going to accept this monthly payment crap for the work I do."

"Okay, you're right. They will pay that much for your services. Let's go inside the library. We can use one of their Internet connected computers. I'll transfer a half a million dollars to your account and show you that your balance has an additional thirteen thousand seven hundred dollars for this months payment."

The two men walked to the front door of the library and Pendergast grabbed Rudy's arm. "One thing, don't get any ideas yourself. The folks I'm dealing with have contacts of their own. They can squash you easier than you're going to squash our New York amateur."

Chapter 27

Friday, March 18, 2005, 7:47 PM

The entire task force assembled while Jocelyn donned the earphones and positioned the microphone connected to Ninth Generation's equipment that would duplicate Charles Rayburn's voice.

Peyton Bender kept circling the large meeting table until he collared Donald Corbbitt who happened to cross his orbital path. "Are you sure she's ready for this, Don?"

"The software and hardware works perfectly. Since the senators are on the defensive and we're dictating our requirements to them, we should be able to manage the content of the conversation. Ms. Hafner is a professional and has been role-playing as Charlie Rayburn all day. We've all taken turns throwing curve balls at her and she's done a marvelous job with the trial runs. So yes, I believe we're ready as we can be."

"How is she feeling?"

"She's nervous, but that's to be expected," Corbbitt replied. "She did ask earlier in the day for a little breathing room when she's actually on the phone with Senator Horne. Joshua hooked up some monitoring equipment in the adjoining room. I'm going to be in the room with her as a back up."

"How's that going to work?"

"I'll have a large pad of paper and a marking pen to guide her if it becomes necessary."

Bender just nodded his head in approval. "What are we waiting for then?"

"Just your permission to proceed, Peyton."

"Hell, you've got that. We can't turn back now."

Don Corbbitt sat across the table from Jocelyn with his paper and marker at the ready. The rest of the team moved to the other room.

"Jocelyn," Dale Perkins from Ninth Generation said in her earphone. "Would you please say a few words so we can do a final check on the voice emulation software and electronics?"

"I'll do my best to convince Adrian Horne that I'm the real blackmailer, Charlie Rayburn," Jocelyn said directly to Donald Corbbitt, but her voice sounded exactly like the taped voice of Charles Rayburn.

"Jocelyn, you sound just like him. So don't worry, you'll do fine."

"Thanks for your confidence in me, Don," Jocelyn said softly, but again the equipment made her sound like Charlie Rayburn.

Don smiled, and pointed to the telephone. "Go ahead and dial."

Jocelyn took a deep breath and punched in the numbers for Senator Adrian Horne's unlisted home telephone.

"Hello," a young woman said after the third ring.

"May I please speak to Senator Horne?"

"Hey dad, it's for you."

"Well, I told you before to ask who it is," a distant male voice said.

"May I ask who's calling?"

"Just tell the senator it is his friend from New York," Charlie said.

"Dad, it's your friend from New York," the young woman bellowed.

"Son of a bitch," the distant male voice said.

Jocelyn looked at Donald and shrugged her shoulders.

"Gerald, what the hell is wrong with you. You shouldn't be calling my house, especially now."

Donald put his finger to his lips indicating that Jocelyn should say nothing.

"Pendergast, is that you?"

Donald smiled, and waved his hand indicating that Jocelyn should continue.

"No, it's Charlie from Bolton's Landing," Jocelyn said, resuming her electronically created impersonation.

"I thought we had ten days?" Horne said.

"I'm just calling for an update. Are you guys going to pay up?"

"Yes, we'll pay you the money. What other choice do we have?"

"Good, there's no point in making this into an ugly scandal with all the money floating around. When can I expect the money?"

"Look, we want to end this as bad as you do. It takes a little time for all of us to scoop up a million dollars each. I'm waiting on one more senator to call back now. Once he does, I'll get in touch with you."

"Don't jerk me around, I might have to increase my demands."

"Look, why don't you come down here, and we'll discuss this face to face?" Senator Horne asked, trying to force the issue.

Jocelyn looked at Donald, who gave the thumbs down signal.

"No way, Senator. I'm not getting in the middle of a pack of wolves. I want the money delivered here. Then I'll hand you the tape, and we'll be done with this."

"And just where is here?"

Since the primary purpose for the telephone call was to determine the location for the money drop, Donald just nodded for Jocelyn to proceed. "Here in Bolton's Landing of course, at Senator Howard Champion's home. I can give you directions if you need them, Senator."

"I know how to get there," Senator Horne admitted.

"Senator, let's say you'll be here by five in the afternoon on Monday with all the money."

"What if I don't have it all by then?"

"Then you'd better call me. If your reason is good enough, I might wait. Watching you guys squirm after this tape is broadcast nationwide is almost worth the eight million dollars. So you'd better hurry."

Jocelyn hung up the telephone without saying good-bye to her friend in Washington.

Peyton Bender led the others from the adjoining room. "Excellent, Ms. Hafner."

"Thank you, sir," Jocelyn said, as she let out a huge sigh.

"Joshua, your end of this worked perfectly. Very impressive."

"Thank you, Mr. Bender. Oh, we're going to start building a voice file for Senator Horne by using this conversation."

"Do we have any plans to use Senator Horne's image or voice in the future?" Peyton asked, who hated being surprised when his neck was on the line.

"No sir, but it's hard to tell exactly what is going to transpire during the investigation. If we get started immediately and if you and Agent Corbbitt decide it's necessary, it will decrease the amount of preparation time. We'll simply be ready sooner."

Peyton nodded, "I like how you think, Joshua."

"If I might make a suggestion," Joshua said. "I don't know how much videotaping you do in the course of interrogating suspects, but it might be useful to get as much on tape as possible for future deceptive productions. If it is never used it won't be a problem, but if the need arises you'll have something to work with."

"Great idea, Joshua, that will work as long as it doesn't get in the way of the investigation or other productions that you might be making at the time."

Joshua raised an eyebrow. "I'm not suggesting that you alter the normal course of investigation, just consider making more videos for our purposes here. As far as interfering with other productions, we're capable of making more than one at a time, Mr. Bender."

"You know, Don, if Mr. Koweleski isn't careful, he's going to make himself invaluable around here."

Don laughed. Joshua Koweleski had no way of knowing that it was the best compliment that Peyton Bender had ever given anyone.

"If you folks will stand down for a few minutes, Don and I have a few things to discuss."

Peyton waited until Ms. Hafner and the Ninth Generation personnel left the room. "Don, it looks like you're right on target. Aside from the senators responding to the blackmail demand, we know for sure that Gerald Pendergast is behind this whole scheme."

"Yes, but I don't believe for a minute that Senator Horne is going to show up with eight million dollars in the trunk of his car.'

"Me either. There's too much at stake here for these powerful men, and they can't take the chance that they'll be hit on again for more money in the future."

"Their response has to be with muscle," Corbbitt said.

"So far you're right on track with your analysis of this whole business, Don. We're getting close to the time rein these people in. I'm going to get you some help for your rendezvous in Bolton's Landing and meet with Assistant Director Pincher in Washington. Arresting all of these senators at the same time is going to make an impact on his staff load."

"Great, Peyton. Let's just hope that Gambrelli slides out from under a rock, I'm willing to bet that he'll be the muscle involved in Bolton's Landing."

"I was pleased to hear Horne admit that he knew Gerald Pendergast. It really ties up a lot of loose ends."

"Well, that did a lot for me too, Peyton, I was making a huge assumption that proved to be correct."

"You've always showed great instinct in this business, Don, that's why you're the best I've got here."

"Thanks, Peyton, but something is still bothering me about all of this."

"What's that, Don?"

"We know that Gerald Pendergast is definitely behind both the senators and Common Cause executives. Peyton, what I don't know is who is behind Gerald Pendergast and what they're really up to?"

Chapter 28

Sunday, March 20, 2005, 11:04 AM

"Don, I'm worried about you," Jocelyn said on the telephone from her Manhattan hotel room.

"Thanks, but don't worry, this is all part of the job."

"I'm sure it is, but this Gambrelli seems like such a goon, he's capable of doing anything."

"That's why we've got to get him and lock him away."

"Still I'm worried. I love you and can't bear the thought of you being hurt or killed."

"I'll be fine, there's a van filled with special agents from our Albany Field Office just minutes away. I've got the proximity sensors out so nothing larger than a raccoon can get near the house without us knowing about it and there are video cameras and microphones inside the house. Hopefully we can catch Gambrelli in the act."

"Just be careful, and come back to me in one piece," Jocelyn said as she fought hard to keep from crying.

"It's a pity you're not here with me. There's a wonderful view of Lake George through a large picture window," Don said to divert Jocelyn's attention and minimize her concern. "Senator Champion certainly knew how to relax. With the panoramic view, a few snow flakes, and the overstuffed chairs here, I'd have trouble staying awake."

"Oh great, now I'm worried that he'll sneak in on you while you're dozing."

"I'm actually set up in a garage under Charlie's apartment, except for a few daydreams about you, I'm wide awake."

"That's sweet, Don, but pay attention and don't get hurt."

"I will, dear, please don't worry. I've handled guys like Gambrelli before."

Sunday, March 20, 2005, 8:12 PM

The trouble with stakeouts based on hunches was that you were never sure where, when, how, or even if the one you were waiting for would show up. Sitting alone in the cold garage it was easy to drift mentally far away from the reality that a ruthless killer could appear at any moment.

While he was hiding behind Senator Champion's Lincoln Town Car in the garage, someone shining a precisely aimed flashlight through the roll-up door window might catch him napping. The proximity sensors placed around the house only provided enough warning if you were alert enough to see the flashing red zone lights.

Twice, deer wandering in the monitored zone triggered the warning system causing him to tell the back-up Albany team that there was a zone intruder. Both times, he cancelled the alert as the deer scampered towards the partially frozen lake.

After tedious hours waiting alone, his ears still strained to hear the faintest sounds, but his eyes were virtually worthless now in the evening hours with only a few sources of artificial light. He made a mental note to bring night vision equipment on the next rural stakeout.

His mind, needing stimulation, played tricks on him. In total silence, distant sounds seemed more ominous than they were. After several hours, boredom always took over and staying alert became much more difficult.

He longed to be with Jocelyn again. He thought back to the joyous time they had together and the delicious moments he spent holding her in his arms, kissing, and finally enjoying their first intimate moments.

He closed his eyes and savored the wonderful mind picture of Jocelyn's perfect body, her soft supple skin, and the sweet fragrance of her hair. He remembered the hunger in her kiss and the way they moved together, each one giving to the other unselfishly, soaring higher and higher until he thought his heart would explode from unbridled passion.

He remembered in the soft light of the room, the beautiful glow on her face. When her body trembled and she whispered his name, he felt that the most beautiful experience in his life had just occurred.

He opened his eyes and saw the read alert light flashing.

"I've got an intrusion alarm, in the western quadrant," Corbbitt whispered to his backup team.

"Copy," Special Agent Allan Crosby said.

"If it's him, let's catch him inside the house, we can hold him for breaking and entering if nothing else."

Corbbitt threw an old tablecloth over his electronic equipment, preventing the red and green alert lights from attracting the attention of anyone walking by the garage. He moved in the shadows towards the garage window trying to prevent the single bulb outside the garage from shining on his body.

A faint outline of a huge man walking along the shoreline moved slowly towards the main house. The outline seemed to stop abruptly, but Corbbitt soon realized that whoever it was turned and was now walking in the area between the main house and the combination garage and apartment where he was hiding.

Corbbitt slowly turned away from the window and keyed the microphone again. "I think it's him." He turned back toward the window in time to see the man walking slowly toward the garage.

For a moment, Corbbitt thought he might have company as the huge man peered into the garage windows and for an instant the single light flashed on the man's face. The huge nose, broad forehead, and square jaw matched the features of Rudy Gambrelli.

Corbbitt pressed himself back against the wall next to a folded stepladder.

"You see anything," Crosby said in his ear at the worst possible moment. Corbbitt moved his arm slowly to key the microphone twice, but said nothing. It was a signal that meant he heard the statement, but could not answer.

Gambrelli backed away from the garage a few steps. He looked back at the apartment above the garage and then toward the main house. Both buildings were completely dark and the absence of barking dogs, music, or other sounds gave the impression they were both unoccupied.

"He's moving toward the house," Corbbitt whispered.

"Copy. He probably figures he's going to have to wait for Charlie to come home."

"He's going up the stairs at the side of the house."

"Copy."

"He's checking under the door mat and flower pots for a key."

"Copy. Too bad we didn't leave him one."

Corbbitt watched Gambrelli smash a small window that was next to the front door and reach through to unlock the door. "He is inside now, broke a window to get in," Corbbitt said.

"Copy. We'll follow him with the low-lux cameras."

"Copy," Corbbitt said.

"Subject is standing inside the door, apparently just listening," Agent Crosby said as he watched Gambrelli on his monitor.

"Copy. I'm leaving the garage to get closer. Let me know if he suddenly heads for the door."

"Copy. Subject is checking downstairs rooms very quickly. Be advised that the subject has a handgun."

"Copy," Corbbitt said as he removed his weapon from its holster and clicked off the safety. "Let me know when he's upstairs. Minimal responses from me, just keep feeding me information."

"Copy. We're moving closer."

Corbbitt keyed the microphone twice and used the time to creep up the five stairs to the wooden porch. He stopped behind the closed front door and waited for Gambrelli to check the upper floor of the house.

"Careful, Corbbitt, he's on the other side of the door. The staircase is to the left of the door."

Through the broken window, Corbbitt could hear the steps creaking as they individually flexed under the massive hulk of Rudy Gambrelli. Corbbitt knew that Gambrelli, a hardened criminal who enjoyed killing, would fight his way out of a confrontation rather than face prison and a likely death sentence.

"He's upstairs now, drawing the curtains in the master bedroom. Okay, Corbbitt, he's got a light on now and walking towards the small desk."

Corbbitt slowly turned the doorknob and opened the door wide enough to gain entrance. He could hear his heart pounding in his ears as he searched for a place to hide in the event Gambrelli decided to dash downstairs.

"He's found the envelope with the tape inside. Watch out, he just turned the light off and is leaving the bedroom.

Corbbitt moved quietly from the front door and the foot of the staircase through to the hallway and into the kitchen knowing that this game of hide-and-seek was potentially lethal. He heard Gambrelli moving down the staircase quickly as if he was sure he was alone in the house and was not concerned about the noise he made.

Corbbitt hid in a large pantry with a folding door that squeaked as he closed it.

Gambrelli's footsteps suddenly stopped as if he heard the noise.

"He's headed for the family room. The envelope is open. Apparently, he wants to view the tape," Crosby said. "We don't have a camera in the family room, Corbbitt."

Corbbitt heard the television audio and decided to open the folding door hoping that the television would mask the sound of the door if it squeaked again.

Corbbitt left the pantry and headed toward the sound of the television and Senator Champion's taped voice.

"We see you now, Corbbitt. The family room is on your right," Crosby said, stating what was obvious to Corbbitt as he crept down the hallway towards the family room doorway.

Corbbitt stood at the edge of the doorway and moved just enough so he could see Gambrelli sitting on a large couch with his feet propped up on a coffee table. He tried to see whether Gambrelli's gun was visible and eliminated the coffee table as one of the possibilities.

"Wow, these senator's are into some deep shit here!" Gambrelli said to the empty house.

Corbbitt moved quickly into the room. "Freeze, Gambrelli."

Gambrelli saw movement behind him reflected in the television screen and turned with his weapon in hand. He fired twice and missed as Corbbitt dove and rolled to radically change the firing angle.

Corbbitt fired once and Gambrelli heard the bullet zip past his head. "The next one goes in your ear, Gambrelli. Drop the gun."

Gambrelli froze, realizing that whoever was in the room with him had the advantage.

"I'm FBI Special Agent Donald Corbbitt, drop the weapon now. Last chance."

Gambrelli let the gun fall to the center of a couch cushion.

"Keep your hands up and walk to the wall straight ahead," Corbbitt ordered.

"What's this about?" Gambrelli asked, trying to lengthen the time before he was spread-eagled against the wall.

"This is about breaking and entering, it's about the murder of Senator Howard Champion, and the murder of Margarita Rosario. I'm charging you with these crimes and placing you under arrest. Move up against the wall spread your arms and legs. Rudy, you know the routine. Do it now."

"Agent Crosby, support requested now," Corbbitt said into the microphone.

"Copy. We're rolling up to the house now."

Gambrelli turned quickly and caught Corbbitt by surprise. Gambrelli's meaty hand struck him in the side of his head. The massive blow sent him flying backwards and his weapon slid toward the doorway. Gambrelli dove for his gun on the cushion. Corbbitt lunged for Gambrelli's legs and managed to stop the forward progress of the huge man. Gambrelli kicked violently to shake free. Corbbitt winced from the sharp pain in his left shoulder as Gambrelli raised his leg to strike again. This time Corbbitt grabbed the leg and turned it hard to flip Gambrelli onto his back. Gambrelli's head hit the hard wooden floor with a sickening thud.

Corbbitt jumped on the advantage, striking Gambrelli once in the face breaking his nose. "That's for Margarita Rosario," Corbbitt said, raising his arm and striking Gambrelli in the face again breaking several of his teeth. "That's for Senator Champion," Corbbitt said and raised his arm again. "And this ..."

"Is enough, Agent Corbbitt," Allan Crosby said as he stopped Corbbitt from striking Gambrelli again.

Corbbitt looked at Crosby and realized that indeed it was enough. "Thanks, Allan, you saved me from killing this guy. Cuff him for me, will ya, and read the bastard his rights," Corbbitt said as he waited for time to dilute the excess adrenaline in his body.

Chapter 29

Monday, March 21, 2005, 6:45 AM

Gerald Pendergast looked at his watch, and grimaced, none of the senior executives thought there was enough work to do to report to work early. He followed his secretary's written formula for making the perfect urn of coffee, coffee that he desperately needed after a fitful night and little sleep. The entire project depended on Gambrelli getting the videotape and the little weasel before he could injure men of power and position. He poured himself a cup from the strong end of the half-filled urn.

He grabbed his briefcase and extracted a personal organizer. The organizer was essentially a minicomputer that made the first computers seem as retarded as one-celled amoebas with just enough sense to cling to life.

He used a pencil as a pointing device to punch a few buttons that would first align the machine to the company's wireless network and then to the Dubai Bank in the Cayman Islands. After checking with the small file that helped him remember the account information, he keyed in the account number and password. Within a second another screen appeared offering various selections. He pushed number one to capture the account balance. The screen read three hundred eight million four hundred twelve dollars and eighty-seven cents. Aside from the legal costs to get him through the Senate inquiry and trial, and residual expenses to manage the final part of a scheme that he helped develop, the money would all be his.

He looked out the window and mused. All of the headache, stress, and endless harassment from the FBI, Securities and Exchange Commission, the press—all of the anger from enraged employees and investors would soon be an ugly memory. The delayed Senate Judiciary Committee investigating into the bankruptcy should be a breeze since he purchased the required cooperation from the committee members. It would still take a little luck, good lawyers, and a huge sum of money to minimize the risk of a guilty verdict. Perhaps, if the Attorney General played it just right, there might not be any risk at all.

All that was required now was Gambrelli's expertise to protect the senators from the amateur blackmailer. If Rudy did his job right, they would all get out of this without scandal or a prison sentence. They would retain the money for their individual contributions and go on their merry way.

He looked at the small screen again and beamed. Three hundred million dollars was the reward for the months of unbelievable pressure and soon he would be able to enjoy the luxuries and freedom it provided.

A soft but familiar knock on the door interrupted his reverie. "Yes, Heather."

"Good morning, sir."

"Good morning, you're in early."

"Yes, I mentioned that I have a dentist appointment in the afternoon. I just wanted to get a jump on the day."

"Well, you're more dedicated than the others around here, Heather."

"Thank you, sir. Do you want some more coffee?"

"Yes, if you don't mind."

"Right away, sir," Heather said as she started to back away from his door and stopped. "Sir, it might not be my place to say anything, but there's this guy pestering security."

"I'm sure they'll handle it," Pendergast grumbled.

"I hope so. It's just that—well the guy claims to be the new president of Common Cause."

"What!"

"Yes, sir. People are arriving in droves to report to work. Security is really backed-up because of this. They don't know what to do."

"It's probably just some crackpot, there's always something weird going on in this city."

Heather nodded and went to fetch another cup of coffee for her boss.

Pendergast shook his head and looked at his bank balance again to regain the delight he had before Heather's interruption.

His eyes widened as he saw the balance change from over three hundred million dollars to one dollar and eighteen cents.

Monday, March 21, 2005, 9:05 AM

Jocelyn winced when Don looked up from his paperwork and turned his head in her direction.

"Pretty, huh? Well, you should see the other guy."

She came closer to him and he covered up the portion of his report that justified the need for firing his weapon while apprehending a suspect.

"You're eye is black and the whole side of your head is swollen. What about your vision?" she said with genuine concern.

"Oh, I'm fine. This looks much worse than it really is."

"What happened?"

"Gambrelli was a lot faster than I expected. He's as big as a refrigerator, but lightning quick. I got in a few licks of my own. We took him into custody last night after the Glens Falls hospital checked him for a concussion and taped his broken nose."

Jocelyn studied his injuries. While the black and yellow discoloration on his face from Gambrelli's punch did nothing for his appearance, she felt the natural attraction tug at her and she fought a natural urge to hold him. "So the tape we made worked."

"Yes, beautifully."

"Do we need to get busy on another one?"

"Not at the moment," Don said. "I've primed Gambrelli with a little information that we have and convinced him that his buddy Pendergast set him up. He said something about money Pendergast and his friends owed him, and that he was just trying to get him killed or imprisoned to avoid paying up."

"So much for criminal loyalty," Jocelyn said.

"Gambrelli's been advised by his lawyer that he might face the death penalty. So it doesn't surprise me that he's telling all," Don said.

"What's next?"

"It's time to knock Gerald Pendergast off his royal throne."

Monday, March 21, 2005, 9:11 AM

An immaculately groomed man with dark brown hair, thin mustache, and penetrating eyes entered Pendergast's office. A security officer stood outside the door waiting to see whether there would be a confrontation and the need for New York City Police.

The man looked directly at Pendergast, opened his briefcase, and ceremoniously presented Pendergast with a single sheet of paper. "Sir, this is from the newly elected Common Cause board of directors. My name is Akbar Muhammad, I am the newly appointed chief executive officer."

Pendergast snatched the paper from Muhammad's hand. "So you say! Let me see that." He looked at the paper that duplicated what Muhammad just said. It included fifteen signatures of individuals who claimed to be on the board. Pendergast noted that Muhammad's signature was among them.

"Don't think for a minute that you can just walk in here and take over with a single sheet of paper, mister. No one has said a word about this to me," Pendergast said in a rage.

"I understand your position. Frankly, I'm sorry that events warrant your removal," Muhammad said in a voice that was calm and just above a whisper so that Pendergast had to strain to hear him. "If you will call the telephone number in Dubai, you will get confirmation that I am indeed the new chief executive officer."

Pendergast grabbed Muhammad's business card and looked at the number.

"Is there a problem?" the security officer said, noticing Pendergast's rage.

"You bet there's a problem. Get this man out of my office."

"Sir, you are upset and acting unprofessionally. You are in fact in my office. You may take the rest of the day to gather your personal effects. Meanwhile, I need to talk with the existing senior staff as a group and then meet with them individually."

"You'll do no such thing, and I'm not going anywhere."

The officer grabbed Muhammad by the arm. "Buddy, I don't know what you're up to but it's time to leave."

"Officer, I am a non-violent person. You're talking to the new chief executive of this company. While he's confirming this on the telephone, I'll wait outside the office," Muhammad said calmly. "If this is acceptable, no complaint to your security company regarding your action will be made."

The security officer looked helplessly at Pendergast for direction. Pendergast scowled but nodded his head in agreement.

"Mr. Pendergast, during your last moments with the company, do not destroy any files, issue any policy statements, or transfer funds belonging to the company. In fact, do not take so much as a pencil that belongs to the company. I'll wait outside now while you call Dubai."

Pendergast slammed the door and lunged for the telephone. His hands were shaking so violently that several times he hit two buttons at the same time and had to redial. The telephone stopped ringing after the fourth ring.

"Hello," Pendergast shouted. "Who am I talking to?"

"I am Jobran Al-Tarabolsi. I've been expecting your call," a man with a soft and nearly musical voice said.

"Oh Mr. Tarabolsi, I didn't know I had your telephone number," Pendergast said to one of the foreign investors who purchased Common Cause. "What's this all about?"

"It is simple. Mr. Akbar Muhammad is the new chief executive officer. His credentials are valid."

"Why am I suddenly being replaced?"

"It may seem sudden to you, but we have planned this all along."

"Why? What have I done?"

The telephone line was suddenly silent as if additional time was required to formulate an answer. "Mr. Pendergast, a man with flexible principles is a man with no principles at all. We cannot take the chance that your ambitions will betray us, like you have betrayed the previous owners."

"But I worked in your behalf, I did all of this so that you and the others could get the company at a bargain price and make money on it forever."

"Yes, and we do thank you for that. But you did all of this because of the money we waved in front of you, and such a man who would ignore the responsibilities entrusted to him cannot remain with us."

The rage within Pendergast intensified. "You can't do this to me! What about the money in the account, you've drained it dry."

"What money? What account? If you'll check again, you'll see they no longer exist."

"You owe me and I'm not going to let you get away with stealing the millions you guys promised."

"We owe you nothing. You see we have the company and the influence you bought for us. What we don't need is you."

"I'll take this to the police. I'll tell everything I know."

"Perhaps you will, but what of it. Our purchase of the company won't be reversed and they cannot touch us. At best, you would only be a minor inconvenience and we have ways of dealing with such trivial problems."

"Well, we'll see about that!"

"Mr. Pendergast, some of the people we employ delight in hearing the screams of people they inflict pain upon. Be very careful what you do. We can whisk you out of the country easier than you might think and most Americans find the prison cells in the Mid East most uncomfortable. Believe me, in the end you would kiss the feet of the man who would use a bullet to end your life."

"You can't do this to me."

"We've already done it. Now step aside and let Mr. Muhammad tend to his responsibilities. If you'll control yourself with regard to the business we've conducted in secret, we're prepared to offer you a modest stipend."

"Oh! A modest stipend, huh! All right how much."

"One thousand dollars a month," Tarabolsi said calmly.

"One thousand! I can't live on a thousand a month in New York City."

"That's up to you. Perhaps you can find employment elsewhere."

"Not with what's happened here, no one will hire me," Pendergast shouted.

"Perhaps you should have thought about the consequences of what you've done. Good-bye, Mr. Pendergast."

Pendergast dropped the telephone receiver on the floor and slumped in his chair in total defeat.

Monday, March 21, 2005, 10:45 AM

Donald Corbbitt entered the Common Cause office building with Special Agent Malcolm Vondra, a recent addition to the New York City Field Office. Although Vondra appeared a little overzealous, Corbbitt sensed that he would soon blend in with the other agents. The rigorous training and background checks required by the Bureau meant that he would soon be up to speed and handling his portion of the case load.

The security officer greeted Corbbitt with a friendly smile and inquired about their destination.

"Well, things are in an uproar there this morning."

"What happened?"

"Apparently the CEO got canned. The new guy just showed up to take his place. It caused quite a stir here a few hours ago."

"What happened to the former CEO, Pendergast?"

"I know who you mean. I think he's still up there, but the new guy wants him off the property as soon as possible," the officer said.

"We need to talk to Pendergast before he decides to make himself scarce, Malcolm," he said, hustling his new colleague off to the bank of elevators. "It figures, the very day when we want to pick this guy up, he's ready to bolt."

They took the elevator to the eleventh floor and noticed instantly that the air seemed to be heavy with tension and stress. One look at Pendergast's secretary, Heather Pollack, confirmed that she had had better days at work.

"I was going to call you about what happened here today, sir," Heather said. "It's been very hectic. With Mr. Pendergast being fired, and his replacement just showing up from nowhere making all sorts of demands, there just wasn't time."

"That's okay. I understand. Where's Pendergast now?"

"He was here just a few minutes ago. The poor man looks terrible."

"You know him better than anyone else, Heather. Where would he go?"

"I'm sure he's not making the rounds and saying his 'good-byes'. He knows everyone hates him here," Heather said. "You might try the men's room or the rooftop."

"Rooftop?"

"Yes, we all go up there for a break when it's not too windy. If you're going to hunt for him, better take the visitor's passkey for the executive washroom. For the roof, take the elevator to the twenty-second floor and then take the staircase into the tower."

"Thanks, Heather," Special Agent Vondra said.

They checked the executive men's room on the way back to the elevator bank without finding Pendergast. Corbbitt had the uneasy feeling that his new colleague was going to see a tragedy on his first case assignment.

"This elevator's taking forever," Vondra said. "We could probably run up the stairs and get there quicker."

"Perhaps, Malcolm. What happens after you run up eleven flights of stairs and suddenly you're required to use that energy? You may not get enough time to catch your breath."

"Gotcha. I guess there's a lot to learn in the field, and I know that you're the best in our office."

"Thanks, but I bleed just like anyone else and I'm still learning everyday myself," Corbbitt said as an elevator door opened in front of them.

On the twenty-second floor a stairway next to the bank of elevators led upward as Heather described. The normally closed and locked door to the roof showed signs of significant abuse. Corbbitt guessed that building occupants desperately needed the breath of fresh air, a view of the Manhattan skyline, and relief from the pressure-cooker environment called work.

They climbed the steel stairs and peered out on the windblown rooftop. A solitary male figure, partially hidden by air conditioning equipment, stood fifty feet away. He was very close to the three-foot retaining wall.

"Pendergast," Corbbitt yelled.

"Maybe he can't hear you because of the wind," Vondra said.

They moved closer to the man and Corbbitt confirmed that the man was Gerald Pendergast.

Pendergast raised one leg over the barrier and sat on the edge straddling life and death.

"Pendergast, stop! You don't have to do this."

Pendergast turned his head toward them. "I don't, huh?"

"Call security, Vondra. Tell them we have a potential jumper on the roof. Clear the street and sidewalk on the west-side of the building."

"Gotcha," Vondra said, but continued to look at Pendergast.

"Do it now, Vondra, and get back up here. I might need your help."

Vondra sprang into action.

"Look, Pendergast, we know what you've been doing here at Common Cause but let's not make this any worse," Corbbitt said, trying to convince Pendergast not to jump.

"You don't know the half of it, Agent Corbbitt. Aside from all the misery I've caused everyone, I've lost my job here at Common Cause and now the bastards who I helped steal this company for aren't going to pay me as they promised."

"I understand you're under a lot of pressure over all this, but consider if you jump, that you might land on some poor soul below. Do you really want to be like your buddy, Gambrelli and kill indiscriminately."

"Oh you know about him, do you?"

"Yes, I'm here to arrest you for your part in Senator Howard Champion's murder. Gambrelli is afraid of a possible death sentence. He's been telling his part of the story. Did you know that Gambrelli killed Margarita Rosario just because she helped him make the cigar that killed Champion."

Pendergast thought for a moment. "All the more reason for me to jump and get it over with."

"Pendergast, there's a way you can redeem yourself."

"How's that?"

"Tell the world what you know and who is behind you. Do that so this won't happen again," Corbbitt said as he inched closer to Pendergast.

"Corbbitt, you have no idea how ruthless these people are. Look, down in my briefcase there's a personal organizer, its got all the account details of who's involved in this," Pendergast said as he put his other leg over the edge and sat facing oblivion.

"Look in a file called 'Bigbucks' and use 'CCCC' as the password to get the information you need to put an end to this," Pendergast said, talking over his shoulder.

"I'll do that. What else am I going to find in there?" Corbbitt said, moving quickly behind the man.

"My stupidity," Pendergast said as he leaned forward to push himself from the ledge.

Corbbitt lunged and managed to get three fingers under Pendergast's suit jacket collar. Corbbitt strained under Pendergast's weight and managed with his other arm to push against the barrier to keep himself from going with Pendergast.

"Thanks for trying, Corbbitt, you're a good man," Pendergast said as he raised his arms and slid out of his suit jacket.

Corbbitt watched Pendergast fall along the building wall until his head struck a protruding ledge. His body caromed off the ledge away from the building and landed on the top of an armored vehicle that was delivering cash to the first floor bank.

"Corbbitt, security is clearing the area," Agent Vondra said.

Corbbitt stood and faced his new colleague. "He's gone," Corbbitt said and dropped Pendergast's jacket.

Chapter 30

Tuesday, March 22, 2005, 9:11 AM

Using his cell-phone, Akbar Muhammad placed a call to the first senator on his alphabetical list. He could picture the man fumbling for the cell-phone reserved for private personal communications.

"Good morning, Senator Brenner," Akbar said.

The telephones were silent as Senator Brenner tried to recognize the strange voice. "Who is this?"

"I'm a new friend of yours. My name is Akbar Muhammad, I'm the new chief executive officer of Common Cause Communications Corporation."

"What happened to the other guy, eh, Pendergast?"

"Let's just say he failed in his attempt to soar over us in Manhattan yesterday."

Again, there was silence while Senator Brenner interpreted what he really meant. "All right, assuming that this is true. How did you get this number?"

"I received your special telephone number from Jobran Al-Tarabolsi. Mr. Tarabolsi is, or should I say was, a special friend of the late Gerald Pendergast."

"Well I don't know any Tarabolsi."

"Yes, that is understood. Mr. Tarabolsi is part owner of this corporation, but he is also responsible for transferring to you the sum of ten million dollars," Akbar said calmly.

The silence on the telephone lasted longer. "Tell Mr. Tarabolsi that nothing has changed. I've committed to help Common Cause get through the Senate Judiciary Committee hearing."

"Yes, that is understood. Mr. Tarabolsi requests that you call him at your convenience, sometime within the next six hours. Remember that he is a businessman and that in most cases in business sooner is better than later," Akbar said.

"Well, I'm not going to call some foreigner over this issue of Common Cause. It is not proper behavior for a United States senator."

"Mr. Tarabolsi is not a man to be trifled with. You may say that he orchestrated Pendergast's failed attempt to fly without even trying. I would hate to think what this man could do if he wished to exercise the power at his disposal."

"Are you threatening a United States senator?"

"Not at all. I am merely suggesting that it would be in your best interest to honor Mr. Tarabolsi's request. I should point out that he is aware that it is unseemly for a United States senator to take a bribe," Akbar Muhammad said, waiting for the senator's response.

"All right, let me have his telephone number."

"Thank you, Senator Brenner. You'll find Mr. Tarabolsi is usually very accommodating and easy to do business with. Here is his number in Dubai."

Akbar Muhammad gave Senator Brenner the number and hung up the telephone. He sighed, and dialed the next senator on his list. He made a note to contact the Attorney General later. There was no point in rattling him this far away from the next presidential election.

Tuesday, March 22, 2005, 11:21 AM

"Agent Corbbitt, this is Pauline Dryfus, Senator Champion's office manager."

"Yes, Ms. Dryfus, I was about to call you. We've arrested the man who we believe is responsible for Senator Champion's death."

"I still can't believe he's gone. Does this monster say why he had to kill such a fine man?"

"We're questioning him now. I can't go into the case details, but he's worried about a death sentence. What did you want to tell me?"

"You asked me to keep my eyes and ears open around the other senators' staff members. I'm not very good at such things, but I can tell from their behavior that something is wrong."

"How is that?"

"Well, Senator Yost from California is normally the Senate comedian. You never see him without a huge smile and his lightning wit around here is legendary. Just an hour ago I saw him in the hall, and he not only ignored me, but bumped into me without even turning to say a word."

"Interesting, anything else?"

"I made a point of calling my counterpart in his office just to see if I could detect what was behind his sudden change in temperament. Ginny, was very abrupt with me and that's so unlike her."

"So whatever is going on has rubbed off on the staff?"

"Yes, it seems that way," Pauline said. "I know that's not much, but I thought you should know."

"Thanks, Ms. Dryfus, I really do appreciate your help."

"Agent Corbbitt, thanks for catching the guy who killed my dear friend," she said with a sniffle.

Corbbitt hit the save button on the computer knowing that the reports needed more information for Peyton Bender's update. He needed to thank the special agents in the Tampa Field Office for their help on the case and Isaac Saltzman for his knowledge and help in bringing this case to the President's attention.

It was also time to call José Rosario and tell him that he arrested a man believed to be his wife's murderer.

Tuesday, March 22, 2005, 2:59 PM

Senator Raymond Brenner delayed making the call to Dubai as long as he dared. He hoped for some revelation, some Divine Guidance, or support from other senators who might be subject to the tug of the marionette string that suddenly tightened around his neck. He dialed nine, seven, one, for the United Arab Emirates, four for Dubai, and then Tarabolsi's number.

On the third ring a woman spoke, "Hello, caller from the United States. May I please have your name?" she said with a thick accent.

"Senator Raymond Brenner," he answered impatiently. "How did you know I was from the United States?"

"Mr. Tarabolsi has business worldwide. This line is reserved for his interests in the United States."

"Oh."

"Excuse please, Mr. Tarabolsi is currently on the telephone. Please hold. I will tell him you are waiting."

Senator Brenner drummed his fingers on the desk. No doubt, others already had their arms twisted by Tarabolsi. He wondered if all his colleagues waited until the last moment to call and the arm-twisting resulted in a minor strain or complete arm amputation.

"Excuse please. Mr. Tarabolsi indicates only another minute is required and requests that you remain on hold."

"I'll wait," Senator Brenner said reluctantly. He wondered if this was an Arabic ploy to demonstrate power and dominance by placing him on hold. The telephone played some Arabic melody in his ear.

"Ahhhh, Senator Brenner, I know you are a busy man and I am sorry to make you wait," Jobran Tarabolsi said in a voice that oozed sincerity.

"It's all right, Mr. Tarabolsi, but what is this all about."

"Yes, you Americans always want to get right to the point," Tarabolsi said. "That is different than our custom where we try to establish an air of cordiality before discussing business."

"I'm sorry, I am not well versed in your customs and traditions, sir."

"Perhaps one day you'll have the opportunity, but as you say in your country, let's move on."

"All right," Senator Brenner said. "I understand your organization wants some flexibility and cooperation from the Senate Judiciary Committee. I've committed to provide what you require."

"Things are often different than what they appear, Senator."

"What do you mean?"

"Simply, that we don't really care if your greed-driven company executives are found guilty and serve the rest of their days in prison. Frankly, you can tie the remaining ones together and roast them over a slow flame."

"That's pretty harsh, Mr. Tarabolsi."

"They've demonstrated a total lack of trustworthiness. In my country, their punishment would be quite severe."

"So this is not about softening the Judiciary Committee's inquiry into the Common Cause bankruptcy."

"No, my dear sir. With Mr. Pendergast's assistance we engineered the entire take over of the company, your cooperation is required in other areas."

"Our cooperation does not extend beyond this issue, Mr. Tarabolsi," Senator Brenner said gruffly.

"Really? I think your cooperation extends to whatever issue interests us, Senator Brenner. I don't believe your career as a politician can tolerate the revelation of a certain financial transaction that exists between us."

"Are you blackmailing me?"

"That's what you Americans call it. We simply look at it as purchasing your cooperation."

"It amounts to the same thing," Senator Brenner bellowed.

"If you insist, but let's not quibble over this and discuss what is required of you."

"Required! I don't like your implication that I have no choice in this."

"Senator Brenner, after our conversation when you have time to reflect on your position, you'll find that you really have no choice but to cooperate."

"We'll see about this," Brenner raged.

"I suggest you remain calm and listen to our requirements. Perhaps our needs are not as difficult to bear as you might think," Tarabolsi said.

"All right, I'll listen," Brenner said, knowing that there was no alternative.

"Since the creation of Israel as a country in 1948, the United States has continuously supplied foreign aid, loan guarantees, favorable trade relations, and of course significant contributions to their military prowess."

"Oh my God, you expect me to intervene in our long-standing foreign policy."

"Senator Brenner, we're not asking for heavy-handed action by you or your colleagues. We expect you to support our position on these matters, continuously. We expect you to aggressively reduce or eliminate the flow of money and military power from United States to Israel. Our ultimate goal is to remove your country's protective shield from the Zionists in our midst. Your voting record and the results of your persuasive efforts with other senators will be monitored."

"Impossible," Brenner said.

"In addition, you will actively support the creation of a Palestinian state and provide them with enough aid to ensure they become a viable nation."

"It's totally out of the question," Brenner fumed.

"Really? Your government did it for Israel and you will do it again for the Palestinians."

"And if I fail to accept your requirements or fail to achieve the desired results on this impossible mission, you'll expose me for taking your money?"

"Of course, Senator, but that might be the least of your concerns in this matter. It seems to me that one of your Judiciary Committee members died recently.

"Were you responsible for Senator Champion's assassination?"

"Senator Brenner, I've stated our requirements. Please begin immediately. Good-bye."

The photograph of Thomas Jefferson's nineteen-foot bronze statue stared back at him. Alone in his office Senator Brenner wept for the first time in decades.

Tuesday, March 22, 2005, 7:45 PM

For the second time in a week, Senator Adrian Horne held a caucus of senators affected by the latest revelation. A written agenda for the meeting was hardly necessary because each man understood the ramifications of the two-pronged attack on their reputations. Each hoped their collective wisdom might prevent their constituents from learning that they were far from exemplary in the office entrusted to them as representatives of the people.

"Gentlemen, we have a lot to discuss here this evening. So let's get started," Senator Adrian Horne said. "I'm out of booze from the last time we met, so unless you brought some with you, we're limited to soft drinks and water."

"Probably for the best anyway, we need to focus and figure a way out of this," Senator James McCabe said.

"If I may continue. I did some checking into recent events concerning Common Cause. Gerald Pendergast committed suicide by jumping off a skyscraper in New York. He did this after having his job taken away by the same group that paid us the ten million dollars and talked with us this afternoon."

"Incredible!" Senator Marvin Douglas said. "It's hard to believe that we've fallen victim to this incredible scheme."

"Yes, and let's not forget the amateur blackmailer. That's what's so unnerving about all of this. Gerald Pendergast agreed, reluctantly, I might add, to deal with this guy Charlie. Since he's no longer with us, there's no way that I can find out what's been done about this."

"Yes, and we've missed the accelerated deadline demanded by the blackmailer. I've been watching the news all day for some evidence that he's gone to the media. And so far, the FBI hasn't pestered me. How about it? Anybody here had a brush with the FBI today?" Senator David Yost asked.

"It looks to me that we're starving for input here," Senator Kenneth Wren said. "If Pendergast sent someone to deal with this problem to fetch the tape, maybe there's a record of an incident. Who knows, Charles Rayburn might be dead. If that's the case, one part of this massive problem is over."

"Conversely," Senator Petrie said. "If Rayburn releases the tape, our involvement with Tarabolsi won't matter much. We'll be of no use to him without our vote and influence in the Senate."

"Especially if we're in jail," Senator Sandor Mahady said.

"I'm pretty good with the Internet, maybe I can find out if there's any report of a death in the Bolton's Landing area recently," Phillip Petrie said. "Maybe one of us could call the police station and see if there was any activity at Champion's house."

"Searching the Internet is not a bad idea. Just remember that the absence of news doesn't help us one way or another," Senator Horne said. "As far as calling the police goes I'd think twice about that. Right now we're isolated from any event there. Let's try to keep it that way."

"Let's deal with the other problem by assuming we've heard the last of Charlie. Is anyone here going to yield to Tarabolsi's demands?" Senator McCabe asked.

"Israel is the only democracy in the area. We've been supporting Israel for years and frankly, their intelligence support and ability to take action saved us a lot of grief. Without them, Iraq would have nuclear weapons and probably used them."

"Wait a minute," Senator Horne interrupted. "Let's not turn this into a political posturing contest. The real issue is if we're going to knuckle under to any of Tarabolsi's demands in the first place."

"No, you wait, Adrian. This may be your home and you're the chairman and all, but our necks are on the chopping block too," Senator Brenner said. "I don't know what he said to you guys, but he made it very clear to me that we were going to cooperate with him, or there was a distinct possibility that we'd wind up like the late Howard Champion."

"There's nothing to indicate that Tarabolsi had anything to do with Champion's death," Senator Horne responded.

"Perhaps, Adrian, you know something you're not telling us about Senator Champion's death," Senator Marvin Douglas challenged.

Adrian reeled at the accusation that threatened to unmask the truth about his lie that set up Senator Champion's death. "I know you don't care much for me, Douglas, but let's rise above petty bickering to get out of this mess. Okay?" Senator Horne said in an effort to regain composure.

Ideas became debates. Debates became arguments. With the intervention of quick thinking neutral senators, arguments stopped short of physical altercation. When all present were exhausted, Senator Adrian Horne knew that when the sun rose, scandal would reign. In the absence of a last minute miracle, each senator would choose a path without regard to the consequences that decision would have on others. Wednesday promised to be nothing but chaos and the United States Senate would never be the same.

Chapter 31

Wednesday, March 23, 2005, 8:15 AM

Donald Corbbitt shook Joshua Koweleski's hand before the team meeting that Peyton Bender organized. "Joshua, you've done an amazing job here. I just wanted to thank you for your skill and dedication."

"Actually, I thought we were going to do a lot more. Is Mr. Bender going to dissolve our task force?" Joshua asked.

"I think so, but I wouldn't worry if I were you. With your innovations there will be more work to come."

"I never thought we'd go all the way to the President of the United States though. He's all but guaranteed a government contract, so I think you're right," Joshua said. "Are you going to make some arrests now?"

"I think so. We've got enough information to support prosecution of the Common Cause executives and our group of corrupt senators. Peyton and I are traveling to Washington to confront them about all of this. I think you'll see many special elections across the country. What are your plans?"

"I've got to take some time off at Mr. Hammond's insistence. He gave me a nice bonus and a week's vacation. I'm going to ask my girlfriend, Bethany, to marry me. Maybe we'll go to Mexico on our honeymoon."

"That's wonderful, I hope it works out for you. I'm thinking of doing the same myself," Don said and looked at Jocelyn as she entered the conference room.

"Wow, are you a lucky man."

"There's a few things we need to talk about, but I have to admit, I've never fallen for anyone as much as her," Don said quietly.

"What are you two boys whispering about?" Jocelyn asked.

"It's a guy thing, Jocelyn. We were telling each other about the beautiful women in our lives," Joshua said.

"Just how many women in your lives are there?" Jocelyn asked, putting them on the spot.

Both men flushed as Peyton Bender entered the conference room followed by Dale Perkins, and Deborah Clements. "If we can get started," Peyton Bender said with his traditional prod to begin the meeting immediately.

While people were still taking their seats, Bender began. "First, let me say this has been one of the most successful operations performed by the personnel in this office. I'm going to write an Operations Report that specifically talks about using Ninth Generation's reality duplicating software to destabilize organized crime. The work done here has been exemplary by all members of the team.

"Ninth Generation personnel have concluded their demonstration and speaking as an assistant director of the Bureau we welcome further opportunities to work together on other cases. I'm sure that other branches of the government like the Central Intelligence Agency will also make good use of your software and equipment.

"Thank you Mr. Bender. It was a pleasure to assist the Bureau with these cases," Joshua said.

"Ms. Hafner, your journal entries helped me keep track of operational progress and were invaluable in the reports I submitted to the President of the United States. Your ability to learn a new task well enough to fool conspirators was most impressive. If you have no objections, I'd like you to stay a few days and help me prepare the Operations Report," Peyton said. "I have examples of similar reports that will help you get started."

"Thank you, Mr. Bender, I'm glad it all went so well and I'd be happy to help you," she said but smiled at Don across the table.

"I might add that none of what we've accomplished would have happened if it weren't for Special Agent Donald Corbbitt's instinct and perseverance. At an early stage in the investigation, he recognized that Senator Champion's death was directly connected to the Common Cause bankruptcy. Again, his performance and insight clearly makes him one of the top special agents in the Bureau."

Donald Corbbitt smiled as the others nodded in agreement. "Thanks, Peyton," he said.

"Since you've all signed the confidentiality agreement, I might as well tell you what the end game is for those individuals involved with the murder of Senator Howard Champion, and those involved with the manipulation of Common Cause into bankruptcy.

"So far we've arrested Rudy Gambrelli for murdering both Senator

Howard Champion and Margarita Rosario. Gambrelli's arrest proved Agent Corbbitt's theory. Eight senators on the Senate Judiciary Committee were involved to whitewash Senate inquiry.

"The link to Common Cause was undeniably the Company President, Gerald Pendergast. Just before Pendergast killed himself, he suggested that Agent Corbbitt look at a personal organizer for details associated with the case. The information acquired from the organizer implicates eight senators, three remaining Common Cause executives, and one additional high-ranking government official. I won't tell you who that individual is at the moment because the President of the United States needs to be the first to know."

"It looks like you guys are going to cause your own earthquake. This news is going to rock the government very hard," Joshua said. "When are you going to spring the trap?"

"We're going to start the tremors this afternoon. I've been talking to Washington, Assistant Director Pincher already this morning. Are you ready for this, Corbbitt?"

"Sure, I'm really interested in what our elected officials have to say about all this. What about the Common Cause executives?"

"Small potatoes. I'm going to let Special Agent Vondra get his feet wet. I'm sending him and three other agents over to Common Cause this morning," Bender said. "Again, good job folks. I couldn't be more pleased. If there's nothing further, let's get on with the day's business."

Corbbitt caught Bender's eye while the others left the conference room. "What is it, Corbbitt?"

"Since our trip isn't until noon. I'd like a few hours off to take Ms. Hafner to breakfast."

"If you don't, I will," Peyton mused. "One thing regarding your case with Ms. Hafner, Don."

"What's that?"

"Don't blow it. I doubt that you'll ever find anyone like her again."

Tuesday, March 22, 2005, 12:10 PM

"How are we going to handle this?" Corbbitt asked Peyton Bender as they were boarding the airplane that would take them to Washington, D.C.

"I've got to sort all this out with the Director and if he doesn't lop off my head, we're both supposed to see the President later in the day. Assistant

Director Pincher is up to speed on all this and will provide support to bring in the senators. See what you can find out when they have them in custody."

"This is going to hurt a lot of people."

"Not to mention the people's confidence in their elected leaders," Peyton said.

Peyton's cell-phone chimed.

Corbbitt watched Peyton's eyes widen as he talked to his counterpart in the Washington Field Office, Harold Pincher.

Corbbitt moved aside so that others could board the airplane and waited until Peyton finished talking. "What's up?"

"It's all ready started. In the last hour Senators Yost, Brenner, Wren, and Mahady just made individual announcements that they are resigning. Pincher's agents brought them in for questioning, but their lawyers are speaking for them."

"What about the others?"

"Nothing yet, his men are checking."

"Will this change our plans any?"

"Unless something happens by the time we land, I'm going on as planned. You can see if the ones in custody have said anything useful to say about their activities. Remember the staff in Washington is not as familiar with this as you are."

"This is going to be a wild day in Washington, and the media's going to have a feeding frenzy," but Corbbitt saw that Peyton was absorbed in thought. He grabbed Peyton's arm to get his attention and pointed towards the airplane. The stewardess was ready to close the cabin door and urged them to get onboard.

Tuesday, March 22, 2005, 2:30 PM

Upon arrival at Washington's Reagan Airport, Peyton received another update from Assistant Director Harold Pincher. The four senators in custody cited their fifth-amendment right to remain silent as advised by their lawyers. Peyton heard the anxiety in Pincher's voice as he relayed the latest events over the telephone.

"You guys must have really uncovered something juicy here," Pincher said. "At this rate we're going to run out of senators. Senator Petrie from Massachusetts tried to commit suicide. He's over in Walter Reed Hospital now in critical condition."

"What about the other three on the list?

"We're still trying to track them down. They didn't show up at their offices this morning or we would already have them in custody."

"I've got Corbbitt here with me. Where can he be most useful?" Peyton asked.

"Is that Donald Corbbitt? The same guy who shot his mouth off on national television."

"Yes, the same one. But give him a break. He was under a lot of stress that day, and if it wasn't for his persistence and instinct no one would have done anything about this conspiracy," Peyton said in support of his best special agent.

"We have the same problem you do in New York with our case load and inadequate staff levels. So I can use him with all that you've uncovered in the Senate. Since there isn't much to do with the senators in custody, see if he can locate Senators Douglas, Horne, and McCabe."

Although Corbbitt heard only one half of the conversation, Peyton's instant retort to Pincher showed the difference in the two supervisors. Peyton's interpersonal skills with his staff far out-shined Pincher's.

"He wants you to track down Senators Douglas, Horne, and McCabe. If they've decided to flee or hide, it might take some time. Personally, I think Pincher's an ass and he just wants you out of the way."

"There's something that's bothering me about this," Corbbitt said. "They've had our videotape since last Tuesday and all of a sudden they're taking drastic action."

"What's your point?"

"We know the linkage between the senators, Common Cause and through Pendergast to Gambrelli. The point is that we've had Gambrelli cooling his heels for two days now, Pendergast is dead and there's no way they could know whether Gambrelli was successful or not."

"I get what you mean now. If Gambrelli was successful, there wouldn't be a risk to them. Since they have no way of knowing why are they suddenly admitting guilt," Peyton said, completing Corbbitt's thought.

"Something else has happened to force their hand. Something these men are more afraid of than the scandal or spending time in jail. It's possible there is another dimension to this whole business, Peyton."

"I'll keep this in mind. Give me a call if anything develops."

Tuesday, March 22, 2005, 4:33 PM

After a brief stop at the FBI Washington Field Office, Corbbitt tried calling Senators' Douglas, and McCabe only to get the answering machines at each residence. With no solid plan in mind, he drove to Senator McCabe's townhouse in Georgetown only to find no one home. With so much happening in Washington, Corbbitt thought that his boss was right and he was on a fool's errand trying to check the obvious locations.

He punched in the address for the Douglas's home on the car's navigation system. With the Washington traffic fighting forward progress, it took nearly an hour to reach Potomac and the sprawling Douglas home.

He turned left into the long driveway and stopped the car near the house. He saw a woman on the outside of the house peering through a window. She suddenly turned and ran toward his car. Corbbitt rolled down the passenger side window.

"What's the trouble?"

"My husband, Marvin has locked himself in his study. He's slumped over on the desk."

"You're Mrs. Douglas?"

"Yes. Can you help me?"

"Yes, of course. I'm FBI Special Agent Donald Corbbitt," he said, showing the distraught woman his identification.

"The telephone in his study rings constantly. What's happening?"

"Let's see what's going on first, Mrs. Douglas. Your husband maybe in a lot of trouble, but that will have to wait."

Corbbitt followed Mrs. Douglas through their palatial home and pointed to the study door. "I've been out all day, first at the hairdresser and then to play bridge. He's been awful moody the last week or so, but he gets that way from time to time."

Corbbitt looked at the six-panel door and the fine woodwork surrounding it. "There's a dead bolt here Mrs. Douglas, I'm going to cause some damage if I break in."

"Just do it, I'm really worried about him."

Corbbitt used his weight against the door. It took three attempts before the deadbolt casing finally broke through the surrounding wood and the door popped open.

Senator Douglas' head and shoulders were down on a desk that dripped vomit to the edge onto a Persian carpet. Immediately, Corbbitt checked the senator's pulse. "He's alive, but with the amount of alcohol he's consumed, you'd better call an ambulance." Corbbitt looked at the empty bottles on the desk and floor. "From the looks of it, he's had four bottles of whiskey."

Mrs. Douglas dialed nine-one-one and requested an ambulance, while Corbbitt tried to awaken the senator. Together they moved him from his desk chair to a near by couch and waited for the ambulance.

"Does he do this often, Mrs. Douglas?"

"He does drink a lot, but I've only seen him like this once before. Let me get something to wipe up the mess," she said as she saw the damage the acidic vomit was doing to the carpet.

Corbbitt thought it was interesting that Mrs. Douglas was more concerned about the furniture and carpet, than the cleanliness of her husband.

Corbbitt took advantage of her absence to look around. Under a partially filled whiskey bottle that lay on its side was a small piece of paper with eleven digits. He copied the numbers and wondered what they meant.

"Why do you think he did this, Mrs. Douglas?" Corbbitt asked when she returned with some rags and a bucket of water."

She looked at him and suddenly felt embarrassed. "I'd ask the maid to do this, but she's not here today. What did you ask me?"

"Do you know any reason for him to do this?" Corbbitt repeated.

"No, all I can say is that he came home and was really upset, and went right out again after Senator Horne called him last night."

"You have no idea why he was upset?"

"No, sir, and I don't pry into his business. I learned that a long time ago."

They heard a siren approaching and soon an ambulance pulled into the driveway. Mrs. Douglas greeted them and showed them where her husband was and told them how much he drank.

The paramedics checked the senator's vital signs and tried to calm Mrs. Douglas who was now putting on a good show of wifely concern. Douglas, still in a drunken stupor only grunted once as they lifted him from the couch onto a rolling stretcher for transport to the ambulance. One of the paramedics suggested that Mrs. Douglas follow the ambulance to the hospital in Rockville, Maryland, so that she would have a way to come home later in the evening.

Corbbitt stood in the driveway and noticed that the door to the Douglas home remained open. He went back into their home where the smell of alcohol and vomit prevailed. He checked under and around Senator Douglas's desk. There was nothing but the eleven numbers that he already copied.

While the numbers could represent many things, the obvious use was a telephone number. That was worth checking. With the aid of a telephone book's information section he determined that the first three numbers corresponded to the country code of the United Arab Emirates and the fourth number directed the call to Dubai.

"This really doesn't surprise me at all," he said to the empty house.

He noted the time and date of his call for his report and using the senator's telephone, he dialed the number.

On the first ring a woman with a heavy accent spoke, "Hello, caller from the United States. May I please have your name?"

Corbbitt altered his voice but realized that it was unlikely that the woman would know that he wasn't the senator. "This is Senator Marvin Douglas, there's something I forgot to tell him," Corbbitt said.

"Mr. Tarabolsi is sleeping and is not taking any calls at this time unless it is a matter of utmost urgency. Is your information of this nature?"

"Well, no it is not."

"Then will you try again in about six hours?"

"Thank you, I'll do that."

He hung up the telephone knowing that he made the connection between the senators and the real source of money.

Using his cell-phone, he called the Washington Field Office to get someone over to the Rockville hospital. He also placed a call to an intern back in the New York Field Office who could get him answers quickly. He needed to find out about Mr. Tarabolsi and determine what was really going on with the senators.

Tuesday, March 22, 2005, 6:56 PM

Senators Brenner, Yost, Wren, and Mahady, their lawyers, the Bureau Director, Peyton Brenner, and Donald Corbbitt, stood as the President of the United States entered the conference room in the west wing of the White House.

"Gentleman, please be seated," the President said. "I've had to postpone a dinner meeting with the newly appointed Ambassador from Spain, so let's make this time worthwhile."

The senators braced themselves for a verbal beating from the President they knew they deserved. "If I've learned nothing else about this job, it's that there's no point in spending time on finger-pointing. Senators, you know what you've done, and you've done the honorable thing by stepping forward and resigning. You've taken the first step towards redemption and that's to your credit.

"If you choose to remain here, so that I can fully understand the ramifications of what's happened, forget about fifth-amendment rights. Also forget about cover-up ploys and tricky legal maneuvering," the President said as he raised his hand and pointed to the door. "Because on this side of that door none of it will help you one bit.

"The only way I can use the power of this office to protect the people of this country is by completely understanding the truth," he said and stared at the individual senators before him. "To you it was a simple bending of moral principle to fatten your bank accounts, but as you've seen, evil entraps even the best and the brightest when they forget their responsibilities.

"Senators, I need to know right now, who is behind this and what was their motivation?"

Immediately, the lawyers started whispering in their respective clients' ears. Special Agent Corbbitt passed a single sheet of paper to his boss who read it and passed it on to the Director of the FBI.

"Mr. President, I believe Agent Corbbitt can answer one part of your question. It may jog the memories of others," the Director said with a tone that indicated his disgust of the situation and the guilty senators.

The President read the paper and looked at the senators again. "Ok, now tell me about your involvement with Mr. Jobran Al-Tarabolsi."

Again, the lawyers whispered to their clients.

"Enough," the President said in disgust. "I'm not conducting a trial here or a witch hunt. I have a responsibility to protect the people and you're going to tell me without a ten-minute delay for every question I ask you. Senators, you know deep in your heart you've done wrong. Help me repair some of the damage you've done."

"Mr. President, my client has rights. If he discusses this with you, it may be used against him in court," Yost's lawyer said.

"Quite right, counselor, you may take your client into the other room and it will be recorded that he did not wish to cooperate. Just remember cooperation goes a long way with the judge when it becomes time to pronounce a sentence. So, maybe it's time to stop the crap."

"Mr. President," Senator Yost said, "I'm going to tell you what you want to know. I hope the others do too."

"You may stay, Senator Yost, if you're willing to talk to me without your lawyer and just tell your version of what happened."

Yost, seeing no other choice, nodded to his lawyer who got up and left the room.

"All right, if any of the rest of you want to discuss this with me, I'll listen to you one at a time. For now the rest of you can decide in the adjoining room what your level of cooperation is going to be."

In the next hour and a half four senators told all they knew about Common Cause, Gerald Pendergast, Jobran Al-Tarabolsi, and the ten million dollars that each received.

The President listened and took a few notes. Each senator added another layer of what the President would later call a web of financial terrorism. Their confessions confirmed that the ultra-rich and powerful developed another method to attack the United States of America.

Tuesday, March 22, 2005, 6:56 PM

The Director, Walter Lowery, and Attorney General, Eric Ethelridge, entered the Oval Office. "Come in and be seated," the President said, directing them to the two chairs in front of his desk. "It's not been one of my better days in office, but there are times when you can laugh and times like today when you want to cry."

"I know what you mean," Ethelridge said.

The Director just nodded.

"Terrible to see men with such talent, charisma, and inner drive throw it all away with one careless decision that entraps them and their families."

Both of his visitors agreed.

"After struggling hard to win the people's confidence and the respect of all those around them, with one act it all vanishes," the President said. He pulled two sheets of paper from the center drawer and placed them ceremoniously on his desk. "I wonder what drives a man to do such a thing?"

"I'm sure I don't know," the Director said.

"What about you, Eric?"

Ethelridge suddenly feared what the President might say next. "Well, I don't know either. I expect in most cases it was greed."

"Greed in some cases, perhaps, Mr. Attorney General, but in other cases I believe it is the quest for power. Would you agree that's possible, Walter?"

"Yes, Mr. President, some men would do anything for power. We've seen it happen before."

"What would you do if a trusted colleague of yours, took a huge sum of money in exchange so that others might influence the foreign and domestic policy of the United States. Especially, if he had designs on being the next president?"

Eric Ethelridge could feel the sweat rolling down his back. "I'd probably have to fire him," he said with a broken voice.

"If anyone in this country has the responsibility to follow the Constitution and the laws enacted by Congress, sir, it's you," the President said as he handed Ethelridge the first sheet of paper. "Wouldn't you agree, sir?"

"Yes, Mr. President," Ethelridge said in a whisper.

"Then why did you accept fifty million dollars from the Common Cause chief executive officer?"

"I did no such thing."

"Don't lie to me, sir. That's a verified copy of an account statement from the Bank of Dubai, in the Cayman Islands. The statement came from the late CEO of Common Cause, Gerald Pendergast and it's got your name next to it."

The blood drained from Ethelridge's face and the paper in his hand oscillated as his hand shook.

"Are you going to sit there and tell me this isn't true?"

"No, sir, sadly it is true."

"Here's something you probably don't know, Mr. Attorney General. You thought you were getting the money from Common Cause to help shield the bunch of swindling crooks they call executives. But that's not the case, is it, Mr. Director?"

"No, Mr. President, unfortunately it is not."

"Eric, do you really believe someone is going to give you fifty million dollars and not want to extract your political life-blood sometime in the future? It turns out the money really came from a consortium of ultra-rich investors who are now trying to use their wealth to gain a foothold in this country. Their ultimate aim, sir, is the destruction of our way of life. In other words, it is a form of terrorism—financial terrorism."

"I had no idea, believe me, sir," Ethelridge whined.

The President handed him the second sheet of paper. "I'm not asking for your resignation. I am demanding it. Sign at the bottom, and get out of my sight."

Chapter 32

Sunday, April 10, 2005, 6:32 AM

Don looked over at Jocelyn to make sure that she was still sleeping and then slid carefully out of bed. It was quite an honor for the President to invite him to Sunday brunch and even more gracious of him to extend the invitation to his friend, Jocelyn. He decided to give her a few more minutes of sleep and use the time to think of how much more he enjoyed life since meeting this beautiful woman.

He felt suddenly like a gyroscope spinning out of its frame, with Gambrelli indicted on two counts of murder, the remaining senators located and arrested, and a ton and half of report writing completed, his case responsibilities vanished. In the absence of critical demands from the Field Office, precious time became available. They finally had the opportunity to talk, question, and understand one another's dreams, needs, and personal limits.

He reached in his suit jacket pocket and found the small case that held her engagement ring and sat in the chair next to the window. He looked at the ring and placed it on his little finger. The early morning sunlight illuminated the single one-carat diamond. Instantly the room walls caught and the reflected light from the diamond's many facets. Dozens of sparkles danced around the room as his finger moved in the sunlight.

He pondered the magic of this ring and the lives that soon would change. He thought of the change in his lifestyle and what would be required of him to ensure Jocelyn would feel loved the rest of her days. He put the ring back in its box and tucked it back in his jacket.

Since their first intimate moments together, he thought of the many ways that a man might propose marriage to a woman. Other men might propose in front of thousands at a baseball game or climb a mountain and beg on bended knee, but Jocelyn was an exotic combination of simplicity and elegance.

Finally, he decided that a beautiful setting and honest words from his heart would be all that was necessary. He knew the perfect venue for his sole approach to married life. He peeked through the curtains and the bright sun struck him in the face. It looked for the moment that Washington's fickle spring weather would cooperate and contribute to this memorable day.

He looked at Jocelyn's face for a moment then drew closer and kissed her on the cheek. "Good morning, sweetheart. It's time to get up," he said softly in her ear.

She opened her eyes and smiled. "A gal can get used to this alarm clock, you know."

Sunday, April 10, 2005, 11:47 AM

Two hours with the President and the First Lady made Jocelyn and Don feel like royalty. The President told the entire story of how Special Agent Donald Corbbitt rose to the occasion again to protect the citizens. Corbbitt was amazed at the President's ability recall details of events associated with the intertwined cases of Howard Champion's assassination and the corrupt behavior of the Common Cause executives.

Jocelyn was shocked, when she heard from the President what Jobran Al-Tarabolsi and his organization wanted in exchange for the money they paid to bribe the senators and the Attorney General.

"Fortunately, our people and our system of government are strong," the President said. "We've survived scandal such as this before, and each time we show the world the metal we're made of."

"Can't something be done to take Common Cause away from the crooks who stole the company?" Jocelyn said.

"Perhaps, if we can get them on racketeering charges," the President said. "If nothing else, I can make sure they have a tough time doing business in the United States."

"I don't believe the government ever reversed a corporate take-over, but it seems to me that getting money back to the original investors would serve justice and certainly wouldn't hurt your party's reputation," Don said.

The President looked at his watch, wiped the corners of his mouth with a napkin, and stood. "I must ask to be excused. There's a flare up in North Korea this morning."

"Thank you, Mr. President, for inviting us," Jocelyn said.

Don shook hands with the President and First Lady and offered his thanks.

"I meant what I said before, Donald, we need more people like you who work tirelessly to do the right thing."

"Thank you, Mr. President."

The President left abruptly, but took with him the idea of bolstering his ratings by aggressively attacking the new owners of the Common Cause Communications Corporation.

A few minutes later they found themselves by the White House guard shack on Pennsylvania Avenue.

"Are those new shoes killing you, Jocelyn?"

"Not at the moment, why?"

"Let's bask in the sunshine a little and go for a walk."

Jocelyn, sensing that this was important to him, readily agreed.

They walked arm in arm stopping now and then to look at the spring flowers near the Ellipse or to watch children flying kites near the Washington Monument. They walked toward the Tidal Pool lined with fragrant cherry trees that were in full blossom. Pigeons scurried around their feet as they walked along the path that curved toward the Jefferson Memorial. It was the kind of day where the cool water of the Tidal Pond and Potomac River tempered the heat of the early afternoon sun.

Don selected what he thought was the best view and searched the depth of his soul for the right words to say to Jocelyn. He edged her to the side of the curved path between two cherry trees.

"Jocelyn."

"Yes," she replied and turned toward him.

He looked into her eyes. "Jocelyn," he paused, reaching for perfection that could only be born in his heart. "Jocelyn, I've judged this to be the right moment and the right place to ask you something that is very important and comes from my heart."

He noticed her eyes glistening as she hungered for him to continue.

"Although our time together has been limited, I cannot help but notice how incredibly sweet my life is when I am with you. I want you to feel confident in my love and devotion to you. Jocelyn Hafner, I ask the same love from you. If you can do this, not only at this moment, but forever, Jocelyn, then marry me, and become my wife."

"Mr. Corbbitt, you may keep that one square inch I gave you. I accept your offer of marriage. I want you as my husband and will love you the rest of my life," Jocelyn said without hesitation.

He removed the engagement ring from its box and showed it to her. "Then accept this ring as a token of my love," he said as he delighted in the expression on her face.

She looked at the beautiful diamond solitaire and tears flowed freely down her cheeks.

He reached for her hand and had little difficulty sliding the ring on her finger. They shared a sweet lingering kiss to seal the agreement while a gentle breeze showered them with tiny cherry blossom petals.

Epilogue

Monday, July 4, 2005, 10:14 AM (local time, Dubai)

Jobran Al-Tarabolsi looked down from his penthouse suite in one of Dubai's ultra-luxurious hotels. Soon he saw his white Lincoln stretch limousine pull out from the underground garage and make a right turn. It was a beautiful automobile with a curved couch, and a vast array of communications, and video equipment to permit monitoring his vast holdings in real estate and security investments spread over the world.

He hoped that the last minute change in plans to take alternate transportation to the airport would prove unnecessary, but his security force was seldom wrong. Fortunately, through the grace of Allah and the revelation that a CIA operative entered the city just hours ago, it seemed wise to follow security's recommendation. Such a pity, he thought, to lose such a fine machine.

The explosion lifted the heavy automobile high in the air. The street below broke into chaos as the blast propelled automobile parts through shops and human flesh. The window in front shook violently from the shock wave that took a second to reach his elevation.

He spoke to a nearby aid to order another limousine and send the driver's widow his regrets with a sufficient sum of money so that she and her children would not have to beg in the streets. He could have stopped the destruction and death of his trusted driver, but for the present, he thought it best for the Americans to think that they were successful in their assassination attempt.

The explosion was a message from the President of the United States whose heavy-handed tactics warned them not to launch another attack on American interests. He added this to his list of talking points for the next meeting with his friends from Singapore, Frankfurt, Kuwait City, and Tokyo. As for the failed plan to subvert the United States government they would have to understand that it was impossible to foresee that a terminally ill woman would draw such attention from the FBI.

Printed in the United States
32532LVS00006B/49-51